THE ENTITY'S CHOSEN

TIMOTHY J. O'LEARY III

SCRIPTOR HOUSE
The Epitome of Greatness

Scriptor House LLC

2810 N Church St, Wilmington, Delaware,19802
www.scriptorhouse.com

Phone: +1302-205-2043

Paperback ISBN: 979-8-88692-066-6

E-book ISBN: 979-8-88698-067-3

Contents

In Memoriam

SGT JAMES PAUL O' LEARY, PRISONER OF WAR

KOREAN WAR

JANUARY 22,1931-JUNE 13, 1951

I dedicate this work to my son, Michael, and my very good friend, J Hunter King. They both have shown enormous leadership ability and untiring dedication toward helping others in need. Michael and Hunter have always generated sincere enthusiasm and a willingness to assist those who demonstrate continued interest in the learning process.

Michael's personal example is one of instilling responsibility or one's actions and, for youth who are fortunate to learn from his wisdom, to seek knowledge through failure.

Hunter has been instrumental in his ever-present empathetic ability to seek the very best in all for others. His work with youth programs has resulted in a significant impact on the lives of those he has touched. His influence has been far-reaching and has offered a lasting legacy attesting to his ability to lead and show sensitivity toward those who have witnessed his kindness.

Michael leads so that others may follow. Hunter determines the leader, so that others may learn.

My life has been enriched as a result of their presence.

Tim O'Leary

OTHER WORKS BY TIM O'LEARY

Non-Fiction:

Nowhere to Run: A Story of Maternal Abuse and Recovery

FICTION:

The Portal The Entity

The Entity's Child

The Dimensional Gateway

Tim O'Hara: His Athletic Life and Times

Collaborative Non-Fiction Work with Shelly Lynn O'Leary:

Crying in silence: A Story of Cerebral Palsy and Its Effects on Seizures.

This is my sixth sojourn into a science fiction military time travel fantasy. Putting these works together has been hugely satisfying. The characters have mostly been identified and developed previously in The Dimensional Gateway Trilogy. I have taken the opportunity to promote personalities that are endearing to the reader. And, most certainly, to my Wife Lynn, who has challenged me repeatedly to write another book about Shawn Crawford, a protagonist with whom she enjoys reading about in a world challenged with a stiff political agenda, pacified by a hero who refuses to take prisoners.

I have introduced a new character, Commander J Hunter King. He embodies the Warrior Way, in contrast to Lieutenant Colonel Shawn Crawford's cavalier attitude. However, he shows more restraint and a degree of ambivalence towards structured military orientation. As Shawn and Hunter are so very far apart in their perspective in the ways of military decorum, they are yet so very similar in their demand to promote an awareness of respect shown to others. This forms the basis for their chemistry. This is the essence of their dedication toward humanity and the rights of all.

Enjoy the moment!

CAST OF PRINCIPAL CHARACTERS

COMMANDER ELLA CARUSO: Australia's top scientist and resident expert on the workings of Portals, and Shawn Crawford's primary assistant in understanding the intricacies of time travel, having traveled through the Dimensional Gateway herself. Additionally, she is a member of the Australian Department for External Affairs. Time-Era Origination: 2074.

FLIGHT SERGEANT WILL CARUSO: The Plane Captain of the F-42A Tiger Shark and F-142B Leopard Stealth Fighter Aircraft in the Royal Australian Air Force. This highly-intelligent and detail-oriented crew member is known for his carefree attitude, and meticulous problem-solving skills, which he applies to all Fixed-Wing and Rotary-Wing Aircraft make and types. His exceptional support to the Royal Australian Air Force's Aircraft Fighter program earned them the Meritorious Service Medal. Additionally, they are a member of the ENTITY's Inner Circle. Time-Era Origination: 2074.

SERGEANT CRYSTAL CRANSON: The Chief Administrative Assistant and Gatekeeper for Marshal Allison Morrison in the Royal Australian Air Force. This highly efficient officer may come across as harsh and unyielding, but beneath the surface lies a heart of gold and boundless inner kindness. Additionally, she serves as the Chief Guardian to Colette Roberts-Crawford in the absence of Lady Christine Roberts. Original Time-Era-2074.

SIR STEVEN SHAWN CRAWFORD: The Air Marshal of the Royal Australian Air Force, a former Lieutenant Colonel in the United States Army, husband to Lady Christine Roberts, and father to Christopher and Colette. This accomplished pilot has flown a range of helicopters, including the OH-58D Kiowa Warrior, UH-60 Black Hawk, and RAH-66 Comanche Attack Helicopters, as well as the F-42A Tiger Shark and F-142B Leopard Stealth Fighter Aircraft.

Despite his impressive accomplishments, he remains a moral, modest, and humble contributor to all aspects of personnel involvement. A chief expert in the understanding of Portal/Wormhole events, he is the principal deterrent to assassination attempts on the lives of various historical figures.

Additionally, he is an audacious and fierce devotee of protecting the rights of the oppressed, having been twice awarded the United States Medal of Honor and recognized as a hero of the Third World War. A Seventh Degree Black Belt Martial Arts Specialist, he is an expert in the art of silent killing, and fluent in eight foreign languages.

As a former Delta Force Black Ops Operator and triple ace in fighter aerial combat, he is a force to be reckoned with. He also holds a Doctorate Degree in Advanced Aeronautical Engineering and Quantum Mechanics, with minor degrees in Economics and Chemistry from Georgia Southern University.

He is a member of the Australian Government Intelligence Agency and is known for his love of a good Beef Wellington dinner. His exceptional abilities and accomplishments have earned him the favor of the ENTITY. Time-Era origination:2014.

TODD DIGHELLO: A part-time musician who has contributed to famous scores like "The Star-Spangled Banner," he is a CIA operative and time traveler who works for the ENTITY. He also serves as the principal organizer in an operation to abruptly cease hostilities during the Third World War in 2018. Original Time-Era-Always.

AMELIA EARHEART: Held a record in gyro altitude flight, she is the first woman to fly solo across the Atlantic Ocean and complete an around-the-world flight with the assistance of Shawn, Christine, and Christopher Roberts-Crawford. A pioneer aviator who champions women in aviation, she is married to Baron Von Richthofen. Time-Era origination: 1939.

ROBERTO "BOB" JESUS GONZALES: A highly respected helicopter pilot, Unit Historian, and OH-58D Pilot-in-Command for the 341st Aviation Helicopter group, he is back-seat flight radar intercept officer for MAJ Derek Peterson in the F-22A Raptor Stealth Fighter. He also holds the rank of Air Commodore in the Royal Australian Air Force, piloting the F-42A Tiger Shark Stealth Fighter, RAH-66 Comanche, and AH-1G Cobra Attack Helicopters. He was awarded the Distinguished Flying Cross and Silver Star for his exceptional aerial performance against enemy forces. A principal character, paternal influence, and mentor to Shawn Crawford, he is affectionately called the "chief." Time-Era origination: 2014.

LTC WILL MARSHALL: The Executive Officer (XO) for the 257th Air Force Fighter Wing in South America, and the chief assistant to COL Jackson Elliott, he helps promote the commander's administrative intent in all operations. He is a known "free spirit" within the senior command structure. Time-Era origination: 2014.

ALLISON MORRISON: A Marshal in the Royal Australian Air Force and the Commander of the Sydney Maritime Defense Force, she is an exceptional and charismatic leader in the ongoing struggle against the African Federation Forces' incursion into the Australian continent. She is Michael O'Leary's wife. Time-Era origination: 2074

AIR CHIEF MARSHALL MICHEAL O'LEARY: A former Lieutenant Colonel in the United States Air Force, he now serves in the Royal Australian Air Force as the Senior Commissioned Officer. He is also a fighter pilot mentor to MAJ Shawn Crawford during his transition from OH-58D Helicopters to the F-42A Tiger Shark Stealth Fighter; and gained Fighter Pilot Ace status during conflicts in the Korean War and World War II, where he was wounded in action. He is married to Allison Morrison. Time-Era origination: 2053.

CPT SHELLEY O'LEARY: A formidable force in aerial combat against enemy fighters, she pilots a YF-23A, Sea Avenger, and Sea Scorpion Stealth Fighter Aircraft in the Royal Australian Air Force. He is a close platonic friend and confidant of Sir Shawn Crawford. Time-Era origination: 2074.

MAJ DEREK PETERSON: A 257th Aircraft Fighter Wing member, piloting a YF-23A, a Black Widow, and an F-22a Raptor Stealth Fighter Aircraft, he is a double ace during World War II and the Korean War with a record in downing enemy aircraft. A friend of Sir Shawn Crawford, Christine Roberts, and Bob Gonzales, he is a member of The Entity's Inner Circle. Time-Era origination: 2014.

BARON MANFRED VON RICHTHOFEN: Amelia Earhart's husband, he is a World War I fighter ace with 80 credited "kills." Time-Era origination: 1918.

LADY CHRISTINE ROBERTS: A Lieutenant Colonel in the Royal Australian Air Force, she pilots the F-22A Raptor and F-42A Tiger Shark Stealth Fighter Aircraft. Despite being born in 1991, Colette's military lineage is impressive—her ancestor was a Triple Fighter Ace who scored more than 15 "kills" during World War II and the Korean War. She is married to Sir Shawn Crawford. Time-Era origination: 2014.

CHRISTOPHER ROBERTS-CRAWFORD: The son of Sir Shawn Crawford and Lady Christine Roberts, he is known as "Little Obi Won".

With a remarkable skill set, he speaks fourteen languages fluently and holds a seventh-degree black belt in martial arts. At the incredibly young age of 12, he became the world's youngest fighter pilot to earn the coveted title of Ace. He has a sister named Colette, and is also referred to as the offspring of the ENTITY. Time-Era origination: Always.

COLETTE ROBERTS-CRAWFORD: The daughter of Sir Shawn Crawford and Lady Christine Roberts, she was known for being precocious, sassy, brilliant, and loving. She has a brother named Christopher and is recognized as the daughter of the ENTITY. Time-Era origination: Always.

LTC BRIAN TIMMONS: As an Operation Officer in the Royal Australian Air Force, he is highly detail-oriented in anticipating and planning for Marshal Morrison's intent in executing wartime operations involving the Avenger and Sea Scorpion Stealth Fighter aircraft. Time-Era origination: 2074.

ENSIGN J.G TIMOTHY O'HARA: One of the greatest athletes to ever play basketball, baseball, and football, he established high school and collegiate records in all three sports. During his freshman year as a quarterback, he led the United States Naval Academy to victory over Florida State University in the Sugar Bowl by calling every play at the line of scrimmage by himself. In addition to his athletic achievements, he is also an F-35 Lightning II Advanced Stealth Fighter Pilot who earned the status of "Ace" after shooting down six enemy aircraft. He is a friend of Sir Shawn Crawford and a fellow member of the Australian Government Intelligence Agency.

FAMOUS HISTORICAL PERSONALITIES: Abraham Lincoln, John Fitzgerald Kennedy, Martin Luther King Jr., Robert Francis Kennedy, and Mahatma Gandhi are pivotal historical figures who dedicated their lives to serving their countries and pursuing world peace. Thanks to the efforts of Shawn Crawford in thwarting all assassination attempts against them. They were able to continue their monumental, significant, and life-changing work for the betterment of all. Shawn Crawford is the final member of this distinguished group of historical figures who influenced the world's final peace and harmony. Time-Era origination: Various.

THE ENTITY: Also known as Obi Won, His Blueness, His Greatness, and His Vast Blueness, he is the father of Christopher and Colette Roberts Crawford. Serving as the Principal Guardian in the cosmos, he sustains world peace through Sir Shawn Crawford's participation in any assignments and events occurring throughout the world. Time-Era origination: Always.

COMMANDER J HUNTER KING: A charismatic leader in special operations, he is an expert in SEAL/Delta Force operations and fluent in seven languages, with a specialization in Arabic and Swahili. He also holds a seventh-degree black belt and is a master in the Art of Silent Killing. In addition to his martial arts skills, he holds dual Doctorate Degrees in International Studies from American University and Advanced Fusion Quantum Mechanics from Massachusetts Institute of Technology [M.I.T]. Impressively, he built his first mini-jet fighter at the young age of 11. He is married to the equally charismatic Kathleen and is a veteran of the African Wars between 2079 and 2081. Time-Era origination: 2074

PROLOGUE

As LIEUTENANT COLONEL Steven Shawn Crawford and Commander J Hunter King ducked behind the embankment by the Parisian canal and withstood the chips of concrete flying over their heads, their immediate thoughts were those of their missed meals and dessert at the Château Du Lac Restaurant. Hunter referred to his friend, Shawn, as a "Coach". The feeling of entitlement was mutual, as they both had spent time working with youth sports. The term "Coach" was a moniker to be appreciated. At this very moment, however, there was no appreciation shown for missing the Châteaubriand and the Cherries jubilee!

Man, Shawn thought, I have just to do a better job at this CIA job of mine! And here was his best Buddy, Commander King, who was more preoccupied with the more mundane things like how he was going to dispose of the bodies who were making his life as slightly difficult at the moment!

And King at this very moment was thinking, 'What's up with this interrupting a card-carrying spy having a quiet evening where he could spend more than five minutes dining at a top restaurant in Paris with *me mate, Mon*! He hadn't even had enough time to break the French bread! I have just to go to Church more often! He looked over at Shawn, who has unwrapping a packet of fig newtons from his side pockets. He offered one to King.

'Coach, how long was this in your pocket? Several more bullets chipped more of the concrete abutment away overhead.

'I put them there on Saturday, a month ago.'

One of the terrorists cursed in Ukrainian at his running out of ammo.

'I'll pass,' said Hunter.

The Uzi bursts were coming few and far between now. Shawn sighed. Well, at least their ammunition conservation was a bit more tolerable, in that they had no idea about conserving ammunition.

'You know, Coach' Crawford said. 'I wonder what the airline rates are going for these days for booking a trip to the Island of Bermuda right about now?'

'Well, my Friend, I bet they're fairly cheap. And, I would also bet that Kathleen and Christine would love to soak up some sun and go shopping in Hamilton. But do not, I repeat, do not get me on one of those suicide motorbikes . I still have briers sticking out of my butt, the last time my bike wanted to do a cross-country against my will.'

They both got up suddenly and began firing at open targets. Two of the terrorists went down. A third came at Hunter with a 12-inch blade. Commander King told Crawford that this one was his.

As the attacker thrust his knife forward towards King's heart, the Commander continued his conversation with Shawn about the Bermuda bike caper. Shawn threw down another fig newton.

'Ah yes, I remember that moment well, *mon, Ami*! All I could think of at that time was, *'Me Mate, Mon*! Did he ruin the bike, *Mon*!'

The blade never got within 24 inches of the former SEAL. King took his body into a squat position and, at the same time, swept his right leg toward his attacker's calf. The man went down quickly on his back and hit his head on the concrete roadway, rendering him totally unconscious.

Shawn quickly went through the pockets of the downed terrorist while looking for intelligence paperwork he could find. He was also looking for food. Man, was he hungry, or what?

'Who are these guys, anyway? I heard that the Ukrainians and Serbians had joined forces on the Rive Gauche, but these guys really hated one another ! It had to have something to do with their *capos* getting together, with the motherly dowagers finally convening with an understanding that each would not come to their pinochle card games with daggers in their underwear! My life will never be the same!'

He quickly stood up and came face to face with a final-terrorists who had stationed himself at the far end of another concrete barrier across the road to the right and adjacent to the Canal. Hunter turned quickly in the direction of the threat, pointed his Beretta at his newest uncovered target, and put a two-shot burst into the man's forehead. The assassin toppled backward into the canal.

'He doesn't do the back-stroke very well, does he coach?'

The last assassin had a compatriot who popped up all of a sudden and came at Shawn while wielding a very long knife.

'My turn!' shouted Crawford.

For the moment, Shawn thought that this would be exactly what he needed to cut the French bread roll on his table. Need to focus, Shawn.

Crawford stood with a smile on his face. The second assassin lunged at him and was surprised that his knife point had come up empty. As the knife arm swept past the pivoting Crawford, the would-be assassin's momentum carried him to point 90 degrees to Shawn's front.

Crawford took both of his hands and placed them on both sides of the attacker's head. As he twisted the man's head sharply to the left, he heard the "snap" of the assassin's spinal cord. Crawford released the body, and the individual collapsed onto the sidewalk.

A nanosecond later, a shot rang out behind them. For a moment, Shawn mistook the spatter of ketchup on his white shirt to be his own blood. He decided that the round fired was not intended for them and that he most certainly would have to get his shirt to the cleaners at the earliest possibility! He began thinking about his lunch six hours earlier at that quaint inside French restaurant with Commander King. Shawn had ordered 'pommes frites', and he was most certain that there was an extra squirt from the ketchup container that had most definitely gone awry! He now knew why Hunter had ducked when he did!

Shawn turned around slowly and saw yet another assassin lying on the cobbled rocks to the side of the restaurant and 15 meters behind him. He was not moving. Holding in the shooter's hand was a silence PPK/S Caliber 9 mm kurz/.380 ACP. He stood looking back at Crawford and King with a smile that could only have been honed by Shawn Crawford himself.

'What took you so long?' said Crawford.

Standing in front of Shawn and Hunter 20 meters away and looking at them both was their partner, Timothy O'Hara.

O'Hara was dressed like a beggar and sported the requisite facial hair to sell his disguise.

'Well, I thought you were going to enjoy the great French cuisine, including the "desert du jour!" I didn't want to interrupt!' offered O'Hara.

Shawn picked up the knife. He looked around. The police had yet to arrive because of the shots previously fired. In matters such as these, bystanders would hesitate to get involved for fear of reprisal. Knowing this, Crawford calmly straightened out his shirt, and walked back into the restaurant. Hunter followed him inside after checking the last attacker's clothing for additional intel.

They sat back at their table. Shawn put the knife by the bread loaf and proceeded to canvas the menu. Hunter took a quick glance outside and watched the local gendarme arrive at the grisly scene. The waiter arrived and they ordered.

Timmy O'Hara then disappeared into the shadows.

It was another magical day in the life and times of Shawn Crawford, Agent, Australian Government Intelligence Agency, a.k.a., Spy, and J Hunter King, SEAL/Delta Force Operative, and fellow coach.

F-22 Raptor Advanced Stealth Fighter Courtesy of owips.com

YF-23 Black Widow II Advanced Stealth Fighter Courtesy of militaryphotos.net

FRIENDSHIP AND FAMILY

The accident involving Shawn, a fellow pilot friend from another Time-Era, and the pilot's father was traumatic at best. The O'Hara's and Shawn had been driving to the Sydney Maritime Base Officers' Club following the arrival of Tim's father Patrick from the Time-Era in 2011. They were to meet Shawn's wife Christine and their two children, Christopher and Colette.

On the way to the Club from the airfield, they were broad-sided by a reckless driver running through a stop sign on Base. Tim O'Hara, his father Patrick, and Shawn had perished instantly in the crash. The paramedics were called as soon as it happened by a young airman who happened to witness the accident. They were too late to save them.

Christine, Shawn's wife, and her children, Christopher and Colette, arrived at the accident scene while on their way to the Club to join her husband. Christine immediately went over to the curb. Young Christopher and Colette, Shawn's children, immediately exited their vehicle and calmly walked over to where the three individuals had been thrown from their totally demolished military vehicle. The two children were the Progeny of The Entity.

As they walked over to the three inert bodies, they witnessed the paramedics place sheets over the three bodies, acknowledging that the three had perished in the accident. When the paramedics saw the children approach, they immediately blocked their access to the bodies. An Air Policeman stepped forward.

Christopher and Colette merely looked at the Air Policeman. He stepped aside. Christopher instructed his sister to go over to where their father Shawn lay. He moved over to the O'Hara's, Christopher and Patrick.

Both children knelt beside the victims, with Christopher between the bodies of the O'Hara's. As if on cue, they immediately placed their hands on the bodies of each O'Hara. Colette, with tears beginning to well in her eyes, placed both of her hands over her father's heart. Both children knelt in that position for 30 seconds.

All of a sudden, a bluish light descended upon both children and then down over the bodies of each victim. The hue intensified slowly at first and then increased in intensity. Encircled both of the children and the inert bodies lying on the ground.

Soon, the light was so intense that those within it were lost from sight. The light remained in this state for more than two minutes. Individuals began to congregate in the immediate vicinity. They stood in awe at what they were witnessing.

Within the light, Shawn opened his eyes. He felt his body rise ever so slightly. With the bluish tinge still wrapped around him, he noticed "Entities" moving toward him from a distance. They began to take shape as they grew nearer.

Finally, one particular "Entity' appeared to walk ahead of the "others". His attire was robe-like, with a bluish color likened to the encompassing light about Shawn's body. He seemed to float toward him and stopped a few feet in front of Crawford.

Behind this "Entity" were human figures that Shawn found difficult to recognize. The figure before him smiled warmly, and then stepped forward and wrapped Shawn in his arm.

'We are all so very proud of you, Sir Shawn Crawford,' he sensed the "BEING" saying. At that point, the group behind began to advance toward him. The body of individuals appeared to swell as they moved forward. All at once, their movement stopped.

The "Entity" before him smiled warmly and then said, 'Shawn, those you see before you are the souls whom you have saved as a result of your previous heroic efforts in preserving the lives of famous personages, such as Presidents Lincoln and Kennedy, and others. Each individual stands before you to pay homage to your sacrifice made on his behalf.

'With this evidence of gratitude fosters a further request for additional measures in correcting still yet more injustices in your world. We ask that your work not be done, but be a continuing mission of significant importance to eliminate that which others choose to take advantage of in a world fraught with greed and selfish ambition.

'Shawn, your love for all and everything that you hold most dear is a total measure of your importance toward ensuring that peace may rule in the place of anarchy. We wish for your dedication toward influencing the promotion of well-being for all, in concert with the elimination of everything that serves to promote selfish behavior, and that you continue your mission on our behalf.'

When the light dissipated, Shawn opened his eyes and rose weakly to his knees. 'Anyone got the number of that truck?'

'Father,' said Colette, 'Please remain still for a few moments. You're going to be fine. The O'Hara's are also unhurt. Christopher is administering to them now.'

Shawn looked over and saw that Christopher was quietly talking to both Tim and his father Patrick, both still lying on the ground. After a few moments, Christopher asked for the paramedics to come over and check the O'Hara's and Shawn for any residual concerns. Ninety seconds later, the medics could find nothing physically wrong, notwithstanding that all individuals should have died in the crash. They strongly urged that the three accident victims go immediately to the Base Hospital Emergency Room for a full, comprehensive evaluation before going home for the evening.

Shawn went over and checked on Patrick and Tim. They both appeared to be fine, but Shawn thought that it would be better to make sure by visiting the ER. The O'Hara's declined the strong urging on Crawford's part to be checked out. Tim especially wanted to celebrate his father's arrival and ask Shawn to forego any further pleading about driving over to the hospital.

Crawford yielded to their wishes and arranged with the air policeman on the site to have the vehicle towed to an appropriate location. He grabbed Patrick's bag from the demolished car, and they piled into Christine's SUV and drove over to the Club.

As weird as it sounded, they were all able to enjoy themselves in celebrating Patrick's arrival in Australia. By all rights, they should not have even been in this position a half-hour before, but here they were as though nothing had happened.

Midway through the celebration, Patrick indicated that he had a few words he wanted to share. He first thanked Christopher and Colette for their life-saving assistance on the road. Patrick also thanked Shawn for the sacrifices he made in taking his son Tim under his wing and for going back in time to retrieve him from the 20th Century. He knew that he had left a grown-up daughter, Meghan, behind. But he also knew that her life was reasonably complete and hoped one day to be able to see his son, Michael, play ball for the New York Yankees once again.

Tim O'Hara and his father Patrick had arrived in the future, via their goodness shown to others in the early 21st Century. This appeared not the only prerequisite for the O'Hara's, especially for Timmy O'Hara, US. Naval Academy Graduate and Pilot of the advanced F-35 Lightning II Stealth Joint Fighter. It was his humility that endeared him to so many in and around his life.

Young O'Hara had been an athletic Prodigy at the Naval Academy. He took over the quarterback position for the Navy Varsity as a First Year Midshipman and led his team to a Sugar Bowl victory over Florida State University. His ability to lead was shown on that football gridiron. So much so, that the varsity coach, after witnessing Timmy's uncanny ability to read defenses earlier that season, allowed the young O'Hara to call his own plays at the line of scrimmage.

His ensuing three athletic years prior to graduation were successful as well. Shawn Crawford, the Agent of the Entity, had been the instrument for transferring the O'Hara's from the year 2012 to 2087. And, in that time of transference, both O'Hara's had moved from the Northeastern United States to the continent of Australia to enjoy, not only the good that was to experience there; but also to share in the challenges facing Australia in the years to come.

2053 Prefecture Air Force F-42A Tiger Shark Stealth Fighter Courtesy of wallpaperpimper.com

A FRIENDSHIP FOR THE AGES

Young Timmy O'Hara had first encountered Sir Shawn Crawford after skimming the waters over the Persian Gulf. O'Hara was being aggressively pursued by an advanced Iranian jet fighter in the vicinity of the Gulf of Hormuz. The Iranian had skipped his bread and tea for lunch and wanted to have young Ensign O'Hara for a mid-afternoon snack instead. He wasn't going to be afforded that opportunity, or luxury, however.

Ensign O'Hara and his F-35 Lightning II Advanced Stealth Fighter were abruptly intercepted instead by a cloud formation that appeared out of nowhere. Within that cloudy mist, was a bright bluish hue. After traversing the cloud, Tim O'Hara found himself far removed from the Persian Gulf location and absent an Iranian bandit at his six o'clock position. He soon found himself in the vicinity of the Australian Continent.

When he looked over to his left, he was rewarded with the smiling face of none other than Sir Shawn Crawford, a.k.a., LTC Shawn Crawford, a.k.a., Air Marshal Shawn Crawford. The Australian Government had conferred upon him so many titles that he wasn't certain who he was when he rolled out of bed each morning! His daughter Colette was the only one who could keep him straight day in and day out.

Shawn waved his hand from the cockpit of his futuristic fighter, the F-42A Tiger Shark. With that wave came an all-knowing smile that told young Timmy O'Hara that the Shark pilot knew exactly what young Timothy was going through at that very moment.

'Hey, Guy,' radioed Shawn. 'You appear not to be only lost, but it appears that you are lost. Well, my friend, let me ask you a question, and it is important that you answer it correctly the first time. How do you like your Beef Wellington prepared? Personally, I like mine on a plate, but that's just a preference.

O'Hara looked at Crawford like he had two heads! 'Well, Sir, for starters, where am I? And, it's medium-rare on a plate as well.'

Crawford chuckled, 'I think I already like you, my young pilot friend! O.K., that cloud and light you exited a few minutes ago was famously referred to around here as the Portal. You have jumped into another Time-Era. Given that you are "driving" a shiny new F-35 Lightning II Advanced Jet Fighter, I would put you originally from the Time-Era somewhere between 2011 and 2011. How am I doing so far?'

'Sir, you are absolutely right about the date. I was being chased by an Iranian Fighter when I encountered your "portal". I broke out back there and am still wondering where I am now.'

'You are about to be my guest at the officer's club at the Sydney Maritime Air Defense Base in the year 2087. My "chariot" that you are ogling over is called an F42A Tiger Shark Stealth Fighter. It has been around since the 2050s. I myself used to be an OH-58D Kiowa Warrior Helicopter Pilot back around 2014 before I saw the light of day and decided that I wanted to test the old adage, "Speed Kills"! Now, off your nose, the runway you see in Sydney. Let me smooth the way for you to land before you run out of fuel or are shot at by one of the ubiquitous Sea Scorpion jet fighters. Now, if you think my aircraft is nasty-looking, wait until you see one of those "beasts"!'

Shawn made the call to Sydney Approach Control, who directed both aircraft to descend and maintain 1,000 feet. When they got to within 10 miles of the base, Approach told Shawn to contact the Tower on the assigned frequency. Crawford got clearance from the Tower to land, and Shawn told his F-35 pilot to drop back in trail so that they would make the landing together. The tower was so advised.

Once on the ground, Shawn taxied over to the hangar where he housed the Shark. He stopped short of entering and spooled down his engines. He advised Tim to do the same.

F-35 Lightning II Advanced Stealth Joint Strike Fighter

Courtesy of community.warplanes.com

Once the aircraft were chalked just prior to the engines winding down to a stop, Shawn and Tim exited their aircraft, after a brief exchange of personal information from their respective cockpits. Crawford walked over to the F-35 and extended his hand to Ensign J.G. Tim O'Hara and officially welcomed him to Australia.

Shawn's plane captain, Flight Sergeant Will Caruso, greeted Crawford by quipping, 'I see you have adopted another wayward pilot from the "bowels" of The Portal, Sir Shawn!'

'Hello, Will. Allow me to introduce Ensign Tim O'Hara. Mr. O'Hara, please meet the best Plane Captain in the entire world, both past and future. Will, the young good Ensign, and I have just made an acquaintance ourselves just before you arrived? He is a Connoisseur of Beef Wellington, so I know immediately that I shall vouch for him in any group or venue.'

'Sir Shawn, it sounds like an appropriate vetting. Mr. O'Hara, let me be one of the first to welcome you to our humble continent, the World of rambunctious kangaroos and sedate women.'

'Thank you, Will. My interception in the Air by LTC Crawford was indeed fortuitous. I suspect it could have been worse.'

'Believe me when I say this. Mr. O'Hara, there is no worse interception than by LTC Crawford.'

'Will, I truly feign being hurt. Moving along then, Ensign O'Hara and I have an important meeting with the Marshal.

Australian Navy F-72B Sea Scorpion Advanced Stealth Fighter

Courtesy of seltech.wordpress.com

Would you be so kind as to tow both aircraft into the hangar? Or, if you wish, you may play with the buttons inside the cockpit and find the right ones to ground taxi both fighters inside. Your choice.'

'I think I can manage both.'

And so, the friendship between LTC Crawford and Ensign J.G. O'Hara began. Their relationship would be one of the adventures and deadly association with the world of terrorism.

Over the many ensuing years of peaceful coexistence of nations over much of the world [certain hotspots would always appear to flare up among the Third World countries], Australia's Continent continued as the watchdog in the Southern Hemisphere.

The Marshal's Office stressed aircrew training in the F-73B Sea Scorpion and not before too long, the Aussie Pilots were rated as being the top aviators in the advanced fighter tactics.

The man behind this push, forever demanding the most out of its pilots through rigorous training programs, was Air Chief Marshal Michael O'Leary, a time-era transplant from the year 2053. Upon his arrival in Australia with Major Shawn Crawford, Shawn Crawford respectfully addressed the Air Chief Marshal as Lieutenant Colonel Michael O'Leary, which was his official military ranking at the time. This was made possible thanks to The Entity, which allowed them to travel through its Portal in the same aircraft. Shawn viewed Colonel O'Leary as a surrogate father figure, and the Colonel mentored him through his transition from flying helicopters to piloting advanced fighter aircraft. There was a mutual respect that was unshakable between them. Shawn's saving his Mentor's life during an aerial confrontation with a fighter from the African Federation of States solidified their bond of friendship in perpetuity.

COMMANDER J HUNTER KING

THE AK ROUND just missed his right ear. It's a good thing I didn't have my ear ringing this morning, he mused sarcastically. As he ran a random route through the Cambodian Jungle, he had to watch out for the vines that snaked around the ground surface.

He came abruptly to a halt and looked down from the top of a 25-foot cliff. Below were running rapids from a river that flowed down from the mountains to the north. King heard his aggressors moving closer. He had no choice. He jumped, and with youthful athleticism, turned his body into a head-first vertical position and hit the water below. It was deep enough as he barely scraped the bottom of the river bed.

He swam underwater toward the bank on the near side from where he jumped. He let the water carry him along the bank until he came to a tree overhang that completely masked his position. He heard the Cambodian terrorists talking above him and also heard them depart the area. They were unable to spot him and decided to move parallel to the river to try to find him, or his body.

King knew approximately where he was from the map he carried in his leg pocket. There was a small village located about three "klicks" from his position, now maybe a little less as the water had pushed down the river. It was nearly 1100 hours. He would make his way toward the village that was reputed to be non-committal in the country's fight for control by both the government and the terrorists. He was hoping to get a little rice from them as he hadn't eaten in over 24 hours.

King waited long enough to ensure that his adversaries had left the area, and he then swam diagonally toward the opposite bank. The village was now perhaps less than 400 meters from his departure from the river. This had been a horrendous day. Murphy's law was alive and well in Cambodia! He wondered what the word "Murphy" was in Khmer, the official Cambodian language.

Commander J Hunter King, United States Navy SEAL, and Delta Force had begun this mission three days ago when he reported to San Diego, California, and the Naval Special Warfare Command Headquarters. Intelligence sources in Phnom Penh reported a major terrorist leader to be in the country's capital for a meeting with other local terrorists "capos". The individual had been elusive for a very long time. Here was an opportunity to finally take him down. Commander King was tasked to do just that.

He had flown commercial to Cambodia's capital and had met with his local contact to get an up-to-date status briefing regarding the whereabouts of the target. There was a supposed meeting to be held in the "bush" when the leader was going to inspect the field operation camp located to the southeast of Phnom Penh. The coordinates of the exact location and the time of the inspection were afforded to King.

He was to be dropped off two kilometers from the camp and make his way to the site at least 24 hours prior to the arrival of the terrorist leader. His contact dropped him off for 28 hours at the designated location and the King stealthily moved toward a location where he could establish his "hide", settle, and waited for the moment to take down the leader. His field of view was ideal. He was on a slight incline. The wind was negligible and not presenting a factor. Just before taking the shot, he would again assess that variable. The round trajectory would have to be considered, as well as the distance to be the target.

King was wearing a military jungle ghillie suit that blended in with his environment perfectly. He settled in the next 24 hours. He was equipped with standard sniper gear, which included the Mk 13 MOD 5 sniper rifle, ammunition, a knife, binoculars, a compass/GPS, a water bladder, a whistle, insect repellent, a mini thermometer, food rations, first aid supplies, ear protection, a penlight with a filter, chemical mace, campo paste, a strobe light, a pencil and notebook, a hand-held radio, and a laser range finder.

The day was hot and he was sweating profusely. Any movement he would make was done in an extremely slow, exaggerated motion. Insects were having a "family get together", but he was trained to ignore their bites and annoyance factor overall. He settled in for the wait.

Map of Southeast Asia Courtesy of

www.geology.com

The night went by with little activity, and he was able to doze here and there. His light sleep was simply that, for he would awake with any kind of activity in the camp. When the sun came up, he was in the process of finishing an energy bar washed down with some water from the bladder. Terrorist activity in the camp was beginning to pick up slightly. It appeared that the leadership down below was getting a bit annoyed with the regular "low-life" soldier and pushed them to get things looking like they were going to inspect the King of Siam. The perception was everything, Hunter thought.

At 0900 hours, a convoy of vehicles pulled into the make-shift compound. A slender Cambodian exited the three-quarter-ton military vehicle as one of the camp's underlings reported to him. He barked at the latter soldier and demanded to speak to the officer in charge.

A moment later, an officer appeared from one of the huts and walked slowly over to the visiting dignitary. In the meantime, Hunter took his binoculars and identified the officer as the one he was there to assassinate.

He secured the binoculars and all of this loose equipment very slowly and settled in behind the sniper scope. He had lased the hut nearby, so he had enough data to set up his shot. The distance to the target was 400 meters. Wind direction and velocity were negligible. He knew the ambient temperature. Hunter made a slight correction for the angle of the shot and settled into a comfortable position behind his Mk 13. He sighted the cross-hairs on the head of the terrorist. He slowly squeezed the trigger.

The rifle "bucked" as he fired off his round. As the bullet was fired at such tremendous velocity (3,070 feet per second), it arrived at the target with a slight deviation was negligible. His target was struck in the forehead, he was propelled backward with such force that he was pushed back six feet.

As soon as the King made the shot, he slowly moved backward and behind the low mound upon which he had stabilized his Mk 13. He literally slithered to a point where he would be totally masked when standing upright. He then quickly vacated the area.

After traveling 100 meters, he pulled his PRC-77 radio and made his extraction call. Once he received the familiar double-click from the operator at the other end of the transmission, he moved toward the coordinates where a helicopter would pick him up. He needed to get there in a hurry. King couldn't afford to eat for this meeting. He wasn't. As a matter of fact, he arrived at his pickup coordinates at precisely the same time as the arrival of the aircraft. And none too soon! Vehicles were approaching the LZ and would arrive at his location shortly.

The helicopter didn't bother to land but hovered momentarily 12 inches above the ground. King opened the rear crew compartment and climbed in, at the same time he threw his gear to the other side behind the pilot's station. Even before he latched the door shut, the helicopter nosed over as the pilot applied forward cyclic while pulling up on the collective. The aircraft shot forward and then up into the sky after moving through the translational lift.

Commander King in His Side
Courtesy of snipershide.com

The vehicle arrived at the clearing site from behind and began firing its AKs at the retreating aircraft. Nothing vital was hit, and the helicopter cleared the three lines and was soon out of sight.

The Commander donned a set of headphones and told the pilot that he was "up".

'Did you have fun back there? Commander? There's a sandwich and a thermos of coffee in the netting behind my seat. Help yourself. Tips are always appreciated.'

'Thanks, it's much appreciated. And, I just tip my boonie hat to you!'

Looks like the timing was just about right. I see you had invited some "friends" to see you off. Oh, and don't mind cleaning up back there. The maid will be the first thing in the morning.'

'Shawn, they were really after you since they knew you would be the pilot driving this "limo" out of the area this morning. Don't know how they knew. It couldn't have been the Cambodian leaflets I passed around Phnom Penh yesterday with your photo on it!'

'Commander, you are always thinking of me. I don't know how to thank you. So, I won't.'

'What time is Happy hour, Shawn?'

'Hunter, I'm always happy, every hour of the day! Would like some

cashews?'

'Now, how long have you had those in your flight suit, Shawn?' 'Well, let's see. I was born 25 years ago, so…'

'I'll pass, Shawn. Thanks anyway. What time do we get back to the Base

camp?'

'We'll be there in 20 minutes. Let's see. We have 15 minutes of fuel

remaining. No, just kidding. How's your family, by the way?'

'Kathleen keeps winning this trip to all kinds of places as a result of his doing so well in her job. This time it's Hawaii. How about you? Are you going to travel anywhere in the near term?'

'No, not really. They're trying to keep me fairly close to home. Being the disreputable character that I am, it's important that I maintain my image. I would hate to disappoint. Besides, I'm traveling today. I'm "driving" Mr. Daisy!'

'And Mr. Daisy does appreciate it. I'll be rotating back to San Diego when we get back to the Base camp. How much longer do you have in the country?'

'They won't tell me. I overheard the Adjutant telling the S-4 that my leaving was going to be sometime after "hell freezes over". Kind of hard to imagine when that will be when one is in Cambodia! Whenever it is, Coach, I know that we will definitely work together again. I read the tea leaves, as they were floating in my coffee the other morning.

FUTURE ASSIGNMENTS IN THE GOVERNMENT INTELLIGENCE SERVICE

ONE PARTICULAR BEAUTIFUL summer morning in early February, many years later and into the future, sir Shawn Crawford was called into the Marsha's Office. After checking with Marshal Morrison's Gate Keeper, Sergeant Crystal Cranston, Shawn entered the Commander's Office.

Inside was LTC O'Leary, Todd Dighello, the Director of the Australian Government Intelligence Service, and the Australian Prime Minister. Shawn was asked to sit down on the couch.

Crawford looked at the group assembled and said, 'Does this have anything to do with the dinner roll I took in the officer's Club the other night?'

'Shawn, this has nothing to do with your Beef Wellington plate and any and all meals at the Club,' Morrison chuckled. 'The Prime Minister would like for you to consider a proposal of national concern. Prime Minister, Sir, please fill in Sir Shawn regarding your thoughts as they relate to national security.'

'Thank you, Marshal Morrison. Sir Shawn, we have reports from covert operatives around the world that there is a move undertaken by terrorist cells to infiltrate the continent of Australia for the purpose of bringing down our Continent's tallest skyscrapers. We believe that there will be a coordinated attack within the next few months.'

'Australia currently has six buildings at least 800 feet in height. It is believed that our two tallest buildings, the Q1 on the Gold Coast, 1,058 feet and 80 floors, and the Eureka Tower in Melbourne, 975 feet with 91 floors, are the proposed targets for these terrorists. Both structures are relatively dated, as they were erected in 2005 and 2006.'

'We are asking you to assist us in a manner, unlike anything you have done for us in the past, Sir Shawn. I'm sure you remember Special Agent Todd Dighello. Agent Dighello will fill you in on the specifics of this very important undertaking to preserve and protect both life and property here in Australia.'

'Thank you, Prime Minister. Colonel Crawford, it's nice to see you again.'

'I wish I could say the same about you, Mr. Dighello,' replied Shawn.

'Listen, I know that you still hold Agent Colette's death on the Isle of Capri against me. And, I apologize if you feel that I mistook her importance for indifference. Please believe me that I was saddened by her loss. She was an exceptional Field Agent, one that has been difficult to replace. But in my line of work, death often comes as well as tragically. Each and every agent in the intelligence service knows the total risk involved with any mission and at any time in that person's life. It may sound callous to many who do not live out experiences day in and day out, but it's absolutely necessary to move on to survive in this day and age. So, Colonel, can we move on at this point?'

'O.K., Mr. Dighello, I'm listening.'

'The terrorist brigade's planning cell is located somewhere in Paris, France. The leadership, we believed, has begun to finalize plans to infiltrate Australia in the next three months. We have strong evidence that they have not gained entry here as yet . What we want to do is take out their leadership in Paris, thereby "cutting off the head of the snake", as it were.'

'This is the mission that you have conducted successfully in the past. As a matter of fact, one successfully completed mission caused the cessation of hostilities, culminating at the end of World War II. We would like for you and one other individual to travel to France and take out this leadership body. Will you do this for us, Colonel?'

Shawn looked at Dighello and the others in the Commander's Room. He remembered the last time he had undertaken an assignment of this nature. Shawn had managed to infiltrate the Chinese headquarters with the help of a covert national. It had seemed easy to accomplish at the time, but, all in all, he considered himself fortunate that the mission had gone as well as it did. There was a great deal of luck for these things to go smoothly.

'O.K., I will do it. Who do you have in mind for the other person to go along with me?'

'That person will be up to you. Everyone around here knows what an excellent judge of character you are, with your feeling toward me as the exception. But, perhaps one day, you will come to know that you can trust me explicitly as well.'

'It's important that we have you and the other person in Paris by this weekend. We will all have the appropriate deceptive personal documentation for you both by tomorrow afternoon. We will need to know the name of your partner by the close of the business today. Do you have any questions for us, Colonel?'

'No, not at the moment. I'll have a name for you by 1600 hours this afternoon.'

'Splendid. Let's plan to get together here in the Commander's Office tomorrow at 1300 hours. Until then, thank you, Colonel Crawford. There will be many people thanking you also when this assignment is completed. Until tomorrow, Prime Minister, Marshal Morrison, Air Chief Marshal O'Leary, Colonel.'

Agent Dighello turned and walked out of the office. The Prime Minister thanked Shawn for his service in advance and departed as well. Crawford was left looking at two of his favorite people in the world.

'Sir Shawn, what's going through your mind right now?' asked Morrison.

'My choice of an accomplice, Marshal. I want Ensign O'Hara to go with me.'

'Are you certain that Tim is the right choice?' asked Colonel O'Leary. 'Sir, I believe he is. Of course, he'll have to learn "on the fly" so to speak.

But, I do believe that he can handle any situation that comes his way. He has shown an interest in martial arts, and I've been working with him.

As I've said, he is definitely a quick study. I need to talk to him right away. Ma'am, Colonel, if you both will excuse me, I'll be with Ensign O'Hara for the next couple of hours. I will report to you both by 1500 hours today.'

Tim and his father Patrick were at their quarters when Shawn pulled up into their driveway.

Young O'Hara was working on the engine of his used car that he had purchased recently. His father Patrick was mowing the lawn in the front of the home.

'Colonel, it's good to see you. Care to have a beer with us?' asked Patrick O'Hara.

'No, Sir, but thank you just the same. I need to talk to Tim for a few moments. Hey, you, can you break free from that Rent-A-Wreck for about ten to fifteen minutes?'

'Sure, Sir Shawn. Dad, I'll be back shortly. Want to go in my "limo" Colonel?'

'Ah, no, thank you just the same. Does that thing have four tires, by the way?'

Tim looked at his askance. Wipe his hands. And followed Shawn to his SUV.

Crawford left the Base and drove down to the local beach. They both got out of the car and walked up to the peer that jutted out some 15 meters into the water. They walked to the end and sat down on an empty bench. Shawn looked out into the ocean for a long moment. Tim knew something serious was going on with Crawford, and he let him have his moment to reflect briefly before he started to tell him what was on his mind.

'Tim, I've been given an assignment by the Prime Minister and an Agent of the Australian Government Intelligence Service, Todd Dighello. I have worked with Agent Dighello one time previously, and it had to do with a mission that caused the cessation of hostilities during the Third World War. When I completed my mission successfully, the War ended a few days later.

'The reason I'm telling you this is that I have been given another assignment and I need someone to accompany me to see it through. It has to do with ensuring that the safety of the people of Australia is cared for, as well as protecting the Country's infrastructure. I would like to have you with me on this assignment.'

'There is a terrorist cell meeting in Paris, France this coming weekend that I had my partner need to neutralize. The terrorists are finalizing plans to blow up at least two of the highest buildings on the Gold Coast and Melbourne. Our internal transportation infrastructure system may also be at risk.

'Timmy, I am asking you to come along because I have the utmost confidence in your ability to watch my back. Now, I know you don't have any experience in spy craft, but I also know, as I told Commander Morrison and Colonel O'Leary, that you are a very quick study.

'The clock is ticking, and I was told by Agent Dighello that I needed to have the name of my partner by 1600 hours today. Is this something that you are willing to take a risk with because it will involve a great deal of that?'

O'Hara looked at his friend and said of course he would come along. He told Shawn to tell him what he needed to bring, and he would ensure that he would be ready when the time came to leave the country for Europe.

'Shawn, If you want me to go along with you. I'm there. When do we leave?'

'Tomorrow, we have a meeting in the Commander's Office with Dighello. He will have all the appropriate documentation for each of us to gain access to Paris, as well as the location of the terrorist meeting location this weekend. On our way over, we will go over our plan of action in detail. You once told me that you speak French like a native, did you not?'

'*Mais, oui, Monsieur!*'

'*Tres bien, mon Ami*! How do you think your father will react to this?'

'Dad is a Patriot, Shawn. And such patriotism extends to wherever he calls

"home". He loves it here, and finds all of you simply fantastic!'

'Super, the feeling is definitely mutual, most assuredly. O.K., let's get you back to your place. Do you want me there when you break it to your father?'

'No, but thanks anyway. Knowing my father as I do, I have no problem in that way with anything new that I attempted to get involved with. Dad has always trusted my judgment.'

'Let's plan to meet up in the Commander's Office at 1250 Hours tomorrow, Tim. I'll notify Agent Dighello who my partner will be. By the end of our meeting with him tomorrow afternoon, we'll be all set to go. Be prepared to leave as early as tomorrow on a flight out of Sydney in the Tiger Shark. On the way, I'll transition you into the airframe. It's always safe to have two rated pilots in an aircraft.'

'Sounds good to me, Shawn. And thank you for your trust in me. It means a lot, coming from you.'

'Timmy will see you tomorrow. If you need to talk about anything this evening, give me a call.'

THE FRENCH CONNECTION

WHEN SHAWN AND Tim meet with Agent Dighello in the Commander's Office the following afternoon, the Government Intelligence Agent had all the appropriate paperwork for both. Fake passports, French currency, French nationality papers, and location for ingress were provided. In addition, there were two safe house locations in the event that their cover was compromised for any reason.

Dighello gave them the name of their contact person and the location of their meet. The contact would have additional handgun firepower in the form of a Beretta with silencers. A bag of extra French currency was to be found in each safe house in the event of its need . Another contact would meet them at the safe house.

The point of the ingress would be Beauvais–Tillé Airport, a 65-minute drive into Paris. The Tiger Shark would plan to arrive in the early morning hours, when the airport was known to be closed due to aircraft traffic being non-existent. Beauvais–Tillé would re-open for incoming and outgoing traffic at 0630 hours. Their contact would meet them at the north end of the tarmac by an old deserted hangar.

Their route of flight would take them in a westerly direction, and therefore they would be "chasing the sun" the entire trip. Shawn calculated the route of flight in terms of hours at mach-5 speed and at 20,275 meters. Winds aloft at that altitude would be relatively negligible. He back-tracked his egress location and time of arrival with the known prevailing winds and calculated that they needed to leave Thursday evening to make the rendezvous with the French contact at the appointed time and location.

They departed on time and had no problems.

Shawn didn't waste any time with Timmy's transition. They went through a quick series of aerial acrobatics and then simulated emergency procedures. O'Hara's familiarity with flying the F-35 Lightning II allowed him to quickly pick up the subtle differences in procedures. An hour into the flight, Shawn was satisfied with Tim's progress and checked him off.

'Timothy, you now have the controls. I'm going to grab an hour's worth of sleep. We should be landing in Madagascar in 90 minutes for fuel. If I'm still "sawing logs" after 60 minutes, wake me up with a whiff of pizza!'

'O.K., Shawn. Didn't know you brought pizza long for the ride. Where do you have it stowed?'

'In my leg pocket, Timmy. Can't you smell the pepperoni pizza from your right seat?'

'Ah, no I can't, Shawn. Do you normally pack pizza in your flight suit?' 'Only if I can't take a vegetarian one with me. Nighty night!'

They re-fueled in Madagascar and were quickly on their way to their next destination, Beauvais–Tillé Airport, France. Along their route of flight, Shawn went over the plan to infiltrate the house and upstairs room where the terrorists were to make their final plans to wreak havoc in Australia. Their flight plan time was right "on the money" as they landed at 0200 Hours local time. The field was deserted.

The Shark made an abbreviated short-field landing to minimize the landing roll and quickly taxied over to the airfield apron adjacent to the civilian Fixed Base Operations [FBO].

There was an abandoned hangar at the extreme end of the tarmac. The door was open, and the lights were off. Shawn cautiously applied enough power to the twin turbines to put the F-42A inside the structure. There were no other aircraft inside.

As soon as they stopped the aircraft and applied the brakes, a vehicle arrived at the entrance of the hangar and stopped. The driver shined his lights in their direction. It went on and off three times.

That was their contact.

Tim and Shawn deplaned . Tim closed the hangar door. They quickly went over to the waiting vehicle, a black sport utility vehicle. When Tim got to their contact, he was surprised to see that she was a woman, and a beautiful one at that.

Shawn quickly spoke to her in French and asked if she had the requisite clothing for them to change into the back of the vehicle. There was no need for introductions in the spy business.

'*Mais oui, monsieur. La-bas,*' she pointed to the rear seat area. Shawn and Tim quickly got into the back seat and rapidly changed into the clothing provided. Their contact got in behind the wheel, started up the SUV, and drove off the tarmac to a small access road leading to the A-16, the main artery from Beauvais–Tillé to Paris, 56 miles away.

After a quick 61-minute ride, they arrived at one of the safe houses. They were dropped off and were met by a male contact at the door, who quickly ushered them into the darkened foyer inside. Their female driver left immediately.

The contact leads them up a flight of stairs to a room where two other individuals were sitting at a table and pouring over paperwork. After a quick greeting all the way around, Marcel, the French Security Agent, gave Shawn and Tim the specific meeting location where the terrorists were to effect their final plans.

Following a detailed discussion of what the two Australian Government Service Agents could expect, they were provided with Beretta 92SD handguns with attached silencers affixed to the end of the barrels. C-4 explosives serving to blow the building up were also given to them, along with detonators, detcord, and an explosive device to a timer. Tim and Shawn were then led to another room where the beds and linen are positioned on either side of the room. The Frenchmen then said that the beds were for them to get some rest. Security in and around the safe house was assured.

Shawn thanked the Security Agent and the latter left the room. The two Australian then went out to their beds and, without saying a word, laid down and went quickly to sleep. It had been a long night, with a longer day to follow.

The next morning, Shawn and Tim ate a spartan breakfast and went over the detailed planning with the French operative. At 2200 hours that evening, the *Al-Qassam* Brigades were expected to meet at the address the operative had given them. They would be dropped off two blocks from the location of the Brigade's meeting and move on foot toward the building. Following the sanction of the terrorists present, Shawn, and Tim would calmly walk a half-block and enter a Renault parked in an alleyway shadow. They would then be driven back to the airfield to the Beauvais–Tillé Airport to depart the country in the F-42A.

At precisely 2200 hours, Shawn and Tim were dropped off at the designated location, and they proceeded on foot. They pretended to walk unsteadily while portraying two drunks holding bottles of wine and walking down the street. They were in a bar area where such behavior was commonplace, and they mixed in nicely with those others, leaving in a state of somewhat lacking in the state of sobriety. Their faces were smeared lightly with lampblack to portray a "scruffy" appearance. Their clothing was worn and soiled. They played the part perfectly.

Beneath their garb, they carried their Beretta 92SD weapons, as well as the C-4, and accessories that would be used to assassinate guards outside the meeting room. Contrary to popular belief, knives were not the best instruments to use in the art of silent killing. Their use created a noise factor from the victim that could easily alert others in the area. A single shot to the back of the head was the mode of choice.

There were no guards standing watch outside. Had there been, their presence would have seemed suspicious to any local law official passing by the building. Shawn could expect sentries inside, however.

They both went to the side alley and spied the fire escape ladder attached to the side of the building. As Tim was a better jumper than Shawn, he managed to catch the lower rung and pull himself up onto the first stage. He assisted Shawn.

They quietly climbed the steel scaffolding and located an unlocked window on the third floor. It led to a hallway. They let themselves into the building. The meeting was thought to be on the second floor. Being a floor above was advantageous because the guards in the second-floor hallway would be looking for any possible threat as opposed to that coming from above.

Shawn and Tim walked quietly down the stairwell to the second floor. Door hinges in these old buildings notoriously creaked, and Shawn had come prepared. He applied some fast-setting compound spray on all three door hinges and waited 45 seconds for the chemical to set.

He opened the door slowly and took a peek down the hallway. There was one guard looking out the window to the street below. Another was dozing in the chair that was leaning against the wall beside the door leading to the room where the supposed meeting was being held. Shawn could hear voices coming from inside the room.

Shawn signaled Tim that he was going to draw the guard by the window over to their door. He told O'Hara to portray a drunkard when the guard came over to open their door. Shawn then kicked the molding at the bottom of the wall and waited for the guard to come over to check on the noise in the landing.

When the door opened, Tim lay on the third-floor stairway and feigned to be asleep. He held the bottle of wine to his chest. When the guard's head became visible, Shawn fired a silenced shoot to the back of the terrorist's head. As he crumpled forward, O'Hara quickly reached out and grab the body before it had the chance to hit the floor. He quickly searched the man's clothing for any intelligence paperwork they could take with them. Crawford looked back into the hallway. The other guard was still dozing. Shawn and Tim were wearing running shoes to temper the foot noise within the building. As Shawn approached the dozing guard, he reached into his pocket and pulled out a garrote. He quickly replaced it around the guard's neck and strangled the man. Before his body could hit the floor, O'Hara grabbed him and noiselessly dragged the body over to the stairwell. Tim, once again, checked the guard's clothing for any intelligence he could take back with them. He then laid the body beside the other dead terrorist while Shawn was quickly putting the detonators and C-4 together outside the room where the planning meeting was being held. He set the timer for five minutes. When the clock started, Shawn started his stopwatch. They quickly made for the stairwell and down to the bottom floor.

They exited the building and feigned their stumbling routine, but at a slightly faster clip. They rounded the corner, crossed the street, and found the alleyway where their contact sat waiting in the black Renault compact sedan.

The vehicle started moving before Tim could close the rear door. Shawn checked his watch. 15-14-13-12-the Renault was now 50 meters away from the building. 9-8-7-80 meters away from the structure. 3-2-1-. There was a huge explosion that rocked the Renault 110 meters away. Shawn and Tim turned around and witnessed a huge fireball mushroom into the Parisian night air.

Nothing remained of the building.

Timmy looked over at Shawn and asked, 'Do you think you used enough C-4, Colonel?'

'Yes, I do believe you are right, Little Obi won. We should have brought more!'

'Sir, had you used just a little more, France would have been no more. On second thought, perhaps that would have been a good thing! I hope our contact doesn't understand English!'

'Don't worry, *Monsieur*, he does not,' said the driver, dryly. Timmy and Shawn looked at one another and broke out laughing.

'Marcel, you have the driest wit of anyone I have ever known. You would make a martini jealous!'

'That's very good, Sir Shawn.' Said the driver now in perfect English. 'I studied at Georgia Southern University in a quaint little town called Statesboro. Do you know about it?'

'Do I know of it, Marcel! My goodness, they have a statue of me in the middle of Sweetheart Circle! I bought all of my degrees there. When were you there?'

'I graduated in 2078. Most of Statesboro, Georgia is all GSU right now. RJ's Restaurant on South Main Street is still there. I believe Randy Nessmith the owner, still entertains the locals and guests with stories of GSU football prowess during the early years of the 21st Century. Randy's a great guy, he must be close to 115 years old now, Sir Shawn! I think he is closer to 120, *Mon Ami*! And *Monsieur* Mike Philips, the manager, is a lot younger at 108.'

'Bet they don't look a day over 73! Just young pups.'

'I want to thank you both for ridding the world of this terrorist scum this evening. The world is but a little safer to live in, these anarchists are eliminated. I know that your Homeland of Australia and its Government are indebted to you for your intercepting plans to create a great deal of national suffering.

'Marcel, it has been young Timmy's and my pleasure. We happened to be in the neighborhood this evening and thought we would stop by for a little French snack. We are entirely glad to be of assistance. Please call us again when you anticipate having as much fun!'

'Ah, of course, *mon Colonel*!'

They arrived back at the Airport at Beauvais–Tillé at midnight. After a quick goodbye to Marcel, Tim, and Shawn changed back into their flight suits, climbed aboard the Shark, and started the twin turbines.

'Tim, you have the takeoff and much flying back to Australia. All of that C-4 aroma has made me a bit sleepy. You don't mind, do you?'

'Not at all, Colonel. I thought we could do a few barrel rolls on takeoff. What do you think?'

'You know, I tried that the first time I had the takeoff with my Mentor aboard. His gray hair turned a beautiful shade of white on that one! Whatever you wish to do, young Obi won.'

O'Hara taxied to the action with the prevailing winds and started an immediate takeoff roll. He got 25 feet in the air and immediately did two barrel rolls! Crawford nearly had a heart attack!

On the ensuing climb out, Shawn said dryly, 'Has anyone seen my heart?'

'Colonel, I believe it is presently in your throat!'

The remainder of the flight was uneventful, up until they left Madagascar on their final leg toward Sydney. They were jumped by three African Federation Stealth Fighters.

O'Hara didn't ask for permission to take evasive action. His Naval Academy Fighter pilot training kicked right in. Shawn let Tim take over the aircraft totally. He would be his other set of eyes in the cockpit.

Tim dumped the noise abruptly and lost 2,000 feet in a moment's notice, and then executed a hard left-hand turn and completed three barrel rolls in the interim. The stress on the Tiger Shark airframe was enormous. He could hear Shawn grunting loudly in the right seat.

Timmy then brought the nose up and jinked back hard to the right. He kept the F-42A coming around. Two of the three Africans were relatively new at this game of aerial "cat and mouse". O'Hara was able to line up to the right quadrant of one of the aircraft, got a steady tone, and announced, 'Fox ONE!' He immediately went after the other fighter, who decided he didn't want to play any longer and dove for the ocean.

O'Hara whispered, 'Oh no, you don't! You want to play rough, Dirtbag?

We're going to play rough!' another steady tone and 'Fox Two.'

The F-42A threat acquisition radar started blaring. The third fighter was working his way around O'Hara's left. Tim decided to make the other pilot's job more difficult by banking a very hard left and bringing the stick up against his flight suit. The Tiger Shark soared as O'Hara's added thrust.

He pivoted sharply to the right and then downward. The two aircraft passed one another with a combined speed of 1500 mph! Tim banked left this time, a very hard left! He was able to cut the angle down to 90- degrees. Timmy kept his left-hand bank in and soon found himself too close for another missile shot. He announced, 'Going to guns!'

He fired off his 20 mm cannon and completely sheared off the African's vertical fin and rudder assembly. The impact of the rounds hitting the fuselage at that juncture caused the African fighter to rotate into an uncontrollable flat spin. Ten seconds later, the pilot managed to overcome the enormous inertia inside his cockpit to blow his ejection seat. A parachute opened five seconds later.

O'Hara then looked at Shawn and asked, 'Colonel, do you have anything to eat?' It was then that Crawford knew that Timmy O'Hara was a Man after his own heart if he could even find his heart after all that!

THE GOLD COAST AND NORTHERN ENVIRONS

AFTER LANDING AT the Sydney Maritime Defense Base, a landing that Timmy O'Hara absolutely nailed perfectly, he taxied the aircraft over to the hangar. Both Crawford and O'Hara were greeted by Flight Sergeant Will Caruso.

'Welcome back, my two Wayward Cavaliers! Did you enjoy Paris? What a lovely City, is it not? Caruso stressed the very last with a thick Parisian accent!

'Will, we wanted to stay longer to enjoy the cold, but had to break away, I'm afraid. We did manage to make some new friends and did also manage to say "Adieu" to some others who, as it turned out, had no sense of humor at all! They went out with a Bang, as it were!'

'Oh, and Will, my young friend Timothy here, bagged three African Fighters just off the Madagascar coastline on our way back. It would really be a nice gesture if you could add three more African States Flags on the side of the fuselage. Perhaps even affix them in a way that identifies Ensign O'Hara as the culprit for their demise!'

'Absolutely, Sir Shawn! Congratulations Ensign O'Hara! Did you get any assistance from Colonel Crawford during the aerial ballet?'

'No, Will, I did not. He sat there the whole time eating a piece of pizza. I do believe one of my three barrel rolls in a row caused some of his pizza sauce to get on his flight suit, though.'

'Well done, Ensign! It's time for Sir Shawn to do his monthly laundry now, anyway. Lady Christine refuses to wait on him and his two lovely children won't get near him beginning the fourth week!'

'Gentlemen, I do believe that this is what is called a "full-court press"! I'll have you know, and good authority at home will back me up on this, that I do my laundry after five weeks, and not four. And yes, it is sadly true that my Children are never around to hug me after a week and a half. Could it be the mouthwash?'

Sergeant First Class Caruso chuckled and turned to Tim O'Hara, 'Ensign, a certain female Sea Scorpion fighter pilot came around the hangar about an hour ago and was asking about you. I believed she said that she would be at the Officer's Club right now for lunch. Her name was CPT Shelley O'Leary, if memory serves.'

'Will, your memory is always serving,' said Shawn. 'Young and chaste Timothy O'Hara is above such earthly pleasures as dining with a young lady, who is obviously acting extremely forward. Ensign O'Hara will absolutely have none of this chicanery!' offered Crawford.

'Am I correct, Ensign? Ensign? Was that Timothy O'Hara leaving in a rush and most probably heading over to the Officer's Club, Will?'

'Sir Shawn, this young man is a real gem. And so is Shelley O'Leary. It would be great if they would hit it off with one another.'

'Will, I do believe that they are way ahead of you, myself, and everyone else on this Base, except for the remaining members of my wonderful family. Speaking of which, I need to file my report with Marshal Morrison and then head over to my quarters. Will, we'll talk to you later, my young guru!'

Ensign Tim O'Hara entered the officer's club dining room and immediately saw CPT Shelley O'Leary alone in a booth and eating a salad.

'May I join a beautiful lady for lunch?' O'Hara demurred.

'Why, I was just thinking about you, my fearless Warrior. I understand that you and your sidekick Pancho went on an international junket. How was it?'

'Shelley, Paris in February is not what it's cracked up to be. There were, however, some fireworks that made the trip somewhat interesting. Anyway, how are you?'

'I'm doing great, thanks! Have been training in the Sea Scorpion for the past couple of weeks. A lot of gunnery practice over at the range. Other than that, I'm catching up on my reading. I've got this book called The Portal, which is the first in a trilogy series about advanced fighter aircraft involved with time travel. Pretty awesome storyline! The guy who wrote it is a terrific author!'

'When you're done with it, I'd like to borrow it, if you don't mind.'
'Absolutely. Are you going to have some lunch?'

'That salad looks awfully good. I think I'll order one of those.'

They talked about life in general around the Base. After eating, Tim asked if Shelley wanted to go for a walk. She looked at her watch and decided she had plenty of time before she needed to get back to operations, where there was a briefing to be conducted by the Operations Officer, LTC Timmons.

They strolled along the boardwalk, which offered a beautiful view of the sandy beach and ocean waves crashing onto the shore. They found an empty bench and sat down.

'You know, it's been very interesting reading about individuals in the history books. Individuals who have accomplished tremendous feats and have found their way here through The Portal. You, for instance, are mentioned for your athletic abilities in multiple sports, especially at the Naval Academy.

'Sir Shawn is the same way. To read about his exploits and his accomplishments and actually meet the individuals, such as yourself, Shawn, and Lady Christine, are present experiences that are immeasurable in terms of importance. And, I am awfully glad to have met you. I enjoy spending time and talking about your past. It is truly fascinating!'

'Well, thank you for that, Shelley. I truly don't place any importance on my past accomplishments. What I have gained from athletic events is the knowledge that you are only as good as your team. And, I've found that this applies to how pilots work together to reach an endpoint. I suppose I have always been a part of a teamwork structure that fosters the mandate that everyone does his job to the best of his ability. Success generally is the endgame accomplishment.'

'Well, I need to get going. LTC Timmons wants all of us pilots in the briefing room on time. It was great spending a little time with you, Tim. We should do this more often.'

'That would be great. I'll look forward to the next time. Talk to you soon, Shelley!'

Crawford had, in the meantime, reported to Marshal Morrison's Office by checking in with Sergeant Cranston out front. After being told that she was not in the meeting, Shawn knocked on the outer door and entered when given permission.

Morrison was sitting in an easy chair. Colonel O'Leary was opposite her on the couch. They seemed like they were deep in conversation.

'I hope I didn't interrupt anything,' said Crawford.

'No, not at all, Sir Shawn. Please have a seat. How did the assignment go for you both?' asked O'Leary'

'It was a success. Let's say that Paris, France is now a conversation piece in that it has a new crater where a building once stood. The cell was neutralized. We did bring back some intelligence that suggested that more meetings we're going to be held in different locations, not in Paris, but all over the world. If Agent Dighello wants these neutralized as well, someone is going to be awfully busy.'

'These are difficult times. When are you expected to report to Agent

Dighello?' asked Morrison.

'I am heading over to his downtown office right now, Ma'am.' Colonel O'Leary then asked, 'How did Ensign O'Hara perform?'

'Like a pro, sir. As a matter of fact, and this is really the reason I came up here to speak to you both, we were jumped by three African Federation Fighters just south of Madagascar on our way in. Timmy bagged all three.'

Morrison looked at O'Leary and said, 'Looks like our friends to the north are not wanting to play nice any longer, Michael,'

'True, we'll have to step up our Intel in Jakarta and try to find out what they are up to. Shawn, thanks, and welcome back. You didn't, by any chance, bring back some of what wonderful Parisian bread, did you?

Crawford reached down and unzipped his lower leg pocket in his flight suit and extracted a small loaf wrapped in a protective cover. He gave it to Marshal Morrison, who inspected it closely.

'Don't see any bullet holes in it, so I guess we won't have to worry about lead poisoning when we break bread this evening, Michael,' Allison Morrison quipped.

'Ma'am, I would never present such an inviting packet with more than two bullet holes. I believe the flight surgeon stresses to stay away from any bread that has more than three bullet holes in it when I offer it to someone after a mission. Got to run. Enjoy the bread!' Crawford chuckled.

Shawn arrived at the Parliament Building 20 minutes later and rode the elevator to the top floor, where the Australian Government Agency Service was located. He identified himself to the outer office secretary, who announced him to Agent Dighello inside. Crawford walked into his office.

'Shawn, welcome back! I heard that you and Ensign O'Hara were highly successful. Congratulations. How did young O'Hara do?'

'He worked out well. He has an intuitive sense of himself. I think his talents are wide-ranging. After watching him these past few days, I'm convinced he is able to do anything he sets his mind to. He's that good.'

'Fantastic. Is there anything you want to go over with me as an after-action from the past few days?'

'We were able to pick up some intelligence from the couple of the terrorists that we sanctioned before the building blew. Here are a couple of documents I wanted to give to you. It appears that Paris isn't the only location where cells are busy calculating their next moves.'

Agent Dighello looked over the paperwork and then looked up at Shawn. 'I think, according to this, I may have more work for you to do for us if you are still so inclined. You, of course, work directly for Colonel O'Leary under Marshal Morrison. If you believe that this "wet" work is something that interests you, we certainly can use your talents.'

'You know, I really did enjoy the intrigue of it all. Yes, I would like to be of continued service whenever you need me. Would Ensign O'Hara be able to assist me in any additional assignments?'

'Absolutely. You both seem to have good working chemistry. This is something hard to find quite often. If O'Hara wants to continue, then we certainly would love to have him join us in this global fight. I will talk to both Marshal Morrison and Colonel O'Leary about the both of you. You're having access to your high-performance aircraft is most definitely a plus. Let's meet in a couple of old days at the Base in the Commander's Office. This will give me time to go over the intelligence you brought back with you.'

Dighello got up from his chair and extended his hand to Shawn and said, 'Thank you so very much for your accomplishment, Sir Shawn. You continue to make a difference in this world. I will see you again in a couple of days.'

Fifteen minutes later, Shawn walked into his home on base. Christopher and Colette came over to him and gave him a huge hug. 'Where is your mother?' Shawn asked.

'Did she go flying alone?'

'No, father. Auntie Amelia went with her. She thought that Auntie would like to fly on her own. Mother was going to feel her out to see if Auntie was amenable to transitioning into advanced fighter aircraft from her Lockheed Electra.'

'Oh, really! I wish I could have spoken to her before she left. Young Ensign O'Hara shot down three African Fighters on our way back from Europe early this morning. It appears they are gearing up for something that I wanted to let your mother know to stay to the east northeast of Australia for the time being. Did she say when she was going to be back?'

'She told us it would be an hour and a half flight.'

'And the Baron, what was he up to today? He didn't want to tag along?'

'No, father,' said Christopher. 'He is having a book signing at the Base Bookstore this morning. Did you know that he wrote his book about his World War I fighter exploits?'

'Actually, no, I did not. Did he say anything about mentioning me in his book? I mean, it really should go without saying, right?'

'Father, you are absolutely correct; it should go without saying,' said Colette impishly and with a huge smirk.

'O.K., O.K., You two, I yield! How about I take you over to the officer's

club for lunch? How does that sound?' 'Yea, Pizza!' both children yield.

After the three of them returned from lunch, Christine had still not returned to their home. Shawn called over to the base and was patched through to the hangar.

'Flight Sergeant Caruso, how may I help you, Sir?' said Will on the Phone.

'Hi, Will, it's Shawn. What time do you expect Christine back from her flight? I understand she took the Leopard out for a spin with Amelia. Any ETA back at the base?'

'Sir Shawn, they're overdue by a half hour. Their flight plan took them to the north of Sydney and slightly west. They are dispatching an aircraft in ten minutes. They were about ready to call you to let you know what's going on.'

'O.K., I'm coming over. Could you make sure the Shark is all set to go?'

'She's fully fueled and armed, Colonel. I will have her on the tarmac and ready when you get here, Sir.'

'Christopher and Colette, I am taking you over to Commander Morrison's Office. I need to check on the status of your mother's flight. I'm sure that Sergeant Cranston won't mind watching you when I'm gone.'

'Father, is it about Mother?'

'Yes, Christopher. She is overdue from her flight, and I'm going to see what I came to do to sort all of this out at the airfield.'

'Father. I am going with you.' Said his son.

'Christopher, I think it's best that you stay with Colette.'

Christopher reached over and grabbed his father's arm lightly, looked into his father's eyes intently, and said more softly, 'Father, I am going with you.'

Shawn looked back at his son for a long moment and said, 'O.K., You're coming with me. Let's go, you two.'

They got into Shawn's SUV and drove over to headquarters, where Shawn and the two children went up the stairs to commander Morrison's office. He checked in with Sergeant Cranston and asked if she could watch Colette briefly while he tried to get a handle on his wife's flight situation. Sergeant Cranston's eyes lit up when asked because she simply adored Colette. The feeling was mutual. Shawn asked if he and Christopher could see the Commander. Cranston said that Marshal Morrison was not in, but that Air Chief Marshal O'Leary was inside. She told them to go in.

'Shawn, Christopher, what a surprise! How are you two?'

'Hello, Sir. Have you heard that Christine and Amelia are overdue from their training flight this morning by almost two hours now?'

'What! No, Shawn, I was not informed. What did her flight   plan suggest?'

'She filed a flight to the north northwest. I didn't get a chance to tell her about Ensign O'Hara's and my mixing it up with three African fighters earlier this morning on the way back from my assignment. Had I done so, I would have advised her to fly due east and away from any potential threat. I took a look all at the SITREP [Situation Report] for activity occurring in the lower area of Indonesia. They appear to be ratcheting up their presence, specifically, guerilla activity in a pocket around East Timor, on Jaco Island, to the east of the mainland. It's possible they may have a very limited presence on Melville Island, off the coast of Darwin.

'I'll be watching the intelligence reports as they come in. Tell me what's happening at this very moment to locate her.'

'Sir, they've launched an aircraft to fly her suspected direction of flight. But since it was a BFR flight plan with no air routes involved, she could be anywhere within the cone of 15 nautical miles on either side of her intended flight line. I'm taking Christopher with me in the F-42A to see if I can assist in any way possible in finding her location. I don't have a good feeling about this, Colonel.'

'Colonel O'Leary,' Christopher said as he looked intently into the Air Chief's Marshal's eyes, 'I feel my presence is going to be needed in bringing mother back safely.' He said nothing more.

Colonel O'Leary knew better than to argue with The Entity's son. The young teenager at 13 years of age was prescient. He was also dual-rated in the Tiger Shark and the Leopard, and was already an Ace in aerial combat against aggressor forces. Anyone who knew Christopher understood never to argue a point with him. Besides, he had already brought his father back to life several times.

'Keep Operations posted while you both are in the air. I presume you have Colette taken care of with Sergeant Cranston. I truly hope that everything will turn out well. Good luck.'

Shawn and Christopher did a quick pre-flight, knowing all too well that Will had done, preparing the Shark for flight. After takeoff, they flew in a north-westerly direction at 2,000 feet. Ten minutes later, they spotted the first aircraft in the air over land. It was a four-engine transport, and the F-42A quickly overcame it and flew ahead.

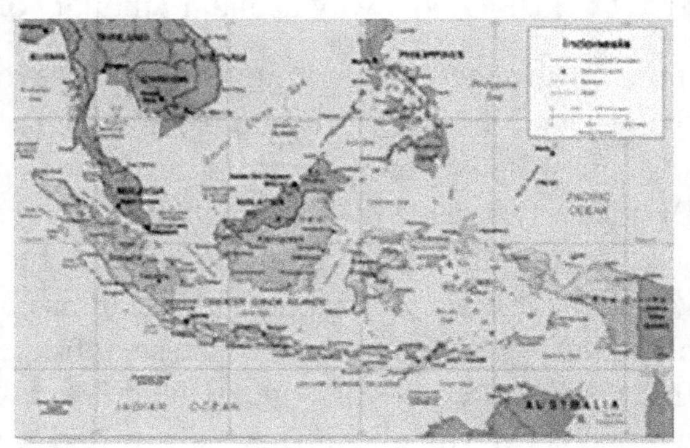

MAP OF INDONESIA

En.wikipedia.org/wiki/File: Indonesia/2002_CIA_map.png

Shawn reached the northern edge of the continent and still had not seen anything in the way of an aircraft. Christopher had been making calls on Guard in the blind since they reached the 50 nautical mile mark away from Sydney. Still nothing from the radios. Crawford then remembered something very crucial.

Quite a long time ago, Christine and Shawn had decided to install special beacons aboard their aircraft that would activate when the other fighter sent out a signal. Either fighter did not have to be on the ground or in the air; it could be in either space. Shawn did not know why he hadn't thought of it earlier.

The device operated similarly to a homing signal that would "reach out" from one aircraft and search for a specific and distinct signal emanating from the other fighter. Their signals were akin to high frequency, or HF signals, much like an ADF instrument used for limited and non-precision instrument approaches under total weather-like conditions. The actual hardware was different, however, in that the receiving and sending emissions were specifically oriented only toward these two aircraft. The stealth-like covering of the fighters was one of no consequence when one of the fighters was searching for the other. The signal was powerful enough to reach out and "capture" the other aircraft to a distance of 200 nautical miles; it was that powerful and innovative.

After flying for 45 minutes, Crawford began getting an intermittent signal from the Leopard. It was weak at first, and Christopher was the first to notice it, as all of his senses were acutely elevated and more sensitive than a normal being was. The beacon signal became more and more pronounced and steady in tone. Five minutes later, the direction-finding actuator kicked in and the arrow in the instrumentation began telling Crawford what direction he needed to turn to keep it centered. There was a distance measuring equipment feature, or DME, that indicated the total nautical mile they needed to travel before being on top of the aircraft. They were within 5 NM at this point with the needle pegged on the center line. Shawn began slowing the aircraft down. They were now over one of the northern Islands of the Australian Continent, Melville Island, located off the coast of Darwin.

'Father, break left!' yelled Christopher. His son sensed the anti-craft missile before it was launched. At this altitude, had Christopher not been along, Shawn and the Tiger Shark would have been "toast"!

Crawford banked sharply on his son's instinct. The missile barely missed the Shark's airframe underneath. As they were so slow to the ground for a fighter, a proximity fuse, if any, did not have time enough to engage. The light from the exhaust left Crawford momentarily blinded.

Christopher saw his father's dilemma and immediately took control of the aircraft. He banked back to the right and lowered the nose to reduce the angle of impact for any further incoming missiles fired from below.

Shawn's son continued bringing the F-42A around to the line-up on the proposed launch point of the missile. The old adage, "where there's smoke, there's fire" was appropriate. Christopher was not going to let the attackers get off another shot at them.

Map of Australia

He got to within 50 meters of the aggressor's location when he launched an air-to-ground missile. Both he and Shawn were rewarded with a tremendous explosion on the ground. They had hit an ammunition dump. They overflew the location of the fireball. And that location was adjacent to what the beacon inside the Shark was telling them where the Leopard was in that general vicinity.

Christopher could read his father's mind when he said, 'Don't worry, father, mother, and auntie are not even close to the location of the ammo dump that we just eliminated. Father, I suggest we hover land not far away and make our way over to the general area. The number of guards around the perimeter will increase as we get closer to mother and auntie Amelia.'

'O.K., Christopher, but, you're going to have to execute the landing as I'm partially blinded in one eye from that flash before.'

'I've got it, father. There was a clearing not far from the ammunition dump that would be perfect for the Tiger Shark to hover-land straight down. The trees will mask our location easily.'

ESCAPE FROM DEATH

CHRISTOPHER DEFTLY ROTATED the Tiger Shark thrusters and quickly placed the huge aircraft on the ground. He accomplished an emergency shutdown procedure and everything all of a sudden became quiet.

Crawford extracted a hand-held version of the aircraft beacon from his center console, and they both exited the Shark. Once the device in Shawn's hand was activated, it began searching for the Leopard's signal. Less than five seconds later, it had an unwavering lock, defining what direction they needed to go. The readout also told them the distance [0.3 kilometers] to travel to get to the other stealth fighter. They had a little less than three and a half football lengths to go and get to the Leopard. The ammunition dump continued to cook rounds, which was helpful because it helped to mask their movement easily.

They reached an edge of a clearing and heard men arguing with one another. Every once in a while, a round from the dump would cook off and the men would duck instinctively. They moved closer and saw five men around the fire. Christine and Amelia were on the outer periphery, tied to a tree, and gagged. Shawn's blood began to boil. He then felt Christopher calming influence when the latter placed his hand on Shawn's forearm.

The Leopard was barely visible on the other side of the clearing and looked to be on a road. He couldn't tell if it was dirt or macadam surface.

One of the men left at the fire area and walked over to Christine and slapped her across the face. She then spits in the attacker's face. He hit her again. Amelia reached out with one leg and kicked the man hard above his ankle. He howled in pain and backhanded Amelia with great force. Earhart slumped forward against her ropes and went unconscious.

Shawn had had enough of his slapping women around when tied to a tree. He noted the wind so that the flames from the fire would not give them away. He also noted that there was only one individual on that side of the fire. The woman would be tied up on the opposite side, as well.

When he reached his desired position, he took a small pebble and threw it at the individual sitting on the up-wind side and close to the fire. Shawn's small rock hit the man on the back of his neck.

The individual reached back as if to swat a fly. Crawford grabbed another pebble off of the ground and threw it at him. After the second throw, he and Christopher split in two directions. The rock hitting the man had the desired effect in that he got up and slowly walked in their direction and toward the vegetation.

At first, he didn't see anything, so he walked further into the wooded area until he lost sight. It was then that Shawn grabbed his neck from behind and twisted it sharply. The individual collapsed to the ground, dead.

Four more to go.

Crawford then began counting rifles among the men. Their weapon discipline was atrocious, thought Crawford. No one was even remotely close to their automatic weapons. They didn't have to be.

'Don't move!' an individual said from behind. 'Get up and walk toward the fire.'

Shawn looked at Christopher as they rose from the ground. They were then told to put their hands on top of their heads as they started walking toward the clearing. Shawn's mind was a whirl and looked for any advantage he could think to get. There weren't at this point. He looked at Christopher. He appeared unusually calm.

Their captive yelled out to his companions. They all reached for their weapons as they saw the intruders being led by one of their own. The leader of the group came forward and asked with a sneer how they had gotten to their location. Shawn told him nothing. The leader stepped forward and got in Shawn's face. He then looked down at Shawn's son, who merely looked toward his mother. Christine tied to the tree with a swollen lip looked on in horror at seeing her son standing diminutive in front of a huge-standing individual. Christopher then looked up slowly into the man's eyes and said softly in the captive's native tongue, 'You should let us go right now.'

The outlaw looked down at the boy and broke out in laughter. His compatriots did the same. The leader then took a swing at young Christopher and got to within an inch of the boy's face, but his swing stopped there abruptly. Christopher never moved a muscle but continued to look the man in the eye.

The terrorist then attempted to put both hands on the boy to pick him up. Christopher put his arm straight out in front of him, with his palm facing toward the man. All of a sudden, the leader was thrust violently up against the nearest tree. His back and head bounced off it, and he slumped to the ground unconscious.

Christopher then looked toward the group that was totally startled by the boy's action. They picked up their weapons and began firing at the boy and his father. The rounds stopped on the front of the pair and dropped harmlessly to the ground.

One of the terrorists mouthed the word "DEVIL" in his native language and immediately ran from the clearing. Two others came forward with large knives they had unsheathed from scabbards. Christopher and Shawn spread apart.

'Christopher, I've got the ugly one on the right. You can have "pretty boy" on the left.'

The aggressor on the right came at Crawford with his right arm raised to thrust at Shawn in a downward motion. He got within eighteen inches and, just before he started his motion toward Shawn's chest, the latter pivoted quickly 360- degrees and rendered a powerful kick to the man's chest, stopping his heart. He lay dead at Shawn's feet.

Christopher's assailant came at him with the knife edge pointed at the child's chest in his right hand. At the last moment, the boy pivoted 90- degrees to the right. The knife sailed past Christopher. At the same moment, The Entity's child grabbed the wrist with his left hand as it sailed by and pressed the arm downward, backward, and away from the boy's body. As the momentum caused the terrorists to turn toward Christopher, the boy then thrust a powerful right-hand fist into the attacker's nose, driving it deeply into his brain. The man fell backward in a heap as the boy let the right arm go. He, too, lay dead.

By this time, the only individuals remaining in the clearing were Shawn, Christopher, Christine, and Amelia, who were slowly getting consciousness while still tied against the tree. Shawn ran quickly to Christine and untied her. He held her close as Christopher tended to his Auntie Amelia.

When the women were untied. Shawn went to the pocket of terrorists, as he had done in Paris. He extracted a half-dozen pieces of paper information with dates, times, and locations. He placed those in his flight suit.

'My God, Shawn, I thought you two were dead when they began shooting at you! And then, when I saw the rounds drop directly into the dirt in front of you, I knew that we were going to make it out of here alive! It's nice having friends in "high places"!'

'Auntie, are you O.K.?' asked Christopher.

'I am now, Christopher! How did you manage to find us?'

Shawn looked at Christine and said, 'Do you remember when we put that improvised tracking device aboard each of our stealth fighters? Well, they did indeed work. We had to dodge a missile as we approached, and that further acknowledged the fact that we had found you both.'

'Where is the Shark?'

'It is safely in a clearing about 300 yards from here, Mother. And the Leopard? They must have shot you down, correct?'

'No, they didn't, actually. The funny thing is that we were drawn to this area by an SOS signal coming from the ground. We noted that it was close to that road over there and the surface looked good and long enough to land. We thought we were helping someone who really needed our assistance. When we got out of the Leopard and started walking toward their clearing, we were quickly surrounded by these terrorists. You came along just in time. I don't think we would have stayed alive too much longer.'

'O.K., let's get you over to the Leopard as it's closer. We've got some medical supplies inside. Looks like you've got a "helluva" fat lip there, Sweetheart! Amelia, you're pretty banged up in the face. Are either of you hurting anywhere else?'

'No, Shawn,' said Amelia. 'They hit me several times in the face, but nothing in the body. It's nothing that the Baron won't fix when we return to Base.'

'O.K., this is how we'll play it. I will lead you all back to the Tiger Shark. Christopher, you drive your mother and Auntie Amelia back to base. I'll come back for the Leopard and will take off from the road and will be behind you by a few miles.'

'Christopher, when you get within communication range of Sydney, call operations and let them know that you're inbound. Tell them I am behind you, O.K.?'

'Yes, Father.'

'O.K., are you two alright to walk?'

Christine looked at Amelia, who nodded once. 'We're good go, Shawn.'

The four of them walked across the clearing and over to the Leopard. Shawn extracted some medical supplies and attended to the cuts on the face of both women. When he finished, they proceeded back across the clearing and toward the Tiger Shark.

'Let's do it then. I'll lead the remainder of the way. Christopher, please bring up the rear. O.K., let's go.'

There was no sign of the terrorists on their way back to the F-42A. While Christopher was getting strapped into the left seat, Shawn made sure that Christine and Amelia were settled into the right and jump seats.

Jaco Island, East Timor, Indo-nesia Courtesy of easttimornow. com.au

'Christopher, when you launch, stay at treetop level until feet wet and heading towards the Australian coastline. If there are any other ground-to-air-missiles, you'll be by them before they'll have an opportunity to engage your aircraft.

'O.K., Father. Be careful, Father!'

'Always, my son. Great job back there.' He gave his son a kiss on the forehead, and then he was gone.

Christopher spooled up the two powerful turbines, brought the Shark to a hover after all systems registered nominally, and lifted above the trees. He rotated the thrusters to the horizontal and quickly gained speed while skimming the top of the trees. He was over the Australian coast in a matter of minutes.

When Shawn took off from the road in the Leopard, he climbed to altitude. He headed in a northerly direction toward Jaco Island, said to be uninhabited and to the east of East Timor. The island was approximately 10 square miles and was generally a place where fishermen took tourists to swim and fish. It would be a convenient place for a terrorist cell to do some detailed planning regarding the infiltration into the northern end of Australia.

He arrived at the island five minutes later and circled it quickly. All of a sudden, a stinger missile was fired from the southern end of the island. Shawn dove the Leopard quickly and the missile sailed overhead and detonated some 100 meters to his six o'clock position. As he was heading in a northerly direction, he kept his dive going and banked sharply to the left. He continued out to sea for 60 seconds after leveling off and then abruptly turned back to the right. He lined himself up with a small sandy cove-like area that was unmistakably evident in front of the beginning of the Jaco Island forest. Furthermore, he started taking some small arms fire on the Leopard's run into the coast.

Crawford then fired two air-to-ground missiles, or JAGM, and had them centered in the far tree line on that sandy nook. The explosions that occurred next must have been a combination of his missiles fired and an ammunition dump hidden in the trees. A series of loud reports one after another that lasted a good 800 seconds announced the destruction of a fairly large depot.

As he turned the Leopard back toward Darwin, he saw several individuals with their clothing on fire and stumbling toward the East Timor Sea from the trees. That is for my bride and Amelia, you dirtbags!'

F-93B Leopard Stealth Fighter Courtesy of
myopera.com

THE AFRICAN ASSIGNMENT

SHAWN CLIMBED QUICKLY to 15,000 feet and pushed the throttles forward. He caught up with Christopher just as the Tiger Shark was switching over to Sydney Tower. He was told by the tower to decrease the speed for separation from the F-42A. Moments later, he entered the break and came around to land on the active runway. He taxied to the hangar and stopped the Leopard just as Christopher, his mother, and Amelia were slowly walking into the hangar. A medical vehicle had been standing by, waiting for the F-42A's arrival. He shut down the Leopard's powerful twin turbines and elevated his canopy.

Shawn caught up with the others as medic personnel were going over both Christine and Amelia. Baron von Richthofen had arrived prior to the Shark's touchdown and went immediately to his bride, Amelia. He was incensed that someone would do this to a woman.

Christopher looked at the Baron for a long moment and informed him that the perpetrators were no longer among the living. And that a planning cell on Jaco Island had been neutralized by his father after he launched from Melville Island.'

As Crawford walked up to them, the Baron turned to Shawn and asked if it was true that he had taken care of the terrorists in Jaco Island.

'Baron, who might have told you that, as he was looking at his son, Christopher?'

'Young Christopher just informed me, *Herr* Crawford. It is the truththen?'

'Yes, Baron. I cannot tell a lie. I supposed I got lost on the way back and found myself approaching that little "uninhabited" Island when a surface-to-air missile was thrust in my direction. Likewise, I guess my finger slipped on the switch to loosen two JAGMs at them when I was trying to open a Twinkies bar. My, oh my! You should have seen the fireworks as soon as my missiles hit. Must have been something very "nasty" in the tree line because it went up like a fourth of July celebration in the States!'

'Baron, would you please be so kind as to take Christine over to the O-club? Christopher and I must report to the Air Chief Marshal and file our

SITREP. I believe Colette may still be at the headquarters building, and I will take her to the O-Club with me after Christopher and I have completed our report.'

'No problem, Sir Shawn!'

'Thank you so much, Herr Baron. I owe you a schnitzel dinner!' 'I look forward to it, Sir!'

'Chris,' said Shawn. 'Are you sure you're alright?'

'Yes, I'm fine. You know me. I could have eaten away at that tree I was tied to and freed myself before you arrived. Besides, I could have used the extra fiber in my diet!'

Christopher laughed out loud at that one.

Shawn looked at Christine and then at his son and said, 'Well, my boy, it appears that plant life is no longer safe in this base.'

This got some giggles from Christopher!

'O.K., Chris, I leave you in good hands with the Baron. Christopher, Colette, and I will be back at the O-Club as soon as we can. I can't tell how relieved I am to see you standing here before me, even though you look like Mike Tyson with that extended lip.'

'Watch it, Cowboy! They'll be matching lips here in a second, and the second one won't be on my other side!'

'Christopher, I think I hear the Colonel calling us to report to Headquarters. Luv, we'll see you soon! And, Chris, please no more bar fights. It frightens the children!'

And with that, Shawn quickly moved away from his feisty bride of a few years and hid behind his son Christopher, who was laughing uncontrollably!

'I will see you when you get home!' announced Christine with mocks sincerity.

'Oh, Luv, I simply adore you when you talk--,' and he mouthed the word "dirty" without Christopher hearing it! 'Come along, Christopher, we really must be going. And please, son, stop interrupting our attempts to leave here!'

Christopher then chanted out loud, 'Dirty, dirty, dirty!'

Shawn and Christine groaned, and all the others laughed out loud!

Shawn and his son walked up the stairway to the Commander's Office and saw that Colette was still there with Sergeant Cranston. They were playing some sort of game with dice and colored pieces on a square board with numerous symbols on it. Every once in a while, pieces would change positions. Shawn decided to give up on trying to understand the play of this game.

'Hello, Sir Shawn. And, Christopher! I am truly happy you are safe!',said Sergeant Cranston.

'Thank you, Sergeant. My father and I are here to file our report on what just happened on Melville Island.'

'Yes, Of course, please go right in. the Air Chief Marshal has been expecting you both.'

'Thank you, Sergeant Cranston.' Christopher then borrowed a cavalier line from his father's repertoire of quips and said, 'Sergeant, you really look great! Have you lost weight? You look fabulous!'

'Well, now. You have left me speechless, Christopher! I suppose I have lost a few pounds along the way this past week.'

Christopher smiled warmly at Sergeant Cranston and turned to walk in the Commander's Office.

Within, with the Commander and Colonel O'Leary was Agent Dighello.

Shawn shared the Melville Island experience with the key leadership and concluded with a concern that the terrorists were becoming more and more in evidence across the globe.

'Our intelligence assets worldwide confirm that to be true, Shawn. We have an opportunity to eliminate some of the world's worst terrorists. There is a large group scheduled to meet this weekend in Mozambique,' said Dighello.

'We need for you and Mr. O'Hara to be in Beira along the coast Saturday evening. They are meeting at the Grand Hotel Beira on Sunday morning. You will meet your contact at the International Airport there Friday evening. I believe you and Ensign O'Hara have worked with him in the past, a Commander J Hunter King.'

Shawn smiled at hearing the name. 'Ah yes, Commander King is definitely a face from the past. Very proficient and very deadly. It will be good to work with him once again. He once promised to give me a scooter lesson on the Island of Bermuda.'

'Good, it's nice to know that you two have more than a professional working relationship together. Commander King will provide the incidentals for your OP when you and O'Hara arrive. I'm afraid that this is merely the tip of the iceberg. It would appear that our political system has taken the lead in the world for initiating the elimination of terrorism. As always, we look forward to what you may be able to bring back with you in terms of intelligence.'

Shawn left headquarters with Christopher and Colette to go over to the Officer's Club to meet Christine for an early dinner. When he arrived, sitting at the table were Ensign O'Hara and CPT Shelley O'Leary. They were sitting close to one another and appeared to be totally taken with one another in conversation.

Christine still had a severe puffed lip, but wore it well, Shawn thought. Christopher and Colette ran over to the table and smiled at seeing their mother with Tim and Shelley.

'Did you two enjoy Sergeant Cranston's company?' Christine asked her children.

'Yes, mother, we did! We are going to help her find a nice young man like Uncle Timmy is for Auntie Shelley!'

Ensign O'Hara thought he was going to choke on the piece of bread he was trying to swallow! He looked sheepishly at CPT O'Leary.

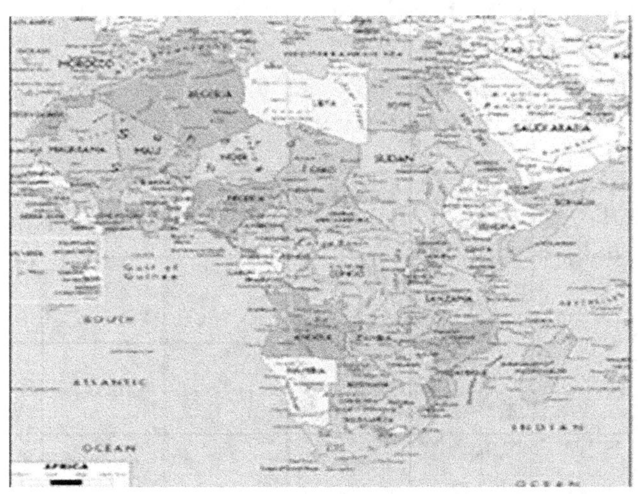

Map of Africa

Courtesy of www.exilon.com/maps/african-continent-maps.html

Shelley seized the moment and said to all, 'Young and handsome Ensign Timothy O'Hara could do a lot worse!' O'Hara then knew positively that he was going to choke on his bread!

Shawn was just getting seated at that moment and asked, 'What did I miss?'

Not only was O'Hara going to choke, but he was going to do it with a thoroughly reddened face!

'Let's change the subject. Shawn, did you get everything straightened out with Colonel O'Leary and the Commander?'

'I did. And Agent Dighello was also present. I'm afraid that I have another junket to go to this coming weekend.'

'Great, father! Where are we going this time?' asked his son.

'Well, Christopher, we'll have to talk about this when we get home. For now, why don't we all enjoy ourselves? Who's hungry? And. Christopher and Colette, I don't want to hear the "P" word for dinner.'

Tim asked Shawn mischievously. 'What's the "P" word, Sir Shawn? As if on cue, Christopher and Colette yelled out, "Pizza!"

Shawn groaned and looked at O'Hara with a look that suggested that he was going to get even for that!

After dinner, Shawn pulled Tim aside and said that they had another mission for this coming weekend, Southeastern Africa, in the Country of Mozambique.

O'Hara then asked if he had any specifics and Shawn repeated what Agent Dighello had told him in the Commander's Office, they were to leave Friday evening. The flight was not a lengthy one in that it was across the Island of Madagascar and the Madagascar Channel. Shawn would get together with Tim the next morning and share with O'Hara the remaining information.

'For the time being, my young warrior, the evening is young, and you have a young lady who values your company. Enjoy yourselves. See you in the morning, Timmy!'

'Good night, Sir Shawn.'

They walked over to where Christine, the children, and Shelley were talking beside the Crawford automobile. They all said goodnight and Tim asked Shelley if she wanted to take a stroll down on the boardwalk.

As they walked, they talked small talk about the past couple of days. They found a bench and sat quietly looking out over the Western Pacific. Shelley leaned over and placed her head on his shoulder and took his hand in hers. She stayed that way for a moment, lifted her head, and looked into those baby-blue Irish O'Hara eyes. He leaned over and gently kissed her on the lips. He put his arm around her and they embraced.

After a long moment, she stood and pulled him to her, and they kissed sensually. Shelley broke the embrace and led Tim over to her vehicle. She drove over to her quarters. They entered, and she led him to her bedroom where they laid down on her bed and slowly disrobed one another, and made love the entire evening.

The following morning, a bright, beautiful summer February morning in Australia, Shelley awoke and found herself alone in bed. A moment later, Tim came into the bedroom carrying a tray of bacon, eggs, toast, and coffee, and a smile.

Shelley smiled back and sat up. She told him to place the tray on the dresser and to come over to her. They made love for another hour and fell asleep in one another's arms. Bacon and eggs would have to wait another morning!

Christopher had been requested to speak to various scientific symposiums two years after he found himself under the loving supervision of the Crawford Family. Colette had yet to come on the scene. His expertise lay in every conceivable aspect of science, but he was most notably sought for his awareness of the workings of the Universe.

Christopher's name was renowned as an expert in quantum physics. He lectured to the leading scientist of the world and concluded each session by answering the various questions as 'experts" sought clarification regarding the finer points of his presentation. Christopher didn't have to write papers on his "theories". They were not theories indeed, but fact, and Christopher was able to prove these facts time and time again. The only limiting factor lay in the closed-minded "intellects" of those who witnessed his lectures. And the majority of these self-professed "scientists" were envious that a 13-year-old science prodigy was proven to be accurate in his assessment in terms of how the Universe functioned. And Upstart he was, but a brilliant Upstart he also was!

So, it was therefore propitious that a scientific delegation wanted Christopher to lecture on some aspect of the Universe as I related to parallel dimensions, such venue for the lecture was to be held in Harare, the Capitol City in neighboring Zimbabwe, at the Crowne Plaza Monomotapa Hotel, world-famous for hosting professional football [soccer] teams and conventions.

Shawn and Christine received the lecture invitation on the following Wednesday through the Australian Department for External Affairs. Christine was aware that the OP was on for Africa that weekend. It was somehow difficult not to imagine the hand of Agent Todd Dighello in the overall scheme of things, not that it mattered at all. The acknowledgement to attend was submitted, and Christopher then became an added influence to the equation for success in Mozambique.

Christine was ambivalent about having her son leave once again for another clandestine mission, this time in Africa. His cover as a guest lecturer was perfect, but it still represented a level of danger that she had yet to reconcile. And truth be known, she was really worried more about her husband. So, having Christopher around in these matters was definitely a plus, as their son had brought Shawn back to life at least twice before. Each time this had to happen was heart-wrenching!

Shawn, Tim, and Christopher took off Friday morning in the F-42A Tiger Shark in lieu of the Leopard because of the Shark's hover-mode- capability. They launched with a full complement of weapon stores. Their time of flight according to the IFR flight plan filed for 22,000 feet was 1 hour 32 minutes on March 4. They were on final approach at the Harare International Airport right on time.

The agenda was to be that they would be met by the Zimbabwe Scientific Community and taken over to their hotel. When they entered the terminal with their individual backpacks after landing, they were met by the country's chief scientist. Inside those packs, and because they knew conclusively that they were going to be treated akin to diplomats, each carried a nine-millimeter Beretta with a silencer attached. Tim O'Hara was introduced as Christopher's understudy.

They were ushered through customs without a check and led outside to a waiting limousine. After some small talk about Christopher's presentation, they arrived at their hotel and were led into the lobby by their host. When the rooms were designated, the chief scientist said that he would be by the following morning to collect them at 1100 hours. Christopher's presentation was set for 1200 hours in the Ministry of the Defense Office Building. It was scheduled to last no longer than three hours.

The scientist asked how long they would be in Zimbabwe altogether. Christopher told him that they would be leaving Sunday evening, as he had a follow-on engagement elsewhere. They had never been to this beautiful country before and wanted to see the historical sites. The scientist then bid them all a good evening, after providing Christopher with his business card and a number to be reached in the event that he had concerns about the following day.

Commander Hunter, their contact, would be meeting them at the International Airport at 1900 hours Saturday, at an adjacent hangar bordering the outer periphery of the farthest fence line on site. Shawn had asked the coach to bring a bag full of snacks.

The following morning, after a full breakfast, the three from Australia were met by the Director of Scientific Affairs for the Country of Zimbabwe. He cordially asked how their evening had been, and he led them to a waiting limousine in front of the hotel. The trip to the Ministry of Defense Office Building was but a ten-minute drive from the hotel.

They arrived at their desired location 20 minutes before Christopher was expected to address the symposium audience. He quickly reviewed his notes before being beckoned forward to take his place on stage and at a centered podium. At exactly 1200 hours, Christopher began his lecture. Tim and Shawn sat in the back of the auditorium.

After 15 minutes of Christopher's expert presentation, O'Hara looked at Shawn and asked, 'Who is this kid and what did they do with Christopher!' Shawn merely looked back, smiled, and nodded!

Christopher concluded his lecture in 2 hours and 45 minutes. He then entertained questions from the floor. There were many who sought clarification regarding many of the issues presented. Christopher answered each one in a manner easily understood. Several scientists merely shook their heads at the responses provided and shook their heads in amazement. Why didn't I think of that, mused many in attendance?

At the conclusion, many attendees approached Christopher regarding his presentation. Each individual was highly complementary and asked if he could e-mail the boy should any questions emerge at a later date. Christopher assured each person that he would quickly respond to any inquiries. He provided his business card with his personal information, including an email address.

At 1530 hours, Shawn, Tim, and Christopher moved from the large meeting area to a waiting limousine to ferry them back to their hotel. Shawn looked at his watch. Perfect timing. The terrorist's meeting wasn't scheduled to begin until 2100 hours that evening. Still, time to review their planning.

When it was time to leave their hotel, Crawford telephoned the concierge to have a taxi available to take them to the Queen Victoria Museum for some sightseeing. Of course, there was no desire to visit the Museum, only to provide the ruse in the event anyone of reputed interest were to ask questions as to their intentions. They each carried a backpack that contained their flight suits. For all intents and purposes, they portrayed tourists anticipating a visit to one of Harare's tourist attractions. They took the elevator to the lobby to await their transportation.

Then the three piled into the taxi, and after traveling in the general direction of the Museum, Shawn asked the driver to pull over. When the driver did so, the three exited the taxi and walked along a "farmer's market" for a few moments until the cab driver was out of sight. Crawford then flagged down another taxi and asked that they be driven to the airport. They arrived there 20 minutes later.

They walked into the terminal building and into the restroom to change their clothing, as they were changing, an individual walked in with no intention of using the facility for its intended purpose. This was further confirmed when the person pulled a silenced pistol and fired a point-blank round at Ensign O'Hara. Tim felt the impact of the bullet as it pressed against his chest, and that was all!

Nearby, Christopher, who anticipated the intentions of the intruder, stood looking at the perpetrator with his left arm out-reached when the round was fired. A blue aura emanated from his palm and appeared to extend to the torso of Ensign O'Hara. He then raised his right arm and thrust it forward with his hand facing the gunman, palm downward. The individual was pushed back with such force that he hit the wall by the door leading into the restroom with a loud thud. He collapsed slowly to the floor, unconscious.

O'Hara simply stood in awe about what he had just experienced.

'Ensign, could you please open my backpack and take out the gray roll "hundred-mile-an-hour' tape and hand it to me?'

When Shawn man-handled the body into a stall, Christopher took the tape and nearly "mummified" the attacker.

'Do you think you used enough tape, Christopher?' his father asked.

They took out a piece and paper and wrote "out of order" in Afrikaans on the door where the unconscious and thoroughly tied up terrorist was "serenely seated" within!

With their change of clothes in their backpacks, they calmly walked out to the F-42A and did a thorough pre-flight of the aircraft. As they were in "Indian Country', Shawn didn't trust airport security to be ever vigilant in and around their craft.

After their thorough walk-around, they climbed into the cockpit. Crawford, sitting in the left seat, initiated the igniters and the twin turbines began rotating as fuel was pumped into the "combustion chamber" at the same time the igniter spark created the controlled "explosion" for the engines. The Shark roars to life!

Crawford made the appropriate ground control call in Afrikaans, and they were cleared to position for takeoff.

In the distance, three military armored vehicles entered the runway, 7000 feet away. They were moving toward the Tiger Shark rapidly. At the rate they were traveling, the Tiger Shark's takeoff distance was rapidly deteriorating.

'O.K., who forgot to tip the maid before we left?'

Shawn pushed the throttles forward. As the F-42A moved quickly down the runway, the vehicles began firing small arms in the direction of their aircraft. Crawford stopped the aircraft's forward momentum and came to a complete stop.

The ground vehicles continued to move forward to their aircraft.

Shawn opened up with his 20 mm cannon and blew one vehicle into the air 10 feet, another off the side of the runway when it overturned three the third vehicles saw the wisdom of "getting out of Dodge" as soon as possible, tried to back up too quickly, and ended up flipping the half-ton vehicle over on its side. It was a bad day all the way around the Harare Driving Academy.

Shawn rotated the thrusters and brought the Shark to an immediate hover, rotated to the horizontal, and shot forward in the afterburner. They were soon cruising southeast bound toward Mozambique at an altitude of 1,500 feet.

When they got to the Zimbabwe City of Mutare just before crossing into Mozambique, Crawford lowered the nose of the F-42A to tree top level after lowering his night vision device over his eyes. O'Hara did the same. Christopher kept him off to monitor the system's instruments inside the cockpit, per protocol. It was another forty-minute flight to the coastal city of Beira, the second-largest city in the country.

The scheduled terrorist meeting was set for the Tivoli Hotel. Their contact, Commander Hunter King, was going to meet them at the far end of the airport that shut down operations at 1800 hours. Their arrival time in Beira was 1915 hours.

Shawn made an abbreviated approach to hover at the designated spot on the tarmac. As soon as he landed, he noticed an area wide enough between two hangars for the Shark to fit. He taxied quickly into position and shut the engines down. They exited the aircraft with their over-the-shoulder bags and were almost immediately met by Commander King.

'Did you boys have a nice flight? And, who do we have here?' King asked when he saw Christopher.

'Coach, this is our backup. Please meet youthful-looking Christopher. He is a dwarf and is 118 years old. Christopher, please bark twice for the coach.'

'Father, I'm not a day over 97. Please do not give the coach the wrong impression. Coach, it's my very distinct pleasure to meet you. Father has told me all about you and how you love to ride motorbikes in Bermuda.'

'Coach, you didn't!' exclaimed Hunter.

'I cannot tell a lie. Ensign O'Hara did!'

Tim was having the most difficult time trying to follow this line of conversation and failing miserably. Commander king recognized O'Hara's confusion and told him that it was more of an outside joke than an inside one! That confused Tim even more.

'Ensign, not to worry. The Coach and I go back a long way, almost as far as 1978! Then there was that time in Cambodia, wasn't there, Coach?'

'Yes, there was. That time when I had to rescue a walking "grass heap" after it had taken out that officer terrorist. They didn't have a welcoming party back then; it was more like an unwelcome departing party!'

'They did get a little excited, didn't they, Coach? I didn't know what the fuss was all about: I only took one of them out! And they want me to go back to their reunion! But, then again, I get a lot after assassinating people.'

'That is what endears them to you, Hunter. Some people never let go of some things.'

'Oh well, here we have another opportunity at sharing our goodwill in Mozambique. Moving right along. The meeting, Shawn, is still set for 2100 hours at the Tivoli Hotel. They are separating nothing. They are conspiring with opulence in mind. I just hope that, when we crash their party, there are enough hors d'oeuvres left for all of us.'

'Not to worry, my hungry friend. I brought some of those fig newtons I saved for us when in France, trying to consume a hearty meal by the canal that evening. And I promised that my fingers have never touched them in the past eighteen months since we were last there.'

It took them five minutes to drive over to the location of the terrorist meeting.

'How do you want to play this?' asked King.

'How rusty are your rappelling techniques?'

'About as rusty as yours. Seems like the last time we did something like that was in Libya many months ago. What do you have in mind, Coach?'

'Since my technique is about as oil-free as yours, we'll go for Plan B. Tim, you and Christopher are going to play father and son looking for your wife. I want you both to approach security and start asking them questions whether they have seen her. Coach, did you bring the canisters?'

'I did.'

'Good. While Tim has security preoccupied, we'll take the stairwell to the top floor. I'm sure they will have a guard posted outside the corridor in the stairwell. After neutralizing that guard and the one most assuredly in the hallway, we'll position the gas after blocking the door from the outside. Did you bring the protective masks?'

'I did.'

'O.K., any questions?'

'Father, what's hors d'oeuvres?'

They all looked at Christopher and broke out laughing. 'Christopher, no worries, I'll find a Fen-way Frank for you somewhere before we leave. Let's do it!'

They all went around to the rear of the Hotel and found the telephone cable, both internal room-to-room and external use to the outside. Shawn applied some acid to the cables and all the lines were conveniently severed. Now, the authorities could not be called, nor could the terrorists within the meeting room call out. Commander King had brought along a scrambler device that would negate any calls made via a cell phone from inside the meeting room.

Tim and Christopher walked into the Hotel, with Christopher playing an Oscar-like performance. He was sobbing, almost uncontrollably, as soon as he began into the Hotel. Hunter and Shawn were watching. Hunter started to say something about Christopher's acting when Shawn cut him off by saying, 'He takes after his mother!'

'I know that, Coach.' Said Hunter smiling.

'O.K., they're in, let's go.'

When the two special ops agents walked into the Hotel, they quickly found the door leading to the stairs. They went inside and began climbing to the top floor. When they got halfway to the top, Shawn pulled out a piece of charcoal, a paper bag, and an empty bottle of wine. He applied the charcoal marker all over his face and then donned a dirty baseball cap. He then shared all the same with Commander King. Anyone now seeing them would identify two bums with bottles of wine in brown paper bags.

They climbed the next several floors with a normal gate until they got to the next to the last landing before reaching their intended floor. Shawn had been right. There was a guard who began to investigate the noise in the stairwell below him.

Country of Mozambique, Africa
Courtesy of Wikipedia, the Free Encyclope-
dia

Crawford put his arm around King, who "did his best to steady his brother-in-wine". As they continued staggering up the stairs, the guard started to come down to meet them. When he was ten feet away from the pair of "winos", King extracted a knife and with a swift flick of the wrist caught the guard in the chest. There was no sound. Shawn quickly reached up and caught him as he was falling forward. He put the body against the wall. Before climbing the last remaining steps to the top, Shawn looked through the pockets of the recently-deceased terrorist for any intelligence paperwork they could take back with them. He noted that, when found, the document was in Arabic, specifically Farsi. This information was all he needed to draw any guard protecting the meeting on the floor. They climbed the remaining stairs to the door leading to the corridor on the last floor.

Shawn opened the stairwell door and quickly peeked around the corner to verify that another guard was standing watch. He was right. He signaled to King that he was going to draw the other guard toward their stairwell door. King gave the "O.K." sign.

Shawn partially opened the door to the floor and said quietly in Farsi for the other guard to come over. His message was that he thought that he heard a noise down below and that he was going to investigate. He wanted some guidance from his compatriot before proceeding down the stairwell, and could he come over to listen to see if he heard the same noise? The other guard said that he should not leave his post and that this had better be worth it. He moved toward the stairwell door.

When the terrorist opened the door, he stood facing a disheveled and smiling Shawn Crawford. Crawford wiggled his fingers as if to say hello. The guard started to raise his AK-74 Kalashnikov Rifle when he was caught from behind by Commander King, who grabbed the unsuspecting terrorist by the head and quickly snapped his neck. Shawn caught the body and placed him beside the other fallen terrorist.

'Now, I want you two to play nice this evening, and, if I hear you fighting again with one another, I'm coming back and killing you again.' 'Nice, Coach. I wouldn't have given them a second "chance".'

They moved into the corridor and down the hall to the door leading into the hotel room meeting. King gave Crawford the canister of nerve gas, and Shawn attached a plastic hose to the nozzle. He placed the end of the tubing under the doorway and just far enough for the deadly gas to take effect. Before Shawn turned the gas on, both he and Hunter donned their protective masks. Once they both cleared the masks, they gave each other the "clear" sign and Shawn opened the canister. Crawford then wedged the door closed. There was absolutely no way anyone was exiting the room by merely opening the door. They pulled out their Beretta and waited.

Before long, there was the beginning of a disturbance, small at first, but becoming more frantic as the seconds dragged on. They heard footsteps approaching the door. There was an apparent struggle as those inside attempted to open the door to escape what they couldn't understand, but that which was threatening lethally.

After three minutes, Shawn withdrew the door brace and forced the door open. With their masks still on, they looked into the room and found some dozen men lying on the floor of the room. Shawn and Hunter went over to each individual and checked for a pulse. There was a moan from the far side of the room. Shawn went over and found one of the terrorists still alive, but barely. He was the only one. Crawford put a single bullet into the individual's forehead.

They moved from body to body and extracted all the intelligence paperwork they could find. Commander King then took out a digital camera and photographed the face of each of the deceased terrorists. Combined with the paperwork they took of the bodies, the photographs would identify those who may have already been previously noted and still wanted by the international community.

They turned on the ventilation system in the room, closed the door, and made their way down to the floor below the lobby that was not accessible by an elevator. Shawn and Hunter exited the hotel via the service entrance to the rear and quickly moved into the shadows. They found their way back to King's vehicle, where O'Hara and Christopher were seated in the back seat.

'Christopher, I was told by a film producer on the way over to the vehicle that you are up for an Oscar for your performance this evening. What do you think, Timothy?'

'Most definitely, Sir Shawn. Watching Christopher, I almost started crying myself. But then, I had to remember that it was my wife that I was searching for!'

'O.K., mission accomplished thus far. I have a nagging feeling that we are far from being out of the woods at this point. As soon as we can get into the air, the better all of us will feel.'

Shawn drove reasonably erratic to conform to what he was seeing in terms of driving habits on the roadway. They arrived at the airport and Shawn drove to the area between the hangars where the Shark was patiently waiting. Once out of the vehicle, Hunter said his goodbyes and hoped that their paths would cross not too long in the future.

After Shawn, Tim, and Christopher strapped into the cockpit, an RPG hit Commander King's half-ton on the passenger side, causing it to flip over. The Commander was trapped beneath the vehicle but was ejected and landed on the ground.

Shawn, immediately seeing what had happened, told Christopher to get into the left seat and Timmy into the right. He exited the aircraft and ran over to his friend, who was lying on the tarmac and unmoving.

Shawn hoisted Commander King over his left shoulder and, with his right hand, withdrew his sidearm and began firing at the approaching threat vehicle. Bullets pinged all around him and on the Shark's osmium-lined body. He managed to reach the Tiger Shark and was then struck in his right shoulder by around fire from one of the aggressor forces. He went down to the ground.

O'Hara then told Christopher to take the controls and to take it to hover once all three of them on the ground were aboard the aircraft. He dropped to the tarmac.

O'Hara reached over to Shawn, who was just gaining unconsciousness.

'Sir Shawn. Can you make it over to the Tiger Shark? If you can, then I'll have Commander King on board right behind you! We have to move now, Sir!'

Crawford got up as if in slow motion and started to move toward the F-42A. O'Hara picked Commander King and followed behind Shawn. Once he had Shawn and Commander King secured, he started to get into the cockpit when he was struck in the leg with a 7.62 mm round. He immediately went down.

Christopher jumped out of the cockpit and was beside him instantly, having seen what was going on below him. Tim tightly brushed Christopher aside and told him to get aboard the Tiger Shark. He would provide the cover fire. He fired his Beretta until the clip was empty of rounds.

As Christopher began to apply power to the aircraft, O'Hara dragged himself aboard the Tiger Shark from under the carriage access doorway. Once he knew that he was safely aboard, he yelled at Christopher to launch. The

Shark accelerated vertically. Christopher's first responsibility was to get out of the "kill zone". As soon as he was clear of the hangar roofs, he applied forward thrust and fire walled the throttles. The F42A responded instantly to the change in thrust as JP-5 fed into the combustion chamber.

When Christopher thought he was finally safe, he caught a mini fireball in his "rearview" apparatus. A surface-to-air missile had been launched. He had not caught it in time, through no fault of his own. The missile hit the Tiger Shark just at the crew compartment. Warning lights flashed all over the console in front of him. They were going down.

Just before they reached 25 feet above ground level, a bluish light flashed downward above them and enveloped the aircraft. After 60 seconds, when the Tiger Shark should have impacted the ground, The Entity's voice interrupted all thought. They were still in the air!

'Christopher, my son. I am going to take you, Shawn, Ensign O'Hara, and Commander King to get medical attention. You performed admirably this evening, Christopher. When you leave this bluish cocoon, you will be on final approach to my home in the year 2112. You will be met by those whom you can trust. I will always be with you, Christopher, my most cherished son!'

The boy said nothing and waited for the bluish light to dissipate. When it did, he executed his approach and landing. A FOLLOW-ME was waiting for him at the nearest taxiway. He followed it to a hangar, entered the structure, and shut the engines down.

Even before he exited the aircraft, three of The Entity's Subordinates were taking Shawn, Tim, and Hunter from the Tiger Shark. Each one of Christopher's crewmates was not moving. Each one of them had no pulse and had perished, despite the innocuous wounds suffered on the part of his father and Ensign O'Hara.

The bodies were immediately placed side by side on cushioned couches. Christopher walked over to where they lay and stared at each dispassionately. The Entities knelt beside each body and placed both hands over the heart and forehead of each aviator.

They remained in this fashion for at least three minutes. Nothing happened. The Entities continued to leave their hands where they initially had placed them.

And then, a clap of thunder announced the presence of the bluish hue, a pale bluish light, bright, but not blindingly so. The Entities had not moved. The pale blue light had not descended over each of the three lifeless bodies. It enveloped them. The blue light rested there for no less than three minutes.

Christopher waited.

MEETING SANCHA

SHAWN, TIM, AND Hunter found themselves far removed from the country of Mozambique when they awoke. And they did so as one. They found themselves in a room with light bluish walls, but walls that were like no other than they had ever seen before. They shimmered as if they were present, but not present at the same time.

A very distinguished being approached and led them to another "room" and asked them to be seated on one side of an elongated table, a dining table. Otherworldly specters come floating into their room and carrying plates of roasted chicken, prime rib of beef wellington, and succulent fish. They poured wine into the goblets in front of them.

When they departed, the guests looked at one another and decided to sort their presence out as soon as they finished eating their dinner placed before them. Shawn wasn't one to pass up a good meal, especially one as good as this one! Besides, Crawford had been in this room twice before and recognized his Host.

After they had been eating for five minutes, this familiar figure to Crawford came into their dining area. He moved to the head of the table. More appropriately, he "floated" to the head of the table! He sat and looked serenely at each of those present. He finally focused his gaze on Shawn. Christopher was standing beside his father's chair and smiling. The Entity's Ambassador acknowledges Christopher with a nod.

'Colonel Crawford, it is always a pleasure to have you with us. It has been some time since we have had the pleasure of your company. Commander King, as this is your first visit to OUR unique existence, I am personally pleased that you have re-acquainted your professional relationship with Colonel Crawford. My benefactor so loves the give and take rendered by Shawn, and it is pleasing to see that he has someone with whom he shares the same joyous wit.

'Ensign O'Hara, we have followed your progress in life. You have shown a softness toward humanity that emanates the true nature of your heart. And that is the goodness that all men should aspire to in order for them to approach self-fulfillment. You have many more good things to share with others, and they will all learn from your humanity and dedication to serving.

'Christopher's intervention regarding your embattled dealings with those who desire to do harm to the overall human existence was fortuitous. I do not have to confirm to you that your mission to eradicate those who do harm to humanity was entirely successful. And, we were more than pleased to be able to mend your wounds and bring all of you to a state of heightened awareness.

'And what do I mean by all of this?

'Few people believe that there is an evil force attempting to conquer parts of the world and establish a stronghold, which would enable it to exert its destructive influence over all humanity and eliminate everything good in the world. As Colonel Crawford has come to realize in the past, this must not be allowed to happen.

'Your assignment to stymie the total interference of all that is good in the World has resulted in success each and every time you have been called upon to change the direction of destiny for the betterment of all.

'As you may have realized, your World in the year 2087 is about to be turned into a hotbed of turmoil, once again. Agent Dighello's thrust to eliminate threats is but a means to squelch a "campfire" as it were. We see your era's struggle as one of eliminating a fire that will eliminate all semblance of liberty for all mankind, and be ruled by those with darkened hearts.

'Shawn, we look to you and the others to act so that this potential end-result may never be realized. In order to accomplish this, we want you to accept another aircraft in your future, and in our time, to assist in achieving what is necessary to perpetuate goodness at the expense of evil. I believe you to be this individual.'

'Shawn, it's good to see you again, my good friend!'

Crawford looked behind him and saw Major Derek Peterson, his old friend, and fellow aviator. He hugged Derek warmly as Christopher looked on with a huge smile. Tim O'Hara and Hunter King both got up from the table and shook MAJ Peterson's hand in turn, as Shawn made the introductions.

'You know, Derek, the last time I was here you treated me as if I had just won the lottery when you presented me with the Leopard. I can't imagine anything better at this point.'

'Well, my good friend, please follow me as I present you with the keys to a very unusual flying machine.'

They walk over to the futuristic hangar. Even more modern was the F-98A Stingray Stealth Fighter, which was truly unbelievably looking in every manner possible. The design was beyond imaginable!

Shawn's first question to Derek, 'Does this thing make coffee too?' brought a huge chuckle from Christopher who said, 'No, father, but it does make Pizza!'

'Oh, groan, please, Christopher and Colette? Please give them my love. One of these days my duties around here may not be so intense so that I can enjoy that beautiful Australian environment of yours.'

'You are always welcome, you know that, Derek. You know that you may "drop-in" literally anytime you, please. I would just love to see you again. Why, we might just arrange for a genuine Australian Luau, not that we have such a feast, but we would arrange it for you.'

'Now, how we get into this thing? Looks like this is going to be an extensive transition.'

'Oh, not really. We have your voice recorded into its mainframe. Everything is "voice-activated". Go ahead, say something to your new Toy!'

'Open, sesame!'

'Shawn,' said a very sweet female voice. 'I'm sure you can be more original. Try again, please.'

Crawford looked at Peterson, who merely smiled back. 'I may be in trouble with Christine with this sultry rendition of Marilyn, Derek. However, I'm willing to get used to it, if she is.'

'Coach, I can talk to her, if you like. Your bride may not be aware that this voice is a perfect replica of your long-lost cousin from Arkadelphia , Arkansas! You do remember her, don't you, Coach?'

'Now that you mention it, she does ring a bell. I'm certain that you're referring to cousin Maybelle. She's probably put in an additional 50 pounds by now. That would have her tipping the scales at a "lean" 420 today. And, I do hope that she was able to replace her dentures. Having that one tooth was a bit frightening. Do you remember the time when Maybelle wrestled that heifer to the ground that morning? Wow, she really made a hamburger out of that four-hoofer! And, at the country fair, she won the Cow Tipping Contest! Truly an amazing woman!'

**F-98 Stingray Stealth Jet Fighter Cour-
tesy of Wikipedia, the Free Encyclopedia**

'Father, when can we go and visit her? She sounds like a lot of fun!' 'Yes, my Boy, tons of fun! But surely, I digress and, Coach, thank you for helping me put everything in perspective.

'Shawn,' the F-98 said, 'If you ever refer to me as Maybelle, I promise I will never show you the ejection seat lever.

'Well, now that we have that understanding, why don't I call you Sancha?'

'It has a nice ring to it, Shawn. Sancha, it is.'

Shawn looked at everyone around him and noted all were nearly doubled over in laughter!

'O.K., Derek, what's next?'

'Ask, Sancha. She is now considered to be your Life Coach, right, Sancha?'

'This is true, Derek. Shawn, please into my den. I chose this term, as you will soon see why.'

And the "den" door opened. Shawn looked at everyone with a bit of trepidation before stepping and entering the aircraft.

What he saw inside was simply outstanding! The inside consoles resembled nothing as he had ever seen before. The pilot's chair sat in the middle of the "cockpit". There were two additional chairs to the front on either side of the pilot's station. Behind, were six 'stations" where passengers could sit comfortably. And, "comfortably" was the operative word. They resembled overstuffed chairs with luxurious padding.

Who would want to leave this place, he thought.

As soon as he said this, a voice said in his mind, 'Why, thank you, Colonel. That is the nicest thing you've said, since we first met 10 minutes ago.'

What? I am hearing voices now.

'No, Shawn, you are not. Let me explain what is going on. Your input may be mind-delegated. You may also issue commands out loud. Either way, your voice actuates my senses, whether you say anything out loud or whether you are thinking it in your mind. You are the only individual outside The Entity's original inner circle who may do this. There is a provision for one additional input person, but it has to be of your choosing. So, before you decide who that individual will be, I would think seriously about your choice. It has to be the right person for all the right reasons.'

'O.K.,' Shawn said out loud. 'And when I've made my choice, how do I go about making this happen?'

'All you have to do is tell me who that individual is. I will do the rest for you. Shawn, do you have any further questions for me at the moment?'

'Yes, how would I get us up in the air?'

'Colonel, all you have to do is think or say it. Brevity is best. If you want to initiate engines, just say, "start engines". If you want to taxi, then say, "taxi to active".

'The first few times, I will assist you with commands. If I don't find the command to be a responsive one, even though I know what you are referring to, I will make a suggestion to you in your mind. Do you follow, Colonel?'

'Yes, I do Sancha. And I do hope that you like that name.'

'Oh, I do. But let's be sure that Christine would be comfortable with it as well. We don't need any untimely discord, do we?'

'No, Sancha, we do not. And thank you for all of this. It will be a learning situation for me, so please be patient.'

'Patience is what I demonstrate best, Commander. And this is the title I will refer to you for you to command this vessel. Now, I do believe your friend is waiting for you outside. I look forward to working with you, Commander.'

'As I do, Sancha.'

When Shawn exited the F-98 Stingray, he looked like he had just gone to heaven!

'Well. What do you think, Commander?' asked Peterson with a smirk on his face.

'How did you know that my title within the aircraft, Derek?'

'Oh, let's just call it intuition, shall we? Why don't you say goodbye to your BENEFACTOR before you leave.'

On the way, Derek motioned that on board the Stingray was a new form of body armor that appeared to repel anything from a rifle round to a crossbow. He suggested that, since there were enough vests for everyone, they also be stored within the Tiger Shark for potential use. Shawn said that he would see that this was done.

Derek led the way back into the rear conference room. To the rear, stood some "old" familiar faces. Shawn's face lit up when he saw these famous personages.

When Tim and Hunter saw who was in the room, they looked at Shawn and asked, 'These people, aren't they the people I think they are, are they?'

'The very same. Let me introduce you two to some of the most influential individuals in the history of mankind,'

'President Lincoln and Kennedy came forward ahead of the others. President Lincoln said, 'Shawn, it is so nice to see you again. You know, Mary Todd talks about you all the time. How have you been, my Friend?'

'Oh, day to day, Mr. President. Sir, may I introduce to you two of my very good friends, Commander J Hunter King and Ensign Timothy O'Hara?'

'Yes, I know both of them, Shawn. Commander, it is my pleasure to make your acquaintance. And yours, as well, Ensign. May I introduce, to both of you, President John Fitzgerald Kennedy! President Kennedy will now make a formal presentation to all three of you. Yes, even you, Shawn.'

President Kennedy came forward and shook Hunter's and Tim's hands and told both of them what a big fan he was of both of them, as they were both Navy men! He then asked his brother Robert Francis Kennedy to come forward with the citations.

The first to be awarded was Shawn himself. RFK read the promotion order that elevated him in rank from Lieutenant Colonel to Brigadier General. This "double" promotion was generally unheard of, but as President Kennedy said as he pinned the star on Shawn's shoulders, 'Brigadier General Crawford was entirely deserving for his total service rendered on behalf of humanity.' Shawn's double award of the Medal of Honor certainly did not hurt either.

Hunter was next promoted to the rank of Admiral Lower Half, the equivalent of Brigadier General on other major services. He, too, was lauded for his significant contributions to mankind during his tenure of service, both in the Navy and in the Central Intelligence Agency.

Young Tim O'Hara earned the "highest leap" in rank as he was promoted to the rank of Lieutenant Commander, or the equivalent of Major. His "second lieutenant" to field grade rank had never been witnessed before in the history of the United States, with the exception of those who earned battlefield commissions during wartime service. Commander O'Hara accepted his award with humility, his hallmark signature.

Presidents Lincoln and Kennedy, Senator Kennedy, and Dr. Martin Luther King. Jr. and Mahatma Gandhi then shook hands with the three promotion recipients. Entering the room was Flight Sergeant Will Caruso. Baron Manfred von Richthofen, and Amelia Earhart. Each individual gave hugs to all three individuals with a sincere "thank you" for their service to the World.

Christopher had left the room as soon as the promotion was made. As Hunter and Tim were talking and mostly listening to stories given by the famous, influential members of the 19th and 20th Centuries, Shawn noted Christopher's absence. He excused himself from the group and left the conference room.

He found Christopher talking earnestly with The Entity's Ambassador.

'Christopher, sorry to interrupt, but I missed you inside the conference room. Is everything alright?'

Both Christopher and the Ambassador smiled warmly at Shawn and told the latter that all was well and that Christopher was merely catching up with the Ambassador. Christopher then excused himself from the Ambassador's presence and returned to the conference room with his father.

Admiral King and Commander O'Hara were enthralled listening to Dr. King and Dr. Gandhi. President Lincoln and Kennedy and Senator Kennedy came forward when Shawn and Christopher entered the room.

'You know, Shawn, whenever you are in the Hyannisport area, you must stop by. The place has been expanded construction-wise. You wouldn't recognize the place!'

'Yes, Shawn. My dear brother has made it into a palatial estate. Seriously, if you are ever in the Cape Cod area, please stop. However, when someone like yourself comes to visit, we will be there to welcome you. And you know that you can bring friends and stay as long as you would like.'

'Thank you, Senator. And to you, as well, Mr. President. I'm positive I would love to see your historic summer place.'

'And, General, I have yet to meet your bride. I know Jackie and Christine would get along famously. Your Wife and mine are very strong personalities.

But they both harbor a softness not seen in many. It would be a very pleasant experience for both of them.'

'Thank you, Mr. President.'

Their guide then suddenly appeared and led them back to the hangar and to their aircraft. Major Peterson walked with Shawn.

'Derek, why haven't you somehow been promoted since I've known you? It somehow doesn't seem appropriate for you to remain a Major when you have given so much to the cause of freedom.'

President John Kennedy

Courtesy of Wikipedia, the Free Encyclopedia

President Abraham Lincoln Courtesy of Wikipedia, the Free Encyclopedia

Dr. Martin Luther King, Jr.

Courtesy of Wikipedia, the Free Encyclopedia

Senator Robert Francis Kennedy

Courtesy of Wikipedia, the Free Encyclopedia

Mahatma Gandhi

Courtesy of Wikipedia, the Free Encyclopedia

'Shawn, look around you. Rank means nothing here. This is where I belong, and I am happy to be of service to The Entity in the way I am asked to serve. General, please do not worry about me. I am right where I should be. Please tell Christine hello to me. And tell her we both have to go up in a Raptor together in a flight of two one more time. Goodbye, my very good, Friend.'

'Goodbye, Derek. We will see one another again.'

Shawn, Tim, Hunter, and Christopher walked over to the aircraft. They now had two to bring back. Crawford considered their situation for a second and said, 'Christopher, I want you to fly the F-42A as lead aircraft. Take Admiral King and Commander O'Hara with you. If I'm going to crash and burn to learn how to fly my beautiful aircraft, I would choose to do it alone.'

'Yes, Father,'

The three walked over to the Tiger Shark. Shawn stood before the F-98 for a long moment. *Did it really mean that I am beautiful, Shawn?*

Hello, Sancha, and yes I did. I think we are going to get along very well with one another. Please open the command module door, Sancha.

All of this conversation took place in Crawford's head. When he saw the hidden doorway into the flight deck, he knew that he was going to enjoy his relationship with Sancha.

As will, I, Commander!

Once Christopher had taxied out of the hangar and began moving to the established active runway stipulated by Ground Control, Shawn then initiated his own movement inside the Stingray.

Start engines, Sancha. Show system instrument as nominal. Contact ground control for clearance to taxi. Initiate taxi procedures and proceed in accordance with the controller's directives.

All of this was directed in thought alone. Sancha complied with each request from her Commander. The Stingray began to move forward and proceeded to the active runway in accordance with the Ground Control guidance.

The Tiger Shark was ion the threshold and ready to take off.

Commander, I have a message from your son Christopher. He is requesting confirmation that everything is satisfactory with the F-98 performance. Shall I contact him in the affirmative, Commander?

Yes, thank you, Sancha. And, Sancha, tell him that I am proud of him.

As you wish, Commander. Sancha arranged for the takeoff with her coordination with the tower.

Commander, we have been given permission to depart. What are your orders? You may proceed, Sancha.

Thank you, Commander. The F-98 A Stingray is rolling.

The takeoff speed was unbelievably quick. But Shawn never felt the backward push into his seat with the advancing speed. It was as if the aircraft was standing still. There was no sensation of movement.

The F-98 rotated and immediately retracted its landing gear. It climbed amazingly fast to the altitude established by Departure Control.

Commander, what are your orders?

Sancha, inform the Tiger Shark that we will assume the lead position. Communicate to Christopher, and we will pass him on to his starboard side. Advise him to assume combat spread information.

As you wish, Commander.

The F-98 passed the Tiger Shark on its left side and settled into a flight lead status. The flight continued for another 20 minutes. During that time Shawn took the opportunity to get to know the Stingray by asking Sancha operational questions pertaining to all aspects of aircraft performance including ammunition stores, ceiling limitations, maximum speed, and stall indicators. Sancha responded in a clear, concise, and understanding manner. Shawn began to feel more comfortable.

The Entity's cloud enveloped them without notice. They were within The Entity's grasp for no more than 30 seconds. Both aircraft broke out into the clear, found themselves over a countryside teeming with combatants facing one another 75 meters apart.

Sancha, determine the Time-Era we have found ourselves in, please.

Very well, Commander. We are presently in the last decade of the fifteenth century, circa 1494. The forces you see below you are the French forces under Charles VIII of France and facing the Papal States Military, led by the Son of Pope Alexander VI, the Duke Giovanni de Candia Borgia

Sancha, please transmit this information to the Tiger Shark.

Sancha relayed the specific information to Christopher aboard the F-42A. Tiger *Shark acknowledges receipt, Commander.*

Sancha, please relay to Christopher that we will land both forces on the battlefield. The Tiger Shark is to face South; we will face North. Once we have hovered to the ground, I want the Shark to fire a missile into the trees above the Army. We will also fire a missile over the heads of the forces led by Charles VIII.

Yes, Commander. Tiger Shark acknowledges the directive, Commander.

Very well, Sancha. Proceed to an equidistant point in the middle between the two armies. Has Christopher done the same in the F-42A.

Christopher acknowledges, Commander. O.K. Sancha land the F-98, please.

Proceeding to the requested touchdown point, Commander.

Sancha, please relay to the Shark to fire the missile upon touchdown. We will do the same. In addition, have all personnel dons the new Kevlar protective vest following the missile launch. 60 seconds following the missile being fired, I want all personnel to exit the aircraft with automatic weapons and flight helmets on. They are to stand at port arms until a follow-on order is issued by me. Acknowledge.

After a moment, Sancha came back to Shawn.

Commander, Christopher, acknowledges all.

Once both aircraft were on the ground, a missile was fired above both armies. A minute later, the Shark's aircrew exited the F-42A and stood facing the Armies of the Papal States. Shawn stood facing King Charles VIII.

Both groups of warriors on either side looked at the strange machines in awe. Many were seen to cross themselves as a gesture to protect themselves against something the devil himself had made. Many to the rear began moving away from the battlefield. Shawn, via his headset, told Hunter and Tim to move forward and to the duke commanding the Papal militia. Shawn walked toward King Charles VIII.

While walking toward the leaders of both groups, Shawn instructed Hunter to advise Papal armies to go back to the Vatican and remain there. There would be no more fighting today, or at any other time.

Shawn stopped 10 feet before the French King, who was still mounted on his horse. One of the King's men raised his crossbow and, before he could let loose an arrow, put a bullet between his eyes. The man fell backward to the ground and lay dead with his eyes open.

'Your Majesty, it is time for Your Liege and his Army to march back to France. Should you persist in the attempt at senseless slaughter, I will assure Your Highness that you will see the sunset this day; Shawn stood his ground.

King Charles VIII looked back at his captain lying dead on the ground behind him. He turned toward Crawford and said, 'You are but one man, *Mon Ami,* if that is needed, what you are. I have 25,000n behind me. Why should I be ordered by you or anyone else from your extraordinary party?'

Sancha, please fire a 30 mm cannon burst over my head and into the

trees from left to right behind the king's army. On my mark. Acknowledge.

'Admiral King, the good King Charles VIII, is reluctant to yield to his most sophomoric behavior. This is a little example of what may happen to his army should he persist in his petulant behavior. Just a heads-up, Admiral.'

'General, I love it when you talk dirty!'

Whenever you are ready, Commander.

'My Liege, if you would be so kind as to direct your attention to the stand of trees behind you, I will attempt to dissuade Your Highness from any further attempt at irrational behavior.'

You may proceed, Sancha.

All of a sudden, there was a burst of fire from the F-98A Stingray. The trees behind the King's army were completely cut down halfway up their trunks. It was an awesome sight and an extremely frightening experience for every French soldier on the battlefield. It lasted for 20 seconds and just long enough to get everyone's attention. More than half of the 25,000 broke ranks and scattered to the right and left. King Charles was very much intimidated but decided to play one last card.

'Monsieur, I could take you, hostage, right now and your plan would be foiled.'

Shawn lifted his Uzi and put a three-round burst into the nearest general, one that Shawn disliked immediately due to his hostile demeanor and constant sneer.

'I would like your Highness to make an attempt. The next burst of fire from my weapon will be to arrange Sire's face so that it will appear ugly than it is already. Your "chess" move, your Highness.

King Charles VIII then did an about-face with his horse and ordered his army to retreat to the north.

Meanwhile, on the other side of the field, the Papal Army cheered in triumph. Admiral King then pointed his automatic weapon skyward and fired several rounds into the air.

'Duke, you will command your troops to refrain from any further overzealous celebration. There are no winners or losers today. And there will be no more dying today. Your Army will return to the Vatican and you will report to your father the Pope that Rome will spare. The warlike intrigue of the day is finished, do I make myself clear, Duke?'

Duke Giovanni de Candia Borgia stepped forward in defiance and stressed that he took no orders from "peasants". King smiles within his helmet and went nose-to-nose with this up-start and said that today, the Duke was the peasant and he was nobility. Admiral King stepped back one step and unceremoniously took the butt of his weapon and struck the Duke squarely in the jaw. The Duke's eyes rolled back into his head and he went down to the ground unconscious.

'Who is the second in command in this "ragtag" Army of yours?'

An officer came forward timidly and identified himself. Admiral King informed this individual that he was now in charge and that he should have someone collect the Duke and cart him back to Vatican City.

'Yes, My Lord!' exclaimed the officer.

When the Duke was suitably positioned for transportation, Admiral King cautioned the leadership that further bloodshed would be dealt with harshly. He wisely counseled the new commanding officer that the official word of the day was "PEACE".

'Yes, My Lord! The Vatican Army then moved to the rear smartly.'

Very soon, there were no armies present. Shawn came forward to meet the others near the aircraft. They removed their helmets.

Commander O'Hara kept a vigilant eye out for anyone of either Army who felt that he may wish to wear the mantle of Hero for the day. He need not have worried.

'Well, now, that was fun! Does anyone have anything to eat?' asked Crawford.

Christopher stepped forward and presented his father with a Twinkies bar. He then handed one to the other two aviators

'Christopher, my son, you are ever the resilient one!'

'I try, Father. Mother always told us that you are a Twinkies fan. She also shared with me that Suzie Q's were also on your list of the most important food groups known to man.'

'Coach, is that right?' asked Admiral King.

'Coach, that may be slightly exaggerated. I did eat a box of Suzie Q's in one sitting once. But, I assure everyone here, that it was entirely by accident!'

They all looked at Shawn Crawford and broke up with laughter!

'What?' he said.

A CONFLICT RENEWED

THE FLIGHT OF two launched in the late-15th Century, and all hoped for the best. But, if history was any lesson to be learned from, the conflict to oust Pope Alexander VI was not going to happen. As history foretold, this Pope would succumb to a horrible malarial infection in August 1503.

Shawn led the sortie out of the past century and directed Sancha to identify The Entity's unique cloud formation. She isolated it from the myriad of other clouds present that day in 15th Century Northern Italy. Shawn directed Christopher to advance the F-42A to his right wingtip. They entered the cloud together

Once inside, Shawn heard the voice of The Entity address him with laughter. 'Young Jedi Knight. It is good to have you with me again!'

'Hello, your Wickedly-Large Blueness! I was wondering if I would ever come in contact with you again. As I did not hear from you prior to entering the conflict between the Vatican's minuscule militia and the enormous body of King Charles VIII, I thought for a second that you were vacationing in Bermuda! Have you ever been on one of those motorbikes they serve for tourists here?'

'Oh no, Shawn! Ever since Admiral King piled his bike into the "pucker brush" that time on the Island, many who witnessed the event refused to go near a motorbike for at least three weeks. He set the Island Bermuda Bike Industry back a hundred years, even before they even considered the invention of motorbike! As a matter of absolute fact, the Hamilton Times reported the following day that his entry into "thorn country" received a 9.9 rating from the Bermuda Judge, with a degree of difficulty nearly unparalleled in the "tourist industry". Of course. My young Jedi, who was quickly surpassed by the Author of this book when he "dumped" his bike twice within a five-minute period of time.! His bride Lynn refused any and all spousal conveyance and was "saved" by a "knight" who offered her safe haven back to her destination! That episode not only made the Bermuda Papers but was highlighted in the London times two days later.

The Author not only "lost face", but refused to show it for weeks to follow!'

At that very moment, the astute Author noticed all of his Characters looking outward from the pages.

'And now to the business at hand. What do you have for us that may assist you with your greatness?'

'Shawn, I will release you and Christopher's aircraft to your home continent. It is time for you to go home and enjoy a well-deserved rest. You have done well; your leadership ability has overcome many shortcomings in this world past and present. There is still work to be done. There is a cloud on the Australian horizon that will test you. With the help of Commander O'Hara and Admiral King, I am confident that goodness will prevail. As always, I will be with you, my young Jedi.'

Shawn's release of the cloud with the Shark "in tow" and the Sydney Maritime Defense Base in sight gave him a feeling of calm. They all needed the rest. He looked forward to spending time with his family for a few days.

He made the call to Sydney Approach Control and was soon handed over to the Tower for landing sequence. When Crawford, actually Sancha, settled the F-98A Stingray beside the Leopard, Flight Sergeant Will Caruso stood there in awe of his new "toy" to care for.

'Colonel, no, wait, I see now that it is General Crawford, where did you

pick up this lovely piece of work? As if I didn't know, "Commander"!

I already love this guy, Commander. It will be a pleasure having him around!

Yes, Sancha, he is definitely one of the very best there is. One could not hope for a better aircraft maintenance technician in the whole world, or universe, for that matter. I am surprised that he did not maintain your systems at "Entity World"!

He did, Commander. He is merely playing you like a fiddle!

Well, then, I supposed it was my turn to enter the contest of dueling fiddles!

'Hello, Will. Yes, please meet the F-98A Stingray Stealth Fighter. She is indeed a very special, lovely lady. *Keep it up, Commander!* Will, I have the distinct pleasure of introducing you to Sancha. She is a voice-modulated controlled fighter who refuses to allow the pilot to do anything at all. She is one magnificent lady.

'Sancha is totally independent. One may only access the internal compartment via the voice recognition feature. Once an individual is able to access her via a key transformational auditory-biopic integrated sequencing design system, the crew member may relate to Sancha via telepathic means.

She will sense a dangerous situation before it has begun to surface. Sancha is beyond state of the art, Will. Sancha has redefined the word "art".'

'Sir, would you be able to explain all of this to me in English? From what you are telling me, I may not be able to work on her at all.'

Shawn, please relay to young Master Caruso that which he already knows. He will be able to access my mainframe, as one of very few to be able to do so. All Entity Relations such as Major Peterson and Christopher, even Colette, are automatically permitted access. There is one other individual outside the MASTER's Inner Circle that you may wish to have available, my ability to communicate. You may choose that person at any time, Commander.

'Sir, did you hear my concern?'

'Uh, yes, sorry, Will. I was listening to Sancha relay to me the answer to your question. As you are already a member of The Entity's Inner Circle, you automatically have access to Sancha. Does that answer your question?'

But how is it possible for someone to make this happen, he thought?

Hello, Will. I know you can hear me because I just "heard" you think, how am I doing this far, my Handsome Technician?

Will feigned nearly dropping his teeth! Shawn couldn't help but laugh.

'Sir, did you "hear" her say something in my mind?'

Will, how is this? Now, you and I may communicate with one another without having to say anything. Are my thoughts registering with you at this moment?

Yes, Sir Shawn, they are! Simply amazing! I am definitely going to take good care of this young lady! It appears that I'm going to have to watch my thoughts from now on! Oh, and, thanks for playing along with me. I knew this beautiful aircraft under another name at one time. She is one sexy machine!

Oh, Will, you and I will get along famously, said Sancha.

O.K., you two, I will leave you to love birds alone. But, Will, please do not neglect the Shark or Leopard. You know how cranky they can get when left alone for a while!

Goodbye, Commander!'

Goodbye, Sancha.

Shawn drove over to Headquarters with Christopher, Admiral King, and Commander O'Hara. He reported to Colonel O'Leary, who noted the change in rank for both Crawford and O'Hara. Shawn introduced Admiral King to the Colonel.

'Well, it seems as though to make rank around here one has to get out of

the office more often. Admiral, it's a pleasure to meet you, Sir.'

'Colonel, you don't have to be formal with the Coach up here. Up until a day ago, he was merely a Commander. And now he chews gum and speaks at the same time.' Shawn quipped.

'Thanks, Coach. Coming from Mr. Twinkie himself, that's quite an endorsement.' Hunter responded.

'Now that you have all of that out of the way, tell me what happened. And don't forget to shed some light on that new aircraft you brought in with you. You didn't "steal" that, did you, Sir Shawn?'

'No. Colonel, I did not. Christopher did. MAJ Peterson did say to give you his best regards, however. But I get ahead of myself.

'We were able to tie in the elimination of the terrorists in Zimbabwe with a science lecture given by Christopher in Harare, Mozambique. Of course, we ran into a little trouble getting out of Harare Airport. We managed to damage several of their antiquated trucks on the way out. They'll probably need somebody to work in the near future.

'When we landed in Zimbabwe, Admiral King was there waiting for us. We drove over to the hotel where the terrorist meeting was being held. Commander O'Hara and Christopher provided just enough deflection so that Hunter and I were able to gain access to the stairwell leading to the top floor. We proceeded to take two of the guards out and then sent a steady stream of nerve gas into their meeting room. It was over before we knew it, and they realized it!

'When we got back to the airport, we were about to board the F-42A when another group of terrorists was waiting for us. Each one of us was hit, with Christopher being the only one not taking a round. After ensuring that we were all in the Shark, Christopher took off and almost immediately encountered The Entity's Portal.

'When we broke free, we were in The Entity's backyard. All three of us actually perished before we were brought to medical attention. It was then that we were resuscitated by The Entity's Subordinates.

'After conversing with some old Friends, Major Peterson took us over to the Stingray. The fighter is a voice-activated system. It's an extremely advanced system, and fun to "drive". And now, here we are, Colonel.'

'Well, I am pleased that you are all alright. I'm afraid that while you are gone, the African Federation has reared its ugly head once again. Intelligence sources indicate that they are massing their troops in Kupang, East Timor, just north of Australia's Ashmore and Cartier Islands. They're getting a little too close to home for Marshall Morrison's sake. And I share her deep concern.

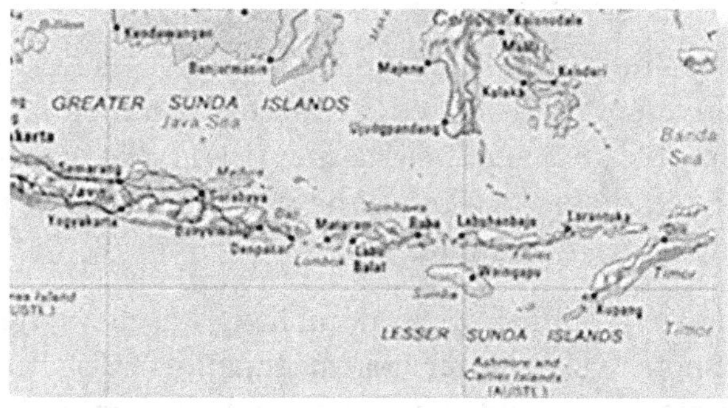

Greater and lesser Sunda Islands, Indonesia

Courtesy of lostpedia.wikia.com

'All pilots are restricted to Base, and we've beefed up our reconnaissance sorties out of Darwin. We are also moving some of our F- 72B Sea Scorpions to our forward operating base there.

'Bob Gonzales is already on a station with his Comanche Helicopter. I know that you need the rest, but I'm afraid it's going to have to wait. 'Admiral, what is your service background training-wise in a nutshell?' 'Well, Colonel, I am a former SEAL and Delta Force Operative.I've been in this part of the World in the past, Sir. As you may know, Colonel, the SEAL mission has always been clandestine. I will assist you in any way I can, Sir.'

"Great, I do think that we are going to use your expertise. We need to know more about what is going on in Kupang. I would like for you and Shawn to get into Kupang using your Delta Force experience and get us some "hard" intelligence. And, Gentlemen, we need it as soon as we can get it so that we'll know what we're dealing with here. Are you two up to it?'

'Absolutely, Colonel. Hunter and I have worked with one another in the past, many years ago. We were both coaches for a Little League Team whose players could have anyone for lunch anytime. In contrast to that experience, I do believe this will be a "cakewalk", right, Coach?'

'You got it, Coach! Colonel, we will leave whenever you want us to.'

'O.K., then. I need boots on the ground by tomorrow after dark, around 2200 hours. Shawn, pick your aircraft. I'll let you two figure out exactly what you need to accomplish your mission. And Gentlemen, thank you for this. The information you bring back with you will most certainly save lives. Good hunting, Gentlemen!'

As they walked out of the headquarters, both Christopher and Tim said that they wanted to go along with them. If not for an active role, they would do anything required in a supportive manner.

'O.K., but I want you both to be sure about this. Christopher, there is no Pizza in Kupang. Will you be able to make it a couple of days without it?'

'I will try very hard, Father. Of course, I can always carry a few slices in my flight suit as you do with your Twinkies, Father.'

'Oh my, I've been hit by a Twinkies monster! Alright then, let's meet this evening in my quarters at 1900 hours. Coach, you're staying with me tonight.

'Roger that, Commander!'

Shawn, Hunter, and Christopher drove over to Shawn's home. At the door, they were met by both Christine and Colette, who jumped into his father's arms.

'Chris, meet a very good friend of mine. Admiral J Hunter King, former SEAL, Delta Force Operative, Lover of Snakes, and Tamer of Little League Players! Hunter, this is my lovely Bride Christine, F-22 Raptor and F-42A Tiger Shark Pilot, and this little rugrat is my darling daughter Colette, a.k.a., Whirling Dervish!'

Colette got down from Shawn's arms and walked over to Hunter and asked him to bend over toward her. He did so, and she planted a wonderful kiss on the Admiral's cheek.

'I am so glad to meet you, Admiral King. I have been waiting for this moment for a very long time now. You are everything I thought I would be. Welcome to our home, Admiral.' Colette said graciously.

'Colette, I am, first, pleased to make your acquaintance, although you have me somewhat baffled that you appear to know me, and I am not you.'

'Admiral, there was a time when you were in Chad, Africa, on a Delta Force mission. Is that not so, Admiral?'

'Why yes? That's correct, Colette. But how could you know? That mission was classified Top secret!'

'Admiral, remember that little girl with a dirty face that you found in the dilapidated wooden structure the day before your unit pulled out? That little girl was me, Admiral!'

'But how is that possible? The rebels burned that structure not five minutes after I left it. It appeared that the little girl I saw in that building had already perished in the village fighting that occurred in the morning. If I had known that you were alive, I would have carried you out of that small building and taken you out with me.'

'Admiral, had you turned around and picked me up, I would not have been there.' And Colette left it at that.

'Hunter, there are so many things to understand with this family of mine. But, believe me when I say that I am only totally blessed to have each one and, in time, you will understand what we are all about.

'Now, having spurned the element of intrigue to new heights, I do believe we should all relax. Coach, please have a seat in the leaving room. Chris,

Christopher, and Colette, please join us. Coach, ask away any question that might pique your interest.'

'I would ask how all of this possibility came to be. That is, how did this most extraordinary family find a way to achieve such a very special bond?'

'Hunter,' said Christine. 'Shawn and I flew together in an F-22 Raptor in South America. He was flying OH-58D Kiowa Warrior Helicopters at the time in support of drug missions. When a joint service mission came down, Shawn and I found ourselves flying together. In the other raptor was Major Derek Peterson. His back seat was a close friend of Shawn's, CW5 Roberto "Bib" Gonzales.

'Christopher came along following Shawn's mission to India when he saved Mahatma Gandhi from assassination. He was stowed away from The Entity's Inner Circle and landed right in our lap. When that happened, our world turned out in a very positive manner. Colette arrived a year later. And here we all are!'

'I have witnessed some very spectacular events in my time, but never as significant as those I've had the privilege of seeing within the past month. I must be blessed to be in the presence of some very extraordinary people.'

'And as are we, Admiral. You compliment my father in every way possible, without even trying. Your past friendship bridges the gap of a lack of understanding of where the other person is coming from to a recognition of each other's strengths, representing an awareness of what is required to survive. This is the nature of your special relationship, Admiral. And this is something for which to be very proud,' admitted Christopher.

At 1900 hours, Commander O'Hara came over with his father Patrick.

'Sir Shawn. I hope you don't mind my tagging along with my son. It gives me some extra valuable time to spend more time with him. He tells me that he's off on another assignment with you and Admiral King, and Christopher. I believe you are also going.'

'Mr. O'Hara, it is not a problem. I apologize for not spending more time with you since you arrived. It's been hectic around here the last couple of months. Sir, may I ask about your background? Did you spend any time in the military?'

'Yes. I retired from the United States Army as a Lieutenant Colonel. I did fly helicopters for 15 years, vintage models of course. They were the UH-1H/V Iroquois "Huey's" and the 0H-58A Kiowa. I only got 2,200 flight hours, and a bit of combat time, not much. Really missed flying, though. If I had another opportunity, I would jump at it in a heartbeat!'

'Well, Colonel, I think we just may be able to arrange something like that for you. You probably have yet to meet a good friend of mine, former Chief Warrant Officer 5, and now full Colonel, Bob Gonzales. He is our resident Comanche Pilot and can do great things with a helicopter like "shake hands, sit up, roll over, beg for attention". I can say that without him present, none of that is true at all.

'What is true about Bob Gonzales is that he can make the helicopter do some pretty fantastic things in the air. When it comes to helicopters, he truly does "walk on water"!

'You'll get a chance to meet him when he returns from the Darwin area after all of this African Federation foolishness is over. I do believe you and he will get along quite well.'

'Well, that is very generous of you. I certainly look forward to the experience of meeting him and possibly getting back into the air again.'

'Why don't we get started with our planning for our little jaunt to Kapang? We will take the F-98A Stingray. There is plenty of room for all of us. Oh, Timmy, may I choose one other individual outside The Entity's circle to have access to Sancha's voice command availability. And I want you to be that person. This will give us a total of four individuals here in the base that are capable of flying/maintaining the F-98. The fourth person is not present with us this evening and that is flight Sergeant Will Class Will Caruso.

'Kupang is all commerce and industry. It is noisy, unkempt, and entirely loose in ways that deter tourists from visiting. It has begun to try to turn this image around. We should therefore fit in very nicely.

'There should be more than the usual troops in the downtown section. A good place to start gathering intelligence will be in the local bars. Coach, you and I will roam through a couple of these establishments to see if we can find more definitive information relating to the threat's intentions.

'As the area outside the city center is apt to be more unstable, Tim and Christopher will remain with the Stingray. You both will have "eyes on the ground" as it were, through the F-98's ability to map our progress. Sancha has a feature where she is able to monitor the status of each individual with whom she is able to communicate. A cockpit feed allows you to see what we see. If at any time we feel we need an extraction, we will signal you to come to us.

'Now, this is a fly-by-your-pants type of operation. Our mission is intelligence gathering. It is not to confront the enemy. Do you have any questions?'

'What type of information are we looking to gather, General?' asked Tim.

UH-1H Iroquois "Huey" Helicopter
Courtesy of Wikipedia, the Free Encyclope-
dia

'We want to try to get an idea about unit locations, strength, and means of mobility. If we could get some definitive timeline in terms of when they plan to kick off their little operation, that would be a bonus. I envision no more than four hours maximum on the ground.

'We will come on low and pick a suitable landing spot for the F-98. I have a topographical map that will show the best place to set the aircraft, not far from where we need to be.

'Time of flight from Sydney will be two hours. We'll coast in a north-westerly heading at 80,000 feet for the first hour. The remaining time will be descending to our touchdown point. I suggest that everyone get a good night's rest. We plan to launch tomorrow at 2100 hours.

'O.K., that's it, unless anyone has any questions?' There were none.

The next morning, Crawford and King reported to the Commander's Office in the Headquarters Building. Marshal Morrison and Air Chief Marshal O'Leary were there. Sergeant Cranston told them to go right in.

'Sir Shawn, it's good to see you. And you must be Admiral King. It is my pleasure to meet you and welcome you to Sydney. Michael has shared much about your assignment in Africa. We're pleased that everything went well.'

'Thank you, Ma'am. Shawn must take all the credit. I merely stood back and watched "expertise" at work.

'Ma'am, before you comment on that comment, I have to admit that I bribed him with a box of Twinkies.'

'Yes, well that certainly does make sense as General Crawford's exploits are fundamentally based upon his ability to satisfy his diet,' Morrison said with a smirk.

'And, by the way, congratulations to you both regarding your recent promotions. Every time you return from a mission, Sir Shawn, you enter this headquarters with another elevation in rank. Before long, the Australian Prime Minister will have to abdicate because of a forthcoming title of "King" bestowed upon you by The Entity.'

'Well, once again, Ma'am. If you had ever seen "Your Greatness", and my reluctant desire to provide him with both Suzie Q's and Twinkies, you would wonder why my position in life merely stops at "King"!

They all chuckled. 'O.K., "King" Shawn, what do you have for us this morning?' Morrison asked with a smile.

'Ma'am, Colonel, we will be launching at 2100 hours this evening to discern what the Africans are up to when we get to Kupang. Admiral King and I will go into the city and evaluate the African military presence, as well as ascertain its plan of action in the immediate future. Christopher and Commander O'Hara will remain with the F-98 Stingray as a backup.

'The F-98 is an innovative machine in that it reacts to voice commands, but only from select individuals. Myself, Christopher, Flight Sergeant Caruso, and Commander O'Hara are the only people capable of accessing its computer systems. This is the reason Christopher and Tim will remain behind in the event that we require immediate extraction.

'Our time on location will be a maximum of four hours. If we get the Intel that we need prior to then, then we will return immediately to Sydney. I have taken the liberty of communicating via secure SAT phone with Air Commander Gonzales and have requested his on-station alert status in the Comanche. Bob's assistance may be necessary, even though I'm not counting on needing it. It's nice to know that there will be back up, if necessary.'

'Very well. I wish you, gentlemen, the best of luck. Please report when you return. Good hunting!'

The afternoon after lunch was spent in the hangar operations room going over the plan and verifying that the F-98 was ready to fly. There really was no need for the latter concern, as it appeared that Flight Sergeant Caruso and Sancha were getting along "famously"!

'What do you think, Will? Will she fly?'

Commander, I will have you know that Sergeant Caruso and I have been sharing information about you.

Oh, *no! Will, you haven't told Sancha everything about me, have you? Sir Shawn, only the salient parts. Other than that, your Knight and Shining Armor reputation has been preserved! Well, that certainly makes me feel so much better!*

'Oh, Coach, don't mind my dutiful Plane Captain here. We were just "brainstorming" with Sancha about how best to succeed in getting us as close to the city location as possible. Weren't we, Plain Captain!'

'Absolutely, Sir Shawn! Admiral, you'll have to excuse the royal nobility in our midst. Sometimes, he has a tendency to digress in his thought patterns, and it's up to me to translate his true intent.'

'Yes, I've been around the General in the past, when to say he has "gone off the deep end" would be to suggest that he was wading in a kiddie pool!"

'Why, thank you, Admiral. I didn't know you were around the pool area when we were in Bermuda at that resort. And I paid those three years old big bucks to keep an eye out on my behalf. Wonder if I can get my $2.50 back.'

Sir Shawn, did you need your "swimmies" in that pool, or did you feel safe going in above your ankles?

Sancha, I'll have you know that I am an excellent swimmer in two feet of water!

The F-98 took off at 1200 hours and rapidly climbed to 80,000 feet. Admiral King, Commander O'Hara, and Christopher were impressed with the comfort level within the cockpit cabin. It was "palatial" compared to any other fighter command center.

After one hour at the outer edges of the atmosphere, the F-98 made a severe descent for a straight-in hover landing at the prescribed landing site, per the operations plan.

Right to the minute, the Stingray was over its landing site and set down, with all external lights extinguished and its internal "cockpit" bathed in infrared lighting, within a couple of trees that masked the city limits of Kupang. Admiral King, Shawn, and the others synchronized their watches and Shawn relayed to Sancha to ensure that their whereabouts were known to Tim and Christopher at all times.

Wilcox, *Commander!*

Crawford and King change clothing to look "the part" as riffraff in town looking for a little fun, they enter the city in the street. Soldiers carrying AK-74 assault rifles accompanied a mounted M72 machine gun that was attached to a crossbar in the middle of the vehicle.

There were few soldiers in any of the bars, and Crawford began to think that this city would end in a failed attempt for Intel. Three-quarters through the main city street, they happened across one bar that had several soldiers sitting by themselves at a table. Shawn recognized their rank as junior officers who may have sneaked away for a short period of time to enjoy a little fun.

Crawford and King entered and found a table close to the booth where the officers are sitting. Shawn and Hunter recognized that they were Algerian, as they spoke Arabic with a northern African accent. As both were fluent in the language, they sat at the table, ordered a drink, and pretended not to listen to what the soldiers were discussing.

'This operation cannot fail!' one officer said to others. 'They have no idea that we are planning a full-scale invasion through the Wellesley Islands at the southern edge of the Gulf of Carpentaria. Along with our fighter support. After our special operations people eliminate their communications network in the immediate area, Sydney will have no idea that their homeland has been invaded. This is going to be a "cakewalk".'

'Yes, but I think waiting for three days to launch the attack is too long a time to wait! There is much room for error by waiting. We should strike immediately!'

'No! Let us have faith in our leadership. They know exactly what they are doing! We must not deter from their mission wisdom. Brother, enough of this serious talk. Let's enjoy the time that we have together!'

Shawn signaled to Hunter that it was time to leave. They had heard enough!

They meandered down the city street in the direction of the hidden F-98. On the way to its location, Shawn received a message from Sancha that their location had been discovered. Tim and Christopher had exited the Shark and, when O'Hara was starting to repel the African soldiers who had discovered their aircraft, he was shot several times in the chest.

Christopher had immediately fallen on top of his body. A very bright blue light descended over them both. When the light disappeared, they were both gone from sight.

The African soldiers, frightened at first, then attempted to gain access to the F-98. Sancha had emitted an electrostatic charge around the airframe that, when touched, repelled the invaders backward at least 20 feet. They were rendered unconscious and unmoving.

Sancha, report!

Commander, the Stingray was discovered, and Commander O'Hara attempted to repel the soldiers, more to negate their communications of their discovery of their superiors. In the process, he was shot several times.

Your son, Christopher, went to his aid and shielded O'Hara's body with his. Christopher was shot several times in the back before a light blue, intense light arrived suddenly and wrapped itself around both Tim and Christopher. The soldiers were rendered immobile by my electrostatic emission surrounding the F-98!

Sancha, we need to deport this area immediately. Are the repelled soldiers still immobile? And, if so, how many? And where are they located?

Commander, there are four altogether. They are still immobile and are located at your two o'clock position. 10 meters from the Stingray. 'Coach, let's get this body aboard, and let's get back to Sydney. 'What about your son and O'Hara?'

'If I know anything after being involved with The Entity for the past so many years, Christopher and Timmy are well-taken care of. Trust me, Coach!'

After they loaded the African unconscious bodies aboard, Shawn directed Sancha to initiate a low-level takeoff from s hover to reduce the exhaust signature of the Stingray. Once in the air, Crawford told Sancha to assume total operational control of the F-98 and expedite its arrival at Sydney's defense base.

In the interim, Shawn and Hunter securely duck-taped the four soldiers to the internal fuselage.

Commander, this feels utterly revolting! Do you have to attach these vermin to my internal siding?

Sancha, sweetheart, and, do not mistake my term as being one of endearment, for it is mentioned only in a Platonic manner, it is important to ensure that the Admiral and I do not have to deal with unexpected occurrences while en route to Sydney.

Sancha was able to get to Sydney in a historic flight time from northern Australia in 47 minutes! When asked about how she achieved this monumental feat, she refused to comment on the grounds that it might incriminate Commander Crawford!

When the Stingray landed, Air Police Forces were present to remove the "prisoners" from the aircraft. Shawn turned the aircraft over to Will after saying mentally to Sancha, *Well done. You are truly a friend.*

Good luck, Commander. I am prepared to leave any time you desire to retrieve both Tim O'Hara and your son Christopher. We will talk soon, Commander.

Shawn and Hunter walked up to the operation, where Morrison and O'Leary were waiting. Patrick O'Hara and Christine came into the room moments later, with Colette in tow.

'Shawn, we heard that Christopher and Commander O'Hara were wounded during the mission! Where are they, Shawn?' Christine exclaimed hysterically.

'Christine, Patrick! Please know that they are safe. Let's all sit down. Chris, Sancha, the F-98 voice module system, monitored the whole situation. Patrick, let me tell you that your sin is safe and in good hands. No, let me say that he is in great hands!

'Both Tim and Christopher sustained wounds during the mission. Tim first, followed by Christopher. When our son was hit in the back, after protecting Timmy from further injury by falling on the Commander, they were both protectively secured in The Entity's Blue Light.

'Now, Patrick. Although it may seem difficult to believe, I would like to request some time to spend with our daughter, Colette. She will try to persuade you that our son will be returned to us in a very short period, completely healed. The wounds that were sustained have been healed in a similar manner to the injury we encountered when we first arrived in Sydney.

'Colette, Honey, would you please help Colonel O'Hara try to understand that his son is going to be fine?'

'Yes, father,' Colette said with a smile.

'Colonel, father was absolutely correct. Your son Timothy was truly alive and well. Sir, please walk with me momentarily and I will explain.'

'Marshal Morrison, here is the Intel that Admiral King and I gathered while we were in the city.' Shawn, with Hunter's input, proceeded to debrief their mission in front of Morrison and O'Leary.

'Michael, it's time that we took the initiative and initiated a strike against the hostile unit stationed in Kupang. They are in violation of the Indonesian

Peace Accords by occupying a sovereign nation's soil. This has happened before and, I vow, this will be the absolute last time that this happens!'

'I'll take care of initiating the alert order for our fighters to mobilize. Let me take care of this right away. If we can get them in the next 36 hours, we will have trumped their invasion card. I'll ensure that there is a suitable protective mix of fighters for offensive purposes, as well as to make certain that our borders are protected.'

'Thank you, Michael. In the meantime, I will ensure that the Prime Minister is apprised of this on-coming threat possibility.'

Shawn and Hunter then walked over to where Colette was talking quietly and with a reassuring tone to Patrick. Colonel O'Hara nodded finally when Colette had finished explaining to him just exactly what was going on with Commander O'Hara at the very moment. Patrick smiled at Colette, gave her a hug, and said "thank you".

'Colonel,' said Shawn. 'Tim will be returned to us, as Christopher will. I will personally ensure that both our sins will be with us, 24 hours have elapsed. Hunter, let's get back to the hangar and re-visit the tapes that captured the confrontation outside the F-98 while we were gone.

'Christine, don't worry. We both know what The Entity can do. His protective blue light was merely a means of insulating both Christopher and Tim from further harm. I promise you that I will get them back for all of us. Let's go, Coach!'

They motored over to the hangar where flight Sergeant Caruso was doing a post-flight maintenance check on the F-98. He looked up when the two general officers arrived.

'Sir Shawn, the aircraft is fully prepped and ready to go any time you are, Sir.'

'Thank you, Will. Coach, ready to take a little ride with me?' 'Put me in, Coach!'

Shawn gave directives to Sancha during the taxi from the hangar to wheels-up at the end of the active runway. Crawford directed Sancha to climb to 35,000 feet and to begin looking for The Entity's cloud formation. They didn't have long to wait.

They were enveloped quickly and completely within the Entity's domain.

MEETING ALEJANDRO

'HELLO, YOUR VASTNESS! We are here to pick up our two wayward Aviators. Of course, you wouldn't happen to know anything about their situation, would you?'

'Hello, my two favorite general officers. Christopher and Timothy are alive and doing well. Your son, Shawn, is a hero in the way he protected Commander O'Hara. I will take you both to them.'

'Thank you, Almighty and Wise Blue Meanie! We can't wait to see them again. And, thank you for taking them away from their attackers so swiftly.'

The F-98 exited the cloud formation and found itself in familiar "territory", the 22nd century. The Hindu Tower operator cleared them for landing and Shawn complied with total directives. They were on the ground quickly and taxied behind a "follow me" vehicle into their familiar hangar place.

Out of the aircraft, they were met by one of The Entity's minions, who led them into the huge room with shimmering light blue walls. A familiar form came "floating" toward them and welcomed Shawn and Hunter back to their ethereal domain.

'Sir, it's nice to see you again. You know, I could dress up this place a little with portraits of myself, but I don't think your shimmering walls will hold a nail.'

The Entity's ambassador chuckled. 'Shawn, we miss your humor when you are not here. Although, Senator Kennedy's needling of his brother Jack does create some comic relief. And, President Lincoln has come "out of the closet" to display a very dry wit. Of course, the struggles of Drs. King and Gandhi attempting to understand one another to keep us constantly wondering their speech patterns spawn from different languages!'

'Yes, Sir. I know the feeling. Trying to understand Shawn sometimes does lend itself to something akin to Saturday Night Live Comedy Show! Oops, sorry, Coach!'

'Hunter, I am truly offended! O.K., I'm over it. Now, where would my wayward son and the young enterprising Naval Officer be at this moment, Your Floatness?'

'At the moment, Christopher is conducting a science lecture in front of all the very famous personages. I do believe he has lost President Lincoln along the way, as the President has dozed off and is being propped up by then Senator. Christopher's knowledge of the Universe is unparalleled in your world, but fairly simplistic in its understanding on our own. Come with me.'

They walked into the room and saw Christopher talking to those seated around a conference table. When he saw his father walk into the room, he stopped mid-sentence and excused himself while he walked toward Shawn.

He embraced his father as everyone stood. President Lincoln   mumbled

something about, 'Is it over already?'

Christopher's "Audience" came forward to greet the two aviators. Admiral Hunter went immediately to Commander O'Hara and asked how he was. Tim responded with a smile and said that he never felt better and hadn't realized he had been shot several times. All of a sudden, he had been outside the F-98 trying to repel the enemy soldiers and then found himself here in the conference room. When trying to make sense of it, Christopher explained what had happened. They told the young officer that his father would be a spoon arriving to take them back to the late 21st century and to Sydney.

President Lincoln came forward as the Elder Statesman of the group and welcomed Shawn and King.

'We were just being lectured to by your son, Christopher. He has a fantastic mind. Although, I must admit that my understanding of anything he said was lost on me after his opening sentence. It's so very nice to see you both again.'

'Thank you, Mr. President. I understand what you're saying about Christopher's subject material. Whenever I have trouble sleeping at night, I ask Christopher to come into our bedroom and begin the lecture about the universe. I'm usually sound asleep within a minute and a half after he begins.'

Christopher lightly kicked his father in the shin but smiled when he did so.

'Ow, that didn't hurt at all!' he hugged his son warmly.

Shawn approached The Entity's Ambassador and asked if there was anything he needed to do to assist His Vastness in anything humanity required to continue in the quest for world peace. Crawford was told that further "assignments" would be forthcoming. He thanked Shawn for all of his efforts to date. The Ambassador hinted that Shawn's team was now complete, with one exception.

'What might that be?' asked Crawford.

'Commander O'Hara's father Patrick has shown a deep interest in flying helicopters again. We know that you have mentioned to him about getting together with Air Commander Gonzales to make this happen. It is imperative that Colonel O'Hara effect a transition into the helicopter that we ask you to take back to your base in Sydney. This will be the aircraft that Colonel Patrick O'Hara will command in the near future. We ask that you make this happen, Shawn.'

'Absolutely! I'll take it back and Commander O'Hara can log some time in the Stingray Fighter. If there is nothing else for us, please, lead the way to the aircraft.'

'Hi, Shawn! It's good to see you again, old friend. I'll be taking you over to the Vampire. How have you been?' asked Colonel Derek Peterson.

'Derek, it's good to see you! Sorry, I didn't hear you come into the room. It must have had something to do with the awful snoring coming from the "Guest" here, listening [or sleeping] to Christopher's presentation on the salient points of the workings of the Universe! Son, please don't kick a very old Aviator again!'

Derek laughed at Christopher's feigned "hurt" expression.

'Derek! What's this: a promotion to full Colonel! Well deserved! It's about time your efforts have been rewarded. Before long, you'll be commanded to this organization. His blueness better watch out because I'm sure He can hear your footsteps fast approaching to take over His position!'

Shawn, you're too kind, but I don't think that will ever happen. As a matter of fact, my promotion to full Colonel is a direct result of your thought the last time you were here that suggested I should be promoted. I really have to thank you for this.

'Well, my friend, I am so very glad to assist in getting you the reward you richly deserve! Now, about this new and innovative helicopter, can you show it to me? I hope it's not going to kick my butt?'

'Oh. I don't think that is going to happen. You may like so much

flying in the "weeds" again that you will want to give up flying Sancha!'

'Well, I wouldn't go that far. But the Vampire does sound intriguing. I'm anxious to see it!'

The Sikorsky Vampire Attack Helicopter
Courtesy of airnewstime.co.uk

They got to the hangar and walked to the far side. There, before them, was a totally awesome helicopter! "Sleek" was a word that barely did it justice. It was a single-pilot gunship that was totally automated, just as Sancha was. It responded to voice commands like the F-98 and was capable of mental communication as well.

'Shawn, say hello to your new aircraft!'

'Wow, Derek, this is one "sweet" rig! What are all the parameters?'

'It cruises at 280 knots. It's capable of doing over 350 knots with an accelerated booster injection system inserted into the twin combustion chambers. The name of this "beast" is whatever you choose. Just like the Stingray, it will respond to all commands provided by The Entity's inner circle. So, Flight Sergeant Caruso is capable of communicating with the aircraft.

'In addition, you may pick two other individuals outside the circle to access its communication systems module. I presume that may be Colonel O'Hara and Air Commander Gonzales. However, that is entirely up to you, my Friend.'

'Well, first, I do believe I will sign the name "Alejandro" which

alludes to the "Defender of Mankind"

'Well, chosen and very appropriate. Let's go over the features of "Alejandro".

Derek went over pre-flight procedures as well as start-up protocol. He indicated that emergency procedures were essentially the same as any other helicopter, with one exception: Alejandro would initiate and execute each one incurred. This aircraft was totally automated. He did everything but provide room service. Of course, there was a provision to ensure the comfort of the pilot in all situations, but that did not mean either a "back-rub" or "complimentary Twinkies"!

Crawford pouted for a second and then got over the disappointment,, especially about the Twinkies situation! 'O.K., Derek, anything else I need to know that I could share with both the Air Commodore or Colonel O'Hara?'

'There is an ejection seat system available for the pilot in extreme emergencies. The angle of ejection is controlled automatically by Alejandro, who determines the best and more suitable degree of ejection that affords the maximum opportunity for survival. This would be a nice feature to know about should the aircraft suffer a catastrophic failure during flight.'

'Nice to know. When we have to "punch out" are there snacks somewhere in the ejection pod so that one may not only admire the view on the way down but may also ensure that the impending landing occurs on a reasonably full stomach?'

'I will leave that feature for you and Flight Sergeant Caruso to work out.

Next, you'll expect a "hot plate" installed!'

'Well, a guy has to eat before being potentially captured. The worst thing that could happen would be for the enemy to take his Twinkies nourishment away when he arrives in all of his glory!'

'Any other systems questions that need to be addressed before you take the Vampire out for a familiarization flight?'

'No, I think that Alejandro and I will get along with no problems. And wait until I get "him" home and introduce him to Sancha! Whoa, I do believe there are going to be fireworks in the making in the hangar that night!'

'I don't even want to go there, my friend! O.K., Shawn, let's get started with an orientation flight. I know you haven't forgotten how helicopters work since you've fallen in love with fighters.'

As Crawford was recognized by the aircraft through the initial intervention by The Entity, all Shawn had to do was to submit an appropriate command to "Alejandro" to get started. He mentally directed the aircraft to open the pilot's command station, and Alejandro complied. As Crawford got himself properly seated in the comfortable command chair, he heard Alejandro request the next command in his head.

Welcome, General Crawford. What are we going to accomplish during this flight?

Good morning. Alejandro. This morning is an orientation flight so that you may instruct me on the pertinent features of the operation of your aircraft. Is this acceptable to you, Alejandro?

Sir Shawn, I will execute any and all directives provided that lend themselves to your personal safety. All you have to do is to suggest in your mind to start engines. Further instructions are anticipated should you be incapacitated during any flight segment. What are your directives, General?

Start engines, Alejandro. Notify ground control of our intentions to hover the taxi to the active runway. Indicate that you have the automated weather information. Inform ground control of our direction of flight [westerly], our mode of flight [VFR Local], and our initial altitude upon leaving the control area. How to copy, Alejandro?

Copy all, General. Are you prepared to proceed?

I am, Alejandro. Initiate the process outlined, please. Wilcox, Commander.

As Shawn taxied to the active runway under the control of Alejandro. Shawn directed that he assumed personal operational control of the aircraft. Alejandro released the controls to Shawn by saying, 'You have the aircraft, General.'

Shawn responded, I have the aircraft," indicating that Crawford had taken over the control of cyclic, collective, and anti-torque pedals of the Vampire, unlike the OH-58D Kiowa Warrior that Shawn was used to flying before he transitioned to the F-42A Tiger Shark several years ago.

Crawford held short of the active runway and awaited a jet fighter to make its approach and landing. Once this was accomplished, Shawn informed the Vampire computer that he would execute the takeoff. The Vampire acknowledged the directive.

Crawford hovered onto the active and was cleared for takeoff, with the announced customary warning of "caution wake turbulence". Shawn announced that he was clearly left and right above and initiated his takeoff.'

Once he reached an altitude of 750 feet above ground level [AGL], he was cleared to proceed on course and to contact Departure Control on a specific set frequency. Shawn switched over and announced to the controller that his intent was to go over the gunnery range for training. He was cleared on "hot" as no other traffic was scheduled for such training that day.

Crawford set a course for the range that was located 15 kilometers to the southwest of the airfield. His aircraft was fashioned with a full complement of air-to-ground rockets.

Once in the vicinity of the range, he made an announcement in the clear that identified his aircraft, altitude, and established range time, not to exceed one hour, in accordance with the established training SOP [Standard Operating Procedure] for the base. He also announced his ammunition usage while firing off the range.

After firing his rockets, coupled with masking and unmasking, low-level target acquisition procedures, and nap-of-the-earth [NOE] flight, he had exhausted his allotted time on the range. There were "fast-movers" now scheduled to train within a 15-minute period of time, and he definitely wanted to be done before they arrived at the station.

Alejandro, take us back to Base. Upon receiving approval to land, I will assume operational control of the aircraft. With aircraft control procedures between pilots strictly observed.

Very well, Commander.

When Crawford completed his flight, he met Christopher, Commander O'Hara, and Admiral King in the hangar. The indicated his intent regarding the return flight to Sydney via The Portal. Commander O'Hara would be the Aircraft Commander aboard the F-98A Stingray. He would follow in the Vampire Helicopter. Christopher was the overall Mission Commander for the return through The Portal. They launched a half-hour following Shawn's return in the Vampire.

When they reached an altitude of 23,000 feet, restricted because of the top ceiling altitude of the Vampire, they entered The Entity's cloud.

As Christopher was the mission commander for the return flight, The Entity made his presence known to him, but Shawn was able to listen in the conversation.

'Christopher and Shawn, we have an atrocity that cannot be ignored in the mid-20th century during the American involvement during World War II in Belgium on December 17, 1944. It is commonly referred to as the Malmedy Massacre, especially occurring at Baugnez. Commander O'Hara, you may remember from your history that this atrocity committed by the German troops led to the massacre of 84 American prisoners of war in the open snow-covered fields there. These Americans from 285th Field Artillery Observation Battalion were ambushed by the Germans on their way to reinforce the 7th Armored Division at St. Vito. 120 Americans were gathered in the field. The Germans lined them up and began firing at them, killing 84. When fired upon, some prisoners feigned death, but they too were shot in the head.

"We need you to stop this massacre from occurring. Please utilize any reasonable means possible to preserve the lives of these American Soldiers. There are individuals who would suffer due to this atrocity who would later contribute to world peace. It is most important that their lives be preserved.

As always, we will be with you.'

The landscape before them was snow-covered, definitely winter. Below them, an American convoy of trucks was moving at intervals down the frozen dirt road. Off to either side, at a distance of 50 meters, in the tree line, were some 25–35 soldiers waiting for the convoy to approach in their "killing zone". The Germans.

'Timmy, you have operational control, as well as the firepower between us. You make the first gun run in and I will follow. Let's continue to provide fire support until the convoy is clear of the German ambush. On my mark: Go!'

The F-98 swept toward the tree line and let loose a series of rockets that completely decimated the centerline of the Germans. They began to fall back. A small contingent on either side remained and fired after the departing Stingray. Shawn easily targeted these individuals and stopped at a hover and fired continuously into the wood line until the German threat was no longer able to mount an offensive.

Shawn told Tim that he was going to set the Vampire down and see if he could talk to the convoy commander. As he did so, the lead American command jeep pulled off the side of the road and waited for the "strange aircraft" pilot to emerge. After Shawn climbed out of the Vampire, he walked calmly to the convoy Commander, a Captain, and introduced himself.

The captain recognized his rank as a general officer, and immediately rendered a salute. Crawford returned it and asked if his men had taken any casualties. The captain indicated in the negative for Shawn's aircraft and the other "strange ship" had done all the damage for them.

'Great! Glad to hear it! Had we not come along, this would not have gone well for you and your men, Captain? The Germans were lined up in a perfect ambush position. Your unit in a Field Artillery Operation Battalion, is it not?'

'Yes, General, it is. Sir, what unit are you with? I, for one, had never seen aircraft as yours, or the other one for that matter, before in my military career. And I thought I had memorized every friendly and enemy aircraft in this Theater of Operations.'

'Well, Captain, let's say that these are experimental in nature. We are in the process of testing them in a threat in the environment. I'd say that we've done pretty well today, wouldn't you?'

'General, I can't thank you and the other crew enough. I'd like to forward a report to my Higher Headquarters if you don't mind. You are General Shawn Crawford, I see. And what do you call that aircraft of yours, Sir?'

'It's called a helicopter, Captain. It's fairly futuristic in design. I, myself, am slowly getting used to flying it.'

And that moment, Alejandro sent Shawn a mental reminder that it was time to leave, as soon as the good General was ready to depart.

'Captain, I am holding you and your Unit back from reinforcing the 7th Armored Division. I'm certain that they can use your assistance as soon as possible. Captain, it's been my pleasure talking with you, as well as providing the firepower necessary for you to continue on to St. Vito. I wish you and your men the best of luck.

'Oh, Captain. I'm going to go out on a limb here and predict that this War in Europe will come to an end on May 8, 1945. And another prediction: Adolph Hitler will commit suicide in his Bavarian Bunker on April 30th, a week before. Write those dates down. I think you'll find that I will be right on the money, plus or minus 24 hours. The War is almost over, Captain. Less than six more months. Tell your men to hang in there, O.K.? All the best, Captain, and keep your head down.'

Alejandro, please open the command module. Communicate with the F-98 that we are ready to depart. Information Commander O'Hara that we will meet at 3,500 feet at a heading of 270 degrees. Acknowledge.

Commander O'Hara has been so informed. Commander. Please indicate your readiness to depart.

Alejandro, initiate takeoff and join the Stingray at the assigned altitude.

Wilco, Commander.

After Shawn had taken off, he began his climb to 3,500 feet AGL on a westerly heading. As he cleared 1,200 feet, he was jumped by three Me109 Messerschmitt German Aircraft diving out of a far greater altitude. Crawford directed Alejandro to take evasive action and notify the Stingray that they were being pursued by three German fighters.

Alejandro dumped the aircraft's nose and screamed downward toward the snow-covered fields below. The Vampire leveled off just in time before impacting into a frozen field adjacent to a secondary road heading east and west. The first German fighter was too confident in his chase after the helicopter and was not able to pull up in time. It crashed nose-first in a ball of flames. There were still two aircraft left to contend with. The demise of their flight leader drew no sympathy from the other two German 109s, as they both pursued the strange-looking aircraft.

Just when Shawn thought that his aircraft was going to be locked on by one of the two remaining Messerschmitt German fighters, the Stingray blew one of the Germans out of the sky with an air-to-air missile. The other German decided wisely not to stay in the fight and abruptly turned back to the east, where his airfield was located some 7 kilometers away.

'Well, boys and girls, that was fun! Why don't we call it a day in the 20th century and return to the Sydney Base for a little R&R and a well-deserved Beef Wellington Dinner!'

'And Pizza!' announced Christopher from the Stingray.

'O.K., I'll buy it. I've got your mother's credit card, Christopher, so I'm

willing to make this sacrifice.'

'You're a man among men, Coach!' quipped Hunter.

They were engulfed by The Entity's cloud and the light therein after flying in formation for approximately five minutes. As usual, "His Blueness" was his jovial self, as he addressed Crawford in the Vampire.

'You have done well, once again, My Young Jedi! You never ceased to amaze me with each and every success. Perhaps, one day, you may entertain the opportunity to become a member of our staff. However, this would appear to be a conversation for another time altogether, as of this point.

'When I release both of your aircraft, the Australian Continent will have been under attack from the African Confederation from Indonesia for the past several days. I am going to release you over the City of Darwin and the Forward Air Defense Base located there. Please know that I will always be with you.'

And did he ever release them into the Australian/African confederation conflict? When they departed the cloud, Shawn immediately told Christopher to descend immediately and turn to a heading due South. He told him then to fly a heading of 210 degrees, over the northern edge of the continent, and away from the battle, however momentarily, until he could assess the threat situation.

Shawn then made a call on the tactical frequency to the forward controlling headquarters to let them know that their aircraft were available to enter the aerial fight. He immediately got a response asking for his type of aircraft and weapons stores. Shawn responded that he was an F-98A Stingray with a full load of missiles and that there was a Vampire Attack Helicopter also full of complement missiles. The controller directed Christopher to a different sector over the sea to the north of Darwin. He directed Shawn in the Vampire to proceed to the northern coast of Darwin and assist the Comanche in the area with ground troop support. Shawn replied that he was en route to assist the Comanche.

When Bob Gonzales of the Comanche saw the Vampire enter the fray, he exclaimed, 'Where the hell did you come from, and what the hell are you flying soldiers?'

'Hello, Bobbo! Have you missed me?'

'Shawn! How did you get here? No, wait on that! Help me by lining up to my left with a 50-meter separation. We've got some ground troops who need some serious support down there. Do you have a full load out?'

'I do. When we land, do you have anything to eat? Hold on a second while I engage some vermin approaching our infantry down below.'

Crawford fired off two air-to-ground missiles to the front of the advancing Australian forces and literally blew a hole in the African lines. The Aussies proceeded onward and now had the offensive in their favor.

He then peeled off to the left, further from the Comanche, and opened up on the African forces with his 30 mm cannon. It was ugly, but effective. Shawn rotated back toward Gonzales's advanced attack helicopter.

'Now, about that meal that you owe me before you "skipped out of town"! I will settle for nothing less than MRE, "ham and eggs", if you have one leftover.'

'Shawn, look left!' An African fighter came out of nowhere and began to line up with the Vampire. The African had a good tone on his threat acquisition radar, and the Vampire was receiving it well. Just when Shawn figured he "had bought the farm", the fighter was blown out of the sky! Behind it and roaring past Shawn's Vampire was the F-98A Stingray. Sancha never looked so good! He promised to ensure that he would treat her to an extra quart of high-synthetic oil when everything was said and done!

'Father, are you alright? We've got to get this mess under control down there. I am seriously getting hungry for Pizza!'

'That's my boy!'

The Vampire began taking small arms fire from his left. He pedaled-turned the Vampire in that direction and raked the wood line with another burst of 30 mm cannon. A caution light came on, and he looked at it closely. It wasn't anything to be concerned about. It would have been had the light indicated that dinner at the club was closing for orders in 10 minutes.

Christopher had now mind-directed Sancha to seek all African fighters and destroy each one. "Her" ability to recognize an enemy aircraft from great distances allowed Christopher to remain at a relatively safe distance.

The only problem was that the F-98 was rapidly running out of air-to-air, or sidewinder missiles.

His son relayed the message about missile depletion to his father.

'Christopher, how many Sidewinders do you have left?' 'Only one, Father. What would you suggest?'

'Get one more kill by expanding that last missile. I then want you to direct Sancha to keep up the offensive. When you are positioned at the threat aircraft's six o'clock position. I want you to drive that fighter in my direction, as you have the speed, I have the firepower. I can't run with them, but you most certainly can.'

'O.K., Father. My threat recognition radar recognizes at least three African Fighters remaining. Here comes one now, father!'

Christopher directed Sancha to exercise evasive maneuvers. As the F-98 climbed with power, the African tried to mimic the F-98 by going vertical with a Stingray. As the enemy fighter began rotating into a full-power climb, Shawn took the very brief opportunity to target the Africans exposed underside.

Shawn announced "Fox One" and his missile left the helicopter's rails with a near-blinding flash of light. It ran through and struck underneath the fighter near its twin-engine exhaust ports.

There were two remaining African Fighters. One of them began a dive in the direction of Shawn's Vampire. As soon as Crawford saw it approaching a half-mile away, it all of a sudden exploded, with the pieces falling into the ocean below. A familiar voice over the tactical frequency.

'Anyone saw a handsome United States Naval Academy Fighter pilot lately?' inquired Captain Shelley O'Leary, as her Sea Scorpion Stealth Fighter blew by overhead.

'Shelley!' cried out Timmy O'Hara. 'Is that you doing a lot of the gun-slinging up there?'

'The one and only one! What happened? Did you run out of ammunition?'

'That's affirmative, Shelley. But we're working with Sir Shawn, who is flying the Vampire helicopter in the weeds down there somewhere. There's another African out there, isn't there?'

'I've got him. He's all mine. See you folks on the ground.'

They watched as the Sea Scorpion nearly executed a perfect 90-degree angle in the sky. Shelley kept it coming around until she got a good tone and announced, "Fox four" BAM! Pieces of fighters fell apart just above everywhere after her missile hit mid-frame. Just another day at the office!

All of a sudden, all air activity stopped altogether. The Stingray flew to the Darwin advanced Base of Operations and hovered to the ground. It then ground taxied to the ramp where it shut down its engines. Shawn was right behind him and settled the Vampire down beside Gonzales Comanche.

Bob was waiting on the tarmac for all to "deplane". When Shawn secured the Vampire, he walked over to his old friend and gave him a big hug.

'It's wonderful to see you again, Shawn. You've been away so much lately that I thought you must have found another restaurant offering a better Beef Wellington elsewhere!'

'Oh, no. I didn't want to get a terrible reputation for leaving friends behind not once, but twice. How do you like my new "toy" over there?' as Shawn pointed to the Vampire.

'Awesome looking machine! Somebody said its name is "Vampire".

Does that mean it only comes out at night?'

'Only if it wants to! Come over to the Stingray. There is someone I want you to meet.'

After Gonzales gave Christopher a hug, Shawn introduced Hunter to Bob.

'Admiral King and I go back a long way. He's a "snake-eater", SEAL,

and Delta Force. And he even remembers the "secret handshake"!

Hunter shook Bob's hand and said that it was a pleasure meeting him and that Shawn had mentioned Bob several times in the past.

At that moment, CPT O'Leary taxied the Sea Scorpion onto the ramp and parked it adjacent to the F-98A Stingray. After the Engine shutdown, she exited the fighter and went immediately to Commander O'Hara.

Bob noted the gleam in young Timothy's eye and said that he believed that Shelley had finally met her Mr. Wonderful.

'They make a good pair, don't they?'

'Yes, they do, Bobbo! Oh, listen, Commander O'Hara's father is a former Huey Pilot with over a couple of thousand hours of stick time. What do you think about transitioning him into the Comanche? He is itching to get back into flying in the "weeds" again.'

'Absolutely! Would love to have another stick-mate. When things settle down here, I do believe that we are just about at that point, and we can affect the transition. There are still some resisting ground pockets that may take care of themselves now that their air support is no longer among the flying!'

Gonzales was correct in his assessment that the ground troops were outmaneuvered and left with "zero" air support from the African Federation Air Force. After another two days of minimal contact with the threat, the Australian forward forces were able to pull back to Sydney. A more sizable contingent with air power to match was left behind. These troops and airmen would remain in Northern Australia for six months and remain for six. This would enable overlapping command and control without the need to educate an entirely new command and troop structure on the status of any potential threat, as well as intelligence regarding movements from the islands of Indonesia to the north.

Once Shawn and company were safely settled into a normal life of "fun and frolic" at the Sydney Base, Bob Gonzales met Patrick, and they began that latter's transition training into flight qualification into the AH-56 Cheyenne Attack Helicopter.

On the first morning, Bob instructed Patrick about pre-flight operations, where to tug and pull, where to step, and not to. The Cheyenne was a fully-automated aircraft. Although the word "automated" was exactly in reference to how a fast-mover was "automated", it was still miles ahead of flying a UH-1H/V Huey Helicopter.

Bob and Patrick met every day, Monday through Friday, to go over the systems in the morning class, and then out to the range area to log some flying. Patrick was a quick study and had a great "touch" with the Cheyenne. It didn't take him long to fly the airframe as opposed to the other way around. All too often, students were "behind the aircraft" in that they reacted rather than taking control at the outset.

At first, and after an orientation flight, Patrick got comfortable with what the Cheyenne was going to do when applying cyclic input. Gonzales then went through the emergency procedures with him in the morning in the hangar,, and then went out to the range to put the aircraft through its places.

At first, Bob would demonstrate the procedure a couple of times to illustrate how Cheyenne reacted under simulated emergency situations. Next, Patrick would demonstrate the proper method of recovering from an emergency. Autorotations were quickly mastered by Patrick. He was able to show how to land the Cheyenne safely to the ground without engine power.

The autorotation was a basic "diet" of the new student, as he or she had to master a safely controlled landing after an engine failure. There were many students in the initial entry rotary-wing program who simply could not execute a safe autorotation and were subsequently released from the helicopter training program.

All too often, a student would fail to recognize a proper entry attitude and allow the helicopter to approach the final end of the procedure too quickly. At other times, a student would "over-shoot" his designated autorotation point by building up too much airspeed. It was important for airspeed, rotor rpm in the "green", and proper alignment with cyclic and pedal control after adjusting initially for loss of main-rotor authority. Together with wind direction and speed, and an "appropriate" landing site, there were many factors to consider when putting a helicopter down safely under auto-rotational control.

All of these and more considerations were all well and good when practicing autorotations at a military air facility in a peacetime environment. In a wartime situation, however, there were no exercises: there were real-time emergencies. And a pilot had to ensure that he or she got it right first on time.

Once again, Patrick adapted extremely well to the particular nuances of the Cheyenne. He performed each end of every emergency procedure with precision.

AH-56 Cheyenne Attack Helicopter

Courtesy of Wikipedia, the Free Encyclopedia

Bob took Patrick to the Gunnery Range on the fifth day. Gonzales had thought that the training would take at least five days for Colonel O'Hara, who had no prior experience with gunships, to become proficient. However, Gonzales was proven wrong, as the Elder O'Hara quickly surpassed his expectations.

The first day, after being cleared in "hot" to engage ground targets, Patrick completely blew away each and every standing target, better than anyone Bib had ever seen before, except for Shawn Crawford!

'Patrick,' Bob said. 'Do you come out here at night and practice while everyone is asleep? That is phenomenal gunnery! You have a "magic" touch, my friend. Does commander O'Hara know how awesome you are with aerial gunnery?'

'Well, I did hint to him when I told Tim that I was going out to the range in the Cheyenne with you today that I hoped to keep the missiles within the boundary of the continent of Australia!'

'Ah, well, Colonel. I think you may proudly tell your son that there are all kinds of Australian "ground-hugging animals" who are now afraid, very afraid, to see you, my friend, approach the range of gunships!'

'Thank you, Commodore. That's very generous of you. I always wanted to have an opportunity to see what I could do with the ground targets when flying a helicopter. I guess I didn't manage too badly after all!'

'I would say that that was the understatement of the year! Man, you can fly as my wingman anytime! O.K., what we are now doing here is wasting rockets. You have the aircraft, Patrick. Take us back low-level to the hangar. I'm going to take a nap. Wake me when Will Caruso has microwaved the Pizza and is ready to serve it when we have stopped the Cheyenne for the day. Well, done, Patrick!'

'I have the controls, Commodore.'

'And, by the way, from now on it is Bob and Patrick, O.K?'

It was a 20-minute low-level flight back to the Air Defense Base. Patrick announced to the tower his intentions when he got to within 8 miles of the field.

After landing and slowly ground-taxiing into the hangar, Will was standing by the wall nearby and holding a plate of very warm pizza. Patrick just shook his head and marveled at the personalities he was fortunate to have met since arriving with his son weeks ago.

'How was your flight, Colonel?' asked Will Caruso as he handed Patrick a slice of cheese Pizza.

'Well, it went fairly well, I imagine.'

'Will, don't believe a word he said. It went better than well. He shot the "eyes" out of those range targets. I do believe the next time the good Colonel goes to the range, the targets will be shaking in their standards on a completely windless day!' said Gonzales.

After Bob retrieved two slices of the Italian Pie from Flight Sergeant Caruso, he asked the Colonel to conduct a post-flight of the airframe, even though Bob knew that Will would immediately take care of it himself.

'Patrick, I'm going up to Operations to close out our flight plan. Why don't you head home? And well done today, Patrick. Truly awesome! I'm signing you off to fly the Cheyenne any time you want to go up and get some stick time.'

'Thanks, Bob. I really appreciate all the help you've given me. I'll see you sometime soon. Will, thanks much for the Pizza. Blowing up targets really makes me develop a ferocious appetite!'

Understand, Colonel. You're rapidly sounding more and more like Sir Shawn Crawford. I don't know if I can survive having you two around the hangar! Enjoy the rest of the day, Sir!'

Patrick then went over the Cheyenne in a meticulous post-flight. When he finished, he said goodbye to Will and left the hangar. He then drove over to his quarters.

Bob, in the meantime, closed out his flight plan with operations and then drove the short distance to the headquarters building. He climbed the stairs and checked in with Sergeant Cranston. The Commander and Colonel O'Leary were both in.

'Good morning, Marshal Morrison, Air Chief Marshal O'Leary!' 'Morning, Commodore!' said Morrison.

'Bob, if you call me by that title again, I'm going to have a drop you for one push-up. How are you?' asked O'Leary.

'Great, Sir, thank you. I've just completed my transition from Colonel O'Hara into the Cheyenne. He's a natural pilot. I would like to make a recommendation for having an official military transfer of Colonel O'Hara, retired, to the Australian Air Force in active status. Shawn and I are the only pilots who can fly the AH-56. As we all know, General Crawford is having way too much fun with Sancha these days. Having Colonel O'Hara as my Cheyenne backup would make a lot of sense.'

'Yes, it does to me as well, Commodore. Why don't we make this happen the day after tomorrow here in my office? This will give me time to run it by the Prime Minister who, I'm certain, would have no problem with approving our request.' said Morrison.

On Monday morning, Shawn, Hunter, Tim, Patrick, and Christopher were called into Morrison's office at 1000 hours. When they arrived, Air Chief Marshal O'Leary was present with the Base Commander, along with the Prime Minister of Australia.

Shawn immediately quipped that he was being relieved of his service to the "Queen" for having had over his allotted number of Beef Wellington meals for the month to date. He started shaking hands with everyone and telling each individual how much he enjoyed working with each person.

'Shawn, enough, O.K.,' O'Leary smiled. Shawn shirked back into the crowd with a smirk, knowing all too well why all were summoned there in the first place.

Marshal Morrison then introduced the Prime Minister, who began his remarks by saying that Sir Shawn Crawford had indeed set a record for Beef Wellington dinners, lunches, and breakfasts in the past three weeks. And that the general assembly was considering erecting a bust of his countenance in the hallowed halls of the government legislative building to honor such an impressive display of gluttony!

Crawford remarked with all modesty that, since the arrival of the Admiral King, he had been forced to increase his protein diet due to the Admiral's insistence that he, Shawn Crawford, could use the additional beef intake.

'Nice, Coach, really nice,' deadpanned King.

Ignoring the friendly banter, the Prime Minister then began telling everyone present why they were called into the Commander's Office. He asked

Lieutenant Colonel Patrick O'Hara to come forward and stand beside him and Commander Morrison.

'We are so very pleased to have a gentleman who has served his country in America with great distinction. Now that he has found retirement, the Australian military leadership has considered very seriously Colonel O'Hara's prion expertise in the area of rotary-wing aviation and has decided that this individual's abilities should not go "by the road', as it were.

'Lieutenant Colonel O'Hara, it is with great honor and privilege that I confer upon you an officer commission in the Royal Australian Air Force. In addition, I am pleased to promote you to the rank of Brigadier General in the Royal Australian Air Force. Congratulations, General O'Hara!' The Prime Minister next shook Patrick's hand and asked those present to come forward and to render their congratulatory remarks.

When Shawn got to General O'Hara, he said. 'When you get free, let's celebrate at the club and have a Beef Wellington smorgasbord! What do you say?'

'Shawn,' said Colonel O'Leary. 'The newly appointed General Officer will not be joining you for a mid-morning snack. Isn't there something that you could manage to be doing at the moment, such as getting ready for Christopher's symposium in the States on Wednesday?'

'Colonel, I am deeply offended. Does anyone have the time? Must be getting close to lunch!'

Shawn was dutifully ignored as each individual came forward to congratulate Patrick on his new status with the Australian military. Finally, Crawford stood before Patrick and shook his hand warmly, and said that he was truly pleased that he was now a member of The Entity's Circle of favorite people. He then gave General O'Hara a big hug, and then whispered in his ear that he had 20% discount coupons for Beef Wellington night coming up this Friday!

When the official ceremony was over, Bob Gonzales suggested that Patrick take the Cheyenne out for a cross-country flight, and why didn't he take young Commander O'Hara with him to sit in the front seat. Tim thought that this was a great idea, and his father agreed. They decided to launch after a celebratory brunch at the officer's club.

While everyone was enjoying his and her meal, Tim asked his father if he missed seeing Michael, his brother. Patrick said that he did so every day and that he hoped that, because he was now 100-plus years into the future, it would be great if he could travel back in time to see him play Major League ball one more time. Tim then replied that in the world in which they now lived, anything was possible. One just had to believe.

And so it shall be.

A NEW YORK DAY IN THE BOSTON SUN

'THIS SHOULD BE a lot of fun, Dad.', saidTim. 'I've never been in an attack helicopter before. At the Academy, we did a lot of troop transport work my last year, but never something as exciting as this.'

'Well, stay up for an hour or so to give you a feel of what it's like to fly "in the weeds". If you want, I'll let you handle the radios. All set to go?'

'Sydney ground. Cheyenne 56, west ramp, with information Zulu, VFR, 2,000 feet, westbound, ground taxi instructions, over.'

'Cheyenne 56, good afternoon, ground taxi to runway 27 left via taxiway Bravo, squawk 4722, Altimeter 30.09.'

'Taxi to 27 left Bravo, squawk 4722, altimeter 30.09, for Cheyenne 56.' A moment later, ground control said, 'Cheyenne 56, contact Tower 125.9, good day, Sir.'

'Tower 125.9, for Cheyenne 56, good day, Sir.'

'Sydney Tower, Cheyenne 56 is with your taxiway Bravo.' 'Cheyenne 56, roger, taxi to runway 27 left, hold short.' 'Taxi to 27 left, and hold short for Cheyenne 56, Roger.'

'Cheyenne 56, winds are 250 at 10 knots, altimeter 30.09, cleared for takeoff.'

'Altimeter 30.09, Cheyenne 56 is cleared for takeoff.'

Patrick then announced, 'We're cleared right and left and we are clear above. Cheyenne is on the go.'

At 600 feet AGL, Tower came back to Patrick and said, 'Cheyenne 56, contact departure on 124.5, good day, Sir.'

'Over to departure control 124.5 for Cheyenne 56, good day, Sir.'

'Departure Cheyenne 56 is with you out of 800 for 2,000, EFR, westbound.'

'Cheyenne 56 is radar contact, proceed on course.' 'On course for Cheyenne 56, roger.'

Halfway to the range area, the Cheyenne was all of a sudden completely enclosed in a white mist. Patrick held what he had in course direction and altitude. They then entered a pale bluish light and rested in it, as if stationary in space, for 30 seconds.

'Patrick, congratulations on your appointment and promotion this morning! Well deserved! And young Tim, it is good to see you again as well. You know, Shawn would be the first to tell you, I heard your conversation before departing the airfield and that you both wished you had the opportunity to see Michael again.

'Today, I am going to make this happen by sending you back to the year 2008, Michael's seventh year in the Big Leagues with the Yankees. Personally, I'm a Red Sox fan myself, but I have to be careful admitting that around Dr. King,who absolutely adores those braves in Atlanta.

'The Yankees are playing the Red Sox this evening at 1930 hours. You will find a suitable change of clothing in the side compartment in two small Duffel bags I've provided for you. When you break out of my protective cocoon, you will already have been cleared to land at Logan Airport in Boston and will be in the final approach. You will be directed to the "Follow Me" vehicle that will lead you to shut down. Don't worry about refueling. That will be taken care of for you.

'Go into the FBO, change your clothing in the men's room, and out the front door. A cab has been called to take you directly to Fenway Park. You will find two box seat tickets in your clothing, first row, the home plate side of the Yankee dugout.

Michael will notice you there. You won't have to move anywhere to meet him before the game.'

**Fenway Park, Boston Red Sox Cour-
tesy of Wikipedia, the Free Encyclopedia**

'I've also arranged to allow you to gain access to the park via the player's entrance. When you arrive, the Yankees will be taking batting practice. You will see Michael as soon as you find your seats. I want you both to have the most enjoyable time. There is no time limit on your return. Please be comfortable with this. I wish for you both to enjoy this get-together to the fullest. I love you both, and I will always be with you.' And then, He was gone.

It was a good thing that Tim was sitting in the forward seat, or gunner's station, for had he seen his father, the tears streaming down his face.

Everything happened as outlined by The Entity. The Cheyenne broke out on final approach and, after touchdown, was directed to follow the vehicle over to the FBO ramp. Those on the ground watching this advanced attack helicopter taxi were in awe regarding its futuristic design. It was as if ground operations had ceased altogether to allow such an unusual and powerful-looking aircraft to pass by in a regal manner. Had Shawn been in the cockpit, he should have waved and thrown leaflets out to the "poor" advertising that he was there to save them from their flight. That thought brought a smile to Tim's lips. That would have been Shawn: make light his presence to detract from his own importance.

After the aircraft was chalked, Patrick raised the cockpit and he and Tim exited the aircraft. They secured their Duffel bags from the baggage compartment, just as The Entity had said they would be there. Walking into the FBO and to the men's room, they change into some very comfortable clothing. The Entity had got their sizes perfectly and they both looked the part in 2008 Boston. There were even sunglasses provided. When Tim saw these, he automatically, again, thought of Shawn, his mentor, who would have been disappointed at not finding a small box of pepperoni pizza included in the baggage!

They exited the men's room and went out the door and immediately saw a cabbie leaning against his vehicle and holding a handwritten sign that read "O'Hara". Patrick identified himself and his son, and they have then whisked away to one, if not the oldest, American League Parks, Fenway.

They were dropped off at the player's entrance and, when Patrick attempted to pay and tip the driver, the cabbie looked at him with a smile and politely said that the fare had been pre-arranged in a very handsome manner. He wished the O'Hara's a good night and hoped they enjoyed the game.

At the player's entrance, there was another gentleman at the gate. He was also holding a handwritten sign that read O'Hara. Patrick and Tim approached

be silent for just a few moments. Michael then proceeded to tell them about his family, his father, a war hero as a helicopter pilot, and his older brother who was offered a bonus in excess of $10 million to sign out of high school. And that Timmy O'Hara had gone on to accomplish great feats at the United States Naval Academy as a freshman quarterback leading the midshipmen to a sugar bowl victory against the Florida State Seminoles.

He expressed his pride in his brother, who had progressed to piloting advanced fighters for Abraham Lincoln. However, his brother was later presumed lost at sea following an aerial battle with Iranian fighters over the Persian Gulf. Michael continued by stating that the true heroes of the present day were his father and brother, who served as warriors in this great country. Their service allowed for games to take place each day, including the game that was being played at the time.

And then there was silence, as Michael's Yankee teammates looked at him, and then at his father and brother, who admired him openly. And there was the clapping, slowly at first, but riding to a crescendo that would have made any ballpark in the big leagues proud at its intensity.

When it finally subsided, someone noticed quite a knock on the door. The clubhouse attendant went over and opened it. There, in uniform still, stood looking at both of them as both Red Sox players entered the Visitor's Clubhouse.

Tek was the first to speak. 'Thank you for allowing Tim and me into your clubhouse. Wake and I want to personally congratulate young Michael O'Hara for his outstanding day today. You are certainly among the very best there are.

'We are here to acknowledge one of the greatest potential athletes who may have played the game along with his brother Michael. And you, that is a young man standing before you: Timothy O'Hara. I can only tell you this: Wake and I had the pleasure of playing Tim O'Hara many years ago. As a matter of fact, I caught a younger Tim O'Hara in a game in which he not only won, as a Major League Pitcher, but did so convincingly.

'Tim O'Hara disappeared off the face of this earth as quickly as he appeared here today. I'm not insisting that you believe everything I've just said. However, I urge you to pay tribute to Michael O'Hara, his brother, not for what he is, but for what could have been in the context of Major League Baseball history.

'Wake and I thank you for your attention and time. Congratulations on today's win. And that goes especially to still young Michael O'Hara. Timmy, may we speak with you for just a moment?'

The three left the room and walked down the tunnel a short way. Tek stopped and turned toward O'Hara.

'Your destiny has never been in major league baseball. All three of us know that. Wake has something he wants to return to you to keep.'

Tim Wakefield then put the 1898 silver coin in Tim's hand. He then told him that this was a gift from the past and that Tim O'Hara earned it for his devotion to family, and all that was good in the world. He then gave Timmy O'Hara a huge hug and said that he would never forget him as long as he lived. Tek did the same. They both then turned away and walked back to the Boston clubhouse.

When Tim returned to the clubhouse to join his father, Michael was in the process of getting cleaned up. They left the park 20 minutes later and over to the hotel where the Yankees were lodged for the series with the Red Sox. In the dining room, they enjoyed a great dinner and took the opportunity to catch up on Michael's progress in the Big Leagues. His career has taken off since he was called up that first year in professional baseball following his junior year in high school. But Michael wanted to know all about what had happened to his father and brother.

Tim began his journey with the impending dogfight with Iranian Fighters in the Persian Gulf, and how he had been taken away from impending doom by a mysterious cloud formation that sent him well into the future. When he finished telling about his meeting with General Crawford and the other aerial warriors of the late 21st century, he looked at his father. To Michael, this had to be akin to a science fiction intrusion upon one's well-being. Tim responded that it was indeed an intrusion, but one that resulted in all good things in terms of flying and friendships.

He informed his brother that their father was alone and needed him to return, and also had a feeling that their father would eventually find solace in aviation—a passion he had been pursuing for years. He had not been wrong.

Michael said that he had missed them both terribly, and that professional baseball was all that kept him going in their absence. During the off-season, he had played in various leagues, more to keep him preoccupied than anything else. It turned out that he had learned a lot from the various managers and coaches during this interim league play, which only served to improve his level of play in the Big Leagues. After a while, he had given up hope of ever finding them both again and totally immersed himself in the professional sport.

'Well. What are the next steps?'

'What's important is that you are happy in life. I know that Tim and I have found real happiness in our lives in the future. There are things that can never be matched in terms of experience. And those are the things that rest in our memories, never to be left behind. It's the going on that sometimes is the hardest because of those things that we never want to let go of, the familiar events that usually never amount to the same if lived through again. And, often, this is the reason it is necessary to move forward, as hard as it may seem to do.

'I know that I am happy with my life for now. Baseball can never last. I know that. But it is the joy of the now that creates the memories for the future. You once told me that, Dad. So, it appears that we have what will make us complete when everything is said and done. I do know that I am going to miss you both when you leave. But at least I will know that you both are alright.

'When must you return to the future?'

'We can stay as long as we like. You have two more games in this series that I believe both Tim and I would love to see you play. Is that alright with you?'

'Dad, Tim, I am so very glad that you came to see me. I don't wish to push you away. But while you remain here, even for a couple of days I will be so preoccupied with knowing that you are to be gone soon, that I will suffer, not professionally, but emotionally. I know also that because you were able to come back here for me this time, I can now look forward to other times in my future when we can spend time together again. Does this sound cruel to both of you?'

'Michael,' Tim said. 'It does not to me because I feel like I understand.

And I can only speak for myself.'

'Michael, I will miss you terribly. But your happiness in your world means much to me. You are correct in presuming that we will see one another again. Because all things are possible with The Entity. And, Michael, the door swings both ways as well. There may be a time in your retirement when you will be able to join us finally for the remainder of our lives.

I love you, Michael. All the best in your life. Most importantly, I wish you happiness always. I promise that we will be all together again one day for good.'

ANOTHER KENNEDY FOR THE TAKING

PATRICK AND TIM were slingshot from The Entity's grasp and found themselves on final approach to Sydney's Maritime Air Defense Base. It was roughly 1600 hours. After the Cheyenne concluded its ground taxi to the hangar, Shawn was seen talking to Will near the Stingray fighter.

When the O'Hara got out of the helicopter, Crawford sensed more than knew that they had gone through the portal. Tim came over with his usual smile, but his father was rather preoccupied with what had occurred during their sojourn through time.

'Welcome back, you two. How was your flight?'

'Oh, I would say eventually uneventful.' said the young O'Hara. 'How about going to the club and tossing one or two down?'

Patrick told Tim to go on ahead and that he would see his son later at their quarters. Shawn looked at the elder O'Hara for a long moment and then turned to Timmy and said with a smile, 'What about it? Are you game, Timmy?'

'Sure, why not. It's been a pretty emotional day. It would be good to begin to turn it around.'

Shawn said nothing as he drove over to the Officer's club. They found a booth away from much of the noise and Shawn told Tim that he would buy the first round.

When he came back to the booth, he asked Tim, 'Do you want to talk about it?'

'What do you mean, Shawn?'

'Where did his blueness send you today?'

'How did you know that we went through The Portal?'

'Your father had this glazed look in his eyes. Actually, it was more of a sadness than anything else. His vastness has a way of doing that to the ones he loves the most.'

'When we went back in time in 2008, to Boston's Fenway Park for a Yankees game.'

'And you both got together with Michael.'

'Yes, before and after the game. He Set a Major League record by hitting six home runs in the 17-3 Yankees win. Michael was just awesome, and he was extremely happy.'

'I'm sure he was. I know it must have been very hard for both of you and Michael after all of this time. And I'm sure that the door was left open in the way of suggesting that such meetings could very well happen again in the future.'

'Your visit with your brother in The Entity's way of ensuring that your presence here and away from him is a measure of your commitment to stay. And that commitment is all too important in what we do here. And I don't mean fighting the Africans. What I mean is how we influence the past so that the future creates a more harmonious inclusion of all humanity in experiencing a peaceful coexistence. That is the essence of what we are all about, Timmy.'

'Far too long the world has been trying to annihilate itself through countless wars, one right after the other. When we get back in time to change something or save someone, we go back to create a ripple that will influence positive things as an outpouring of how the world should be.

'You must ensure the safety of both pilots, Shawn. As always, I will be with you. And Christopher, enjoy the Pizza!' A timbrous laugh followed with the silence.

Hunter turned to Shawn and Tim as he unwrapped his Beef sandwich

and asked. 'How do you want to play this, Coach?

'Sacha, are you able to get within six inches of the B-24 Liberator and over the access hatch leading into the aircraft? Is that what you wish for me to do?'

'Sancha, are you able to get within six inches of the B-24 Liberator's

top hatchway and match speed and altitude for 15 minutes?'

'Commander, if you wish, I can put the Stingray on top of the liberator and over the access hatch leading into the aircraft. Is that what you wish for me to do?'

'Precisely, Sancha. When you've set yourself up in this position, please advice.'

'Wilco, Commander.'

'Coach, won't one of the planes in the area spot us and contact the

liberator?'

'Not if the key to the mic will affect a transmission, and create a static charge, which may potentially set off the bomb.. They know that. So, I doubt very seriously that this will be a problem, I hope.

'Timmy, you'll take the aircraft while I climb down through our hatch and the liberators. Just monitor the systems; Sancha will do the rest. Coach, be prepared to accept two additional passengers. Christopher, you'll be on standby. Any questions from anyone?'

'Coach, you're sure about this. No way we can intercept the aircraft before it takes off from its base in England?'

'No, the aircraft seemingly has to complete its mission by detonating inside the Fortress of Mimoyecques in northern France. It's important that this mission be a success.

Lieutenant Joseph P. Kennedy, Jr., United States Navy
Courtesy of Wikipedia, the Free Encyclopedia

'I think we all know, especially you, Timmy, who's aboard that liberator. It appears that The Entity has a future in store for young 29-year-old Navy Lieutenant Joseph P. Kennedy, Jr. And, it just may not be the same plan that his father, the former Ambassador to England, may we have in mind.

'But those are politics for another day and for another group of decision-makers.

'O.K., We're coming out of the cloud formation. We should be heading in an easterly direction toward Northern France. There will be an English Mosquito Following the liberator, filming the operation. It will be flown by Colonel Elliott Roosevelt, the son of President Franklin D. Roosevelt.

'Two Lockheed Ventura "mother" aircraft and a navigation plane will be in the sortie mix. Then Mosquito should easily give away the position of the liberator due to its unconventional shape. So, let's be looking for such information.'

Five minutes later, Tim spotted the flight nearing the English Channel. It was 1803 hours. 17 minutes to go before the aircraft would explode.

'Sancha, how are we doing? We need to be at the station in two minutes.'

'Commander, you will be able to open our lower hatch in 81 seconds.'

True to her calculation, Shawn opened the hatch door and saw that they

were immediately over the Liberator's upper hatch door.

Without hesitation. Shawn took a special tool and that The Entity "just happened" to leave with them in the F-98 for the purpose of opening the Liberator's hatch. Shawn gently, so as not to create a spark, but working as quickly as possible, opened the liberator's hatchway and slithered through the opening into the crew compartment behind the pilot's station. He walked gingerly around the explosive device and up into the cockpit. He looked at his watch. 14 minutes to go before detonation.

'Hi guys!' said Shawn with a smile.

Kennedy and Willy were completely startled by his presence!

'Who in the world are you and what are you doing here?'

'I am General Sir Shawn Crawford of the Royal Australian Air Force. Your Liberator with all of us in it is going to die in 12 minutes. You see, gentlemen,

I am here to prevent that. Now, further explanation will have to wait until you are aboard my aircraft.

'Lieutenant Kennedy, if you die today, the Ambassador is going to be very upset with you. Now we have 11 minutes. Gentlemen, let's go, and let's go quickly, and that is an order!'

'We don't take orders from you! What the hell is going on here? We have a mission to execute, General, if that is needed who is!' stressed Willy.

Kennedy then looked Willy in the eye for five seconds and said, 'Listen, you idiot, my gut tells me that this is a real emergency. Get your butt out of your seat! If you want to remain, then that's your choice. But I am not going to hang around here to satisfy your ego!'

They both unstrapped from their seats, got up, and then Willy. Shawn finally emerged after closing the Liberator's hatch and climbed up into the Stingray. He secured the aircraft's lower hatch.

'Sancha, time to get out of Dodge and we need to get out of here immediately!'

'Roger, Commander. Disengaging now!'

B-24 Liberator Bomber

Courtesy of www.aircraft.net

The Stingray abruptly put in a severe bank to the right and climbed like an out-of-control elevator! Three minutes later, the Liberator prematurely detonated, sending a shock wave that partially damaged the Mosquito behind it. With his crewmates injured from the blast, Roosevelt would be able to nurse his Mosquito back to RAF Fersfield.

Sancha leveled off the Stingray and asked Shawn what his directives were.

'Sancha, we are going to Cape Cod, Massachusetts, and to the Ambassador's Summer Home. I'm positive he and his lovely wife will be thrilled to see Lieutenant Kennedy home and safe. Lieutenant Willy, we will drop you off at RAF Fersfield on the way in just a few moments. Now, I know you have questions.'

Kennedy and Willy looked at the Stingray's crew, especially Christopher, as a young boy aboard a fighter aircraft, at least that is what they thought this aircraft was, and just shook their heads in wonder!

'Who are you people?' asked Willy.

'Commander,' said Sancha. 'We are approaching RAF Fersfield.'

'Thank you, Sancha. Lieutenant Willy, we will drop you off on the tarmac. It's been our pleasure meeting such a Navy Hero as yourself. We, the crew of the Stingray, wish you all the best in this War, which by the way will end next May. Good luck, Lieutenant Willy.'

And with that, Sancha opened the command module hatch. Shawn escorted Willy over to the front of the operation building, saluted him smartly, and moved back aboard the Stingray.

By this time, some 30 RAF Fersfield personnel gathered from all corners of the operations and surrounding buildings. A senior RAF officer started to come forward, but Shawn had entered the command module too quickly, leaving a totally bewildered audience, now some 200 personnel, on the ground below. Senior leadership was seen to circle young Lieutenant Willy immediately.

'Now to answer Lieutenant Willy's question as to who we are, Joseph, the following information may be hard to digest, let alone believe.

'We are from the future. I won't sugarcoat our existence by lying to you. You are aboard the most advanced fighter aircraft, the fF-98A Stingray Stealth Fighter from the year 2087. We were sent here to save you, Lieutenant. Historically, your Liberator blew up prematurely over Blythburgh, Suffolk, England. You were killed instantly.

'Now, we know that your father, the Ambassador, has great plans for you to acquire the Presidency of the United States one day. We have just changed history, so we aren't sure how your life will proceed at this point. Suffice it to say that you're being saved today was an intrusion into history by forces far beyond your imagination, or forever, for that matter. Do you have questions, Lieutenant?'

'If they are really from the future, what happens to Jack, Bobby, Teddy, and the others in my family?'

'Joseph. The Kennedy Family legacy is to be full of tragedies. Let me give you it in a nutshell.

'Your sister, "kick", who has just married, will die in a plane crash in France in May 1948.

Jack's wife Jacqueline Bouvier will give birth in 1956 to a stillborn girl, whom they named Arabella.

'Jack and Jackie will lose another child due to complications resulting from underdeveloped lungs in August 1963. The baby was named Patrick Bouvier Kennedy.

'Joseph, Jack becomes the President in the 1960 election, defeating Richard M. Nixon. He was assassinated in November 1963 in Dallas, Texas.

'In June 1964, Teddy survives a plane crash and spends a week in a hospital after being pulled from the aircraft wreckage by a fellow senator. He suffered a broken back, among other injuries.

'Bobby would be Jack's Attorney General and, after Jack's assassination, would run for the presidency in 1968. He, too, would be assassinated in Los Angeles, California during the Presidential Primaries.

'Bobby's eldest son, named after you, by the way, was the driver in a crash that left his female passenger paralyzed. This occurred in August 1973.

'Teddy's son, Edward Jr., would lose a portion of his right leg in November 1973 due to bone cancer.

'Bobby's sixth child, Michael LeMoyne, would be killed in a skiing accident in Aspen, Colorado on New Year's Eve, 1997.

'Jack would have two healthy children, a boy, and a girl. Jack's son, John Jr., would be killed in a private airplane accident over Cape Cod near Martha's Vineyard when his Cessna Piper Saratoga would crash into the Atlantic Ocean with his fiancée aboard in July 1999.

'Teddy's oldest child Kara would die of a heart attack while exercising in a Washington, D.C. health club in September 2011.

'Teddy would die of a brain tumor in 2009 after an illustrious career in the United States Senate. He also would run for the Presidency in 1980 against fellow democrat, the incumbent Jimmy Carter, but would fail in his attempt to win.

First Lady Jacqueline Kennedy

Courtesy of Wikipedia, the Free Encyclope-

dia

'Joseph, this entire string of events has led pundits to suggest the Kennedy Curse. Jack's beautiful wife Jacqueline would remarry to a wealthy Greek National and, following his death, would become the editor of two different literary companies. Jackie passed away in New York in May 1994 at 10:15 P.M. in her sleep from non-Hodgkin Lymphoma.

'And here we are, in August 1944 with your life ahead of you and full of promise for good things to come, Joseph.

'Let me introduce to you some very special people. First is my good friend Admiral J Hunter King. Hunter is a Navy SEAL, Special Ops man called Delta Force Operatives. These terms are not in evidence in 1944. "SEAL" stands for "Sea, Air and Land". SEALS are reported to be some of the toughest warriors on the face of the earth in the 21st century. The admiral is also a Delta Force Operative that conducts clandestine operations all over the world. And they are very good at what they do and very lethal at what they do.

'Next, is young Commander Tim O'Hara, an F-35 Lightning II Joint Strike Fighter Pilot who flies off aircraft carriers when not winging his way through time with me. Tim is an Ace Pilot, having shot down several enemy aircraft. He is a Naval Academy Graduate and was a star athlete for the Navy Midshipmen in his time. His brother was/ is a star first baseman for the New York Yankees.

'And next, is my pride and joy. Joseph, please my son, Christopher. This young LAD is a double Ace and is qualified to fly advanced stealth fighters such as the F-42A Tiger Shark and the F93B Leopard, both aircraft to be developed from your time reference point in or about 2053 and beyond.

'Finally, I would be remiss in not introducing to you the lady that runs this entire operation smoothly, professionally, and completely. Please say hello, Sancha, to Lieutenant Joseph P. Kennedy, Jr,'

'Lieutenant, my database is full of information about you. You are an impressive young man. I am pleased to have you aboard, Lieutenant.' Remarked Sancha.

Kennedy looked the command module over completely and asked, 'Where is this young lady hiding?'

'Lieutenant does not exist in the body. She is a computer wonder. If she had an Avatar, Sancha would have a complexion of Spanish descent and a beauty unparalleled in women, except for my bride Christine, right, Christopher?'

'Yes, Father, Mother is a very beautiful lady.'

'Sancha, say position relative to Cape Cod, Massachusetts, please.'
'Commander, we are twenty-four minutes from touchdown. We are descending out of 30,000 feet and at a speed of 520 knots.'

'Thank you, Sancha.'

'You're welcome, Commander.'

The Kennedy Brothers: Jack, Bobby and Teddy
Courtesy of Wikipedia, the Free Encyclopedia

'Joseph, your parents have no idea that you are coming home today. I imagine it will be quite a homecoming. As you have already completed your 25 combat missions overseas, your discharge papers will arrive in the mail tomorrow. Please don't ask how I know this. There are forces at work in my day and age that are completely mystifying to me, at times. When I needed an answer, I got to my son, who fully understands the nuances of time travel and the missions conducted through the medium of The Portal.'

'Commander, we are starting our descent into the Cape Cod area.'

'Thank you, Sancha. Joseph, when we hover land at your father's estate, we will let you out. We will then depart and leave you to your destiny.'

'But, won't you spend a little time with us? I'm sure I will have additional questions.'

'No, we are unable to remain. We are needed elsewhere. But as a remembrance of our little adventure today, I want you to have this, a souvenir, so to speak.'

Shawn reached out and gave him a "challenge" coin that held the F-98A Stingray logo on one side and what represented a "shining light" on the other side, representing The Portal.

'Keep this, please.'

Ten minutes later, the F-98 set down on the spacious lawn between the house and the Narragansett Sound. Shawn walked out of the aircraft with Lieutenant Joseph P. Kennedy, Jr. as his father began walking swiftly down toward the aircraft. Shawn and Joseph Kennedy shook hands and returned salutes smartly.

'Will I ever see you again, Sir Shawn?'

'Who knows, Mr. President, who knows? Take care, my Friend.'

Shawn entered the command module and the hatch closed. As he sat in his command chair, he said to Sancha, 'On screen, please, Sancha.' 'There you are, Commander.'

And, before them on the wide television-like monitor, was a heartfelt welcoming home given by a father who had missed his son very much. The F-98 slowly pulled away as both Joseph Kennedys hugged one another warmly. The younger Joseph turned and waived in silent gratitude at the departing Stingray.

THE SMALLEST UNIFORM IN THE ARMY

THE COMPANY "L" Unit was pinned down in an elongated field with tall grass. Machine gun fire raked the air overhead. Heating it up lethally. A private in the United States Army and one who wore the smallest uniform in the service was doing his best to keep his head down and body lower! Sergeant Joyce Kilmer had gone forward with Major "Wild Bill" Donovan to survey the positions of German troops from a small hill on which he was prone.

In late July 1918, during the Second Battle of the Marne in France, the renowned Poet was shadowing Major Donovan in order to develop and report back intelligence to fighting 69th Regimental Headquarters. His unit had come under intense fire along the *Ourcq* River near the Village of Seringes-et-Nesles.

All of a sudden, Sergeant Kilmer's head whipped back violently, and it rebounded back in almost the same position prior to the German bullet creasing his skull. The young private, with no regard for his safety, jumped up and ran 10 yards to Kilmer's unconscious form. Machine gun bullets dug into the earth all around him as he kept as low as possible.

He dove toward Kilmer's body and covered it with his own. The private then took a grazing bullet to his left arm but continued to ensure that Sergeant Kilmer was entirely masked by the sniper who had targeted him. He checked for a pulse along the neck's carotid artery. It was there, but weak.

The private took a bandage from his belt and wrapped it around the Sergeant's forehead. It was all he could do for now, as stopping the bleeding was now the most important issue.

He then looked where the automatic fire was originating from and two grenades from his pocket. These were the only two he had, so he had better make them work. He still had to neutralize that sniper.

The private decided to put the grenades aside for the moment and crawled 10 yards to the right of his position and behind a tall oak tree. He removed a brown-colored handkerchief from his pocket, and attached it to a small tree limb he had found lying on the ground nearby. He attached the cloth to the limb.

Carefully extending the cloth at the end of the tree limb to the right of the tree, he quickly peered to the left. His tree limb was struck by a bullet and taken forcefully out of his hands. The vibration and force of the round striking stung his hand, but he found out what he needed to know. He had seen the muzzle flash of the sniper.

The private chambered one round into his rifle and set himself into a solid prone firing position. He calculated the slight wind blowing from right to left. He adjusted his windage, accordingly. His rifle had been "zeroed" so he knew his round-down range would be an accurate shot. He just had to shoot it accurately.

He re-confirmed the German sniper's position via the slight movement of foliage. Even though he had great concealment, his cover was extremely poor. The private looked along his rifle site and held his breath as his finger slowly pulled back on the trigger. The round was fired and it went down range.

The private held his position and watched the foliage move in a way that suggested the sniper had been hit. A German helmet then slowly rolled forward in front of the shooter's "hide". The sniper had been "neutralized". Now, to more pressing business.

The private then low-crawled back to Sergeant Kilmer and re-checked his pulse. It was about the same, if not a little stronger. He looked up and noted that he was up against a tree line that extended toward the German machine gun nest that continued to try to find American GI targets. He said to himself that enough was enough.

So, he collected his two hand grenades and worked his way toward the machine gun by going to the outside of the line of trees—one tree at a time.

He soon found himself abreast of the machine gun position, and to its left, his right. He quickly ran forward with the grenades armed and tossed them both into the bunker housing the German machine gunners, then drove for the ground. The grenades exploded in the German's confined bunker and the firing stopped. It was an eerie silence!

Soon, one American, then another, and another rose from his position in the field and ran forward with a roar. The Private immediately went back to Sergeant Kilmer's prone body and called for a medic to come forward.

One did appear quickly and assess the Poet's physical situation, looked at the bandage that the private had administered to Kilmer, and just shook his head. The medic turned to the Private with the smallest uniform in the Army and said, 'You saved his life by taking quick action with the bandaging. The loss of blood has been negligible. He owes his life to you, Private.'

'Thanks,' he said to the medic in return. As the Private turned to return to his squad, a Lieutenant from the Company came over and told the Private to stop where he was.

'I saw what you did to neutralize that sniper who hit Sergeant Kilmer. That was inventive thinking to "draw" that sniper out the way you did, Private. And to make that shot was equally impressive.

'But what was heroic was the way you took out that machine gun nest on your own, at the risk of your life. The Company Commander has issued an order to have you put in for a decoration that signified your bravery here today.'

'Ah, Sir, that's O.K., I don't deserve a medal or any award for that matter. I was just doing what I was trained to do, that's all. But, thank you anyway, Sir,'

'Well, Private, it's certainly out of my hands. We are proud to have you with us.'

'Thank you, Sir.'

Three days later, after the incident by the *Ourcq* River, the Company was moving forward to engage the German lines once more. It was after dark and the command knew that the enemy was in trenches not too far ahead.

Suddenly, a flare shoots into the sky, lighting up the countryside. The Americans were terribly exposed. The Germans opened fire.

In front of the Private materialized the image, not of a body, but of a young boy. He smiled at the Private wearing the smallest uniform in the Army and approached him. The Private caught a round in the chest and went down to the ground. He was not breathing.

The Boy cradled the Private's body and a bluish light, faint at first, but gaining in intensity, slowly surrounded the Boy and the Private lying in the mud in the French countryside. The light blue hue completely masked both forms. They both disappeared within.

When the light subsided, both the Private and the Boy were gone. The Private's fellow soldiers looked about hurriedly and could find not one trace of their comrade. The subsequent report would go no further than Company Headquarters.

The Private wearing the smallest uniform in the army was Private Timothy James O'Leary, Senior. When he awoke, his wound was nonexistent, nor was there any pain from the bullet striking his person. He looked about him and found himself lying on a very comfortable bed like couch in a room with a myriad of lights blinking and affixed within walls on all four sides.

Staring down at him was the Boy who had appeared to him on the battlefield.

'Hello, Private O'Leary. Please do not be afraid. We are friends. My name is Christopher, and I was sent to protect you during the battle that you last witnessed. As you were wounded, I took the liberty of protecting and saving your life.

'You are present on board an advanced airplane, probably the best way to address your location at this point. The war in Europe is over. The Allies have prevailed.

'Your family has received, on your behalf, the Medal of Honor, the Distinguished Service Cross, the French War de Guerre, and the Purple Heart in recognition of your outstanding and exemplary service to your country and the world, despite your absence. Congratulations, Private.'

'Now, I know that you do not stand on ceremony, Private O'Leary, but you are present en route to meet a relative of yours. Please know that what you are now experiencing will become a thought of the past.

'Each one of us is in awe of your exploits. We wish only to honor you, for you are recognized as a very good man and a man of peace. And Private O'Leary, where I came from, men of your caliber are those who are revered for their goodness of heart. You will soon see what I mean by this.'

'Father,' said Christopher. 'We are ready.'

'Very well, Christopher. Sancha, please initiate a course for the continent of Australia and the Sydney Maritime Air Defense Base.'

'Wilco, Commander.'

Shawn then turned to Private and asked, 'Would you like a cup of coffee?' Private O'Leary said he would love one, since it had been a week since he was able to enjoy a cup.

'Private O'Leary, are you a Beef Wellington man, or, could you be a Beef Wellington man?

'Well, yes, I do believe I could be. I've never had the taste, to be honest with you.'

'Great! Then please allow me to offer you a taste of down under.'

After landing and finally settling within the hangar, Shawn and Christopher ensured that Private O'Leary deplaned properly. Will Caruso was present to welcome him to Australia and asked that Private O'Leary accompany him to Operations. They climbed the stairs and entered a large conference room.

When Private Timothy James O'Leary, Sr. entered the room, there were at least 50 individuals present. They each began clapping in appreciation for his heroic actions accomplished during the First World War. Private O'Leary, the diminutive figure that he was, took it all in stride with a faint smile on his face.

Marshal Allison Morrison, the Commander, came forward and welcomed him to Australia. She then introduced him to the Prime Minister.

'Private O'Leary. I am Prime Minister Donnelly. Welcome to Australia. On behalf of the entire General Assembly, please accept our sincere appreciation for your dedication toward protecting all that is considered sacred in this world, and in yours. And that would be the sanctity of the personal right of each and every individual to live in absolute freedom from oppression.

'At this time, I would like to present to you the awards and decorations that you rightfully deserve. The first award is the highest your Country may award a member of its military forces, and that is the Medal of Honor. I would ask Brigadier Shawn Crawford to present this award, in the absence of your President of the United States.'

After the ceremony concluded and Private O'Leary had received the Medal of Honor, Distinguished Service Cross, French War de Guerre Cross, and Purple Heart, the Infantryman donning the smallest uniform in the US Army appeared weighed down by the multitude of medals and decorations. Finally, Air Chief Marshal Michael O'Leary came forward and introduced himself, with everyone standing at ease.

'It is my distinct honor and privilege, Private Timothy O'Leary, to award you a battlefield commission to the rank of Major, United States Army, as well as your official honorable discharge from military service. Congratulations, Major O'Leary!'

Timothy J. O'Leary, Sr., stood in amazement with everything going on and the awards and accolades thrust upon him.

'It's an honor to be here, I'm sure. Even though I have no idea where "here" is! You are all very gracious. If it hadn't been for this boy, I would not be able to stand before you —completely and at a loss for words! Thank you for your extremely generous acknowledgment.'

And the crowd then erupted in applause! Air Chief Marshal O'Leary then approached Major O'Leary and took him by the arm and into the Commander's Office. They were alone, which is how Michael wished it to be at the moment.'

'Have you ever wondered about your forefather's Major? Who they were and where they are from? I have often wondered about my ancestors and whether they were from polished nobility or bank robbers of irrefutable design.

'I have the occasion to check with an expert here in Sydney in the year 2087. And, yes, you are presently in the future, Major, as ironic and convoluted as that may sound. To tell you how you managed to arrive here is to try to explain a myriad of other things that defy logic and human understanding.

'When I first arrived in the year 2053, even though our years of separation may be significant, I was still dumbfounded. I couldn't make sense of anything I was then experiencing for the first time, notwithstanding the way in which I actually arrived here. Over time, I got used to new and advanced ways of doing things. And it all began to make sense to me. Sometimes, when we are is not quite as important as where we are. I don't know if any of this makes sense to you, or not.'

'What I am trying to tell you is that the family you left behind may be the family that you have come to know in the future.

'I have found that you are my great-great-great grandfather from World War I, the ancestor who witnessed the wounding of the famous Poet Joyce Kilmer. You are the father of Timothy James O'Leary, Jr. who served in the Burma-India-China Theater during World War II as a Transportation Sergeant moving beans and bullets to the allied troops.

'He was the father of Timothy James O'Leary III, who served both in Vietnam as a field Artillery Captain and as a Major and Helicopter Pilot during the First Persian Gulf War in Iraq. He subsequently retired as a Lieutenant Colonel after 27 years of service to his country.

'Colonel O'Leary was the father of Timothy James O'Leary, IV, a Clemson University Graduate and a multi-millionaire World Trader who made money the old-fashioned way: he earned it.

'Timothy the IV was the father of my father, Timothy James O'Leary, V who rose to the Office of Vice-President of the United States. No one here knows of my father's success in politics, a tenure that history will speak well due to his exploits in promoting the demand for human rights and justice.

'I have been in the military all of my life, a Jet Fighter Pilot who has found his happiness in another Time-Era. Shawn Crawford is a protégée of mine. He rose from the rank of Warrant Officer to being knighted by the Prime Minister of Australia. Sir Shawn is now, as you know, a Brigadier General, a rank that he richly deserves.

'Your arrival here is not unlike the arrival of many others before you, Grandfather. They have quickly learned to adapt to their new and, unique to them, surroundings. The majority have quickly acclimated to this environment. But it is not for everyone, especially for those who have strong ties to family and loved ones they have left behind in previous Time-Eras.

'I don't expect you to remain. As a matter of fact, I do believe that your return to the year 1918 is imminent. You still have a family to raise and watch grow. Your son, one of three, Timothy James O'Leary, Jr. will be born on July 27, 1922. If you mention this date and this circumstance to your wife Lillian, I'm afraid she may attempt to have you committed as a result of trauma to the head suffered during the great war!

The World War I Soldier Wearing the Smallest Uniform in the Army, PVT Timothy James O'Leary, Sr., with Great Grand Daughter Shelley Lynn O'Leary, circa 1981

'Grandfather, I am so very proud of you and your accomplishments. This short time we have spent together has been priceless! You will spend the night with the Base Commander and me this evening.

'In the meantime, I know there are many here who would like to celebrate your accomplishment at our officer's club this evening. Let me take you to our quarters. I'm sure this uniform is in need of an overnight "rest". We will have some clothing provided for our dinner at the club this evening. You certainly do fit the reputation of the military individual reputed to wear the smallest uniform in the Army, Grandfather!'

They arrived with Marshal Morrison at 1830 hours. The Officer's Club was standing room only in anticipation of seeing the Smallest Man in the Army during World War I. The first to greet Major O'Leary was Baron Manfred von Richthofen, the World War I German Aerial Ace with over 80 kills to his credit.

Michael noted that Grandpa O'Leary immediately recognized the German Ace and shook his hand in awe.

'Baron, it is my distinct honor to meet you. Those of us in the trenches have only dreamt of having the pleasure of shaking your hand. You, Sir, are/were a legend in our time. Our famous Poet, Sergeant Joyce Kilmer, spoke of you often and how very impressed he was by your persona. He spoke of writing a poem reflecting upon your aerial exploits.'

'That's very kind of you, Major,' the Baron said with a nod and a click on his heels. 'Allow me, please, to introduce my Darling wife, Amelia Earhart.'

'I've read about you, Ms. Earhart. You represented the model for all women to follow in furthering your gender's role in aviation. What was to become of you and your future exploits?'

'Major, well, if it hadn't been for Christopher and his father Shawn. I would most certainly not be here today to shake the hand of another hero of the First World War.' And with that comment, she sneaked a look at her husband, the Baron.

'My dear Timothy, that was a definite compliment coming from my wife, who knows no bounds at taking risks herself. I must say that your presence here today is significant for me because I have never had the pleasure of talking to a brave American Infantryman who fought with such valor in the trenches. May I have a moment to talk to you? Because, Herr Major, you, not I, are the real Hero here. Please let us sit together for a moment and talk about how you were brought here with us.'

As Michael looked toward the two World War I foes talking animatedly with one another, a smile came from his lips. Grandfather would never have this opportunity again to talk plainly with a hero of the Third *Reich*. And the very nice and wonderful thing about what it was like to be at War, and both wanting nothing more than to be at peace.

The following morning, Colonel O'Leary drove his grandfather to the hangar and to the F-98A Stingray. Christopher and Admiral King were there talking to the plane Captain, Flight Sergeant Will Caruso. There appeared to be a discussion about lunch and Pizza.

When the crew members noticed the diminutive World War I Veteran come into the hangar, they dropped their conversation and approached Major O'Leary that he would be returning him to his own Time-Era, and specifically to Warwick, Rhode Island. Where his wife is awaiting his return. Admiral King was going along as an additional crew member.

Shawn walked into the hangar with Baron von Richthofen, Amelia Earhart, and Christine Roberts at that moment. On their heels were Marshal Morrison, Brigadier General O'Hara, and his son, Commander O'Hara. Each individual towered over Major O'Leary. At the last moment, he nodded to Christopher, who retreated a few steps to the side of the hangar and came forward with a foot stool.

'It is now my distinct pleasure,' said Major O'Leary, 'to shake each and every hand in gratitude, and to do so in a manner that I may look directly into every person's eye!'

As each person stepped forward, a broad grin spread across their face, both in appreciation of the lighthearted moment and in admiration of the World War I Soldier who, despite wearing the smallest uniform in the US Army during the war, still had a twinkle in their eye.

The Stingray carrying Major O'Leary, Christopher, and Admiral King took off a half-hour later and flew in an easterly heading in one direction of Southern New Zealand. Before getting over land, the Stingray was "ambushed" by The Entity.

'Major O'Leary, congratulations on a well-deserved promotion and the award of the Medal of Honor. We are taking you home to your family in Rhode

Island. Your heroism in saving Sergeant Kilmer's life will bear fruit in the early 20th Century future. We may meet again, Major.'

Christopher then requested a calculation from Sancha pertaining to the time of arrival in Warwick and to the address where Major O'Leary was to live. There were 10 minutes remaining until touchdown.

The O'Leary lived on a side street. Sancha would have no problem with clearance to hover down to a street below and very close to MAJ O'Leary's home. It was the closest that the Stingray would be able to get to a landing point.

With precision, the F-98s guidance system, with Sancha in an over-watch position, set the fighter down in an empty street. The three individuals exited the aircraft. MAJ O'Leary pointed to a modest home three structures down the street.

Christopher and Admiral King shook hands with Major O'Leary, who moved toward his home. Before he could get to the bottom step, his Wife Lillian opened the door and ran down the steps and into his arms. Major O'Leary, the soldier to wear the smallest uniform in the Army, was indeed home.

A SHEPHERD IN MILITARY BOOTS

THE STINGRAY RETURNED "home' without fanfare. Christopher turned the keys over to Will Caruso, who welcomed both Shawn's son and Admiral King back to Sydney.

The Admiral and Christopher walked over to the headquarters building, a ten-minute walk from the airfield. They both reported to the Commander's office. Sergeant Crystal Cranston ushered them into the middle of a meeting involving the Commander, Colonel O'Leary, Sir Shawn Crawford, Lady Christine Crawford, Brigadier General O'Hara, Commander O'Hara, and young, vivacious, and absolutely obstinate Colette Roberts-Crawford.

Christopher noticed that Colette appeared to be the center of attention.

'What is it? Did Colette not get her daily ration of Pizza?'

'Christopher! How did your journey back in time go? Was Major O'Leary able to rejoin his family in Warwick, Rhode Island?' asked his father Shawn.

'Yes. Father. His wife Lillian was home at the time, and she came running out of the house when she saw us land. It was a really happy occasion.'

'That is super! When you walked in, we were just discussing whether we agree to allow Colette to get her driver's license. What do you think, Christopher?'

Colette gave Christopher the evil eye and the "mean eyebrows" all at

once! Talk about walking into a hornet's nest!'

'Father, I think it's time for Colette to do some transition training in the Tiger Shark.'

You could hear a pin drop! Colette's mouth went slack and nearly hit the floor. Christine turned white in the face, and the remaining dignitaries present broke out in a collective huge grin! Shawn thought it was a great idea! Christine then had an idea that she was going to kill Shawn for having that great idea!

Colette then said, 'O.K., I'm ready! It's a good thing I didn't do my nails this week!'

Christopher nearly doubled over in laughter! 'Father, if you like, I can do the transition training with Colette. I am sure that Commander O'Hara would be pleased to assist me, wouldn't you Commander?'

'Why, of course, Christopher,' Timmy stammered and felt himself wilting under Lady Christine's intense stare!'

'O.K., Boys, and Girls, before we do anything we are going to talk about this. Here and now will not work. We'll work something out, won't we, Luv?'

Christine was not happy. So, everyone decided to call it a day. When they all left, Colonel O'Leary told Marshal Morrison that he wanted to fly once again. He wanted to go through The Portal and back to the Korean War to see if he could locate a relative of his who died in a prisoner of war camp due to Pellagra and malnourishment.

'Michael, you know that I wouldn't keep you from doing what you thought was absolutely necessary. By all means, pursue this issue and resolve it. What is your overall plan?'

'I would like to take Shawn, Christopher, and Admiral King with me in the F-98A Stingray. And I would like to leave as soon as possible, tomorrow, perhaps.'

'Check with Shawn and the Admiral. If they're amenable, then satisfy this need of yours. By the nature of your mission, it won't be a cakewalk by any stretch. Just be careful, Michael. If you need to talk to Shawn right now, go for it. Just let me know what the plan is going to be when it is finalized.'

'I will, and thank you for being understanding.'

Colonel O'Leary drove over to Shawn's quarters. When Christopher answered the door, he asked the Air Chief Marshal what time they were leaving in the morning in the Stingray. He suggested that they bring some warm clothing because Korea was going to be cold this time of year.

'Colonel, please come in. Father is attempting to burn the house down by using the charcoal grille. He'll be just a minute, either walking calmly into the room or sprinting for the door yelling "call the fire department!" It could go either way, Colonel.'

'Hi, Colonel! Shawn said as he calmly walked into the room. 'So, what time do you want to leave?'

'How does everyone know what's going on around here before I even know?'

'Well, Sir, it's like this. When you live with two of The Entity's children, it's like the walls are non-existent. You can look nonchalant about things, but you can't hide.'

'Shawn, I love military history. There is information lacking regarding the status of my great-great uncle, who served during the Korean War and was captured and made a prisoner of war. It was during the extended battle at *Unsan*. SGT James Paul O'Leary was a member of Headquarters Company, 3rd Battalion, 8th Calvary, 1st Calvary Division when his Unit was overrun by North Korean forces on November 2, 1950. The following day, he and some 200-300 American Soldiers were taken captive and carted off to a Prison Camp that was labeled P5.

'There is information that my Uncle Jim perished in that camp from malnutrition and Pellagra. I wish to travel back through the Portal to the night when the Division Commander left behind the soldiers under his command so that I could make a difference to my uncle and the countless others who ultimately perished due to starvation.

'Uncle Jim was given birdseed to eat, Shawn. Bird seed! CPT Kapuan, a Chaplain who was also among the prisoners with headquarters company, made an effort to sneak food to my uncle and other prisoners, but was ultimately caught and executed by his North Korean captors for his humane actions.

'I understand that this is but one of an untold number of wartime atrocities that have existed over time. But this is personal to me. It has stayed with me for a very long time. And now, I have the means to do something about this one event.

'I am not asking for your permission to make this journey. I will proceed without the blessing of anyone here in this Time-Era.'

Shawn looked at his old Mentor for the longest moment, smiled, and said, 'When do you wish to leave, Colonel? You had me at the doorbell. Let's take the F-98 and the F-42 Tiger Shark. Hell, let's take the Leopard, also! And, while we're at it, let's invite CPT Shelley O'Leary and her Sea Scorpion. The more firepower, the better the advantage for success. I know you have no problem flying the Tiger Shark still. Every time I see you around her, I have to get a napkin to make sure you don't drool into the hangar flooring.'

'I'll fly the Leopard with Timmy and Christopher taking the Stingray. Admiral King will be with me. We'll use the F-98 as the command and control ship, as well as an attack platform. In addition, I need to get Christine out of the house. She can go with you and I will "drag" Colette along with me if that would be the appropriate term. I'll transition her along the way. Believe me, she will not present a problem with being a "quick study"! If I know her, she will have everything under control the moment we leave The Entity's cloud!'

'And, oh, by the way, let's have General O'Hara and Air Commodore Gonzales meet with us tomorrow to finalize our on-station planning, as well as CPT Shelley O'Leary.'

'Shawn, I can't thank you enough. This is really important to me. If it's alright with you, let's leave tomorrow evening at dusk. The intelligence reports indicate that the Africans at the moment are toothless and can't find their dentures with radar.'

'Tomorrow it is, Colonel.'

The following day was spent planning in accordance with what history had written about the battle at *Unsan in* Korea. The tactics used by the North Korean 116th Elements were studied in thorough detail. From all accounts rendered, the 8th Calvary Regiment was to be hopelessly surrounded by dusk on November 2, 1950. The North Korean troops effectively blocked any form of retreat across the bridges to the east and west. A couple of blocking positions were established that denied the 8th Calvary Regiment access to the Town of *Unsan,* three-quarters of a kilometer to the east, as well as to key dirt roads leading away from their embattled positions. The 3rd Battalion, 8th Calvary Regiment had been outplayed by the North Koreans and would pay for it dearly over the first three-plus days.

'The 1st Calvary Division Commander effectively abandoned the 3rd Battalion by telling them that "they were on their own". And furthermore, Major General Gay, the 1st Cavalry Commander suggested that those trapped from all sides "use their own judgment in getting out"! There were virtually no egress options available if you look at the tactical map. The dirt roads were blocked, as well as all the bridges. Why the 3rd battalion set themselves up nearly surrounded by water and didn't protect their egress points, the bridges, is way beyond me!'

'Talk about the Pontius Pilate approach,' said Colonel O'Leary. 'The Division Commander just gave up on all of his men! Unbelievable! Someone really dropped the ball on their defensive scheme. In my opinion, the commanders became complacent and over-confident. And this is why we have to do something about saving those that were killed and taken prisoner, as convoluted as that may sound.'

'I'm with you, Colonel. My recommendation is to come in after dark with our night vision devices and effectively breach the North Korean lines attacking from the north, east, and west. With our running lights extinguished, we will be like a ghost in the sky. Our standoff capability with our helicopters, the Stingray, and the Shark at a hover mode will prove to be assets.

'I'll get with flight Sergeant Caruso to ensure that all four Stealth Fighter aircraft and two attack helicopters are prepped, to include a full complement of weapons. I'm betting that our passing through The Portal will not be a problem for Obi Won.'

'O.K., it's almost lunchtime. Let's go all over to the club and get a bite to eat. From there, let's have everyone meet in Flight Operations and go over our Operations Plan to include mission, threat situation, execution, logistical support, and command control. Following this, I would advise everyone to get some rest for the remainder of the afternoon. We will plan to launch at dusk.'

Immediately following the meal at the Club, Shawn contacted Gonzales and asked him to come over to Flight Operations at the airfield 30 minutes in advance of the other aviators for the mission. When Bob arrived, Shawn said he wanted to run a concept by him for their "journey through time".

'Bob, the three AVX Troop Transport Helicopters, they are all operational, are they not?'

'Yes, they are, Shawn. I just transitioned six pilots into the airframe last

week. They've been training in the aircraft since. Why do you ask?'

'I'd like to take these three aircraft with us back to Korea for the 8th Cavalry Regiment troop extraction in and around the town of *Unsan*. We will have the firepower to neutralize the threat, but we'll want to evacuate all the Regiment trapped back toward the reinforced South Korean position. If we can get the wounded out first, it will obviously increase their chances of survival. Can we re-configure the aircraft to support litter?'

'Absolutely! I'll give all six of my aviators a warning order immediately. I'll also ask the Medical Company to provide medical support, as well as the total medical supply package required for a Level III Triage. They'll be at our meeting set to begin within the next 30–45 minutes.'

'Thanks, Bob.'

After eating, Shawn and the others went over to the airfield and went over to the airfield and went over the tactical reports from those two days at *Unsan*. The following aviators were in attendance: Colonel Michael O'Leary, Brigadier General Sir Shawn Crawford, Admiral J Hunter King, Brigadier General Patrick O'Hara, Commodore Roberto Gonzales, Commander Tim O'Hara, and Major Lady Christine Crawford. Captain Shelley O'Leary, Christopher Roberts-Crawford, Colette Roberts-Crawford, and the six AVX Advanced Troop Transport Helicopter Pilots.

Crawford wanted the tactical position etched into all of their minds. He read the following account:

While the US 8th Cavalry Regiment's 1st and 2nd Battalions were under heavy attack, its 3rd Battalion was left alone for most of the night. But by 03:00, a company of Chinese Commandos from the 116th Division managed to infiltrate the battalion command post disguised as ROK soldiers. The following surprise attack set many vehicles on fire while causing numerous casualties among the Americans, most of whom were still sleeping. By the time the confusing fighting had ended, the 3rd Battalion was squeezed into a 200 yd (180 m) wide perimeter by the PVA 345th regiment of the 115th Division. Despite making multiple efforts to rescue the 3rd battalion by launching assaults on Bugle Hill against the PVA 343rd Regiment, the US 5th Cavalry Regiment ultimately sustained 350 casualties and was compelled to retreat, following orders from Major General Hobert Gay, who was in charge of the US 1st Cavalry Division. The trapped 3rd battalion endured days of constant attacks, and surviving soldiers managed to break out of the perimeter by 4 November. By the end of the battle, less than 200 survivors from the 3rd Battalion managed to return to the UN line.

Colonel Johnson had a special interest in rescuing the 3rd Battalion, 8th Cavalry. He had brought it to Korea from Fort Devens, Mass., where only two months earlier it had been part of the 7th Regiment of the 3rd Division. It became the 3RD Battalion of the 8th Cavalry Regiment, and he had commanded it through the Pusan Perimeter breakout battles. By right of this earlier association, it was "his own battalion."

General Gay at dusk made what he had described as the most difficult decision he was ever called on to make-to order the 5th Cavalry Regiment to withdraw and leave the 3rd Battalion, 8th Cavalry, to its fate. Thus, at dark on 2 November the 3rd battalion, 8th Cavalry, had no further hope of rescue.

Just before dusk, the division of liaison planes flew over the 3rd Battalion perimeter and dropped a message ordering it to withdraw under cover of darkness. Over his tank radio, Miller received from a liaison pilot a similar message stating that the men were on their own and using their own judgment in getting out.

Enemy sources later indicated the Chinese captured between 200 and

300 men at Unsan. At the 3rd Battalion perimeter, Chaplain Kapaun and Captain Anderson had risked their lives constantly during the day in attending to the wounded.

'Alright, we've confirmed the historical documents, so there is no need to second-guess what the Chinese will do,' reiterated O'Leary. 'I will protect the western flank around the *Nammyen* River 300 meters in the west in the F-42. This should neutralize the Chinese threat around the 2nd Battalion position, with my boundary line being the hill just to the north.

'Christopher, you and Commander O'Hara are responsible for the eastern sector, northeast of *Unsan,* as well as Chinese units approaching our friends the ROKs to the east of the *Samfen* River. We'll want to ensure that the bridge just to the east of the Town of *Unsan* remains threat free for 1st Battalion use, if necessary.

'Shelley, you'll take the Chinese unit in the area of Bugle Hill and the western edge of Camel Heads bend. We'll want to neutralize any threat units around that bridge area. Ensure that it is last standing because it will serve as an egress point for the 3rd Battalion if they need it. The Sea Scorpion will make gun passes from the northeast to southwest and use the northernmost area of the Camel's head bend as its boundary gun line.

'Shawn, you take the northern approach and hit the Chinese from behind as they approach the 1st and 2nd Battalions in the Leopard. The Leopard will stay to the north of the town of *Unsan* and use the *Samfren* River as its easternmost boundary for its gun passes.

'When the advanced fighters initiate the attack at the same time, I want the troop transport helicopters to land in the vicinity of each Battalion Headquarters. It will be the pilot's judgment in terms of the most appropriate landing site to set down and be as close to the Battalion Headquarters as possible. Have your medical personnel prepared to do what they do best and move as quickly as possible for the initial extraction of the wounded. I will provide you with coordinates to the rear Combat Support Hospitals.

'Are there any questions?'

'Colonel, what do you want to use for a Rally Point after we've hit their units?'

'We'll use Turtle Head Bend and that flat terrain to the top of the Bend. This area should be neutralized by the time we need to use it after CPT O'Leary pays their units a little "visit" in her Sea Scorpion.'

'Roger that, Sir.'

'Now, having said all of that, I will want to utilize our rotary-wing assets for this mission, as well. I know that you are looking to show off in that Vampire of yours, and here is the chance. The same goes for you, Patrick. We want you both to not only complement our firepower support but even more so, to protect the evacuation of the wounded first to the rear. At the same time, however, come prepared to fly. Your rotorcraft should be outfitted with a full complement of air-to-ground missiles. We are going to need you to support the extraction of the wounded to the rear. The secondary mission is to provide the firepower to positively affect your primary mission.

'I want you both to attack the helicopter on the station at all times. Once the evacuation of the wounded begins aboard the AVX transports, providing covering fire for the loading of personnel is paramount. Bob, you are the rotor-craft command and control element for the extraction of Regimental personnel. Now, I know it will be a bit busy down there in the "bushes" with covering the extraction support, but it has to get done. Bob, I'll ask you to put together an annex to the Operations Order from overall helicopter support, to include frequencies to communicate from ship-to- ship. We don't need people "stepping all over one another" when trying to talk over the tactical radios.

'Now, here is a copy of the Operations Order with annexes appropriate to each of your individual assignments, minus rotary-wing support. Keep in mind that this is a battlefield, and is going to be "fluid". Do what you do best and "adapt", keeping in mind that you have your friendly aircraft most likely on both your right and left.

'Egress points for joint fighter strike force and all helicopter assets are included in the annex sections. Make sure you study these carefully   and communicate with one another. Frequencies and call signs are in the SOI/SSI [Standard Operating Instructions/ Standard Signal Instructions] located in the command and control Section of the Operations Order. As mentioned, frequencies for the rotary-wing assets will be forthcoming.

'Are there any questions? Very well, we launch at 1900 hours.'

The sixteen aviators walked over to the hangar, where Flight Sergeant Will Caruso was using a clean rag to wipe off the cockpit windows of the Tiger Shark.

'Will, feel like going for a little ride today?' 'Absolutely! Did I say that too quickly?'

'No, you did not, my Friend. We are going to use your Inner Circle Entity assistance in ensuring that our three aircraft complete the assigned mission. We are going to get shot at, kicked at, spit upon, and maligned with curses that would make an Australian Navy man blush. Are you still game?'

'Sounds like everything I've dreamed of, Sir Shaw. When do we leave, and I do have time to pack the pizza and beef sandwiches?'

'Why, yes, you do. You will be flying with Christopher and young Commander O'Hara for this exercise. I would be entirely remiss if I did not have you bring Pizza aboard for that young, growing PUP of mine. We are going hunting, my Friend. We will be traveling back in time to November 2, 1950.'

'Ah, the infamous embarrassment for the 1st Cavalry Division at *Unsan.*'

'Yes, and we are going to save their bacon and deliver it to them too!' 'As long as we are able to save as many lives in the process as possible, Sir Shawn.'

'Yes, my Friend. You know, Will, that Operation was not only an embarrassment, but it was an abandonment. We hope to reverse the two so that the Division Commander may end up saving some face.'

'And, do you think I will be able to meet the legendary Father Emil Joseph Kapaun, the Shepherd in Military Boots?'

'I am counting on extracting the good Chaplain as well as every other soldier found in harm's way. We both know that it is really not Chaplain Kapaun, but it is Saint Emil Kapaun, as he was canonized by the Pope in the year 2019. Of course, timing is everything.

'What a blessing for all those who knew him and were able to be in his presence. A truly wonderful man. So, Will, we are of the same mind. Save the Chaplain and all others in need. It will be a busy two days for everyone, but it will represent a time when accomplishment knows no bounds, and a simple, hard-working man walks in the footsteps of the Lord.'

The other sixteen aviators came together in a tight knot. Shawn indicated that they now had the maintenance expertise along for the mission when he mentioned Sergeant First Class Will Caruso as an addition to the mission.

He also gave last-minute instructions to all, but to those who had never been through The Portal before. He told the pilots to maintain the heading and altitude they had when they first became engulfed in the cloud. Their positional status in the flight would remain unchanged once they exited the mist.

'Now, who needs what, before we launch this evening?'

Christopher and Colette simultaneously announced, "Pizza and Lasagna!" Will looked sheepishly at Christine, who threw an ocular dagger in his direction!

OPERATION PHOENIX

SHAWN WENT OVER the very last instructions per the Operations Order to include takeoff instructions from the Sydney Maritime Defense Base. He then turned it over to the Mission Commander, Colonel O'Leary.

Colonel O'Leary looked over to where his Bride, Marshal Morrison, stood looking from the rear of the group, and then said, 'Thank you all for taking part in this very important mission. As you can see, General Sir Shawn Crawford has aptly named it Operation Phoenix. It is indeed a representation of a unit rising out of the fires of annihilation.

'And, yes, it is a critical mission for me, but, I think also for all the lives that will be saved due to your efforts in the next 24 hours. I cannot thank each one of you enough. We are embarking on a mission of mercy and thoughtful consideration given to everything our ancestors have sacrificed for us to be able to live the lives we live today. And it is not merely the 8th Cavalry Regiment we are saving, but the life of every soldier who paid for us to live our freedom today. I wish you all Godspeed. I want to see all of you here in this very spot when our mission has been completed. Carry on.'

'Ladies and Gentlemen, we will be starting engines in 60 minutes. Go over the Operations Order, find your interest in the mission, and, if there are questions or concerns, please refer them to me as I am the Operation Phoenix.' Ordered Crawford.

Shelley walked over to Timmy O'Hara and hugged him warmly. 'You

be careful flying with Miss Sancha today. Stay focused. I want to see you back here with me when everyone gets back. O.K.?'

'Shelley, wild horses of Colette's incessant desire for lasagna dinners from my kitchen couldn't keep me from coming back here to you. And this goes both ways now. I know that you will make a difference, but be careful. This could get nasty.'

'On, I love "nasty"! Maybe we can talk "nasty" when we get back!'

O'Hara turned the deepest shade of red as Christopher walked over to them.

'Shelley, you must be talking about the word "nasty" again. The Commander's reaction to that word always seems to produce a Pavlovian Response in the most over manner. Commander, I'll be in the Stingray. Please enjoy your time with CPT O'Leary.'

Christopher walked over to their aircraft with a smirk.

'I can never get anything from that young man! But I have to admit, even though he is sometimes awkwardly prescient. He is always a joy to be around.'

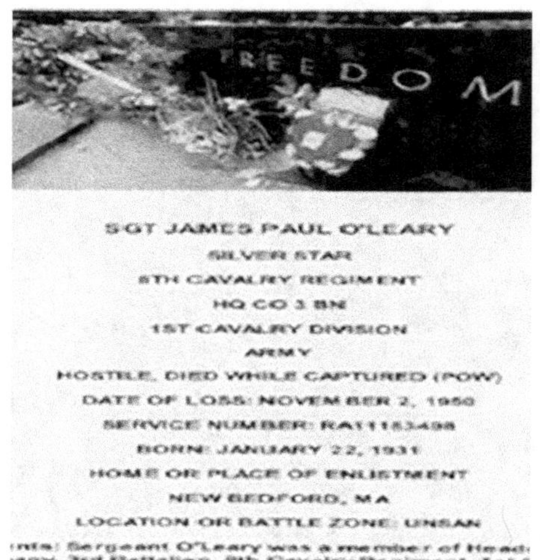

Epitaph for SGT O'Leary www.koreanwar.org/htm/ Korean_war_ project_remembrance.html

Father Captain Emil Joseph Kapaun www.kwva.org/pow_mia/ p_050420_shepherd_combat_boots.htm

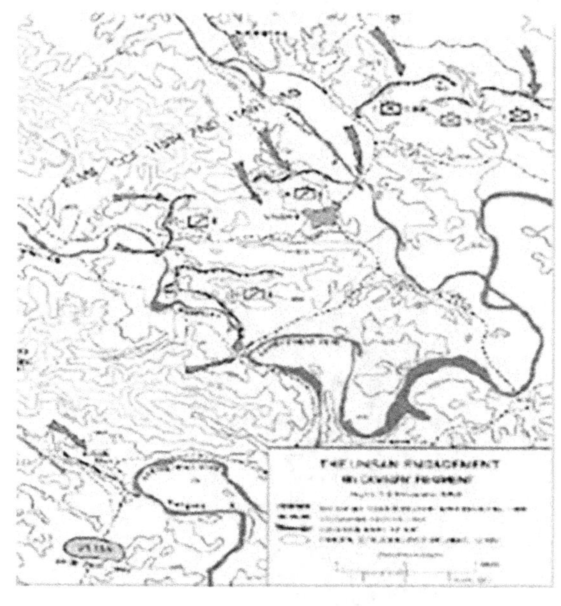

AVX Joint Multi-Role Advanced Troop Transport Helicopter

Courtesy of Wikipedia, the Free Encyclopedia

'Everyone loves Christopher. Well, that whole family endears itself to all who know them. But, listen, be careful, O.K.? I love you, Commander!'

As Shelley walked away, Tim O'Hara knew this Woman was the one he wanted to spend the remainder of his life with.

Shawn and Colette entered the Leopard well before the mission was to begin and started briefing his daughter on the operation of the Leopard Stealth Fighter. As she was not only his daughter but that of The Entity, she was more than a quick study! Colette was a brilliant study!'

'Father, I read the Leopard Operational Manual last night in bed and I do believe I have everything memorized. If you wish to quiz me, please do so.'

Shawn then proceeded to ask her questions about operating parameters, emergency procedures, system instruments, aerodynamic limitations, gunnery, and anything else he could think of to ask her. She responded with the correct answer each and every time.

'Very good, Colette. You appear to have everything down "cold". When we get ready to taxi to the runway, I want you to take full control of the Leopard, including radios and takeoff.

'Yes, Father.'

'Coach,' said Admiral King, 'I do believe she takes after her mother!' 'You see, Father, even Admiral King is able to recognize my talents.'

'Yes, Colette. You have my talents, including those that will reap the benefit of your existence with vaudeville, the next time it comes to Australia.'

'Father, I'll have you know that vaudeville was present in Sydney 220 years ago. They loved me back then!'

'You see, Coach, your daughter truly has been around!'

All aircraft departed Sydney on time, with Colonel O'Leary being in the lead Tiger Shark. In accordance with the Operations Order, there was no "tanking" to be done at altitude. Shawn's not drafting this action into the Support Annex to the Op Plan of meeting with a KC-46 Refueling Aircraft gave testimony to his confidence that Obi won would dutifully take care of all "incidentals" not covered in the overall plan.

Five minutes into the flight, His blueness captured all the strike and support aircraft in His mist. They were not in it for more than 45 seconds. While inside The Entity's protective cover, Obi won's voice through Shawn's headphones.

'Hello, My Young Jedi! I will be brief, as you and your fellow aviators have a significant mission before you. Shawn, I will place your fleet of aircraft five kilometers to the north of the 8th Cavalry Regiment at 0200 hours. The enemy movement will be ongoing, and will be mostly in position for their 0300 initial attacks on the 3rd Battalion Headquarters. And with that, I will leave you, Shawn, for you and Colonel O'Leary to successfully complete your mission. As always, I will be with you.'

All personnel in all aircraft heard the message given to Sir Shawn Crawford by The Entity. There was no need to repeat His message.

'All aircraft ensure that your running lights are extinguished. Check night vision devices ON. Execute the Operation Order in accordance with the established plan on my mark: 5-4-3-2-1, Mark!' announced O'Leary.

All aircraft then re-positioned themselves from their present location to the West of the *Samfen* River. Colonel O'Leary maneuvered the F-42 directly behind the Chinese Communist lines that were facing east in preparation for intrusion into the Second Battalion lines. He had a clear view of the enemy in front of them.

'Christine, please bring up our weapons stores. O.K., thank you.'

'All aircraft, please check in when in position and ready to engage the enemy.'

Shawn indicated that he was in a circular pattern at 2000 feet and was prepared to engage when ready. Commander O'Hara checked in, saying that he was in a position to engage the Communists to the northeast of the Regiment's location. CPT O'Leary was in a circular racetrack pattern at 1000 feet and below Shawn. She was in a position to make her first gun and rocket run on Colonel O'Leary's mark. Gonzales and General O'Hara were in a hover mode to the east of the *Samfen* River, along with the three AVX Troop Transports stationed immediately to their rear.

'All aircraft, on my mark, begin firing: 5-4-3-2-1, FIRE!'

All of a sudden, dozens of rockets streaked into the rear of each of the 115th and 116th Chinese Communist Elements! The fiery trails of the air-to-ground rockets were breathtaking. Both the Communists and the Americans were completely surprised by the onslaught of rocket fire hitting the Communist's positions.

The American troops from the 8th Cavalry Regiment quickly discerned that the rockets being launched were not aimed at them. As the explosions illuminated their surroundings, they soon realized that they were facing a surprise attack by a significant communist force, which threatened to overrun them completely.

Whoever these angels of the skies were, the Americans considered themselves extremely lucky that their aerial allies were there. The total number of communist troops that were decimated, as viewed by the 8th Cavalry regiment in their tactical positions, was simply incredible. The aircraft continued to fire time and time again.

One and a half minutes into the rockets being fired at the Chines, the AVX Troop Transports advanced behind the Vampire and Cheyenne helicopters. Bob Gonzales positioned his Vampire facing north between the 1st and 2nd Battalions. General O'Hara moved his Cheyenne to a position between the 2nd and 3rd Battalions and facing west. The AVX helicopters settled to the ground behind each Battalion Headquarters location, and crew chiefs from each aircraft ran to the Command Posts.'

The Battalion Commanders were stunned at seeing the helicopters land in their "backyards". The crew chiefs reported very briefly to either the Commander or his operations officer and told each officer to get his men aboard the transport immediately! The Commander or staff officer didn't have to be told twice.

The communication between the Cavalry Commanders quickly went out instructing them to get their men aboard the helicopters as quickly as possible, each Battalion Sergeant Major in turn directed his First Sergeant to coordinate the loading of personnel.

Inside the Transport, two additional crew chiefs and two medics were standing by to get the men settled into their jump seats. The wounded at this point were practically non-existent. The planned attack by the Communists was thwarted because the Chinese had more "pressing" issues to resolve at the moment!

While this was going on in the Regimental area, CPT O'Leary was effectively neutralizing the troops stationed on Bugle Hill. This Communist force was, in effect, the command and control element coordinating the total Chinese offensive. With Shelley's Sea Scorpion completely eliminating any direction to the subordinate Chinese unit below, the attacking forces quickly lost the advantage of a coordinated movement toward their American objective.

Shelly then directed her gun-run attack against the Chinese attempting to secure the bridge at the Camel's Head Bend. She meticulously walked her 30 mm cannon rounds, picking off dozens of the communists forming a blocking action on the west side of the bridge. Her objective was quickly met and reported to Colonel O'Leary that her sector was secure.

Shawn, meanwhile, in the midst of firing his rockets, and allowing Colette free rein in the firing sequence, was watching her lay waste to the Chinese to the north of the 1st Battalion Headquarters, while chewing on a Beef Wellington sandwich. In between her firing the 30 mm cannon, he asked Colette if she had forgotten to bring the gray Poupon! She gave her father a side-long glance and mouthed the word "mother" at him! Sawn said no more, for his delicate Bride could be "not so delicate" sometimes when it came to grabbing her husband's accurate firepower!

'Colette, Honey, please remind me to always stay in your good graces!

She bent over between cannon bursts and gave Admiral King a huge kiss on the cheek. Colette absolutely loved the coach and secretly wished that he was single!

She reported to Colonel O'Leary as such and indicated that she was now going to take out Chinese advancing on the friendly South Korean positions. Colette then began her gun runs on the advancing Chinese in the vicinity of the friendly ROK units located to the northeast of *Unsan*. Colette soon had her area completely neutralized.

Meanwhile, small pockets of Chinese began attacking the Americans to their front in an attempt to overrun the 1st and 2nd Battalions. They had nothing to lose, for they were being annihilated to their rear by unforeseen forces. This is when Gonzales and O'Hara in their Vampire and Cheyenne respectively began firing their mini-guns directly at the advancing communists.

Both attack helicopters were sitting at flight idle and monitoring their sectors for such an attack. When it happened., they were ready. They increased throttle to full rpm while sustaining fire on the advancing enemy.

Their cannon firing was withering and absolutely impressive! Communist tanks became visible behind and in front of the advancing Chinese, and they quickly became mounds of funeral pyre! The Chinese communists were caught in the middle. It just wasn't their day. They were completely outgunned and outmaneuvered.

The Transports, in the meantime, were taking the 8th Cavalry Regiment soldiers to prearranged friendly locations in the area of 1st Cavalry Headquarters. The last troops to be evacuated were those of the 3rd Battalion.

'Christine, I am going to hover-land the Shark by the 3rd Battalion Headquarters and ensure that all American soldiers have been evacuated. You have the controls.'

Once on the ground, Colonel O'Leary jumped from the Tiger Shark and assisted the last remaining American forces aboard the only Troop Transport remaining.

When the seemingly last American was onboard, he turned to the only remaining 8th Cavalry Regiment soldier visible and asked if there were any other Americans in the headquarters area. The individual who responded wore a white cross on his helmet and was bleeding from a wound in his left upper arm.

'Colonel, I believe there are a couple more inside the headquarters bunker area. I'm going to find out how many there are.'

'Father Kapaun, you have done enough today. I am putting you aboard the transport so that the medics may address your wounds.'

'Colonel, how do you know my name? I know we have never met before.'

'Father, you may not know me, but I certainly know all about you and your future! Come on, I'm putting you aboard so that you will not suffer the misery of watching your "flock" die in a prisoner-of-war camp. Let's go, Father. I will explain later when you are safely away, I promise you! Colonel O'Leary then led the Chaplain to a waiting crew member, who took him aboard the Troop Transport.

O'Leary then went into the command Headquarters and saw one more American soldier who had been left behind but who was still trying to communicate with his senior headquarters via the established communication system in place. The soldier looked up and smiled.

Colonel O'Leary looked down at him and then at the name tag on his uniform. "O'Leary". The soldier wore the stripes of a Corporal.

'Uncle Jim, it's time to go!'

The soldier with the name tag "O'Leary" looked at the Colonel standing before him and questioned his directive. Not because he said, "it was time to go", but because he had said, "Uncle Jim"!

'Colonel, I don't understand.'

'No need to at the moment. I'm here to take you home to your father and Mother, Timothy and Lillian, and your brother and sisters, Tim, Pearl, and Frances. I will explain all of this when you are safe and away from here. Let's go, Uncle Jim!'

Colonel O'Leary reached down and took Corporal James Paul O'Leary's headphones off of his head and grabbed him by the elbow. He then told the young 19-year-old soldier to follow him.

When they exited the bunker, the two Chinese Communists were approaching. Colonel O'Leary already had his 9 mm Glock out and instinctively put a round center mass in each of the Chinese, who went down to the ground unmoving. Two more approached from his right, firing their weapons. The Colonel took a round in the abdomen and Corporal O'Leary in the chest. They both went down.

These same Chinese soldiers were cut down from behind by Commander Timmy O'Hara, who fired his automatic weapon from ten feet away. Behind Tim was Christopher, who started quickly toward the two fallen soldiers. And behind him magically appeared was Father Kapaun.

As Tim supplied the cover, Christopher knelt down beside Colonel O'Leary who was writhing in pain from the sustained gut wound, one of the most painful ones could experience. Corporal O'Leary was not moving, nor was he breathing. Father Emil Joseph Kapaun knelt beside Corporal James Paul O'Leary and placed his hands over the Corporal's wound, at the same time Christopher's doing the same to colonel O'Leary's.

Christopher and Father Emil stood this way for a full minute. They then looked over at one another simultaneously and smiled as a very bright light bluish hue fell over both of them and the O'Leary's lying on the ground. To those who may have been watching, they were lost in sight. Timmy O'Hara continued to stand guard beside them. He need not have worried.

The Chinese Communists who had advanced to the 3rd Battalion Headquarters position and who were within mere yards of the scene that was developing. Were incapable of firing their automatic weapons due to The Entity's intervention. In addition, there appeared to be an invisible barrier through which they were not permitted to advance, nor did they wish to do so. For they saw what was going on, and they knelt in silent awe. Several of them removed their helmets in respect to what they are witnessing. To say then that all Communists were atheists would have been to suggest that their witness of this supernatural event on the battlefield was a pure hallucination. But all knew better.

Within the hue, Christopher looked over at Father Kapaun and said thank you for his unwavering support for humanity and everything decent in the world. The chaplain, often quick with the soldier's wit, merely acknowledged the highest compliment one might receive with a slight nod of the head and continued to focus on the well-being of the young Corporal.

When the bluish light dissipated into nothing, the four bodies were gone altogether. Commander O'Hara stood by himself as the sporadic fire was heard from crew chief personnel and around the transport helicopters. Soon, even this noise was non-existent. Then, he heard the last of the Transports departing.

As Timmy O'Hara stood there, the throng of Chinese slowly came out of their shadows without weapons and their hands in the air and surrendered. A Chinese Communist Junior Officer came over to O'Hara, who instinctively felt no threat whatsoever from the approaching man. He stopped six feet in front of Tim, turned around, and faced his men, who now numbered around 50. He ordered them to sit with their legs crossed in orderly rows.

O'Hara had lowered his weapon to show respect for what he believed the Officer was doing. The Officer approached Tim and, in perfect English said, 'Commander, I do not know what just happened here. But, what I do know is that something very special occurred and that it was time to put aside the unjust politics of warfare and acknowledge the miracle that had just taken place.

Timmy O'Hara looked him in the eye and extended his hand in friendship. All at once, the 50 strong Communists in attendance and still seated on the ground began a slow rhythmic clapping. It grew in crescendo. It was a huge token of appreciation for the magical event that had just occurred.

'Captain,' Tim said. 'I truly hope we meet again sometime in the future, which may very well be in my past!'

The Officer looked at him quizzically. 'You may have noticed our aircraft. And you probably said to yourself that you've never seen such futuristic-looking aircraft before. You may find this hard to believe, but these aircraft are from the future, Captain. I stand before you from the last year 2087. Incredible, is it not? But true, nonetheless.

'You are a very decent man, I think. And you are an effective leader of men. I see it in the eyes of those soldiers who look at you, who revere you, who would follow you anywhere. You are to be commended, not for all of those things I've just mentioned, but for the reason they exist. And it is here, Captain,' as Tim gently placed his hand over the heart of the Junior Communist Office, 'that your goodness shines. May God keep you forever in His loving embrace, Captain.'

Tim placed his hand on the shoulder of the Officer, smiled, and slowly walked off into the early morning darkness and to his F-98A Stingray. He was alone now, and he had no idea what to tell Shawn and Christine about their son Christopher or the Colonel. Somehow, he knew The Entity would have the answer.

When he got to the F-98, he directed Sancha to fly to the Rally Point. Once on the ground, she exited the aircraft, and to the waiting F-42 Tiger Shark. Christine stood beside the Shark.

'Lady Christine, Christopher, and the Colonel are with The Entity at the moment. Our instructions are to join up with your husband at an altitude of 2000 feet and await the final Troop Transport helicopters for further egress through The Portal and Home. I will ensure that Sir Shawn is made aware of the situation.' Christine knew enough not to question young O'Hara about the status of her son and the Colonel.

Once at the established altitude, Timmy checked in with Shawn.

'General, all aircraft are formed up. Your son Christopher and the Colonel are with The Entity, as I've just so informed Lady Christine.   Sir, you are now in command of our journey home. We await your order, Sir.'

There was a pause for a long moment and then Shawn came on the command net and gave instructions to climb to 3000 feet, combat spread, Rotary-Wing assets to the rear, and 1000 feet below. He gave all a heading of 090-degrees.

Soon the Sydney task Force, Operation Phoenix, was in the warm embrace of The Entity's cloud.

'Shawn. I want you to know that Christopher was enjoying a 12-inch pepperoni Pizza, as we speak. The Colonel wants to get back to his lovely Bride "yesterday". If not sooner! Father Kapaun has shown a desire to stay with us, and we are truly blessed for his decision. The Colonel's Ancestor, young James Paul O'Leary, cannot get enough of the attention he is getting from President and Mrs. Lincoln. What a marvelous young man!

'Your son Christopher and the Colonel will be waiting for you when you land back at your home base. I have to tell you that there are so many good things that came out of Operation Phoenix. Well, done, Sir Shawn. When I release you and your aerial flotilla, Young Jedi, you will be on the final approach. Rest well, Valiant Knight. His blueness will soon be with you!'

'Coach, was that a promise? I mean, we've got to get into some more action here. Let's go motorbike racing. I bet I can beat you to the pucker brush faster than you can get there with a lawn mower!'

'Hunter, there is no one faster at getting into the pucker brush than me. Just ask old friends Debbie, Nancy, and Catherine!

'Time to go home and await the next adventure, which I am most certain is forthcoming, the way this writer works! First, let's get on the ground and see how the boy and the Colonel are doing, I'm sure there is undoubtedly a story to tell!

The Sydney Controller phased in all aircraft, with the helicopters landing directly to their helipads. Shawn and the Leopard with admiral King and Colette were the last to taxi into the hangar. Will, who had been in the front seat of the Cheyenne with General O'Hara, was ecstatic over the just-completed mission. He couldn't say "awesome" enough!

When Shawn got out of the Leopard, the Colonel was there waiting for him. He immediately threw his arms around Crawford and held him for a long moment. He put Crawford at arm's length and said "thank you" one more time.

'Colonel, I was told you were wounded outside the 3rd Battalion Headquarters. How are you, Sir?'

'Absolutely perfect. Christopher did his "magic" and when I awoke I was in a place I had never experienced before. Everything was so modern! I'm sure you know the place I'm referring to. They practically have a plaque in your name!'

'Yes, Sir, I do indeed know the place. I sometimes get the feeling that Mary Todd Lincoln would want to trade her husband in for me! Every time I visit, she offers me some different dessert types. Absolutely wonderful cook!'

'Colonel, I'm glad you're alright. And your ancestor, I heard also that he was wounded at the same time as yourself. How is he?'

'Well, let me introduce you to the young Lad. Jimmy, come over here, Son.' Corporal James Paul O'Leary walked over with a crooked grin on his face.

'Jim, let me introduce the man who made all of this possible. Sir Shawn Crawford, please meet Corporal James Paul O'Leary, my Uncle many times removed. He is having a difficult time adjusting to all of this change, Shawn.'

'Corporal, I am so very pleased to meet you. The Air Chief Marshal here has told me a lot about you. I am pleased that we were able to lend you assistance when we did.

'And, I also heard that you stayed at your communications post until the very last moment, along with father Kapaun. That is tremendously heroic of you! We may have to consider that further, Colonel.'

'Yes, indeed, General, yes, indeed!' as O'Leary looked fondly toward his ancestor.

'Colonel, I'm sure that you have this young man well in tow. I have to report to your bridge, even though I know you have already done so. Corporal, you are truly a Hero. I am so glad that we are here today and in a position to celebrate your arrival at our Base. If you'll both excuse me, I have a family to see, following my meeting with the Marshal.'

Shawn went over to the headquarters and up to Marshal Morrison's office. Sergeant Cranston had left for the day, and Shawn knocked softly on the Commander's door.

'Shawn,' said Morison, who approached from behind, 'I was just getting some copies made. Please come in. I heard that everything went according to plan. Congratulations to a well-executed operation, General.'

'Thank you, Ma'am. Couldn't have done it without the help of a lot of

people. And this is why I'm here, Ma'am.

'There are individuals that I would like to reward for their efforts in making this such a successful outcome. May I make a few suggestions?'

'Absolutely!'

'First individual is CPT Shelley O'Leary. I would like for her to receive the Distinguished Flying Cross as well as a promotion to Major. Secondly, I would recommend a battlefield commission to the rank of First Lieutenant be given to young Corporal O'Leary. He was the last to leave his post and continued to communicate with higher headquarters after everyone else had left the Battalion. A silver star thrown in also would be a nice touch.

'In addition, I would recommend a promotion to full Colonel to Lady Christine Crawford for her outstanding efforts in keeping the mission together at its critical juncture after Colonel O'Leary was literally taken out of the picture.

'Ma'am, please, any time you feel I am out of line, don't hesitate to jump right in!

'Commander O'Hara was seen talking to a young Chinese Communist Officer following the "disappearance of the Colonel and others" via The Entity's assistance. His meeting was seen to dramatically quell further fighting in the vicinity of the 3rd Battalion headquarters.

'I recommend that he also be rewarded with a promotion to Navy Captain. And he should also receive the Navy cross.

'And finally, I recommended the Medal of Honor to your Husband. He, in effect, gave his life for his Country and another human being. I feel that he is totally worthy of such an award.'

'Do you have any other recommendations at this time, General?'

'No, Ma'am, that about covers it! And thank you for your recommendation given to these matters. Now, if you'll excuse me, I believe I have a family to be with. Good day, ma'am.'

'Shawn, thank you again for everything you do for us.'

Crawford rode back over to the hangar and joined his wife, son, and daughter, Colette had a mouth full of lasagna and Christopher was devouring two pieces of pizza at once.

'Why, hello, all! By the looks of the way their two Munchkins are eating their food, one would think that we don't feed them at home! Coach, what do you think?' Shawn asked Hunter who was approaching and who had pizza sauce on his whiskers.

'Well, Coach, I bet I can tell what the favorite food groups are for these two Rugrats.'

'Pizza! Lasagna!' shouted Christopher and Colette in unison.

Christine groaned!

WARRIOR RECOGNITION

TWO DAYS LATER, Sir Shawn, Lady Christine, Commander O'Hara, CPT O'Leary, Corporal O'Leary, General O'Hara, Air Commodore Gonzales, Admiral King, and Flight Sergeant Caruso were ordered to report to the Commander's Office. Colonel O'Leary was already present.

When they were all gathered in Marshal Morrison's Office and were wondering what was going on, the Prime Minister of Australia and his Staff came into the room. Marshal Morrison asked everyone to be seated for just a moment. Sergeant Cranston had arranged for the detail to carry additional chairs into the Commander's Office earlier that morning.

'As we know, the mission called Operation Phoenix was a huge success. I congratulate you all on a job well done. I have asked the Prime Minister of Australia and members of his staff to be present this morning so that we might recognize the heroic efforts of those who contributed to the ultimate success of Operation Phoenix. Having said all of that, I would like to introduce the Prime Minister, who will make presentations to those who ensured the success of Operation Phoenix through their hard work, planning, and execution. Mister Prime Minister.'

'Thank you, Marshal Morrison. I also would like to echo my congratulations on a successful mission. Each one of you contributed significantly to the overall positive results gained through your monumental effort working as a Team. I commend you all.'

'And now, I want to award the following individuals for their part in making this mission so very successful. Would Captain Shelley O'Leary please come forward?

'CPT O'Leary represents the Officer serving in the Armed Forces of Australia as a soldier who consistently goes beyond the call of duty and will give more than what is expected in every task she endeavors to complete. It is my pleasure to award Captain Shelley O'Leary the Air Force Cross for her part played in flying the Sea Scorpion Advance Stealth Fighter against the Chinese Communists Forces during Operation Phoenix. Captain O'Leary, congratulations. I might also add that this award has been presented less than five times in its history. This truly denotes the importance as well as the level of bravery exhibited by its recipient today.'

The Prime Minister then pinned the medal on Shelley's flight suit and shook her hand in gratitude for the service rendered to her country. As Shelley started walking back to her chair, the Prime Minister said, 'Not so fast, Captain O'Leary. I am not through with you yet. It also gives me great pleasure to further recognize your ability to lead others under the stress of combat. As a consequence, the present Australian Legislature has authorized me to promote you to the rank of Lieutenant Colonel, Australian Air Force. Congratulations, Lieutenant Colonel O'Leary!'

Everyone stood as one and congratulate Lieutenant Colonel O'Leary with a loud cheer and clapping that went on for 30 seconds.

Shelley beamed as she returned to her seat. Timmy O'Hara was all smiles and silently congratulated her on her award and promotion. 'Well deserved, Colonel!' he whispered to her.

'Now, there is a young man among us who is new to our Australian service, but performs as though he has been a member of the Australian aviation circles for many years. I would now ask Commander Timothy O'Hara to please step forward.

'Oh, Oh!' he whispered to Shelley as he rose from his chair.

'Commander O'Hara is one of the most versatile young men serving as an attached Member of the Australian Military. As you all know, Commander O'Hara arrived in our airspace just as a certain Knighted Pilot we have among us was opening up a Beef Wellington sandwich while flying his F-93B Leopard Stealth Fighter one morning. Yes, Sir Shawn, we all know about that!'

There were chuckles throughout the room as Shawn mouthed his trademark word, 'What?'

'Commander, it is my distinct pleasure to award you the Navy Cross for your actions in stifling further aggressor forces activity during the time when two of our fellow servicemen were being attended too medically. Your actions are in keeping with the highest traditions of the service and reflect great credit upon yourself, your military unit, and the Australian Department of Defense.'

The Prime Minister then pinned the Navy Cross award on Tim's flight suit and said, 'Congratulations, Commander O'Hara.'

Tim started to return to his seat and the Prime Minister then said, 'Commander, as it is Major O'Leary, not so fast, Commander! As everyone in this room knows, this young aviator, a graduate of the prestigious United States Naval Academy and Star Player on the Midshipmen Varsity Football Team, has displayed enormous leadership ability since he arrived at our doorstep. Commander, we thank you for everything you have accomplished on behalf of this great Country of ours. As a consequence of your actions, I am hereby authorized by the Australian Legislative to promote you to the rank of Navy Captain. Congratulations, Captain O'Hara.'

Everyone stood and clapped loudly for Tim's recognition, which was well deserved.

'I might add, Ladies and Gentlemen, that Captain O'Hara is the youngest serving captain in the history of the United States Navy!'

And, once more, those present gave young Captain O'Hara a resounding cheer!

'Ah, it is my pleasure to recognize a beautiful lady with two beautiful children, who, if I might add, have a propensity for Italian fare. Lady Christine, would you please come forward?

'For those of you who do not know this fabulous woman, Lady Christine Crawford is a Fighter Pilot who has attained Triple-Ace status in the skies all over the world. She is an F-22 Raptor Pilot, has flown F-15 Strike Eagles, and has transitioned into both the F42A Tiger Shark and the F-93B Leopard. When not attempting to keep her husband in line, [everyone looked at Shawn with a smirk, who returned their stares with his "What'?]

Lady Christine cares for the two children of her own and of, who is it, Shawn, His Blueness, His Vastness, Blue Meanie, or all of the above?'

'Yes, Mr. Prime Minister, it is "all of the above"!' said Shawn.

'Lady Christine, your immeasurable support given to Operation Phoenix has not gone unnoticed. It is my distinct pleasure to award you the Air Force Distinguished Service Medal for your total contributions rendered on behalf of your Country.'

The Prime Minister then pinned the prestigious Medal on Christine's tunic.

'Congratulations, Major Roberts!'

When the clapping and the cheering subsided, with whistles from her two children, and Colette shouting out "You rock, Mom!" the Prime Minister kept her close and told everyone that it was time for Lady Christine to be elevated to a status higher in rank recognition.

'I am hereby authorized, once again, by the Australian Legislature to promote Lady Christine Roberts to the rank of full Colonel, Australian Air Force. Congratulations, Colonel Roberts!'

Once again, the cheering for one of their favorite people was enormous! The clapping went on for a full minute. Shawn couldn't remember the last time he had seen his Bride blush with pride. He was so very proud of her!

'Is there an Admiral King in the house?' joked the Prime Minister.

'Yes, Mr. Prime Minister, the Coach is duly present. Sir, we are fortunate to have caught him before he ate his "snake" snacks.' Hunter looked at Shawn and said, 'Why, thank you, Coach!'

'Admiral King, also known as "Coach" among his peers, and Sir Shawn, the "Other Coach of the Lesser Half," as he's affectionately referred to by those familiar with the two Special Operations Soldiers, has been an invaluable addition to our military organization. His leadership style has been a steady influence on many of our junior officers. He is tireless in his devotion to duty, and he is fiercely protective of those whom he holds most dear. There are a few others that I would want to have by my side in an armed conflict.

'Coach, it is my distinct pleasure to award you the Navy Cross for gallantry in the face of the enemy.' The Prime Minister pinned the Award on Hunter's jacket and shook his hand warmly. Colette ran up to him and gave him a big hug followed by a kiss on his cheek.

'Coach, I do hear that Miss Colette wished that you were single.' That brought a huge laugh from those present, following some very loud clapping!

'Coach, you're blushing, you Snake-Eater, you!' yelled Crawford. Hunter just shook his head with a big smile on his face.

'Admiral King, by the authority vested in me by the Australian Legislature, I hereby promote you to the rank of Admiral Upper half. Congratulations on receiving your second star, Admiral!'

A chant began to be heard that went like, 'Coach, Coach, Coach,' Hunter's grin was from ear to ear. He looked at Shawn, who nodded with a smile as if to say, you deserved this, Coach! Congratulations!

'At this time, I would like for Air Commodore Gonzales to come forward. As we all know. Bob Gonzales came to us many years ago with a real American Cowboy, now referred to as Sir Shawn. Coach, among other monikers. Bob has been instrumental in getting our rotary-wing program off the ground. No pun intended! His dedication toward establishing a first-class military helicopter operation has resulted in the qualification of dozens of pilots here at the Sydney Maritime Defense Base. In addition, his acts of heroism have gone unnoticed. Today, I am going to change that to recognize, once a Chief Warrant Officer 5, by presenting him an award that he richly deserves. Chief, if I may still address you as such, it gives me great pleasure and honor to present you with the Distinguished Service Cross in recognition of your extraordinary bravery in the face of extreme danger. You have repeatedly risked your life in service to the Australian military, and your actions serve as a true testament to your courage and dedication. Congratulations, Chief Gonzales.'

Again, there was a huge cheer for one of the most beloved members of the Australian military. Shawn shouted out, 'Hear, hear! Way to go, Bobbo!

When the clamor died down, the Prime Minister requested that Brigadier General Patrick O'Hara step forward.

'General O'Hara has been with us for only a short time, but in this brief period, he has shown leadership ability that has been impressive. We are but the recipients of his greatness in flying helicopters for the Australian military. I had the occasion soon after General O'Hara joined us here in Australia to talk to Air Commodore, Chief Warrant Officer, Gonzales. Bob confided in me that he had seen less than a handful of pilots who could make a helicopter do some wondrous things aerodynamically. And this Gentleman was one of those pilots. And this coming from Chief Bob Gonzales was a testament to General

O'Hara's ability to provide guidance and wisdom to our new rotary-wing aviators in the instruction of advanced helicopter tactics.

'Once again, it is my pleasure to award you, General O'Hara, the Distinguished Service Cross for your bravery in engaging aggressor forces while piloting the AH-56 Cheyenne Helicopter during Operation Phoenix. Congratulations, General O'Hara!'

Patrick's son Tim stood first and loudly clapped for his father. Within a split second of Tim's beginning the ovation, the others in the room stood and clapped heartily for this man who had sacrificed much to dedicate his life to the service of the welfare of the Republic of Australia. Patrick was overwhelmed by the kindness shown by each member of the military in that room that morning.

When Patrick went back to his seat, Tim went over and hugged his father and told him that he loved him dearly. The crowd continued to applaud, this time, for the father and son who had contributed so much for so many.

The Prime Minister continued by asking Flight Sergeant Will Caruso to step forward. Will approached the Prime Minister and was totally surprised at his name being called. He gave Sir Shawn a side-long glance. Crawford merely shrugged his soldiers and smirked at the same time.

'Flight Sergeant Will Caruso is a role model for all enlisted personnel on this Base. He is meticulous in his duties. Thoroughly organized, and most importantly, keeps Sir Shawn completely in line!'

Everyone looked at Shawn and broke out laughing. Crawford merely assumed a martyr's expression of deep hurt, but with a customary twinkle in his eye.

'Sergeant Caruso, there are so many people who rely upon you to take care of their aviation maintenance needs on a daily basis. You constantly rise to each and every occasion by ensuring that all types of aircraft are completely maintained and operationally ready at all times. The aviation community looks to you as a solid anchor to ensure that everything is in place when the suit is up to fly a mission. You are indeed revered for your expertise.

'It is my distinct honor to award you with the Legion of Merit for outstanding performance of duty in all facets of aviation operations. Your actions far exceed the expectations of all who rely upon you to meet the needs of the Australian military service. Congratulations, Sergeant Caruso!'

Will was a definite Favorite among all the aviators, and it was shown when they all rose to their feet, cheered, and whistled. The whistling actually came from Christopher and Colette!

'Before I let this man go, I do have one other administrative piece of business that pertains to Sergeant Caruso. It appears that the certain Knighted Officer in our ranks is adamant about shortening your military title because he suggests that is a mouthful. He proposed a less, using his own words, difficult title in addressing you in the future. Well, the Australian legislature could not agree with Sir Shawn more.

'It is my honor to award you a commission as a warrant officer in the Australian Military by bestowing upon you the title of Warrant Officer Second Class. Sir Shawn also thought it would be nice if you did not start at the bottom of the warrant officer ladder. You may blame him at a time of your choosing, Mr. Caruso! Congratulations!'

Warrant Officer Will Caruso couldn't believe it. He, an Officer! Wow, a day this has turned out to be, he thought! Will looked over at Shawn and nodded his appreciation for being recognized so fully as he returned to his seat.

The Prime Minister continued.

'Each one of these military warrior aviators is a hero in the eyes of the Australian Government. There is one other award that I wish to present. It is a recognition that is not easily administered to a very deserving military soldier, for the award itself does not belong to the Country of Australia. It belongs to the United States of America.

'This soldier/aviator has done nothing short of exemplary service to this Country in each and every assignment given since he arrived here years ago. He has succeeded in every attempt to further the need for peace in this world. His leadership has been outstanding and without his military direction, this country would have been left terribly wanting.

'Colonel Michael O'Leary, please come forward.'

'I am referring to you by the rank of Colonel because that is the military title chosen by the aviators who have witnessed your remarkable achievements since you first met in a general merchandise store in a small French town in late summer 1940. Your association with these three officers, who are present with us today, has taken you through many battles and operations that have contributed to making the world a safer place, one step at a time, even if it may have thinned your hair.

'I am going to ask the Commander of the Sydney Maritime Defense Base, Marshal Morrison, and the wife of Colonel O'Leary, to come forward to assist me in the presentation of this prestigious award.

'Colonel, it is with distinct pleasure and an honor to award you the Medal of Honor for your bravery in the face of extreme danger during Operation Phoenix. As the Operation was close to being finalized, you took it upon yourself, at the expense of significant risk to your life, to seek out any remaining American serviceman left behind at the third Battalion Headquarters. You have subsequently been wounded and even nearly lost your life.

'For your disregard for personal safety and for your commitment to saving the lives of others, it is my very distinct honor, on behalf of the President of the United States, to award you this Medal of Honor. Colonel O'Leary!'

Allison Morrison then took the impressive Medal of Honor and fastened the clasp behind her Husband's neck. She then kissed him on the cheek, coupled with a huge hug. Everyone stood and slapped for a full two minutes. The Colonel stood there with near tears in his eyes as Corporal James Paul O'Leary came forward and gave his Nephew many times a huge hug in congratulations.

When the applause finally subsided, Corporal O'Leary started to return to his seat.

'Corporal James Paul O'Leary, please step forward and stand by your Nephew, with how many "Greats" there may exist before the Family relationship term.

'One of the important and justifiable reasons for Operation Phoenix was to save this young man among others within his Battalion. Corporal O'Leary was the last man at his post in the headquarters bunker. Colonel O'Leary found him still attempting to communicate with higher headquarters on the radio to inform his superiors of the disposition of the 3rd Battalion soldiers under attack on the evening of 2 November 1995.

'Corporal O'Leary nearly lost his life as he finally left the Command Headquarters. He was wounded while proceeding to one of the Troop Transport helicopters. Because of your dedication to serving in the face of grave danger and risk to your personal well-being, it is my distinct honor to award you with the Silver Star. Congratulations, Corporal O'Leary.'

The Prime Minister turned to Colonel O'Leary and asked that he pin the Silver Star on his Uncle. After the Colonel finished fastening the award to the tunic of the 19-year-old Soldier, he shook his hand and gave the boy a huge hug. This time, the applause went on for more than two minutes.

The Prime Minister then told everyone that this award would not do ultimate justice in terms of what Young O'Leary did for his fellow soldiers that evening. And that such leadership should also be rewarded.

'Corporal O'Leary, it is with distinction and in concurrent approval with the Australian Legislature, that you be awarded a Battlefield Commission to the rank of First Lieutenant.

'Congratulations, Lieutenant O'Leary.'

The applause that followed was infectious. Everyone then came forward and shook the young officer's hand and congratulated him on his heroism. The Prime Minister thanked the Base Commander and shook hands with all the recipients, and then left the office with his staff.

Shawn went to each award-winner and shook his and her hand. There were hugs and celebrations on the back. The Base Commander then "suggested" that everyone convene at the Officer's Club, which she had requested to be opened to honor those who received honors that morning.

Shawn, Christine, the children, and the Admiral King went over to Shawn's SUV. There was a huge buffet set up for everyone to indulge in. Off one side there was a small table with pizza and lasagna dishes for "Anyone" who may have been interested.

Captain O'Hara came over to Shawn and asked to speak to him in private.

'Sir, I would have thought that you should have been recognized for everything you have done here, and especially for your major role in putting together the Operation Phoenix Plan. What's up with that, Sir?'

'Well, you know something. I really did nothing but put pen to paper. It was everyone else, including yourself, that made the entire Operation work. Besides, I found out that, when making out the citations, the General Assembly had run out of papyrus!.'

'Timmy, I've been awarded and rewarded. My pleasure is seeing soldiers like yourself gain accolades. I could not have been more proud of you, Captain. The promotion and the award of the Navy Cross were entirely fitting and appropriate. You really did defuse further bloodshed by speaking with that young North Korean Officer. You are commended for your actions.'

'Sir, what are the next steps?' What is to become of first Lieutenant

O'Leary? Is there a plan in place to have him returned to his family?'

'Yes, there is, as a matter of fact. I'm putting something down for our new Medal of Honor Winner to evaluate and, I'm sure, approve. I want 1LT James Paul O'Leary to be back with his family in Massachusetts. They have no idea what is going on with him at this point. I believe we may be able to effect his transition to home life within the next couple of days.'

'And what of Father Kapaun?'

'I truly believe the good father has found a home within the confines of The Entity's World. And that feels right to me. Here is a man of God who will one day in the early 21st Century be canonized a Saint by the Catholic Church and the Pope. What greater honor can there be for a human being, and one who serves God? I certainly cannot think of one. No, Father Kapaun still has much work to do in this world, but with The Entity's assistance.'

'By the way, shouldn't you be with a young newly-minted Lieutenant

Colonel "Driver" of a Sea Scorpion right about now?'

'Yes, Sir, I do believe you are correct. And, thank you, Sir, for everything you have done for me in the way of monitoring and guidance. The benefit to me is immeasurable!'

'Captain O'Hara, you are entirely welcome!'

NEW ENGLAND HOMECOMING

THE NEXT MORNING, Shawn rode over to the Headquarters Building to talk with Colonel O'Leary. He walked up the familiar stairs to the Marshal's office and checked in with her Gatekeeper, Sergeant Cranston.

'Hello, Gorgeous, is the Colonel in this morning?'

'Good morning, Sir Shawn. He went down to the hangar with 1LT O'Leary. You, that young man is single! I do believe I am having a hot flash!'

'Well, before it overruns you, I'd better head down to the hangar. Good talking to you, Crystal; make sure you get that "Flash" looked at right away, O.K.?'

When Crawford walked into the hangar, he saw the Colonel and the newly commissioned First Lieutenant looking over the Tiger Shark.

'Good morning, Gentlemen, and I do use that term loosely when addressing the new Medal of Honor Winner!'

'Shawn, I'm really glad you're here. I want to run something by you. But, before I do that, I want to tell young Jim here that, if he thinks my Medal award is awesome, he needs to know that you've been awarded it twice.'

'Is that so, Sir Shawn? Wow. You must be quite a Warrior!'

'Well, I am outside the house. Within, I run the Daddy Day Care for the family. I'm another Rodney Dangerfield: I get absolutely no respect. Oh, you'll get to know Rodney Dangerfield in your waning years, now that you have them to spend.

'Colonel, what did you wish to talk to me about, Sir?'

'Shawn, we need to get this Lad back to his Family in the year 1950. The Thanksgiving Holiday is coming right up, and I think it would be an appropriately festive time to have him back with his Parents, Brother, and two Sisters.'

'I can't agree with you more, Colonel. When do you want to leave?'

'I was thinking about this evening. Jim tells me that there is a Park behind his parents' home. It has a ball field large enough for the Shark to hover on land. From there, it's a stone's throw to his front porch. What do you think?'

'I'm game. I have no responsibilities around the old homestead this evening. Let me check in with my boss. Have you cleared it with your Bride?'

'I have no problem. She wished young James the very best of luck. His homecoming will remind his Father about the time we took him home to his wife during World War I.'

'O.K., is the Shark ready to go?'

'I spoke with Will a little while ago and the aircraft is fully fueled and armed, not that we'll need the ordnance for this trip. It's always nice to go on a trip when your gun in the holster is fully loaded.'

'Super. If you wish to leave around 1900 hours, I will be here. Let me get my Family ducks in a row, and I'll be back here by 1800 hours. Sounds like a fun trip!'

'O.K., Shawn, We'll see you then.'

When Shawn returned, he had Christopher in tow. As there were a maximum of four seats aboard the Tiger shark, Shawn had no issue with Him coming along after checking with Christine. Besides, it never hurts to have an additional qualified pilot aboard an aircraft.

The F-42 took off right at 1900 hours and got within 15 miles of Sydney when they ran into The Entity's hideaway in the sky!

'Colonel, Shawn, Christopher, and First Lieutenant O' Leary, it is very nice to see you again.'

'Your Blueness,' said Shawn, 'Please not too loud, O.K.? You'll wake up the baby sleeping in the back.'

'Baby, what, Oh, Shawn, I truly love your humor. It's getting fascinating in the future with Bobby continuing to pick on Jack and Mahatma serving Dr. King these exotic foods that Dr. King finds not too exotic1 it's getting to be a real circus back there!

'Lieutenant, I am so pleased that you are on your way home. Father Kapaun sends his well-wishes and would have liked to see you once again. Perhaps another time. And my congratulations on your Silver Star and promotion. Very fine indeed'

'Colonel, congratulations on your Medal of Honor. One more to go and you'll be giving my young Jedi Knight a run for his money!

'And Christopher, I'm glad to see you again, My Son. Unfortunately, I didn't have time to call out for a pizza for your trip to Massachusetts. Perhaps on the way back!

'Colonel, I will take you over to the new Bed-fort Airport, even though you will be landing in Acushnet. I have already cleared the Shark through their airport traffic area.

'Welcome home, young Lieutenant! Your discharge papers will be in your mailbox tomorrow. Please give my best regards to your Father. I fondly refer to him as Grampa now. And, please do say a special hello to your older brother Timothy. I'm sure the Author must be pleased that I thought to ask about him!'

And then silence. 'One day. I'm going to get him to say Auf Wiedersehen!' Christopher giggled.

They broke out over mid-field New Bedford Airport at 1000 feet and Colonel O'Leary started his approach to hover onto the ball field. Being November, the field was empty of people. Shawn donned his night vision devices as did the Colonel just to ensure that they had a clear view of what was going on around them. They landed five minutes later.

It was quiet and the air was chilly. It was going to be a cold November Massachusetts evening. The Colonel opened the canopy and the four exited the F-42. 1LT O'Leary led the other three the 50 yards to his front porch. He rang the doorbell.

When the door opened, Jim's sister, Pearl, was standing in front of him. She looked at him for a second, and her eyes went as wide as saucers. Her hand went to her mouth and she started crying. She then gave him the biggest hug and led him into the home. The other three dutifully followed.

'Pa, Ma,' said Pearl, 'Guess who's coming to dinner?'

The soldier wearing the smallest uniform in the Army during World War I came around the corner and broke into a huge smile!

'Jim, what on earth?' And then he spied Christopher, the Boy who had ferried him home nearly 35 years ago. Grampa then knew how his, so Jim had arrived home.

'Hello, Grampa,' Christopher said. 'How have you been?'

'Hello, Christopher! You haven't grown at all, but then, I should have realized that would be the case if I ever hoped to see you again.'

Colonel O'Leary and General Crawford came forward and introduced themselves, while Jim was with his mother and two sisters. His brother Tim was expected to drop by with his wife Jeanne anytime soon.

Grampa brought the three aviators into the kitchen and introduced them to his other children. When his wife Lillian saw Christopher, she gasped. 'Pa, isn't this the boy who brought you home to me in 1918 from the War?'

'Yes, Ma, it is. This is Christopher. Colonel O'Leary and General Crawford have taken our son Jim from Korea and returned him to us for good. Jim's discharge papers are to be in email by tomorrow.'

At this moment, Jim's older brother Timothy arrived through the front door. When he entered the kitchen, he saw his younger brother and yelled. 'Jim, you're home! When did you get in?'

'Just a few minutes ago. These gentlemen brought me home from Korea.

I'm out of the service tomorrow morning. Where's Jeanne?'

'She's home with Brian, Jimmy, and Michael. I can't stay long. But, you're home for good, right? I'll be back tomorrow morning so that we can catch up. This is fantastic! Did you get discharged as a Corporal?'

Jim looked at Colonel O'Leary who introduced himself, Shawn, and Christopher.

'Your brother earned the Silver Star for heroism at the battle of *Unsan*, North Korea. He was also awarded a Battlefield Commission as a First Lieutenant for saving a countless number of lives when his unit was about to be overrun. But, I'll let him tell you the rest in time.

'We will be leaving, you know. This is your time with your Son and Brother. Jim, I'm going to miss seeing you. I will never forget you. Congratulations on getting your Son and Brother back safely to you. My very best to all!'

Jim then said to his family. 'I'm going to walk them to the door and see them out. I'll be just a minute. It's perfect to be home.'

When they all got to the door, Jim said, 'Thank you for everything you have done for me. I know today that I would have been either captured or dead from that attack on our Regimental location that night. You saved me, and for that, I can never repay you.'

'Listen, Uncle Jim. Just seeing you and ensuring that you survived is everything to me. This door is never closed forever, you know. You've seen the way we work. Nothing is too impossible with The Entity. You take care of yourself. Enjoy your family and life, Uncle Jim.'

And with that, they hugged one another for a long moment. Jim then shook hands with Sir Shawn and Christopher. He placed in Christopher's hand a regimental coin from his unit and asked Christopher to remember him every time he took it out to look at it.

'I will, I'm going to miss you.'

Then, the three aviators walked away from the house and toward the baseball field, where the Tiger Shark stood waiting patiently for their return.

PARIS ONCE AGAIN

WHEN THE TIGER SHARK landed back in Sydney, it was late morning. All three were exhausted and decided to go home to get some much needed rest. Shawn decided to leave the after-action reporting to Marshal Morrison to her Husband.

He and Christopher climbed into their SUV and headed to their quarters. Christopher kept looking at the Regimental Challenge Coin given to Him by 1LT Jim O'Leary. He kept turning it over and over and then looked over at his father.

'You know, Father, Lieutenant O'Leary didn't have to part with this unit piece of his, did he?'

'No, Christopher, he could have kept it for something to remember the unit *esprit de corps* that he experienced with the other members of the 3rd Battalion. And then again, he may have wanted to give it to You for all of your kindness shown to him in the brief time we know him. In any event, it was the gesture that really counts in life. What is important to him now is that he is home with his family. And I know for certain that he feels extremely fortunate that we were able to save him and his fellow soldiers that night.'

'Do you think we'll ever see him again?'

'I firmly believe that everything is possible with your   father, Christopher.'

'Yes, I supposed everything is possible with you, Father!' And he looked at Shawn with the utmost love in His eyes.

When they entered the house, Colette had Admiral King by the hand and led him everywhere she could lead him. He looked up when Shawn and Christopher came in and said to Shawn, 'Ah, the Cavalry had just arrived. What's going on, Coach? How was your trip to the Cape Cod area?'

'Very rewarding, Coach. Lieutenant O'Leary's arrival was well received. We got a chance to see the Doughboy who wore the smallest uniform in the Army and his lovely wife Lillian. His sisters Pearl and Frances were also there when we got there, and his older brother Tim, a Veteran of the China-Burma-

India Theater during World War II, came a short while before we left. Father Kapaun also had served in the CBI Theater, but in 1945, late in the War. Altogether. It was a very rewarding experience.

'That's great. Oh, I heard that Agent Dighello paid the Marshal a visit. I understand that our presence is required in the Commander's Office first thing in the morning. Sounds like another "Boondoggle" to me!'

'Yes, whenever that bad penny shows up, mayhem is not far behind. Why don't I pick you up at your quarter's tomorrow morning around 0830.'

'Sounds great, Coach. To be perfectly honest with you, I'm getting a bit bored with watching reruns of the Adventure Channel. I do believe I need to create my own adventure pretty soon!'

'Coach, one could always find you a scooter to ride near a hedge somewhere!'

'Ah, not the kind of adventure I was looking for, Coach. But, if you hold that thought, you may want to put it in use the next time you cut the grass on the riding mower.'

'Oh, Coach, that really hurts! And so cold!' 'In the morning, young Jedi!'

Shawn rang Admiral King's doorbell precisely at 0830 hours. 'Coach, you're late! I've been up for at least 90 seconds! I do believe you are sleeping terribly.'

'Wonder what the Master Spook has in store for us today, and beyond today. Do you think it could be in some exotic place like the Outback, I'm not referring to the Restaurant of the same name? Perhaps, in Tahiti. Or Maui. Oh, I've got to stop doing this to myself. I'll be a wreck by the time I get to the Marshal's Office. How does my hair look? Am I a wreck,

Hunter?'

'Yes, Coach, you are definitely a train wreck.'

They dutifully checked in with Sergeant Cranston, who told them to go right in.

'Thank you, Crystal. You've done something with your hair, haven't you? Don't change a thing, Crystal.'

'Shawn, I do believe our appointment is waiting for us. Talk to you later, Sergeant Cranston.'

When they walked into the office, Agent Dighello was seated and sipping what looked like a latte. Shawn started salivating. And Captain O'Hara sat in a chair in the other corner of the room from Dighello. When Shawn saw him, Timmy merely shrugged his shoulders.

'Gentlemen,' said Morrison, 'Welcome. Would either of you care for

something to drink?'

'Ma'am, Admiral King will have nothing. I, on the other hand, will have a grande latte with a swirl of mocha whipped cream. Thank you, Ma'am.'

Hunter looked at Shawn for a long moment, as did Agent Dighello. Colonel O'Leary had to turn around for fear of giving his internal laughter away. Marshal Morrison asked Shawn to turn around to accept his order from Sergeant Cranston.

'You see, Hunter, good help is always easy to find!' Hunter stuck his finger right through the middle of the swirl of mocha cream!

'How are you boys doing? Agent Dighello requires the services of three experienced Agents in the field, and he needs them immediately. Agent Dighello, I'll let you take it from here.'

'Thank you, Commander. We have a developing situation in Paris that becomes increasingly troublesome every day, we do nothing about it. There is a terrorist organization that is planning to use nerve gas in the area called Esplanade de La Défense. There are several buildings that present opportune targets for the terrorists to employ nerve gas through the ventilation systems.

'Intelligence has intercepted some "chatter" over the internet that suggests the terrorists may attempt an attack as early as next week. The CIA would like to use you two gentlemen to neutralize the threat.

'There is a meeting to be held Sunday evening in a building not far from the *Esplanade* area. I have the address written down here. Please memorize it. I need to have it back before we leave here today.

'You both need to be in France by Saturday morning to verify the meeting location. It is anticipated that the meeting will involve some heavy-hitting Al-Qaeda operatives. The mission objective is to remove the nerve gas and turn it over to one of our mission specialists. You will fly your own military aircraft into Brussels and then take the train to Paris. You will meet your Paris contact at the train station when you arrive.

'This operation will also take you to the terrorist meeting location and will be waiting for you to exit the *Esplanade* building after you have neutralized the threat. In addition, he will have protective masks and Beretta handguns with silencers for your use.

Esplanade de la Defense

http:/en.wikipedia.org/wiki/File:Esplanade-de-la-defense.jpg#file

'Once you have the nerve gas cylinders secured, you will hand them over to the operative, who will drive you back to the train station.'

'I have a packet for you that includes French passports and currency. Your aliases are in your packet. Once you have gone through everything, destroy anything that may incriminate you once you arrive in-country.

'Do you have any questions thus far?'

'I can think of anything at the moment,' said Shawn.

'Here is the only photo we have of the terrorists. There will be one in your final packet that the contact will give you when he takes you to the building where the meeting is to be held.

'Once you have eliminated the terrorist threat, your contact will drive you to the train station, where you will board a train back to Brussels. Once there, you will be met at the train station by one of our people, who will take you to the airport and to your aircraft.'

'Are the safe houses that we need to know about?'

'Yes, those will also be in your packet. It is absolutely imperative that you take each piece of intelligence, memorize it, and burn it.'

'Well, this all seems so cut and dry. If we can have our packets, then we can be on our way.'

Dighello handed all three aviators, now CIA Agents, a packet with his name on the top right-hand corner.

'Coach, Timmy, shall we adjourn to the "coffee room" at the Club and go over our assignment?'

All three walked out of the room without saying anything else. Once they arrived at the Officer's Club, they sat down with a cup of coffee, and a cappuccino for Shawn, opened their packets, looked at their aliases, and introduced themselves.

'Wow,' said O'Hara, 'My name is *Francois*. And yours, *messieurs*?'

Admiral King identified himself as *Robert*, and Shawn as *Philip*. 'O.K., it looks like we leave from Sydney and take the western route through Saudi Arabia and then into Brussels Airport. I do believe we can bypass Saudi and go all the way to Brussels from here, don't you think, Timmy?'

'Yes, Sir, we can. If we fly Mach 6 at 80,000 feet, we should be in Brussels in two hours and 16 minutes.'

Admiral King looked at Shawn and said, 'How does the boy do that? I mean, calculate our time of flight that quickly.'

Tim responded by saying, 'Well, the distance between Sydney and Brussels is 10,399.62 miles. The speed of sound, or Mach 1, is 760 miles per hour. If you take 760 and multiply it by 6, our mach speed, you come up with a factor of 4560. Taking that factor and dividing it into 10,399.62 miles, you can easily come up with 2.280628421 hours of flight time. Multiplying 0.280618421 by 60 minutes, we can come up with 16.8 minutes, or 2 hours, 16 minutes, and 48 seconds.'

'Huh?' said King.

'Good,' said Shawn, 'Just enough time to have a leisurely brunch along the route of the flight. And the time is right for a fast action movie. Wonderful!' said Crawford.

'Coach, I'll bring the popcorn. What aircraft are we going to take?',

asked the Admiral.

'Since young Captain O'Hara is "driving", I do believe Sancha hasn't been to Brussels in a long time, if ever. Do you like butter on your popcorn, Admiral?'

'Just the light kind, Coach. I'm beginning to look non-svelte.'

'I know the feeling with all kinds of left-over Pizza in the house these days. O.K., moving right along. We have our passports, even though they took a photo of my bad side, straight on, and we have our currency in Euros. A change of appropriate clothing will be nice to get the job done. We'll have to go through customs when we get to Brussels, but I think our passports that are stamped "Diplomat" should suffice our being able to be on our way quickly to catch the train to Paris. What did I miss?'

'Who in Paris do we meet when we get off the train?'

'Let's see. I do believe I have a photo of our contact. No, it's here—right here, attractive young lady. We should have no problem recognizing her. She will have the location of the Paris station when we meet her in Brussels before getting on the train there. It also says that she will ensure our moving through customs is swift and that she will drive us to the station.

'O.K., today is Thursday and we leave Saturday morning. We need to be in Paris at 1100 hours. There is a train schedule here somewhere. O.K., we will be taking the Thalys 9316 train from Brussels to Paris North. It departs Brussels at 0657 hours, and to make the train station, we should back off an hour for good measure to make contact with our driver and allow for traffic congestion to the train station. Plan on departing here, wheels-up, at 0530 hours.

'What did I miss? Coach, Timmy?'

'Coach, our contact at the train station in Paris, do we have a picture?

'Dighello hinted that our Brussels lady will have that information for us. A lot of this appears to be compartmentalized information. It's a "spooky" business for "spooks", I suppose.'

'I think we'll be good to go, Sir. I suspect once we get to Paris and to the

Esplanade, our plan of action will be fluid.'

'Yes, it will have to be in accordance with what we know and don't know at the moment. Let's hope our Paris contact is right on schedule and has accurate information relating to the meeting location. Then it's up to us to execute.'

The three aviators CIA "spooks" spent the following day getting prepared to leave. Shawn went over to the hangar and spoke with Warrant Officer Caruso to check on the status of the F-98. Crawford had called the previous afternoon that they would be departing very early Saturday morning and that he could ensure that Sancha was ready to go.

'She's ready and excited, Sir Shawn. That is a powerful combination when she gets the way! Anyway, you'll have full weapons' stores when you leave here. Never leave home without a few rockets, are what I always say. Let me know if there is anything else I can do for you. I'll be here at 0500 hours to get the aircraft out on the ramp for you.'

'Thank you, Chief! We really appreciate the help.'

The evening before the flight, Shawn was called into Morrison's Office. Dighello and the Colonel were there.

'Shawn, there has been information leaked that the terrorists know you folks are coming to "crash" their meeting Saturday evening. My sources now tell me that they are going to meet in the early morning hours tomorrow. They tell me it's going to be a 0500 start time for their meeting. You, people, are going to leave tonight. And you'll have to fly right into Paris.

'Our contact in Brussels has already taken a train to Paris north to assist in the mission. When looking at a schematic of the *de Gaulle* Airport, there are a couple of places where you may reasonably put the aircraft down without drawing too much attention. Here, I'll give this to you to look over. There will be one of our people waiting for you to land. The challenge and password are: 'It was a beautiful day today." The response should be, 'And it's raining in Bermuda.'

'For the most part, VIPs come into *de Gaulle* generally between 0100 and 0600 hours. So, your unusual aircraft will only draw the attention of local old paparazzi, who suffer from insomnia and can't keep up with the young guys.

'Since they have been forewarned, you can expect beefed-up security. You can bet the location will have changed as well. Our contacts are working hard to get the latest information on the meeting.

'I'll get out of your way so that you can get the Admiral and Captain together. Good luck, and as they say in your trade, Good Hunting!'

Shawn immediately left and went over to the Admiral's and O'Hara's quarters to inform them of the change of plans. He also called Will Caruso and told him that they were going to be leaving at 0230 hours, three hours earlier.

They bought some time because they didn't have to go into Brussels and then take the train to Paris. Shawn could never understand the reasoning behind that strategy at all, I guess the CIA was always extra cautious and saw a "bad guy" hiding behind every corner of a building.

Hunter and Tim had no problem leaving a little earlier. Will was Will. He'd sleep in the aircraft in the hangar if he had to! Christopher never seemed to sleep anyway. Although Christine was being motherly and showed concern about his going at all, he told her that he could be the one with the least potential for getting hurt.

When the four aviators got to the hangar, Will already had the F-98 out on the ramp. The internal system was shown to be functional/operational. Crawford had already filed a flight plan with Operations only, as he didn't want to advertise to the outside world that a fighter aircraft was departing in the wee hours of the morning. As there was no traffic expected into the Base this evening, the evening controllers permitted the Stingray to taxi at will.

Shawn announced that he was rolling, and the F-98 quickly ran down the runway and took off straight up into the air. Shawn leveled off at 80,000 feet. The stars were brilliant at this altitude. They saw a few wandering comets pass by way overhead. It was a beautiful night to be flying.

The time en route was a little less than previously calculated, as Paris was slightly closer than Brussels. They entered the *de Gaulle* Control Zone two hours and six minutes following their departure from Sydney.

They actually landed at a small satellite airfield adjacent to *de Gaulle*. The less conspicuous they could be, with a fighter as advanced-looking as the Stingray, would serve them better. Their contact somehow anticipated their arrival and saw them arrive. The vehicle pulled up alongside the Stingray and the driver got out. An exchange of challenge and password ensued, and both parties were vetted.

She had to be no more than 20 years old, with black hair, dark eyes, and oriental features. She was beautiful. Then aviators quickly got beyond that and focused on what information she had for them. She looked at Christopher, a mere boy, with the slightest concern, but did not question his presence.

Her name was Myra and informed Shawn that the meeting had been changed to a different building, but still within the *Esplanade*. They climbed in her Sports Utility Vehicle, and she drove off into the City. While on the way, she filled them in on the specifics of the meeting and how many they could anticipate being present.

The leader of the group was top-level. Al-Qaeda Operative, high in its chain of command. He, at one time, served as Bin Laden's great, great-grandson, second in command, and considered as entirely ruthless. He had a history of using chemical agents against large numbers of people. Likewise, he was suspected of working with other rogue terrorist elements throughout the globe.

Al-Qaeda's organization had been around for decades and was highly visible during the loss of the Twin Financial Towers in New York on September 11, 2001. They had never been completely neutralized. Years of attempts were made to finally silence their attempts to terrorize the world and deny it peace.

She indicated that they could expect to see at least a dozen individuals present at the meeting. Their meeting would be heavily guarded.

The location of the gathering was on the twelfth floor of a 25-story building. This was considered to be a final meeting before they would break and go in different directions and employ the nerve gas in their geographical areas of concern. The nerve gas canisters were to be present by the end of the meeting and passed out before it convened.

They would take the gas cylinders from the building and filter them through pre-arranged modes of transportation to be subsequently smuggled to the final locations for ultimate use. Suspected targets were to be places of worship and transportation systems around the globe.

Someone close to Myra indicated that the nerve gas cylinders were to be brought up to the meeting in several suitcases. Interceptions might prove difficult as they were expected to be heavily guarded. She said she would point out the supposed entry into the building by those transporting the gas to the twelfth floor after the start of the meeting. The time of the meeting was to work in their favor.

As they continued to drive to their intended building. Myra passed out photos of three key Al-Qaeda Lieutenants. She did not have what she considered an up-to-date photograph of the leader because he constantly changed his disguise. And he was very good at disguises.

Along with the photographs, she gave each of the men a Beretta with silencers, an extra clip of ammunition, and a five-inch stiletto. Myra looked at Christopher, who merely smiled back at her. She then gave each a mini-protective mask that would protect each of them for no more than five minutes against the effects of the gas before the mask filters broke down completely. Myra said that she would station herself in her vehicle in an alley across the street. She would give them 20 minutes once the nerve gas containers in suitcases were carried into the building, and then she would drive away. They needed to be precise in their movements, get the mission accomplished, and get out without causing undue alarm.

When they arrived at the general location, she let each of them out separately, approximately a half-block separating each stop. Christopher exited the vehicle with his father. They each entered the building separately. It was unusual for the main doors to be left unlocked on a Saturday morning in Paris, Shawn thought, but then he noticed row upon row of mailboxes to the right. Parisian citizens needed to check their mail on the weekends.

They all went into the women's room because they all knew at least one of the guards was going to have to relieve himself. They checked their weapons and ensured that the silencers were screwed on, around in the chamber, and safeties on. Then they placed the weapons in their waistband in the back of their trousers that were covered by windbreakers they all wore. Shawn told Christopher to remain with him. The time was 0455 hours. The meeting was scheduled to begin at 0500.

They planned to climb the stairwell stairs to the meeting floor. If they could intercept the canisters from reaching the twelfth floor because they felt they could take the guards, then they would do so. With their elements of surprise, the ratio of success was 2:1 in their favor. If there were more than six guards, they would have to get to the twelfth floor quickly while the elevator ferried the terrorists up to the meeting. From there, it was a fly-by-night plan which made their strategy much more complicated with a decreasing percentage of success. It appeared that their best bet would be to "ambush" the guards on the bottom floor.

'Father,' said Christopher, 'Let me take care of the guards for you.' 'Christopher, no, absolutely not! You are going to stay put, do you understand?'

He merely looked at his father and smiled. Both Timmy and Hunter looked at Christopher's smile and began to get not a good feeling about what was about to happen.

Before Shawn could say anything else, the front lobby doors opened and several men were heard talking in low tones. They immediately made for the elevators. Christopher opened the door before Shawn could grab him and he was out the door.

'Coach,' Hunter whispered, 'Just a second now, O.K., Just a second. "Breath", Coach.'

They heard Christopher approach the men, and He appeared to be balling his eyes out! He was babbling something in Parisian French that was incomprehensible. One of the terrorists started to grab Christopher to backhand Him across the face while cursing him in French.

Before the man could grab him, Christopher put his arm straight out with his palm facing downward and made a "pushing" motion in the direction of the terrorists. They immediately were thrust back against the far wall with such force that they hit their heads against the concrete white cinder blocks and crumpled to the floor. When the others exited the women's restroom, there were 8 terrorists lying on their backs and totally unconscious.

'Father, we need to hurry, we have sixteen minutes before Myra leaves. There are four suitcases altogether. What are we going to do with them, Father?'

'Coach, give me one of the suitcases.' He opened it up and examined the cylinder. They were sealed effectively from leakage, but that seal could be tampered with. 'Coach, come with me to the twelfth floor with your mask. Timmy, stand guard down here with Christopher.

'We will be back in no more than six minutes. Coach, safeties off.'

When they got on the elevator and started up, Shawn hastily outlined his plan. 'They will have guards out on the floor outside the meeting door. When we got to the floor, let the door open and allow the guard to come over. We'll take him out and a second guard, if there is one.

'We then go over to the door leading to the meeting room. Let's make sure our masks are on, cleared, and properly sealed. I'll open the door and toss a canister of this nerve gas inside after breaking the canister seal. I'll then adhere this quick-drying compound to the door crack. Once dried, the door is effectively sealed. We take the stairs down to the first floor and out of the building. The door's opening. Show time.'

They waited five seconds and heard footsteps approaching. Shawn signaled that he was the shooter for this one; he could quickly canvas the hall and take out the other if there was one.

The guard showed his face and was rewarded with a 9 mm round between his eyes. Hunter was out the door before the round dropped the man, and found one other guard in front of a door. Hunter aimed and expertly placed around on the bridge of the man's nose. Two down. They both hurried down to the first floor and to the meeting room door.

They donned their masks, cleared them, and Shawn broke the seal on the cylinder. As the gas was odorless and colorless, one couldn't tell if it was escaping or not. I'd hate to be a canary on this floor, Shawn thought.

He tried the door, opened it, tossed the canister into the room, closed the door, and Hunter immediately began applying the speedy-dry-jelly-like compound all around the door.

They turned and ran for the stairwell, while keeping their masks on until they had started down the stairs. They got to the bottom floor in minimal time, found Tim and Christopher grabbed the suitcases of nerve gas and left the building. Afterward, they spied Myra's vehicle as she gunned it out of the alleyway. She screeched to a stop, popped the trunk, and Shawn and Hunter placed the suitcases in the boot. They got back in the vehicle and then Myra sped away down the street for one block, before she drove more carefully so as not to attract attention. They immediately made for the airport.

Shawn filled in Tim, Christopher, and Myra along the way. When they arrived, they said their goodbyes to Myra and wished her well. She sped off in the direction of the City.

They climbed aboard the Stingray and Shawn directed Sancha to make an immediate takeoff and chart a southeast course back to Sydney at 75,000 feet.

'As you wish, Commander.'

When they reached altitude, Sancha informed Shawn that the fuel gauges read "full'. He had been down that road many times before, Christopher merely beamed a smile back at his father.

'Who's hungry?' asked Crawford. Christopher immediately said

"Pizza1"

'Christopher, I don't think we have any Pizza aboard this aircraft.' 'On the contrary, Commander, please look in our mini-galley.' 'We have mini-galley, Sancha?'

'Yes, Commander, we do. It is right behind you. And I do believe Pizza slices, a lasagna plate, and a Beef Wellington sandwich are all properly heated right about… Now!' and a little bell rang.

'Well, I'll be. I bet you make coffee also, don't you, Sancha!' and at that very moment, another "ding" was heard. 'Coffee is ready behind Admiral King, a soft drink for Christopher, and a grande-latte with caramel swirl whipped cream topping for the Commander. Enjoy, Boys!'

And they all started laughing!

UNEXPECTED SURPRISES

THE STINGRAY TAXIED into the hangar at 0945 hours Saturday morning. It had felt like it had been a lot longer than that as they climbed out of the aircraft. Warrant Officer Caruso was finishing up daily maintenance on the Vampire Helicopter. He came over and asked how their mission had gone, and if Christopher had behaved during the trip.

'Oh, He was a Model Devotee to the mission, Chief,' said Hunter. 'He wiped out the whole terrorist organization with one "air" punch.'

'Well, I've always said never to get on his bad side! Especially when

you're between Him and a ten-inch Pizza!' Christopher grinned broadly.

'Coach, that must have been in the building lobby. Someone must have thrown down a Pizza, and it rubbed Christopher the wrong way! What does he do with beets at the dinner table?'

'Not very well. He keeps asking us to get a dog! But, then again, it would help with the leftovers.'

'Timmy and Coach, why don't you get some deserved rack time? You Navy guys look like you could use some serious shuteye. Christopher and I are going over to Headquarters. I'll wager the Colonel is in the office this morning.'

'Yes, he is, Sir Shawn. I saw his car in the parking lot when I passed Headquarters on my way here a short while ago.'

'O.K., later, everyone. Christopher, let's go. After talking with the Colonel, we can get some brunch over at the Officer's Club.'

Five minutes later, they entered the building and walked up the stairs. They could hear a conversation going on in the Commander's Office. Shawn politely knocked and Colonel O'Leary said, 'Enter!'

Within, was Agent Dighello and the Colonel. They didn't look too happy with one another. They both had stopped what they were "arguing about" and looked at Shawn and Christopher as they entered.

'Sorry, we didn't mean to interrupt. Christopher and I just got back from Paris with Admiral King and Captain O'Hara, and we wanted to report in. I'll come back another time.'

'No, Shawn, stay. You both look pretty tired. We're done here anyway. Tell us about your trip.'

'Well, Agent Dighello, have you received any information about the results of our mission from any of your contacts?'

'Yes, I did, as a matter of fact. Shawn, your mission was a success, probably too much so, we think. Someone came in soon after you left to check her mailbox and saw some six to eight bodies lying on the floor near a far wall in the lobby. She immediately called the police and they, in turn, called for an ambulance. The men in the lobby were carted off to a nearby hospital.

'A janitorial service person who comes in routinely on weekends went up to the twelfth floor and found two men shot in the head. He immediately notified the police, who had just departed the scene. They returned and found a door had been completely blocked with some sort of adhesive compound. They had to use an ax to get inside.

'When they entered, they found twelve men lying on the floor, or slumped over a table. One of the police officers immediately fell to the floor in apparent convulsions. He was quickly removed from the room and the entire group immediately vacated the floor due to suspected nerve gas usage. The way the men appeared to one of the police officers who had served in the French military, the dead individuals in the room perished as a result of a chemical release of a nerve agent. A cylinder had been spotted on the floor not far from the entrance doorway.

'The last I heard, the special unit personnel were going back up to the room with protective masks on. There will be more to follow.'

Shawn said nothing the entire time. After a moment or two, he said, 'Well, I guess that concludes my report to both of you. And with that, Christopher and I are going home to get some rest. Call me if you need me for anything. Good morning, Gentlemen.'

When Shawn and Christopher left the building, Crawford said to his son,

'You still interested in a little brunch, my Boy?' 'Oh yes, Father! I could eat a whole Pizza!'

'Well, Christopher, let's hold that thought and try not to release it to your mother when we get home, OK?'

'O.K., Father, can I still have Pizza?'

Shawn just groaned.

TEACHING THE COACH HOW TO FLY

MONDAY MORNING BROKE beautiful with clear sunny weather. Shawn picked up the Coach at his quarters, and they drove over to the airfield and the hangar.

'What's on tap today, Coach?' asked Admiral King.

'Do I have a surprise for you, my-young-looking and eager to improve his standing in the world, Snake Eater?'

'Oh, oh. Why do I feel that this is more dangerous than it sounds? You know, I'm still a young guy with many more years ahead of me. I'm not due for a knee replacement for another couple of years. My one glass eye still looks good on me, and my arthritic body begs for more pain each and every day I'm blessed to get out of bed. So, what else is there in my life that could be more satisfying?'

'Coach, you are going to learn to fly a helicopter today. Now, I don't want you to get too excited right now. There's plenty of time for you to scare yourself. What I am offering is the opportunity of your lifetime and not just anyone else's lifetime.'

'Coach, I'd rather donate my opportunity to anyone but me at the moment. Is there a reason for this insanity, or do I have to insist upon a psychiatric evaluation for you?'

'Too late, Hunter. I had my update evaluation last week and the psychiatrist indicated that there was still no hope for me. And this is the very reason why I wish to demonstrate to you that my insanity is indeed real! And, I wish for you to feel comfortable knowing that I truly have your best interest in mind, my mind.

'What we can do is start off slow. I don't expect you to get it all in one session. By tomorrow, you'll be excited that you'll want to attempt barrel rolls in the AH-56 Cheyenne.'

'The Cheyenne, really?'

'Did you want to begin with Vampire instead?'

'Does the Cheyenne have a male version of Sancha within its innermost working?'

'I am afraid not, Coach. Only the Vampire has "Alejandro". But, the Cheyenne is really fun to "drive". It really is. Think of it as strapping on a Lamborghini and taking it up to 5,000 feet and screaming your head off! It doesn't get any better than that1'

'Last time I checked, a Lamborghini falls like a rock at 5,000 feet.'

'Just a figure of speech, Coach. If that doesn't work for you, think Volkswagen!'

'I'd just as soon think I'm going to die today!'

'That's the spirit, Coach! And that's the Coach we've all grown to know and love! Here we are. Wait until you get back to your quarters at the end of the day today. Kathleen will be so very proud of you! By the way, is your insurance policy paid up?'

They walked into the hangar and Warrant Officer Caruso had the Cheyenne all ready to go. He was just putting the finishing touches on, making sure the site glass levels were at the appropriate fluid gauge lines.

'Admiral, it's good to see you, Sir! Is your insurance policy paid in

full?'

'Isn't that the second time I've just been asked that question?'

'Hunter, we just want to make sure you've thought of everything, that's all,' Shawn said with a huge grin.

'Sir Shawn, the Cheyenne is fully prepped and ready to go, Sir!'

'Will, thank you so very much. You see, Coach, nothing to fear. I'm going to be right there with you. You don't think I would let anything happen to the father of my children, do you? If I were to "bite the bullet", Christine would absolutely kill me!'

'Shawn, are you sure this is a good idea?'

'Would I steer you in the wrong direction, Hunter?' 'Shawn, are you sure this is a good idea?'

Crawford laughed. 'Will, don't you just love this guy? He's funnier than Don Rickles! O.K., I'm going to have you sit in Gunner's forward seat. The aircraft has a dual set of controls. If I feel that you are going to go beyond the safety parameters, I'll take the controls. When I do so, all you have to do is remove your hands and feet from the cyclic and pedals, O.K.? Let's do it, Coach!'

Will provided Admiral King with a properly fitting helmet and flight vest. He made sure that Hunter was strapped in properly in the front seat as Shawn hopped into the rear.

'O.K.,' said Shawn. 'I'll go ahead and perform the pre-startup checks and get you going on actually flying this beast. We'll fly up to the coast to reward New Castle and stay out of everyone's way and once settled at or about 1,500 feet, we'll transition you into straight and level flight. We'll just take it nice and slow today. It'll be fun; you'll see!'

'Coach, you are definitely buying at the Club later!' 'No worries! I have all of Christine's credit cards!'

They had flown approximately one-third of the distance and were at an altitude of 1,000 feet when they noticed a halted vehicle. The occupants of the vehicle were distributing paperwork through the car window when suddenly, the officer stepped back with their hands raised in the air! The driver got out of his vehicle and pointed a pistol at the officer.

Shawn said, 'Coach, I have the controls.'

Shawn banked the Cheyenne 90 degrees to the left and dumped the collective, at the same time watching his rotor RPM, ensuring that it was still "in the green". He stopped his descent at 20 feet and 100 feet from the two vehicles on the road. Cheyenne's nose was pointing directly at the two men.

As he moved ever so slowly in the direction of the two vehicles, he set the Cheyenne down. Hunter then told the Coach to raise the canopy, which Shawn did. Hunter jumped out of the front Gunner's seat and started to rush the gunman. Shawn armed the 30 mm cannon and fired a short burst over the heads of the two men, who went into an immediate protective crouch. Crawford continued to point the nose at the individuals as Hunter continued to rush forward.

As the gunman started to point the weapon at Hunter, Shawn sent another three-round burst over everyone's head. It was enough for the officer and gunman to flinch. As Hunter was used to having rounds fired all around him, he kept commanding and leaped at the gunmen just as the weapon raised the gunman's arm as the weapon was fired harmlessly into the air.

While still holding onto the gunman's arm, he brought his knee up and connected between the gunman's legs. The man crumpled forward in pain and was no longer a factor. The officer took out his cuffs, forced the man to put his hands behind his back, and applied them to the man's wrists.

As Hunter stayed with the gunman, the officer went over to his cruiser and called for backup. He came back to Admiral King and said that he didn't know who they were, but he owed his life to Admiral King for his heroism.

Hunter replied by saying, 'Sir, do you see that pilot sitting in the back seat of that attack helicopter? Well, believe me, flying with him deserves my heroism. In any event, please, we are just happy to be of assistance to you. Are you all set here now, Sir?'

The police officer said that he had it covered and thanked the Admiral once again. He looked at Shawn and extended his right arm with his thumb pointing upward. Shawn smiled back from the cockpit and returned the gesture. King returned to the aircraft.

After Crawford returned to the front seat and fastened his seatbelt, he closed the canopy and maneuvered the Cheyenne to a hovering position. He then utilized the right pedal to direct the nose of the helicopter towards the north and elevated the collective while concurrently implementing forward cyclic. The Cheyenne started moving forward, picked up speed, and began to gain altitude.

'Coach, now wasn't that fun, or what!' exclaimed Shawn.

'Well, you sure know how to show a guy a good time, that's for certain!' 'That's the spirit, Coach!'

For an additional hour, they journeyed towards the north, with Hunter taking charge of the controls. He adeptly flew the helicopter in various maneuvers, such as flying straight and level, executing banks to the left and right, descending and climbing, making turns while in a descent, and so on. Hunter possessed an exceptional aptitude and demonstrated himself to be a born helicopter pilot.

After the hour was up, Shawn took the aircraft, and they flew back to Sydney. When he ground taxied to the hangar, there were three police cars parked outside. 'Wonder what that's all about?' questioned Crawford.

He shut the Cheyenne down and raised the canopy. Will was walking over to their aircraft with a law official. 'Coach, have you paid my parking ticket in downtown Sydney yet?'

'No, Shawn, I didn't have a parking ticket. Could be a solicitation for

tickets to their policeman's ball. Better hide the donuts, Shawn.'

They both got out of the Cheyenne and stood facing the two individuals approaching.

'Sir Shawn,' said the officer, 'Would you please come with me, Sir? And you too, Admiral.'

'O.K., but really I was meaning to pay that parking ticket fine at the earliest opportunity.'

The officer merely looked back at Shawn and smiled.

'Gentlemen, would you both please get into the vehicle? Thank you.'

As Hunter and Shawn sat in the back seat, Crawford asked the officer what this was all about. He said nothing and proceeded to drive off the Base and over to the Parliament Building.

'Hunter, I do believe that this parking ticket issue is going to have me defrocked.'

'Well, Coach, we've all been frocked in this business in the past. Another day in paradise.'

When they got to the Parliament Building, they were escorted inside and into the main chamber, where the parliamentary process was in a ten-minute recess. The officer looked at Shawn and Hunter, smiled, and wished them both a good day.

An aide to the Prime Minister came toward them and asked if they would accompany him. He led them to a couple of seats in the front row of the chamber. The aid asked them to be patient and that the process was about to begin in another two minutes. He walked away and into a side room.

Shawn looked at Hunter. Hunter looked at Shawn. The Hunter said,

'Ollie, what have you got ourselves into now?'

'Well, I guess we are about to find out. 'Members of the General Assembly began to enter the chamber and moved to their assigned seats. When the room was full, the Prime Minister walked down the middle aisle and over to the center podium. He glanced at the two airmen with a stern look. A Police Officer followed him and sat three seats over to their right. Shawn thought he looked awfully familiar.

'Ladies and Gentlemen of the General Assembly, may I have your attention, please? We are about to take a serious matter into the utmost consideration. As you all know, the Sydney Maritime Defense Base has always been there for all of our citizens in a protective role, to assist in any way possible to ensure the peace and tranquility of the entire Australian population.

'I have recently, 30 minutes ago, actually, become aware of a significant activity that requires the attention of every member present here today.'

Casting his gaze towards the throngs of people, he shook his head and adopted a grave countenance as he addressed Shawn and Hunter. He then requested the Sergeant-at-Arms of the Assembly to approach and guide both Shawn and Hunter to stand beside him at the podium.

They both stood up, walked over to the Prime Minister, and took a place on his right and left. He then looked at Admiral King and asked that he take a place facing him. Hunter did so. He then directed the Admiral to kneel on his right knee before him, to bow his head, and not to look upward. The PM then asked the Sergeant-at-Arms to bring over the sword.

He gave it to Shawn, who now understood what was happening. He smiled at the Prime Minister and nodded.

The PM then began, 'Honored Ladies and Gentlemen of the Australian Government General Assembly, by the power vested in me, I hereby bestow the title of Knight on Admiral J Hunter King for his heroism in the face of danger, for his initiative in protecting a Member of the Queen's Family, and for his dedication toward preserving the sanctity of each and every member of our society. Admiral King epitomes the core belief in our Society that all have a sense of worth, dignity, and the right to live their lives in a manner free from oppression and despotism.

'The Title of Knight is not bestowed lightly. Thanks to the Admiral's rapid evaluation of the peril that endangered the Queen's Nephew, the attacker was eventually apprehended with the assistance of Sir Shawn Crawford, despite the considerable risk to the Admiral's personal safety.

'I would now ask the Queen's nephew, one of our finest and most dedicated members of the Royal Police Force, to come forward and stand beside Sir Shawn, who will now bestow this most sacred honor.'

The Police Officer that Shawn and Hunter saved on the road earlier that day came forward with a huge smile.

The Prime Minister asked all to stand in difference to the great honor about to be bestowed on a member of the Queen's soldiers.

'ADMIRAL J HUNTER KING, YOU are hereby KNIGHTED for your HEROISM [Shawn placed the blade on Hunter's left shoulder], for your DEDICATION to PROTECTING the RIGHTS of EVERY MEMBER of the QUEEN'S SUBJECTS [Shawn the placed the sword on Hunter's right shoulder], and for your WILLINGNESS to SACRIFICE YOUR LIFE ON BEHALF OF THOSE IN EXTREME, [Shawn placed the blade on Hunter's head] CRITICAL, AND SIGNIFICANT NEED, I HEREBY

BESTOW the TITLE of KNIGHT in the SERVICE of the QUEEN. Please stand, Sir J Hunter!'

Shawn removed the sword and Admiral Sir J Hunter King stood and turned to face the members of the General Assembly. They stood as one and cheered loudly while clapping heartily! They continued to do this for a full 90 seconds.

The Prime Minister and the Police Officer then escorted both Sir Shawn and Sir J Hunter out of the chamber and into the outer hallway. When they stopped in the middle of the hallway, the Prime Minister thanked Sir J Hunter for his heroic deed and excused himself to return to the chamber.

The Police Officer turned to Sir J Hunter and extended his hand.

'Thank you for your heroism today, Sir J Hunter. My Aunt, the Queen, has been made aware of your significant action on my behalf. The Queen is going to send both of you an invitation to meet with Her at the earliest opportunity. Once again, I am forever in your debt, Sir.;

And with that, he smiled and excused himself to return to the chamber. Shawn looked at Hunter and remarked, 'See Coach, isn't flying helicopter fun!'

Buckingham Palace Courtesy of http://picture4u.net/ wp-content/uploads/2012/01/Buckingham-palace-london-united- kingdom.jpg

KNIGHT FOR A KING

WHEN SHAWN GOT HOME, Christopher met him at the door. He looked at His Father and grinned from ear to ear. Shawn merely shook his head. He would never be able to figure it out.

'Alright, who told you?'

Christopher smiled even more and raised His eyes to look upward.

'Man, I can't ever get anything from Him! This is a conspiracy, Christopher. You and Colette are probably already packed, aren't you?' he said with a smile.

'No, Father, not yet. How did Uncle Hunter take the ceremony? I'll bet he was more than a little surprised!'

'Well, when the Sergeant-at-Arms presented the Prime Minister with the sword to knight the Admiral, I can almost bet that your Uncle Hunter figured there was no escape and that he was going to "go out" via the Headless Horsemen way!'

'Or in the manner in which the Queen of Hearts kept yelling, "Off with his head!" Well, Colette and I are really very happy for him. I'll bet Auntie Kathleen will be surprised when he tells her.'

'Well, Christopher, YOU know the Coach, he keeps his personal accolades close to his chest. And when a week later, one of Auntie Kathleen's friends tells her what went on rather than Uncle Hunter, then I almost imagine Your Auntie reverting immediately to the "Queen of Hearts"! Oh, and that might not be so pretty! It's a good thing they love one another so much.'

Christopher chuckled at the thought of a diminutive Kathleen King chasing her beloved husband, the King of Snake Eaters, around the house with a sword while saying, "your head is mine!"

'Where are Colette and your Mother, Christopher!'

'They're over at Uncle Hunter's congratulating Sir J Hunter and Lady Kathleen concerning their new titles. So, Uncle Hunter's head is to remain relatively intact, as Auntie finds out from Mother so very soon after the fact.'

'Well, shall we go over and join them? There may be a Pizza in it for

You!'

'I'll drive!' yelled Christopher.

When they got there, it appeared the entire neighborhood was in Sir J Hunter's home. When Shawn saw him, he looked quite forlorn. He turned around to see both Shawn and Christopher standing there, and both of them were smiling.

'Out on the deck, you two!' commanded Sir J Hunter!

'Shawn, how could you get all of these people about our little ceremony at the Legislative chamber this morning? I mean, look at all of these people. Lady Kathleen is running out of finger rolls!'

Christopher. Chuckling, went up to Uncle Hunter and gave him a huge hug. 'I am very proud of you, Uncle Hunter. Please know that it wasn't my Father here, but it was my Father there. He has quite a sense of humor, doesn't he?'

'Well, Christopher, I supposed he does. Anyway, "Lady" Kathleen is half-packed all ready for the trip to London. If these good people had not shown up to congratulate her, she would be sitting in the passenger front seat of our car waiting for us to leave next week!'

Christopher again laughed, 'Uncle Hunter, that's perfect! Just think, you both are akin to being Lords "in the Queen's house". That must be really exciting for you both!'

'Thank you, Christopher. Coach, or should we now address each other as "Sir Coach", shouldn't we be somewhere right about now?' 'I don't think so, Coach.', said Shawn.

'Help me out here, Coach. Once again, shouldn't we be somewhere right about now?' as he pointed to the "gaggle" within the house.

'Oh, yes, you are absolutely correct. I did promise Christopher a lunch full of Pizza and Pizza. Are you boys ready to go? Let me tell Lady Christine that we have an appointment. Be right back.'

After his Father went into the house, Christopher looked at Uncle Hunter and said, 'You know, Uncle Hunter, this is but only the beginning of wonderful things to happen to you. I can't tell you any more than that, but I really think you need to know that information.'

'Well, thank you, Christopher. And, in addition, let me say that your Father means a lot to me. I've learned a lot from him. You are very fortunate to have him as a parent.'

'Yes, Sir J Hunter. I definitely am.'

Crawford came back out and said, 'O.K., boys and boys, I've cleared it with the bosses. Let's go over to the Officer's Club and grab a bite to eat. We can talk about our trip to "Merry Olde …" when we get there.'

On the way over, Shawn said, 'You know, Coach, we can go flying again tomorrow, if you'd like. I am free now that everything is settled down outside the confines of our fair continent. What do you think?'

'Well, to tell you the truth., I kind of enjoyed the flying, not that I did that much myself. Sure, why not. It will help me to stay out of the "crosshairs" of people wanting to ask me about my new status in life. I'll let Lady Kathleen handle the "press" for all of that. What time tomorrow morning?'

'How about I pick you up at 0700? I know the "press" won't be around

at that time in the morning. How's that sound?'

'Works for me, Coach. Now I wonder what Christopher is going to have for his O-Club meal?'

'Pizza, Lord Hunter!'

When they found a table and ordered lunch, Shawn asked about the trip overseas. 'I suspect the best way to go is to fly commercial. Don't know if Kathleen would want to travel by military stealth aircraft. What do you think?'

'Coach, she would absolutely love it! I would suggest we take Sancha. Kathleen and Christine would have a kindred spirit in the F-98A Stingray. Besides, flying commercial would take all day. We could be in London in two or three hours. And, if we left at night, the Ladies would love the view of the stars at 80,000 feet.'

'Wow, great idea. Let's do it. As the Stingray can take up to eight people comfortably, why don't we invite Timmy and Shelley to come along? They may not have seen London before. I'll check with them this afternoon and throw a "Warning Order" at them since we don't have the date for our audiences with the Queen yet.'

Crawford did check with the young couple, and they were enthused about the prospect. Shelley said would query her chain of command about the near future possibility. Tim said that he would jokingly check with his boss [Shawn] about being able to make the trip. The invitation was not long in coming.

The Prime Minister was with Marshal Morrison and Air Chief Marshal O'Leary as Shawn and Hunter walked into the Commander's Office. Crawford had been called by the Colonel the evening before to report to Morrison's office no later than 1100 hours the following morning. Hunter had also been called.

Both Crawford and King were speculating as to why they both were directed to report. Shawn thought it was because he nearly botched the "Knighting" by coming very close to severing the Coach's ear when going from left to right shoulders. Hunter thought rather that it was the wrong Police Officer they saved.

When they entered the Commander's Office, the Prime Minister welcomed them both and said that he had received the Queen's invitation for them to visit with Her Highness the following weekend. The PM gave each of them a packet that consisted of "Do's and Don'ts" when meeting and addressing Her Highness. It was stressed not to put their hands on the Queen, as some completely ignorant and arrogant President of the United States did at the turn of the second decade in the 21st Century. Of course, that President was forgiven because everyone knew that he indeed was the King of the United States. Everyone had forgotten that he had anointed himself one day while taking a breather on the basketball court, following his erratic jump shot getting stuffed by his chief of Staff, who was summarily fired. Oh well, they do come, and they do go.

There was a specific dress code, and Shawn was warned not to bring any clothing that smacked of Hawaiian. No one had to tell Sir J Hunter how to act when in the presence of Her Highness. This, of course, was not lost on Shawn after leaving the office. Then again, his two wonderful children always suggested that they had seen a kaleidoscope with less color compared to their Father's choice of wardrobe on the weekends.

Prior to leaving, Crawford indicated that Captain O'Hara and Major O'Leary would be accompanying them on the trip and that they would all be traveling via the F-98A Stingray Stealth Fighter. All thought that was a great idea for the young couple to enjoy themselves together away from the Base. There were bets here and there as to when the wedding engagement was going to be announced for the two Aviators.

In addition, Colonel O'Leary mentioned to Admiral Hunter that their traveling back to San Diego, California a year ago to bring Kathleen to Australia had turned out to be a great idea. Kathleen was turning out to be a tremendous assist to the other aviator's wives because of her organizational and personnel skills. She had rapidly developed a reputation for coordinating events at Base I in an extremely thorough manner.

During the week prior to the London trip, Shawn and Hunter went flying in the Cheyenne every day. The Coach caught on quickly when it came to exercising emergency procedures and had an uncanny touch with acquiring a weekend to the British Isles, Shawn told Hunter to fly rear for the entire sortie. When the flight was over, Hunter ground taxied the aircraft to the hangar and raised the canopy. Shawn was not moving in the forward seat. All of a sudden, Admiral King heard snoring coming from Shawn's station.

'Ah, Coach, we're home. Could you please help bring in the groceries?'

Shawn awoke with a start and said, 'O.K., Sweetheart,' Then he remembered where he was and looked down at Hunter. Admiral King asked how long he had been asleep and Shawn, after looking at his watch, said for the last 45 minutes. Crawford then asked the Admiral how he had done.

King looked at Crawford for the longest moment and broke out laughing.

'What?' asked Shawn.

'Coach, climb down from there, and I'll critique your flight, O.K.?' 'O.K. Hunter. Geez, I hope I passed and didn't get a pink slip!' 'Coach, you did just fine.

On the morning of the flight, a Friday, everyone convened at the hangar with excitement. Baggage was stowed and a final checklist of what to bring was made and verified. Everyone had what was necessary to impress Her Highness.

Commander. I understand that we are going on a "boondoggle" today. Warrant Officer Caruso has input the flight plan per your instructions yesterday. I have never been to London Heathrow before. How do I look?'

Sancha, you look absolutely lovely this morning. Please don't change a thing. Has the Pizza been stowed for the Rugrats?'

Yes, Commander, as well as the Beef Wellington, Lady Christine's cottage cheese, Lady Kathleen's yogurt, and two garter snakes for the Admiral to munch on during the trip.

Excellent, carry on, Sancha. Wilco, Commander.

'O.K., everyone, we're all set to go. Please remember: smoking is not permitted in the lavatory. For those who are good, there is an extra bag of peanuts. The in-flight movie is "Godzilla Eats Japan". My apologies for it being a rerun. Does anyone have any questions?'

Hunter raised his hand.

'No one, O.K., let's saddle up!'

Once everyone was settled in, there was a tremendous air of excitement surrounding the trip. All were in a terribly great mood and looking forward to two wonderful and memorable days in the Queen's Capitol

Shawn designated Captain O'Hara as the Pilot-in-Command. O'Hara felt honored and requested that Sancha taxi to the active for takeoff. Sancha did all the radio calls prior to launching from the active runway. Whenever Sancha was scheduled to depart days in advance, controllers for ground, tower, and departure flipped to see who could be on duty so that they could 'manage" her departure. Her following was huge because of her voice that was a cross between Marilyn Monroe and Angelina Jolie.

Timmy really had very little to do during the flight. Once at cruising altitude, 90,000 feet, they all marveled at the beautiful start shining so very brightly in the upper half of the stratosphere. Shawn explained that roughly 40 tons of meteors enter the earth's mesosphere every day. That the layer was the one far above them, so there was no possibility that they would run into meteors at this altitude. But he did admit that, at 90, 000 feet, they would be able to see meteors consistently during their flight track to the British Isles. Just as he said that, several meteors entered the mesosphere and disappeared from sight. It was simply an awesome sight!

The flight time to London was scheduled for 2 hours and 19 minutes. After 30 minutes of flying, Sancha mentioned to Shawn and Timmy telepathically that the food was ready to be eaten.

'Ladies and Gentlemen, Sancha had just informed me that the in-flight meal to go with those delicious peanuts is ready to be served. As my two children have unknowingly volunteered to serve your meal, they of course will graciously partake of their Pizza last. Coach, Sancha has brought along a couple of garter snakes for you to chew on.'

'Well, I cannot thank you enough, so I will not even try.'

'Seriously, Coach, we have a surf and turf meal for you. Please everyone, once you get your meal, do not wait for me. O.K.?' He looked around and everyone had already taken two or three bites out of their food.

Sancha provided the individual's favorite food item. She had used Colette as her sounding board to determine the menu for each traveler. The food turned out to be more like a gourmet meal than something one would expect during a commercial flight. It was that delicious.

Shawn then quipped, 'Now, I know we have a good conscientious group here, so I don't expect to find any one of you throwing any wrappers out the window. Our CHILDREN have, once again, unknowingly volunteered to do KP following a meal.

'For the exciting Godzilla movie, I have headsets available for the nominal cost of $125.00 Australian dollars. What', Shawn said as everyone threw their napkins at him.

Commander.

Yes, Sancha, Timmy answered.

I am getting reports from Heathrow that a terrorist cell is expected to create some sort of havoc in the City of London on either Saturday or Sunday.

Thank you, Sancha, Timmy responded. He looked over at Shawn, who merely nodded to him. Christopher and Colette raised their eyes slightly toward their Father.

'Everyone, Admiral Hunter will now provide back rubs, but only to Lady Kathleen. Lady Christine has graciously accepted the task of not giving me "the time of day".'

Colette and Christopher laughed as they picked up the plates and silverware.

Commander, I have started our descent into Heathrow. We are still 40 minutes out from the field.

Roger that, Sancha.

Timmy then announced that they were roughly 35 minutes from Heathrow Airport. All unaccustomed to flying aboard the F-98 were surprised at how quickly the trip had gone by. Shawn then briefed everyone concerning what would happen after they had landed.

'We will all remain in the aircraft and await the customs official. He will come aboard and collect one of these from each of you. I have taken the liberty of having it filled out before we departed on our trip. All you have to do is sign it. Coach, your "X" in the signature block will be acceptable. This will save us a little time.

'We'll then get our bags from the compartment and go into the terminal, where we will be met by a member of the Queen's staff. Two limousines will then take us to our hotel.

'We will be staying at The Savoy hotel. It's a world-famous Hotel with incredible Edwardian and Art Deco interiors alongside a Gordon Ramsay Restaurant. The stunning rooms, my Bride will like, feature elegant, marble bathrooms. Each spacious room is filled with the highest quality amenities, including Loewe flat-screen TVs and an iPod docking station for the Rugrats. The marble bathrooms include chrome fittings and giant shower heads. I am looking forward to turning on one of these because it's time for my fifth-week shower! [There was much clapping from the group!] Some rooms have fantastic views of the Thames River. The Savoy Grill serves a range of classic grill dishes. There's also modern French cuisine within an Art Deco setting with river views. The Savoy is less than a five-minute walk from the famous British Museum and the Royal Opera House.

'Now, tips for that information may be left in the glass jar by the exit door to this fine aircraft. Oh, and Christine, Luv, they do offer babysitting services.'

'That's great, Shawn. Christopher, Colette, and I will be able to go out

and leave you with someone, so we don't have to be worried!'

That literally "brought the house down!" 'Freezing, Luv. Freezing.'

Shawn rebounded and said, 'Our audience with the Queen is scheduled for 1100 hours tomorrow, to be followed by a luncheon on our behalf. Sir J Hunter will be presented with his Knight credentials. And, no, I will not be handling a sword during the entire ceremony. I know some of you are concerned about me, and I want to say right up-front that I do appreciate your sentiment. And besides, that peace of Sir J Hunter's ear I cut off during the ceremony in Sydney has added miles to Admiral King's

Nobility and Recognition.'

When the Stingray landed, it garnered looks from every conceivable spot on the runways and tarmac. The fuel vehicle pulled up beside the "spaceship-like" aircraft. The driver had no idea where the fuel port was located and waited for the pilot to exit the craft.

Shawn was the first one out, and the fuel truck driver approached him and in a cockney accent asked where he could put his fuel line to replenish the tank. Crawford thanked the man and said that it wouldn't be necessary.

The other passengers deplaned and grabbed their bags from Sancha's baggage compartment. A member of the Queen's Court came driving over to the F-98 in one of the limousines and introduced himself. A second limousine then came around the corner of a terminal building and stopped behind the first vehicle.

'Sir Shawn, my name is Sir Robert Lindsey of Her Majesty's Court. We are here to take you to your hotel. We trust that your flight from Australia was uneventful?'

'Yes, it was, Sir Robert. Thank you for asking. Allow me to introduce my entourage. This is my Bride Lady Christine, Sir J Hunter King, his Wife Lady Kathleen, our Pilots, Captain O'Hara, and Major O'Leary, and my two children, Christopher and Colette. Entourage, may I present Sir Robert Lindsey of Her Majesty's Court.'

Christine looked at Shawn and mouthed, "ENTOURAGE!" He merely looked back sheepishly, shrugged his shoulders, and mouthed the word "WHAT?"

'Sir Shawn, if you, Sir J Hunter, and your wives will ride in the first limousines, your children, and the Pilots may ride behind in the second vehicle. Well then, if you are all ready, why don't we get started, shall we?'

Shawn looked at everyone and did a quick clap motion to his ENTOURAGE, indicating that it was time to go. Hunter, who was nearly doubling over in laughter at Shawn's antics, looked at Christine and saw that she was very close to placing a hand grenade down his shorts! Hunter

didn't think his friend was going to survive this trip!

They arrived at the Savoy Hotel Ritz 25 minutes later. The extravagance and glamor of it all were simply breathtaking! They checked in and got their room assignments. The two "Knighted" couples each had a room, as did the Children. What was awkward in front of everyone was how Tim and Shelley were going to handle their room assignment. Both proceeded to accept their one room with aplomb and as if they were an "old" married couple.

Sir Robert then gave Shawn and Hunter each a packet outlining the series of events to occur an hour from that point. He indicated that their limousine transportation would be back to pick them up and take them to lunch at the Le Gavroche. He gave a courtesy bow with a smile and left the building.

At the elevator, while they all were waiting for it to arrive at the Lobby, Shawn was heard faintly humming "Here Comes the Bride". Christine kicked him in the ankle and smiled at Timmy and Shelley, who merely smiled back.

Their rooms were all on the same floor, and Shawn asked if everyone could meet down in the lobby for 50 minutes to await their transportation. When the Crawfords entered their suite, they were stunned by the historical French Renaissance opulence. Their "living room" was big enough to have a soccer game! The bathroom was simply ornately enormous! Shawn thought that he might need a bicycle to get around from room to room.

TWO KNIGHTS AT THE OPERA

AFTER ALL GOT settled in, they met at the pre-arranged time of 10 minutes in the lobby, with Timmy and Shelley arriving five minutes before the limousines pulled up. As they were walking to the vehicle, Shawn asked how all enjoyed their rooms. The Children said theirs was huge! Their Father responded that his living room had a "bus stop" because it was so big! Colette responded with, 'Really, Father?'

'Colette, that is what is called a "Gotcha"!' Christopher replied.

They arrived at the Le Gavroche Restaurant and were more than impressed at the interior design and overall "richness". Their service was amazingly prompt. The meal was first class with more than ample portions of food.

The afternoon was scheduled for "free time". While Tim and Shelley went off by themselves, the "Knighted" Couples and Children decided to do the sightseeing by going to the British Museum. After a full afternoon of playing with tourists, they went back to the Hotel. When they got to their rooms, they found huge baskets of fruit and beautiful floral arrangements for the ladies. Shawn found a Beef Wellington Sandwich with side dishes on the table, and it looked like it had just been taken out of the oven. A decanter of tea was set off to one side.

Three minutes after Christopher and Colette walked into their room, a knock on the door sounded. Christopher opened it and a young man in a tuxedo handed him an extra-large Pizza on an ornate silver platter. They were in Pizza Heaven!

Sir J Hunter found a sumptuous leg of lamb meal fit for the royalty that he was. Lady Kathleen was treated to a skilled-cooked shrimp with Romesco sauce, and Lady Christine was provided Swainson House Farm Duck with turnip and bittercress.

When Tim and Shelley had returned from visiting sights and a leisurely walk along the Thames River, they also found fruit and a wonderful floral arrangement that was synonymous with couples getting engaged to be married. The meaning was not lost on both Timmy and Shelley.

Shawn called everyone at 1630 hours and indicated that Sir Robert had left tickets for them to attend the Presentation "Don Giovanni" at the Royal Opera House. The presentation would begin at 1900 hours. Appropriate attire had been provided and was in the closet of each of the individual rooms. Shawn had been told that sizes should have been perfect for all to wear, and that any formal wear not proper would be exchanged immediately. Sir Robert would be by at 1830 hours "to collect" the Australian Party.

When everyone met outside their rooms to go down to the lobby together, the group had transformed into more than a semblance of aristocratic nobility. Even Shawn dressed up well. When Christine kept looking over her shoulder, Colette asked her mother, 'Who are you looking for, Mother?'

'I was looking for you, Father, because this gentleman standing beside me looking so handsome cannot possibly be my husband!'

'Coach, I do believe that is the Zinger of the night!' Hunter remarked.

'And, Coach, the night is still young!' responded Shawn.

The ladies were all elegantly dressed. Christine wore a T by Tadashi One Shoulder Chiffon Gown that made her look absolutely stunning. Kathleen was wearing an Adrianna Papell Crystal Brooch Ruched Jersey Gown that was breathtaking.

Shelley had on an Eliza J Beaded One Shoulder Satin Dress that had several men in the hallway nearly suffering whiplash when she passed by and on her way to the elevator.

And Colette wore a Pisarro Nights Beaded Kimono Sleeve Dress that her Father thought showed too much knee! He went over to her and asked her if she needed a shawl for the knees, for it was going to be drafty in the theater.

This elicited no response from his daughter. For some reason, Shawn felt like a whipped puppy dog this evening!

Sir Robert was right on time and, as usual, was impeccably dressed. They all slid into the limousines. When the two limousines arrived, they were placed in a queue for exiting the Theater. It took a full five minutes for their vehicles to arrive at the red carpet entryway. The ladies were out first, followed by the gentlemen. Shawn and Christine waited for their children and, when they departed their limo, Colette was in hysterics and looking at Commander O'Hara. She then gave a sidelong glance to her father as Tim's face turned red.

'What was that all about?' asked Shawn.

'Father, Commander O'Hara is so funny. He is just trying to take care of your interests in the dress code you would like to propose for me. He said that if you had your way, I would be wrapped up in a black cloth like a Mummy! Of course, that is far from being true, isn't it, Father?'

Crawford looked at his beautiful daughter and refrained from telling a lie, and therefore said nothing. However, he proposed a life ambition to his daughter by suggesting that she apply for a Missionary position in the South Pacific, as he had heard that Togo was seeking candidates.

It was at that time when Colette was saved by her mother, who insisted that they needed to enter the Theater, so they could be seated for the beginning of the play.

Their seats were toward the front of the theater, with a wonderful view of the performance. Timmy and Shelley sat in the middle, with each child beside them. Next to Christopher sat Kathleen and Hunter. Shawn and Christine were next to Colette.

As the Play was about to begin, screaming was heard coming from the lobby area, followed by gunshots. It appeared to be mayhem out there, Shawn thought. He quickly looked at Hunter and they both exited the rows and ran back toward the lobby. Kathleen and Christine started to say something, but their Husbands were gone from sight almost immediately. Everyone looked to the rear of the audience with apprehension. Christopher looked over at Colette and the latter mouthed the words, "It's the time!" Christopher nodded once and they both got up and quickly stepped in front of the women and ran into the lobby.

'Christopher, Colette!' shouted Christine. Christopher stopped all of a sudden, looked at his Mother, and said with a stern voice she had never heard Him use before, 'Mother, you will stay right where you are!' And then he was gone from sight to join his sister in the lobby.

There was more firing and more screaming! From the wings of the auditorium, two men clad in black with like-colored hoods fired their AK-74 assault weapons into the air. The audience, still seated, all crouched in their seats, with much more screaming from the main floor.

Queen Elizabeth II. Born: Elizabeth Alexandria Mary Windsor

Courtesy of: librarising.com

The terrorists stood there for a second and looked toward the front row of attendees. One of the men spied on whom he was searching for and moved toward the front row. A man from one of the rows attempted to tackle the terrorist and was kneed in the nose for his effort. He collapsed unconscious to the rug flooring.

There were whimpers of fear heard throughout the auditorium. Christine looked behind her and back to the lobby, and still, there was no sight of her Children or Shawn and Hunter.

In the meantime, Crawford and King had quickly removed themselves from the auditorium and stopped by an entry door and peered into the lobby. There were two terrorists pointing their weapons at the crowd. They appeared to be waiting for something or someone.

Shawn looked at Hunter, who returned his gaze as if to ask what do you suggest. Shawn signaled Hunter to follow his lead via special forces hand signals. King nodded once.

Shawn opened the door calmly and walked into the lobby. Hunter did the same. As Shawn walked forward, he looked at Hunter and spoke with him as if they were in the middle of a normal conversation.

Both terrorists moved toward both men and shouted something in Arabic that both Hunter and Shawn knew to be, "Get on the floor!"

As Shawn feigned incomprehension and gave the impression that he now was totally afraid by overtly showing cowardice, the man approached him with the AK-74 gun butt in a horizontal to floor position and brought the weapon back to strike Crawford in the head. The other terrorist was about to mirror what his cohort was going to do to Shawn by slamming his weapon into Hunter's skull.

Shawn and Hunter had them right where they wanted them!

As Shawn saw the rifle butt come forward, he deftly dodged the strike and placed a pressure punch directly into the man's rib section. The air went out of the lung as rib cartilage snapped and was forced into the lung itself. The terrorist grunted and dropped his weapon.

Hunter dropped to the floor as his assailant's weapon came forward to his head. As the terrorist was striking thin air, his momentum carried him forward. King swept his leg and hooked his instep on the back of the man's calf and pulled toward him with tremendous force. The terrorist fell backward and, while falling, let loose a series of rounds from his AK. With nothing to stop his fall as his hands were wrapped around his weapon, he hit the flooring on his back with his head snapping downward with enough force to render him unconscious. Hunter and Shawn had simultaneously taken out the two terrorists at the same time. Shawn then looked at all the Play attendees, put his finger to his lips to indicate silence, and pointed for everyone to leave the building immediately. They didn't have to be told twice.

Meanwhile, Colette and Christopher both had managed to get out of the auditorium virtually undetected in the confusion. Colette walked slowly toward one of the wings of the auditorium and, with a stealth-like motion, approached the man from behind. When she was 18 inches from the terrorist's back, she kicked him in the back of the knee with such force that pain shot immediately into the man's brain pain center and rendered him temporarily immobilized. The terrorist dropped his weapon and grabbed his knee with both hands and went down to the floor.

As the terror was now slightly lower in head level than Colette, SHE picked up the AK and looked at the man, who looked up at HER. She then smiled sweetly and hit the man in the nose as hard as SHE could with the butt of the AK-74. 'Good night!', SHE said to him.

Colette leaned the weapon against the wall, straightened out HER Pisarro Nights Beaded Kimono Sleeve Dress, picked the weapon back up, and calmly walked over to the lobby area.

Just as SHE walked into the lobby with the AK-74, Shawn, and Hunter were finishing up their tasks with the two terrorists. When Shawn had finished indicating everyone to leave the Theater, he turned to see Colette standing there, smiling sweetly, and holding the weapon in HER hands. Shawn and Hunter came over to HER. SHE handed the weapon to HER Father and asked if he really meant to send HER to Togo!

Inside the Theater, Christopher had noticed the final terrorist mowing toward the front row of seats as if he had identified someone of interest. The terrorist grabbed a man and started pulling him toward a side door. Christopher ran to the terrorist screaming and crying while shouting out loud, "Papa! Papa! Papa!'

This action caused the terrorist to stop abruptly and look at Christopher, who had HIS gaze centered on the man being dragged out of the building. Out of the corner of HIS eye, HE saw an opening. Christopher lunged toward the victim as if to hug him. The terrorist reached out with his left hand to push the

BOY away, and Christopher grabbed it and twisted it sharply and outward. His wrist bone snapped.

The terrorist, even though he was in excruciating pain, started to bring his AK to bear on the BOY. As the barrel swung toward Christopher, HE grabbed it and thrust it upward so that it was pointing toward the ceiling. At the same time, Christopher was doing this, HE brought HIS leg up forcefully and made contact between the terrorist's legs. The man let go of the AK-74, with the BOY still holding onto the barrel.

Christopher rotated the weapon deftly in his hands and pointed the rear stock toward the terrorist's head and hit him with tremendous force in the forehead. The terrorist's eyes rolled back in his head and he slumped to the floor unconscious.

Christopher then looked down at the Opera attendee, still on the floor and shaking uncontrollably. Christopher slowly assisted the man to his feet and had him sit down. HE looked him over quickly to see if there were any injuries and found none.

A stagehand came toward HIM, and Christopher asked if he had any strong tape. The young man indicated that he would get some immediately. He came back 45 seconds later and handed a roll of "hundred miles an hour" duct tape to then BOY, who proceeded to truss the terrorist in a truly professional military fashion. He gave the tape back to the stagehand while thanking him with a smile, bent down and picked up the AK-74, and then walked calmly up to the aisle toward the lobby.

There was utter silence in the auditorium as the mass of people all turned their heads to watch this little BOY walk up the aisle cradling an AK-74 Assault Rifle in HIS arms—a little BOY who had subdued with military precision a terrorist who easily could have taken all of their lives.

Christine was standing in the aisle waiting for HIM and HE stopped

before her, looked up, smiled, and asked, 'Are you alright, Mother?' 'Christopher!, Christopher!, my God, YOU just saved us all!'

'No, Mother, not really. I had some help. Colette took care of the other terrorist standing in the opposite wing. I do believe that Bad Guy got the worst of it, as he probably messed up her new dress! I'm going into the lobby to check on Father and Uncle Hunter. Furthermore, I do believe that the situation is under control. Be right back, Mother!'

Christopher walked into the lobby with HIS AK-74 and handed it to Uncle Hunter.

'Father, I do believe a quick announcement from both of you to the audience in the auditorium would be in order. They don't know what to do now, apparently.'

Shawn and Hunter then went into the auditorium and asked for everyone's attention. Shawn announced, 'Please know that everything is alright now. You may all leave the building, but please do so in an orderly fashion. The terrorists have all been subsided. There is nothing to fear. I repeat, there is nothing to fear, and I ask that you exit the building without causing alarm and in an orderly manner. Thank you.'

At that moment, the London Police Swat Team came barreling through the door. Admiral King asked who was in charge. He was directed to a man just coming through the door and into the lobby.

'Sir, my name is Admiral King, Australian Navy. There were four terrorists who have all been subdued. Two are here, and the others are in the auditorium taking "a nap", right, Christopher?'

'Yes, Uncle Hunter.'

'And the terrorist YOU took down is exactly where, Colette, Honey?' 'Uncle Hunter, I left him in the opposite wing. He is still taking a nap.;

'Thank you, Sweetheart,' Hunter said with a smile, as if to say, that's my GIRL!

Colette coquettishly returned his smile with a special one of her own!

This was not lost on Shawn, who appeared from the auditorium and who suddenly had an idea to ask Hunter if he wanted to vacation in Togo for the next 30 years with Colette. This way, he would be able to keep an eye on HER.

The crowd of attendees walked orderly out of the Theater. The Chief of Police wished for Shawn's Party to remain so that he could form a report. As the individuals filed out, many came over to thank both CHILDREN, especially Christopher for his exhibition of martial arts prowess in subduing their more immediate terrorist threat, thereby saving their lives.

The ubiquitous press was present and tried to get an interview with anyone who wished to talk about what had happened within the Theater. Almost everyone spoken to had relayed what he or she had seen regarding Christopher's extreme bravery in the face of mortal danger. News people wanted attendees to identify the young BOY who had saved them all that evening. With Christopher and Colette standing close to THEIR Mother, the TV news reporter came over and asked to speak to Christopher about what happened this evening. Christine denied the request and said that they were leaving almost immediately.

The television reporter would not take "no" for an answer and thrust his mike in the face of Christopher. Christine started to say something in a not-too-kind manner when Christopher told HIS Mother to allow for just one minute with the reporter, but only in the theater alone. Christine reluctantly agreed to it, as she knew her SON and trusted HIS judgment explicitly.

'Alright, Christopher, I wish for you to control the time of the interview, will YOU do that for me?'

'Yes, of course, Mother.'

The BOY and the TV reporter then went into the theater. Christine

turned to Shawn and said, 'Shawn, I don't feel good about this.'

'Luv, if anyone can control a situation, it's our SON. I trust Christopher

just as you do. Let's allow HIM to have this time and space.'

Christopher sat in one of the rear aisle seats and watched the TV reporter.

'Christopher, it's been a long time. How have you been?'

'I've been well, Joshua. Since I joined my Australian Family immediately following the attempted assassination attempt on the life of Mahatma Gandhi, I have, in concert with OUR FATHER's wishes, been able to promote the well-being of peace, and dignity of human rights. My earthly Father is a truly wonderful being. Shawn Crawford has accomplished many great things and has accomplished many great things and has significantly contributed to OUR cause. Tell me, Joshua, what have you been up to?'

'In our parallel Universe, I have faced many significant challenges. At the same time, I have met individual beings who have shown ultimate kindness and consideration in furthering OUR FATHER'S philosophical and practical application in the establishment of order in the Cosmos.

'I already know what has happened here this evening. OUR SISTER Colette has done some amazing things without the knowledge of HER Earthly Parents. I miss both of you. Christopher.'

'Joshua, you have been my BEST FRIEND for a millennium. There will come a time when we will all be together with one another. Be patient, MY BROTHER! Let's go back out front so that the Parents whom I care about so deeply will not worry.

'But before we do that, let me ask you, where will you go next, Joshua?'

'I have no idea, Christopher, But I feel that my time here has been well spent. YOU and YOUR SISTER'S actions this evening, coupled with your earthly parents and relatives, are allowing ME to soon look forward to a change in my existence. Wherever I end up, I know that YOU are close by, Christopher.'

They stood and hugged one another dearly. And they walked through the lobby doors and over to Shawn and Christine for their allowing him to speak with Christopher. Shawn looked at the reporter for a very long moment, smiled, and nodded.

The reporter returned that nod..

A BIG BANG THEORY

WHEN HUNTER AND Shawn had submitted the report verbally, they were allowed to go. In the process, the Police Chief understood that Shawn and his Party would be staying at the Savoy and would be meeting with the Queen in the morning.

Shawn told the Chief not to worry about contacting him at any time at the Savoy.

Sir Robert, who had been sitting near his visiting charges, had noticed everything that went on, notwithstanding the hysteria of the Opera Attendees. At the first opportunity, he went into the lobby and made a phone call to the Queen's personal secretary and informed him of what had transpired at the Opera House. His report was in complete detail, including young Christopher's subduing the terrorist single-handedly.

After hanging up, he approached Shawn and Hunter and informed them that he had just telephoned the Queen's Office and had been told of the occurrence this evening. He then asked if a postponement of the Ceremony to the following morning with the Queen should be seriously considered.

Shawn looked at Hunter who replied that, if Her Highness was still amenable, he preferred that the Ceremony continue as planned. Sir Robert thanked Admiral King for his forthright answer. He then told them that the limousines would be outside in less than two minutes to return them to Savoy.

Christine, Kathleen, Tim, and Shelley were, by this time, standing in a knot beside Shawn and Hunter, with the CHILDREN standing by their Mother. As soon as Sir Robert spied the limousines, he approached his Party and asked that they follow him to the vehicles. They all got in and motored back to their hotel.

'Well, that went well,' quipped Shawn. 'Is everything alright?'

Christine then said, 'Shawn, what were you thinking when you first heard the gunshots and jumped up to go toward the lobby?' Kathleen echoed the same concerned question directed toward Hunter.

'Well, the Coach and I were out of popcorn. And I know how much he badly needs a jumbo container with lots of butter, so we thought we'd take an opportunity while everyone else was preoccupied with the weapons firing. When we heard the "pops" coming from the lobby, I thought the fresh popcorn was just about done and totally inviting. That's pretty much it.'

Christine, with an exasperated look, said with a measured tone, 'Listen, Cowboy, if you ever do something like that again, I will most certainly put an end to your life after someone else has had the opportunity and failed miserably!'

'She's really not angry, Coach. And the red on her face is nothing more than an indication that she totally loves me. Those were really terms of endearment. I do get that a lot.'

Christine looked away with tears starting to well up in her eyes. They arrived at the Savoy 10 minutes later.

When everyone got off the elevator to their floor, Shawn said that he was happy that all were alright. The only people who truly suffered were the terrorists, although one bystander seeking to help suffered slightly from a blow to the face. If anyone wanted to talk about what happened this evening, he would be available for anyone to come by at any time.

The Ceremony in the morning would take place as planned. Sir Robert would be required to "collect" them at 1000 hours for a pre-meeting with the Queen before the Ceremony at 1100 hours. Once again, Sir Robert had provided appropriate attire for all to wear. He had indicated that the clothing provided during their stay was now their property to take back with them to Australia, should they desire to do so.

Shawn wished everyone a good evening, and they all went toward their rooms.

'Coach, can we talk for a moment?' asked Shawn.

'Sure, Coach. Where to?'

'Let's go into Christopher and Colette's room.'

Shawn then told Christine and Hunter informed Kathleen that they were going to check on the CHILDREN in THEIR room. Shawn knocked on the door, and Christopher and Colette were waiting for them in the spacious living room.

'Have you both had an opportunity to talk?' asked Shawn.

'Yes, Father, we have.'

'And what have you come up with?'

'Father, Uncle Hunter, we have spoken to Joshua after we arrived here at the Hotel this evening. He tells us that there is a nuclear device that is going to be smuggled onto the Buckingham Palace Grounds during the morning hours tomorrow. As to the method of delivery, it is difficult to say at the moment. It may very well be in the form of a delivery vehicle or some other mode of transportation.

'My feeling is that it will be delivered from the "other side", which will make it more difficult to detect prior to entering the grounds. We do have one advantage, however, and that is Joshua's presence at the ceremony. He is one of two individuals who will be in tune to its presence only because of his close connection with the "other side".'

'Coach, I'm a little confused,' said Hunter. 'What is the "other side" exactly?'

'Coach, it's a parallel universe. It contains virtually the same "entities" that we have in this "side" or plane. There have been stories, television programs, books, and movies that speak to the theory of a parallel universe. It actually does exist. Supposedly, we have our "mirrors" existing there. Unfortunately, they may not be of the identical conscientious demeanor as those of us on our side.

'Joshua was the TV reporter that took Christopher aside after the episode at the Theater this evening. He is from the "other side". Joshua and Christopher have been "best friends" for, what, Christopher, a couple of thousand years?'

'Yes, Father, give or take a hundred years. Uncle Hunter—Joshua is MY BIG BROTHER. He has been all over the cosmos and has served Entities for a very long period of time.'

Hunter looked about the room at the others and said, 'This is playing out to be a science fiction novel to the hilt!'

'O.K.,' Shawn said, 'Back to focusing. Christopher, where is Joshua at the moment? Can YOU reach him, and, if so, can he come over immediately?'

'I'm sure I can get to him, Father. Let me make a phone call.'

A few moments later, Christopher got off the phone and told everyone that Joshua would be over in less than 5 minutes. 'I told him to come immediately to our hotel room,' he said.

'Well, Coach, I guess at a minimum "glowing in the dark" is not an option,' remarked Hunter.

Joshua, Boy Reporter and Millennium Entity

Courtesy of the Author

'Good. I'm hoping that he has an answer to our dilemma because, if not, we're going to be operating in the blind. And, if that's the case, won't be having toast for brunch, we will be the toast!' said Shawn.

'Needless to say, we'll need to keep this information strictly to ourselves. No need to panic about the natives or our Families.If Joshua fails to provide us with satisfactory information, I will approach the Swat Team Commander tonight and give him ample time to position his troops for thorough screening.

There was a knock on the door.

Christopher answered. It was Joshua. The two BROTHERS hugged. Colette came over and hugged Joshua dearly and said, 'HELLO BROTHER! You've been a STRANGER much too long.'

'Hello, it's Colette now, isn't it? I've missed you, Sis! You don't look a day over 200!'

'If I ever said that to Christine, I'd be sucking wind for more than 200!', said Shawn.

They all laughed. Joshua then addressed Shawn, 'You are a wonderful Parent to these two, Sir Shawn. We watch you constantly from the "other side". Your humor is what sets you apart from all others that we watch each day. There is even a book published on the other side that has captured all of your "quips" through the years. You are one of very few who has a dedicated publisher to record all of your exploits to include every bit of the communication process.'

'Wow, that's amazing. Coach, I could get my own Pulitzer one day! Well, enough about me, but, maybe later.

'Joshua, we have a very serious problem that we are hoping you may be able to help us with. There is a nuclear device that is to be planted somewhere in the Buckingham Palace Grounds early tomorrow morning. This device is reputed to be coming from your "side" of the parallel line. The Palace Grounds are quite huge. Is there any way to detect something like this to your knowledge?'

'There may be, Sir Shawn. What is peculiar about such devices that are not present in this hemisphere of the parallax is that there is a "signature" that is quite simple. It is much akin to an ephemeron. Let me explain.

'You are going to find this very odd, but it is the way it is on the "other side". When a device of this specific nature is put together, it is usually constructed by a male "scientist", for lack of a better title. When this male scientist puts together a nuclear device, he leaves his "signature" on his completed project.

'In the past, when we have searched for devices constructed by a male scientist after many years of their being stored, we have utilized female members who are attuned to picking up these signature ephemera. Not every female is adept at picking up the signature of a male "invention". Only a very few are capable of accomplishing this feat, and we happen to have one in this room.'

They all turned their attention to Colette, who merely shrugged while still standing before them in HER Pissaro Beaded Nights Kimono Sleeve Dress.

'Colette, Sweetheart, what do YOU think? Is this something that YOU are able to do?' asked HER Father.

'Sure, Father. I've done it twice before. I'm sure that I can accomplish it once more. It's like being a Bloodhound!' said Uncle Hunter.

'Oh, Uncle Hunter, would do that if you were single!'

Sir J Hunter King Admiral, Australian Navy, United SEAL, Delta Force Operative, turns the darkest shade of RED anyone had ever seen!

'Coach, I do believe we have found a true weak spot!' said Shawn.

Joshua then said, 'The ephemeron is the most distinctive as soon as it arrives from the "other side". This doesn't mean that it can't be picked up hours after it has "arrived". It just makes it a little more difficult, that's all.'

Shawn then turned to Hunter and said, 'Coach, why don't we pay the Swat Team Captain a little visit this evening? We will need a plan of the Grounds to evaluate where a suitable "Hiding place" would be for a relatively "sizeable" nuclear device might be placed.

'Are you kids up for a little adventure? There could be a late-night English-style Pizza in it for you!'

Christopher and Colette were the first two out of the room.

'Coach, I'm going to inform Christine as to our whereabouts. I'll tell her that it has to do with something about an addendum to the report we filed earlier this evening that required information to make it more complete.' Hunter said he would do the same with Kathleen.

They jumped in Joshua's SUV and drove over to the London Police Station. The Commander was still at the station and welcomed the group into his office.

When all were seated, he asked what he owed the pleasure of their company so late in the evening.

'Captain, we have reason to believe that a nuclear device will be on-site at Buckingham Palace tomorrow and will be detonated. As to the time, no one knows. We have reliable information that such an attempt will be made. We would like to assist you in finding this device before it has an opportunity to detonate sometime, we feel, tomorrow morning.'

'By all means, Sir Shawn. We certainly can use the expertise, as well as that of Sir J Hunter. What do you have in mind regarding a plan of action? Needless to say, we need to be all over this scenario!'

'Very well, I believe the advantageous moment to create the most destruction and casualties would be when the Investiture has begun. And that would be 1100 hours. Count on a few late arrivals, and I would project around an 1115-hour detonation. Admiral King, Christopher, Colette, and I will arrive earlier than expected and see if we either can spot something unusual, or give Colette an opportunity to locate the device.'

'Sir Shawn, we will have a full complement of law enforcement officials present, per the norm for the Queen's special events. Dogs will also be on site. Our protocol calls for additional law enforcement three hours prior, so we will not tip off anyone that we are onto something that would disrupt the Queen's Agenda in a catastrophic manner. And we certainly do not wish to panic the public!'

'That sounds great, Captain. Of course, if we capture the perpetrators involved along with disarming the weapon, that would be ideal. My Team's focus will be to locate the device and attempt to disarm it after evaluating the total firing mechanism. We feel that we have a better-than-average chance of accomplishing this. How many security forces have you employed on the Grounds this evening, Captain?'

'As there are contractors and vendors needing to set up all the evening into the morning, we have more than the normal number of law enforcement officials present to verify identities through a comprehensive vetting process.'

'O.K. As far as all of us here are concerned, I'm going to suggest that we get some rest for the next few hours. Captain, thank you very much for receiving us so late this evening.'

'Sir Shawn, we all know of your reputation and that of Admiral King. With Christopher and Colette present to assist, I feel we have the very best possible chance to stop a catastrophic event tomorrow.'

'Thank you, Captain. I will touch base with you tomorrow morning regarding an update.'

The London SWATand the Police Forces were on alert throughout the night. Christopher and Colette informed THEIR Father that THEY didn't feel that there is much chance for law enforcement to come up with anything before the actual Investiture was to begin. THEIR reasoning was that the device would be drawn from the "other side" at the last moment. Where it was presented was perfectly well hidden, and in plain sight. That was how parallel sides worked.

Crawford then said that everyone should get some rest. He thanked Joshua for taking them around and said that he would see him later in the morning. The following day was going to prove to be an adventure for them all.

As Christopher and Colette went to THEIR room after being dropped off, Shawn told Hunter to remain in the lobby for a moment longer.

'It looks like we have a variable that is virtually uncontrollably by us "weak" mortals, Coach. Colette is going to have to rise to the occasion bug time if this thing materializes as we think it will. We talked earlier about the mode of transportation being possibly a truck, or like a vehicle. But what if it's something else altogether? What if it's a device that can be brought over from the "other side" at the last moment? Then, it truly is up to Colette to come through for everyone!'

'First thing tomorrow morning, let's sit down with Colette and Christopher and see if there is any other information SHE can provide that will give us a better feel for what we are going to be dealing with.'

'Hunter, I have an idea. How about going for an airplane ride?'

'What? Right now? Coach, we're not in for another flight lesson, are we?'

'No, nothing like that. But, I may be able to get a better handle on what's to come if we seek the wisdom of SOMEONE we all know and love. Are you up for a little adventure this evening?'

'Put me in, Coach!'

TWO KNIGHTS IN THE NIGHT

SHAWN AND HUNTER got to the airport via taxi cab a half hour later. Sancha was right where they left her.

Sancha, did we wake you?

Good morning, Commander. No, you did not wake me because I was expecting you both. As a result, I have a local area flight plan for one-hour duration. This should be enough time to accomplish what needs to be done. I would think.

Yes, Sancha, I do agree. O.K., let's see if we can get some concrete information to stop a disaster in the making from occurring. I would hate to see your beautiful exterior coat get married in any way, Sancha.

You are all heart, Commander.

'O.K., Coach, Sancha says she's all prepped and ready to go. Let's take her for a spin. Do you want to drive?'

'Ah, Shawn, I do believe you have this one.'

They climbed to an altitude of 5,000 feet and almost immediately were enveloped in The Entity's cloud and blue hue. Shawn sensed an air of immediacy once inside, a feeling he had never experienced before.

'Shawna and Hunter! Thank you for coming! Looks like we have a situation that must be resolved very quickly. The nuclear device is indeed coming from one of OUR parallel sides. It is being delivered by an alter ego of Sir Robert Lindsey, who by the way orchestrated the impending event. To stop this catastrophic occurrence, you must detain Sir Robert from attending the Investiture this morning at 1100 hours. His absence is the key to stopping the nuclear device from going off, and causing significant death and destruction. As always, I will be with you both.'

'That information is certainly good enough for me, Coach. Sancha, we are done here. Please coordinate our return to the airfield and close out our flight plan.'

'Wilco, Commander.'

When they had returned to the Savoy, they turned in for the evening. Sir Robert Lindsey could wait until the morning, now that they knew in which direction they needed to go.

'Sir J Hunter, sleep well. Tomorrow is going to be a good day for the good guys!'

'I do believe you are right, Coach. Catch you in a few hours.'

Shawn got four hours of sound sleep, a long "power" nap for him. At 0700 hours, he left his room quietly and went over to the CHILDREN's room. He knocked quietly. He heard Christopher for him to enter.

'Good morning, Christopher. Where is Colette?'

'Good morning, Father. She is down in the solarium. It's a peaceful location for HER, where SHE is able to replenish the energy SHE will need to stop Sir Robert's alter ego from accomplishing his deadly task today.'

'YOU both know about Sir Robert Lindsey? But how?'

'Father, you don't think that WE would let you and Uncle Hunter go flying alone, do you?'

'Christopher, I don't know how YOU do these things, but it does border on the uncanny!'

'Yes, Father, I know. Sometimes I do these things just to amuse MYSELF.'

'Well, that's nice to know. Putting all of that aside for the moment, Sir Robert is expecting to pick us up in less than 3 hours. I'm going to need YOUR help in defusing this entire debacle. Colette will also play a major part. Let's go see if SHE has had a chance to fully recharge HER "batteries".'

They found HER sitting in a Lotus position in the solarium. HER eyes were closed, as if SHE is in a deep trance. When the three entered the room, SHE continued to sit very still. No one said a word.

'Hello, Father. I've been waiting for you and Uncle Hunter. I'm ready for the "hunt" now. I feel very confident that I will be able to pick up the "scent" of the device once it is on OUR side of the "parallel door". We need to get ready.'

She then got up and walked out of the solarium and over to the elevator. SHE waited wordlessly for the others to join HER. Once on their floor, Colette and Christopher went into THEIR room to prepare for the Investiture. Shawn and Hunter said that they would meet one another in 15 minutes, given their Brides were ready to go by then.

They hadn't seen much of Christine or Kathleen since the episode at the Opera House. Both women had slept soundlessly, which suited Shawn and Hunter just fine. They didn't need the additional potential drama that came with worrying about what might happen.

Sir Robert Lindsey was right on time. The two limousines arrived precisely at 1000 hours. Shawn gave Sir Robert a quick appraising look to see if he could pick up something of Lindsey's face. The latter showed nothing.

They all piled into the motor coaches and rode over to Buckingham Palace. Tim and Shelley riding in the back with Christopher and Colette noticed that the CHILDREN were unusually quiet on the trip over.

'So, how are you TWO enjoying this weekend thus far? Yesterday's excitement propelled both of YOU into the "Hero" class. YOU must feel good about that in the way that YOU saved many lives.'

Christopher and Colette said nothing and appeared to be totally lost in THEIR own thoughts. Tim and Shelley looked at one another and both shrugged. It was best to allow the CHILDREN to have THEIR own thoughts; they certainly deserved them after last evening's experience.

When they arrived at the Palace, Shawn, Hunter, and the Ladies got out. Both Hunter and Shawn looked around quickly. Nothing looked out of the ordinary.

Behind them, Christopher and Colette stayed with one another for a moment, Colette then said something to Christopher who nodded. Colette then went alone toward the left-hand side of the Palace building. Christopher joined HIS parents and HE and the three couples began walking toward the Palace entrance. Sir Robert directed them toward the front of the Palace and walked with them the short distance to the front entrance.

Crawford had seen Colette walk toward the side of the building and, when Christine asked him where she was going, Shawn replied that he wanted HER to check on something for him relating to the Investiture ceremony. SHE was to return very shortly.

When they entered the palace, they were met by the Queen's staff, who directed them to an antechamber. Sir Robert then excused himself and left the room. Shawn watched where he was going and saw him leave the building and turn right at the door, in the direction of where Colette had gone. Crawford excused himself for a bathroom break, left the room, and walked out the door. He caught Sir Robert turning the corner of the building.

Crawford walked quickly to the building's corner, took a quick look around the façade, saw no one, and turned the corner. There was an opened door 25 meters to his front. Neither Colette nor Sir Robert was in sight. He walked quickly over to the open door, stopped beside a huge refuse container, and heard voices coming from inside. He recognized Sir Robert, who seemed agitated.

'Colette, what are YOU doing here? Aren't you supposed to be with YOUR parents? It's not safe to wander around these grounds. Palace security patrols the Buckingham Palace grounds with the Rottweiler attack dogs. The guards generally let the dogs get to the trespassers first, and ask questions later if there is anything left of the trespasser when the guards finally get to them.'

Shawn then heard Colette say, 'Sir Robert, I am sorry, but I was following what looked like a bunny hopping around. I saw it turn the corner of the building, and so I wanted to see where it went. I didn't mean any harm.'

'Of course, YOU didn't. Now, why don't YOU go back over to the main entrance and to the anteroom where YOUR parents are waiting, O.K.?'

'But, Sir Robert, I wanted to see where the bunny went.'

Sir Robert then raised his voice and screamed, 'Colette, I want YOU out of here immediately! Now, get out, please!'

Colette feigned being hurt and started to whimper as SHE moved toward the door. SHE exited, passed HER father with a smile, and continued walking toward the building's corner. A few seconds later, SHE turned it, leaving Crawford outside, and waiting. He had a pretty good idea as to what was going to come next.

'It took you long enough! Where is the device?'

'Easy now, Robert. It is safely tucked away in the rear left corner against the wall under an old tarp. The timer is set for the explosion to go off at 1115 hours. If I were you, I would be certain that your air taxi is available to get well clear of here.'

'What's the damage radius of this thing?'

'Well, it's not the biggest weapon, but it will flatten everything within a radius of 10 kilometers. There won't be anything left of this place, and no one will be able to get close to it for scores of years!'

'Good, It will be good to pay back this egocentric nobility for their pompous demeanor. I've stood it far too long. What about you? I take it you're returning to the "other side" and never to return?'

'Well, I wouldn't say that, exactly. There is always little mayhem to get involved with all over the globe. Even though it's a bit depressing coming over here every once in a while, it's still a change of pace from the utopian design I'm forced to live in "over there".

'Gee, I really feel sorry for you! When are you heading back? Right away, or just after you arm the device?'

'I will set the arming mechanism at 1100 hours for 15 minutes. I suggest you make sure your helicopter is on time, otherwise, there won't be much of you left to glow in the dark at 1115 hours!'

'Alright, I need to get back to my charges in the anteroom before I'm too noticeably missed. Good luck to you. I'd shake your hand, but I don't wish to disintegrate before my time!'

Sir Robert then left the room and walked quickly toward the corner of the building, and then was lost from sight. Shawn opened the garbage container slowly, heard Sir Robert's alter ego rummaging around the room, exited the container, and followed Sir Robert back to the Palace entrance from a distance.

When Sir Robert walked into the anteroom with a smile, he looked around and found Sir Shawn missing. 'Where is your Husband, Lady Christine?' he asked.

'Oh, hi, Sir Robert, I've been in the restroom. Wow, I must have eaten some bad food or something. Mr. Tidy Bowl and I have been rapidly getting acquainted!'

'Mother, let ME take Father out for a brief breath of fresh air right outside. We'll be right back,' said Christopher.

'Thank you, Christopher. We need to be back in here in less than 10 minutes.'

'Yes, Mother. Come along, Father.'

Once outside, Christopher feigned a look of concern while talking to HIS Father in measured tones, 'Colette is ready to take out Sir Robert's alter ego, Father. SHE is the only ONE able to neutralize him. SHE was able to get a positive scent on the device and knows where it is positioned within the room. As soon as SHE is able to eliminate the "other side" entity, you can go in and neutralize the device, but not before. I'M sorry, but it has to be this way for all to come out of this safely.'

'O.K., Christopher. Sir Robert's alter ego will arm the device for 15 minutes at 1100 hours. That is 10 minutes from now. While Uncle Hunter and Auntie Kathleen are kneeling before the Queen in anticipation of the Investiture. I will be prepared to jump on the device as soon as Colette has taken out Sir Robert's Double. I don't have to ask if SHE is ready, do I?'

'No, Father. As a matter of fact. SHE is actually looking forward to it! When Sir Robert yelled at HER, well, you know, Father, woman scorned!'

'Oh, I know that all too well, Christopher. O.K., let's go show our faces so that Sir Robert knows we are in the audience. Once he leads Uncle Hunter and Auntie Kathleen forward and toward the Queen, we can bolt. Let's get back inside.'

They both stepped into the anteroom, highly visible to Sir Robert. Shawn kept dabbing a handkerchief to his forehead, while Christopher kept looking at HIS Father with deep concern. Christine came over to him and asked if he was alright. With Sir Robert now on the way with Hunter and Kathleen and proceeding toward meeting the Queen at the end of the extended red carpet, Shawn looked at Christine and asked her to remain here and witness the ceremony. He was going back into the restroom for another meeting with Mr. Tidy. She told him that she would be inside witnessing the Ceremony and that if he needed her to send one of the CHILDREN over to get her. She then told both Christopher and Colette to wait outside the restroom in the event that THEIR Father needed them.

'You're a Gem, Luv. I'm sure it will pass. Timing is everything, as they say.'

Christine gave him a kiss on the cheek, turned, and walked into the Hall.

Crawford and his CHILDREN then went outside and to the building's corner. Shawn didn't see Sir Robert from the "other side". They quickly walked to the room and carefully peered inside. Sir Robert's alter was in the far corner, arming the device. Colette walked quickly into the room while whistling. Robert's alter turned around quickly and startled at the same time and recognized Colette as his THREAT.

'YOU!!' he hissed. 'I thought I got rid of YOU 400 years ago! I don't suppose YOUR given name now is Penny for BAD, is it?'

'Oh, but you have been the Bad Boy, instead of Penny, Lucius. You can be such a bore, you know that?' as Colette continued to walk resolutely toward HER adversary.

'You are going back this time, and you will never return.'

Lucius charged HER and SHE dodged his thrust and he stumbled badly onto the cement floor. SHE quickly straddled his back, took his head in both of HER hands, and twisted sharply, but held HER hands in place. After 10 seconds, Lucius' spirit appeared slowly at first, and then, more rapidly, until his entire entity was removed from the physical shape lying on the floor of the room. As it rose into nothing, there was a horrible moaning, and then it was gone.

'O.K., Father, it is done.' Shawn hustled into the corner of the room, removed the tarp, and quickly surveyed the nuclear weapon. He located the arming device and the wires leading to the energy source that would provide the impetus to effect the small nuclear explosion. His Doctorate Degree in Quantum Mechanics from Georgia Southern University was finally coming into play as he successfully disarmed the unit. When it was done, he leaned back against the wall, rubbed his forehead, looked at both of his CHILDREN, who stood nearby smiling down at him, and announced, 'Well, that went well! What do we do for an encore?'

Colette and Christopher both yelled in unison, 'Pizza!'

**Edmund Blair Leighton accolade From Wiki-
pedia, the Free Encyclopedia**

THE BERMUDA QUADRANGLE

AS SHAWN, CHRISTOPHER, and Colette exited the room, the SWAT Team came around the corner with automatic weapons drawn and shields up. The Captain came forward and asked Shawn what he, and the CHILDREN were doing back here.

Crawford started to quip that they had been planning a Pizza Party but decided that he would use that explanation at another time for something less serious.

'Captain, you'll find the nuclear device in the back corner and totally defused. The culprit has literally vanished. The most important thing is that there will not be a bad day at Buckingham Palace and London proper.

The Captain signaled for his troops to go inside and inspect the unit. A sergeant came back out and verified that the bomb had been neutralized completely.

'Sir Shawn, you have managed to save a few more than an Opera House of people again today. I do believe I like having you around!'

'Well, Captain, I couldn't have done it without these two CHERUBS! THEY are my right and left-hand ENTITIES, if you will permit me to describe THEM as such! THEY both sometimes do some incredible "other-worldly" things on a periodic basis. I'm just so blessed to have THEM both as my CHILDREN.'

'Yes, Father, and you did promise US Pizza!'

'And then, Sir Shawn, THEY have a way of bringing you back down to earth, don't THEY?'

'Yes, THEY do, Captain. But I wouldn't trade THEM for the world. Captain, you may wish to arrest Sir Robert Lindsey for the part he has played in all of this. I believe in the end you will find that he was indeed the architect who put this entire plan in motion, Captain. Let's go, Rugrats. Let's go see if Uncle Hunter still has his ear intact!'

They arrived as the Ceremony was winding down. Admiral King was bedecked with the official title "Sir" Hunter, and Kathleen was now officially known as "Lady Kathleen"! Both were weighted down with Gifts of Investiture as they turned to walk back down the aisle amidst the applause of the nearly one thousand English men present. It was "pomp and circumstance" of the highest order and was a sight to witness.

Joshua was seen on the fringes during the Ceremony, and Shawn and Christopher caught up with him before he departed. Christopher hugged HIS Brother warmly. 'Let's not stay away as long next time, Joshua. And We have to keep in touch somehow. I must speak with MY FATHER about this.'

'Christopher, YOU know how this works. We go where WE are needed and where WE can make the greatest difference. Believe ME, WE will see one another again before too long. YOU and Colette are extremely fortunate to have Shawn and Christine as YOUR parents. Don't despair, MY BROTHER. Be well.'

They hugged one another for the last time. And then Joshua was gone.

When the newly-appointed Royalty reached the anteroom, Hunter turned to Shawn and said that he didn't feel like 'toast" so he knew that his friend had taken care of "business".

'Shawn, I didn't see Sir Robert anywhere near us when the Ceremony officially began.'

'No, Coach, I imagine his helicopter is about to be run over by a British Tornado Gr4 Fighter as we speak. Colette took care of the Alter Ego with aplomb, and I managed to finagle my way through defusing a nuclear bomb. Just another day at the office, Coach! Congratulations, by the way, to you and your Bride for the newly-installed titles of nobility. This doesn't mean that you are always going to "drive" the helicopter from now on, does it?'

At that point, Tim and Shelley came over and approached Sir J Hunter and congratulated him on his knighthood. Tim then turned to Shawn and said that he had heard that Shawn had come down with a "bug" of some sort prior to the Ceremony commencing. And was he feeling better now?

British Tornado Gr4 Fighter
Courtesy of militaryimages.
net

'Yes, Tim, thanks to my two little CHERUBS, I was able to survive today's onslaught of nuclear indigestion. Oh, just a figure of speech, so to speak. How did you and Shelley enjoy the investiture? Didn't the Coach look suave and dapper and other things?'

Hunter then quipped, 'It's the other things that I could do without, Timmy.'

'Well, why don't we see if Sir Robert's "stand-in" has nothing more for us before we head back to the Savoy for one final night of opulence.;

After 45 minutes of congratulatory remarks from the myriad of guests, the Australians departed for the Savoy and a much-needed rest. Christine remarked that she could stay up all night due to the sound sleep she experienced the evening before. Shawn groaned internally, and Sir J Hunter looked peaked!

The "CHIPMUNK" CHILDREN never required sleep. Timmy and Shelley were completely left "out of the loop" at the palace, so they both were able to get a good night's sleep the night before. Shawn said Sir Coach was dragging but received little sympathy from the "Bosses" Lady Christine and Lady Kathleen. 'Coach, it's going to be a long night!'

And, it didn't make any difference which one of them had made the statement!

The Australian Guests of Honor didn't have far to go to enjoy themselves that evening. The Savoy offered the very best of entertainment, especially when the establishment realized the Royalty that existed and was staying as guests in their midst. A very speedy arrangement was made to have a high-end top-level Band appear at a moment's notice for all to enjoy. All in attendance were not disappointed with the quality at the Savoy that evening!

Shawn and Hunter sat together at one point when "royal noses needed to be powdered" and talked about really relaxing and the venues to enjoy such relaxation. They both agreed that the Island of Bermuda was at the top of their lists, and wished they could experience the beauty of the pink-colored sand out in front of the majestic Elbow Beach Hotel.

Out of respect for the Coach's motorbike abilities, both Shawn and Hunter refused to bring up their inability to negotiate turns that an 85-year-old grandmother took for granted on the narrow speedway roads on that beautiful Island in the Atlantic. They both agreed that better bike maintenance was required for their being able to truly enjoy the wind in their faces at a sizzling 25 mph!

Shawn then offered, 'You know, Coach, with everything still quiet in Australia, I bet we could take a long way back and just have to stop off in Bermuda to check out a mechanical glitch in Sancha's system. Of course, I wouldn't be so bold as to suggest getting into Sancha's systems, but I do feel that we could definitely make this work for us. You know, Coach, a little well-deserved R&R for you after you had to go through this 'awful' Investiture Ceremony. It had to be a terrible and traumatic experience for you. I just don't know how you are able to cope with the aftermath of all the pain. You are a real Saint, my friend.

'That does it! I am treating you to a week in Bermuda so that you can recover from this very trying experience here in London! We need you to be on top of your game in Sydney, Coach. And I do think that this will most certainly be the emotional "tonic" for you to bounce back and be the 'man" that you want yourself to be!'

Hunter merely looked at Shawn and said nothing.

'I'm going to break it to our Brides, the CHILDREN, and to the Love Birds. We will depart tomorrow morning and get to Bermuda by noon time. After a full week of that luxury, our batteries will be re-charged, and we will be ready to go! This is all very exciting!'

The remainder of the party thought it was a grand idea and one of the celebrations for the honors bestowed on both Hunter and Kathleen, not to mention that Bermuda was a well-deserved hero!

And so, another chapter in the life of Sir Steven Shawn Crawford closed. This story ended with a happy outcome, and with a promise that another adventure was certain to find him. And, together with the Coach, in lands lacking in promise but full of healing potential, their knowledge rested in the assurance that life would never be the way it should be. But in that assurance, they would always be able to predict that their journeys would be full of mending hearts, saving lives, and living the life of the consummate Warrior.

In that, and by itself, their journey would simply … be.

EPILOGUE

WITH THE WORLD in the Southern Hemisphere at peace, for the most part, life settled down to a very comfortable and unwelcomed "crawl" for Brigadier General Shawn Crawford. This was not to suggest that his life offered the personal satisfaction of relaxation and discovery of new "hobbies" in the wake of non-existent contentious activity. His experience in a world full of greed suggested that the next "adventure" was but an ignition of jet fighter igniters away from denying the power-hungry in advancing their self-serving goals at the expense of the common man's dignity. He had not long to wait.

In the interim, he and his CHILDREN flew to various venues that solicited Christopher's expertise in HIS understanding of the Cosmos. They made several trips to Europe and to the United States. Each time, Shawn took a different stealth fighter for the purpose of transitioning Colette into the various airframes. As Christopher had already been rated in all three aircraft, the evaluations centered on Colette. She had mastered the F-98B Leopard during Operation Phoenix.

Colette was perhaps the brightest Entity known to Shawn. Even though SHE was his natural-born DAUGHTER, SHE had been "gifted" at birth with the natural elements innate to The Entity's Inner Circle. Shawn noticed that SHE had been 'touched" with such other-worldly power as soon as SHE was born. SHE had always been iron-willed, and precocious. Shawn recognized that his DAUGHTER needed to be constantly challenged. And for a mere mortal such as himself, THIS was challenging!

Crawford decided to have Christopher work with Colette in the form of team-building in the cockpit. In the 1980s, this concept was brought to the forefront in the military, even though it had always been stressed in flight training programs to a much lesser degree. A series of Class-A Military aviation accidents where loss of life was evidenced had precipitated a reinforcement of training doctrine in terms of ensuring that proper communication existed among flight crews. It was all based on the "unbroken chain" concept.

In the aftermath of Class A mishaps, investigating officers concluded nearly 100% of the time that such accidents resulted from a series of events, like links in a chain that, when left connected, invariably led conclusively to the accident itself. After a final evaluation of the accident occurrence, it was ascertained that if that "chain of events", or links in that chain, were to have been "interrupted", such as taking one single link out of that chain, the Class A mishap nearly 100% of the time would have been averted. And that one "link" might be as simple as one question being asked by one crew member and directed toward another to instill an awareness of a potential concern in the process of conducting a flight. This was the concept that Shawn stressed with his CHILDREN, especially Colette.

It wasn't that SHE was reckless. Colette simply showed no respect for potential factors that might position HER in situations that were precarious in nature. It was documented somewhere that individuals showed no fear when conducting dangerous events until they reached the age of 25. Well, Shawn asked himself, how in the "other world" would that apply to Colette whose Entity BEING had already lived more than 2000 years?

He thought he might need psychotherapy before his life was over!

But what Shawn Crawford did not realize was that his DAUGHTER was totally aware and in tune with HER Father's concerns. SHE pushed the envelope because the envelope was there to be pushed!

In the final analysis, SHE truly was HER Father's DAUGHTER!

SUMMARY OF AWARDS

THE FOLLOWING MILITARY Awards and Decorations were awarded to the indicated Personnel, in alphabetical order, following events occurring during the conduct of Operations:

CARUSO, Will, Flight Sergeant: Awarded the Legion of Merit. Promoted to Warrant Officer Second Class. Title: Mr. Caruso.

GONZALES, Roberto Jesus, Commodore: Awarded The Distinguished Service Cross. Title: Commodore Gonzales, a.k.a., Chief Gonzales.

KING, J Hunter, Commander: Promoted to Admiral Lower Half. Awarded the Navy Cross. Promoted to Admiral, Upper Half. Title: Admiral, a.k.a., "Coach"

O'HARA, Patrick, Lieutenant Colonel: Promoted to Brigadier General, Awarded the Distinguished Flying Cross. Title: General.

O'HARA, Timothy, Ensign J.G.: Promoted to Commander; Awarded the Navy Cross. Promoted to Captain, United States Navy. Title: Captain.

O'LEARY, James Paul, Corporal: Promoted to First Lieutenant, Awarded the Silver Star. Title: Lieutenant.

O'LEARY, Timothy James, Sr., Private: Awarded the Medal of Honor, Distinguished Service Cross, The French *Croix de Guerre*, and Purple Heart. Promoted to the rank of Major. Title: Major.

O'LEARY, Michael, Air Chief Marshal: Awarded the Medal of Honor. Title: Air Chief Marshal, a.k.a., Colonel.

O'LEARY, Shelley, Captain: Awarded the Air Force Cross, promoted to Lieutenant Colonel. Title: Colonel.

PETERSON, Derek, Major: Promoted to Colonel. Title: Colonel.

ROBERTS, Christine, Major: Awarded the Air Forces Cross, Promoted to Colonel. Title: Colonel.

AUTHOR BIOGRAPHY

TIMOTHY JAMES O'LEARY, III is a retired U.S Army Lieutenant Colonel with 27 years of active duty and reserve service to his Country. Tim served a tour of duty in both Vietnam and the First Persian Gulf Wars. He is a graduate of the Defense Language Institute in Monterey, California, where he earned a diploma in Italian Language training. Tim is a helicopter pilot with 2,200 hours of flight time in UH-1 and OH-58 aircraft with the United States Army. During Operation Desert Storm, Tim was a medevac pilot with the 217th Medical Battalion. His final tour of duty was as Battalion Commander of the 286th Supply and Service Battalion.

He has a B.A. degree in Sociology and French and holds a Master of Education and Educational Specialist degrees in Educational Administration and Supervision from Georgia Southern College. Tim was a Doctor of Education degree candidate at the University of Virginia in Educational Administration and Supervision. He also had one year of Spanish Language training at the University of Southern Maine in Portland. Tim taught foreign language and social studies in the Georgia public school system for three years, and was an assistant principal at a secondary education school in Virginia.

Tim has run 13 marathons, including the Marine Corps in 19945 and Boston's 100th IN 1996. He has been a baseball umpire for over 40 years and has officiated five Cal Ripken World Series. Tim played varsity baseball in Italy and did a baseball tour with the European Continental Cavaliers Baseball Team in South Africa.

Tim has three children and three grandchildren. He and his wife, Lynn reside in Gorham, Maine.

ENDNOTES

1.   http://en.wikipedia.org/wiki/Sniper_equipment

2.   en.wokepedia.org/wiki/Jaco_(East_Timor)

3.   en.wikepedia.org/wiki.Pope_Alexander_VI

4.   en.wikipedia.org/wiki/pope_alexander_VI

5.   en.wikipedia.org/wiki/Malmedy_massacre

6.   Courtesy of Wikipedia, the Free Encyclopedia

7.   Ibed.

8.   Ibed.

9.   Ibed.

10.   http://www.history.army.mil/books/korea/20-2-1/sn34.html

11.   http://www.booking.com/hotel/gb/the-savoy.en-us.html

12.   http://shop.nordstrom.com/c/womens-dresses/evenin

9 798886 920666